DRAGON FLIGHT . . . DRAGON FIGHT

High above the gray void they flew, bursting out into the dazzling clarity of the upper atmosphere. Beneath them the gray-white vapor spread in all directions, seamed with deep furrows and slow-rolling waves. Like dueling hawks, the dragons repeatedly circled and lunged and disengaged, each striving to get past the other's defenses and wound an eye or wing. Occasionally they drew on the air's latent power to supplement their own, flinging blazing arcs of lightning at one another, summoning sudden gusts of wind to disrupt one another's flight. The green dragon's assaults became more and more frenzied; the red dragon no longer reacted defensively, but fought with savage fury for his life.

Once more they closed in a mass of tangled limbs and wings and jaws, dropping back into the cloud layer. Lightning leaped and crackled around them, illuminating the grayness through which they fell . . .

ACCLAIM FOR *THE STONE OF THE STARS*

"Legendary gods and lost temples emerge from dragon mists. This is writing that calls enchantment forth from the shadows of Time."
—**Andrew Norton**, author of *Beastmaster's Ark*

"A strong contribution to the epic fantasy genre."
—*Library Journal*

Also by Alison Baird

The Stone of the Stars

THE EMPIRE OF THE STARS

THE DRAGON THRONE • BOOK II

ALISON BAIRD

ASPECT®

NEW YORK   BOSTON

For the Trinity College "gang," with fond memories—
Rodney, Gordon, Sherri, Monica, Eric, and Diane

Copyright © 2004 by Alison Baird
All rights reserved.

Aspect / Warner Books

Time Warner Book Group
1271 Avenue of the Americas, New York, NY 10020
Visit our Web site at www.twbookmark.com.

The Aspect name and logo are registered trademarks of Warner Books.

Printed in the United States of America

First Printing: November 2004
10   9   8   7   6   5   4   3   2   1

Library of Congress Cataloging-in-Publication Data
Baird, Alison.
        The empire of the stars / Alison Baird.
            p. cm. — (The dragon throne; bk. 2)
        ISBN 0-446-69096-1
        I. Title
        PR9199.4.B34E47 2004
        813'.6—dc22   2004010410

Book design by Giorgetta Bell McRee

THE
EMPIRE
OF THE
STARS

The World

Melnemeron

Eldimia

Mirimar

Barrens

Hyelanthia

Mari Alma
(Mother Sea)

Mid-Se

Have

of ARAINIA

Nolo Alma
(Little Sea)

Outer
Territories

N
W E
S

PROLOGUE

(Excerpted from Maurian's *Historia Arainia*)

I T IS DIFFICULT FOR US, studying these annals, to envision the events and personages in them, so fantastic do these accounts seem; so remote and even godlike the figures that move in their midst. We must not lose sight, however, of the fact that these beings were as human as we, in their outward forms at least: that Ailia, Damion, Morlyn, and the rest lived and breathed and knew our mortal weaknesses, doubts, and fears. For any chronicler of this strange and wondrous era the principal task must be to clothe those names in flesh.

As to their story, it is elsewhere recounted in full, and a brief retelling of its main points will serve here. When the Queen Elarainia, revered throughout the world of Arainia as the incarnation of its goddess, gave birth to a daughter, the people rejoiced to see prophecy fulfilled: the *Tryna Lia*, Princess of the Stars, had been born in mortal form to deliver them from the designs of the dark god, Modrian-Valdur. When the little Princess Elmiria was still scarcely more than an infant, her mother took her from her home world and conveyed her by sorcery to the neighboring world of Mera for her protection, for Morlyn, the avatar of Valdur, knew that she would one day challenge his rule. Also, it was in Mera that the Star Stone lay. This enchanted gem alone could give the Tryna Lia the power to defeat her foreordained foe. But upon reaching Mera Queen Elarainia disappeared, and the little princess was left, not in the care of the holy monks on the Isle of Jana as both friend and foe would later come to believe, but on the shores of Great Island much farther to the north, where she was discovered by a lowly shipbuilder and his wife. They took the foundling into their home and raised her as their own. And when she grew older she did not seek out her true origins, for her guardians allowed her to believe that they were her true mother and father.

When she was in her seventeenth year, Ailia (as the young maiden came to be called) made a journey along with many other islanders to escape the invading armies of Khalazar, the Zimbouran tyrant king. She and her family found sanctuary in the land of Maurainia, and at the Royal Academy of Raimar she first encountered Damion Athariel, priest of the Faith of Orendyl. She secretly fell in love with him, though such a love was forbidden, but she did not guess that their lives were interwoven by destiny.

Many others were also bound by fate to Ailia. One was the aged woman known only as Old Ana, a reputed witch dwelling in the coastal mountains. The "coven" that Ana led was in truth a secret company of *Nemerei*, seers and sorcerers who practiced the magical arts of elder days, and she told Father Damion of their ways and of the predestined ruler who would one day descend from the stars. At that time the girl Lorelyn, who had fled with Damion from the Isle of Jana when the Zimbouran forces menaced it, was believed to be the Tryna Lia. Damion later came to Lorelyn's aid again when the sorcerer-prince Morlyn, then using the name of Mandrake, abducted her and confined her deep within the ruins of Maurainia's oldest fortress.

The Zimbouran king, who believed himself destined to seize and wield the Star Stone and conquer the Tryna Lia, then captured Lorelyn and with her Damion, Ana, and Ailia. He set off with his prisoners by galleon to the long-lost Isle of Trynisia: for there the holy jewel lay waiting for either the Tryna Lia or the dark god Valdur's champion to claim it. But with her sorcerous power Ana freed the prisoners after landfall was made, and they escaped together into the wilderness of Trynisia. They were joined by Jomar, a half-breed slave who hated his Zimbouran masters and rejoiced at the chance to thwart them of their prize. The Stone lay in the ruin of the holy city of Liamar, high upon the sacred mountain of Elendor, and Lorelyn and her party resolved to find it before the Zimbourans could.

But many perils lay in their path: not only the vengeful king and his soldiers, but also the misshapen and evil beast-men that dwelt on the isle, and the dragons that made their lairs on the summit of Elendor. Morlyn, using his sorcery to take the shape of a great dragon, led the latter in an assault upon Ana's company. For it was his wish that no one should ever come near the Stone, nor awaken its wondrous powers.

Yet though he caused Ana to be separated from her charges, and though he fought Jomar and Damion in the cavern wherein he kept the Stone, and took young Lorelyn back into his power, in the end he was thwarted by Ailia. The maiden, whom he thought a harmless shipwright's daughter, ventured all alone into the treasure-cave, and took from thence the sacred Stone. She was assisted in her escape from Elendor by a great golden dragon, a servant of the celestial realm, whom she freed from the chain with which Morlyn had bound him fast. The semidivine Guardians, whose sacred duty it was to protect the Stone until the Tryna Lia came to claim it, saved her remaining companions. All were borne away through the heavens and reunited in far-distant Arainia—a world that, to them, had become merely a myth.

Morlyn met them there and once more attempted to challenge them, denying them entry to the royal palace of Halmirion. But before the others' wondering eyes Ailia took up the Star Stone and drew upon its power to put the dragon-mage to flight. In so doing she revealed at last her true identity. And before the people of Arainia she was returned to her throne.

But countless dangers still awaited. For Ailia had not destroyed her predestined adversary, and there were on other worlds many cruel and powerful beings whose aid he could summon in his fight against her.

Part One

THE
TRYNA LIA

1

The Dragon Prince

THE FIRE-RED DRAGON BURST OUT of the Ether high in the upper air, his entrance into the skies of this world a bright flash hardly to be seen amid a shimmer of many-hued auroras. All the lands below him were shrouded and still, bound in the ice and silence of Winter-dark. Nothing moved here save for him, and a few furtive creatures in the snow-clad forests, and the remote flickerings of the Northern Lights. Impervious to the bone-bitter chill, he flew on toward his goal: a mountain that stood apart from the rest of its range, as though singled out by fate for the role it had played in history. Its double spire of granite did not reach as high as most of the cloud-piercing peaks beyond it, yet it was by far the most famous. In days of old it had been called Elendor, the Holymount.

To the Elei people who had once dwelt in the valley beneath, its two peaks had loomed like living sentinels: a pair of great beasts or vigilant giants, keeping watch over the city that lay between them on the mountaintop. But Liamar had long since been reduced to ruin, mere fragments of walls and buildings interlaced with shadow. The stone sentinels guarded nothing now, and the people were long gone from the island. All the Elei's fabled treasure lay piled within an immense cavern deep inside the mountain: they had placed it there for safekeeping, ages ago, but now that their ancient race was gone the dragon had claimed their gold and jewels for his own. He dived down to settle on the lower of the two peaks, mantling his wings about him, and staring at the ruins.

There were cries in the sky above him, high and wild: other

Loänan, celestial dragons, greeting him as they flew past and acknowledged his authority. He was their Trynoloänan, their master
and ruler. They thought him one of their own. None guessed at his
kinship with those who had dwelt in the city below, none knew
that even in this shape he had the soul of a man. His dual nature
was a secret he guarded as jealously as any jewel-hoard. But while
he wore this form it wracked him with a torment very near to pain,
as though mind and body were being wrenched asunder. Once he
had dwelt as a man among men, heir to a distant kingdom: Prince
Morlyn of Maurainia. In that far-distant land his name was still
known, his tale told as legend.

He recalled a time when the city below him bustled with life—
for he was old, at least as humans count time: five centuries had
passed since his birth, although in draconic reckoning he was not
yet in his prime and even in his human shape preserved the vigor
of youth. Here in Liamar the Elei had kept the Star Stone, which
they cherished above all their other treasures: the enchanted stone
of the gods, cast out of Heaven in their last great battle. Indeed,
the whole city had grown around it, shrine and fane and lodgings
and fortifications spreading outward in concentric rings from the
place where it fell. But Liamar was empty now, a setting without its
jewel. He had been here in the land of Trynisia when comets
rained down on this world, and he had seen, without regret, the
old Elei realm fall in ruin. The Stone had then been taken from its
sanctum, and hidden in the secret cave. There he had guarded it
after the people fled, and set dragons to watch the hoard when he
was not present. And there it had lain for centuries . . . until all his
plans went awry.

He recalled other scenes more recent in time, shared with him
by the witnesses through the joining of their thoughts. He beheld
soldiers of a foreign land pursuing two men and one aged woman,
the latter bearing the Star Stone in her hand. Winged beasts—not
dragons, but strange creatures half lion and half eagle—stooped
down upon the armed invaders as they followed the fugitives up to
the roof of the central temple. Driving the men back, the creatures
took up the Stone's bearer and her companions and flew them
away to safety. Lastly he saw a young girl run out onto the top of
the taller peak opposite his stony perch, with more soldiers in pur-

suit. And he watched as she too fled the mountain on the back of a golden dragon, outflying the arrows of her foes.

The images faded away from his inner sight, ghosts returning to the past.

The Tryna Lia. Five hundred years ago she had been only a faceless figure within his mind: his prophesied antagonist, according to the Zimbouran priests who had raised him. Over the ensuing centuries he had been able to forget her, but now the shadowy threat had at last become a reality. And yet superimposed on these fearful thoughts was his memory of this girl, whom he had first encountered in the country of Maurainia, then again here on the Isle of Trynisia: a seemingly ordinary young girl, guileless, naive, utterly innocent of her own destiny. But in the hands of old Ana and her sorcerous conspirators, young Ailia was even now being corrupted, carefully shaped into the living weapon that would one day threaten the realm of the god Valdur's servants—and, if prophecy was to be believed, his own life as well. Nor had she any choice in the matter. In the eyes of the Nemerei she was bound to her fate as surely as he, and there was no escape for either one of them but the death of the other. He must find a way to draw her out of her own world, into another where her powers were not so strong. And prophecy said that she would come to Mera with an army, to deliver it from Valdur's servants. If he could but force her hand, make her attempt to fulfill that prophecy before her powers were developed enough, he might perhaps defeat her.

He sprang off the peak and soared skyward on his flame-colored wings, as though seeking to leave his thoughts behind. For if he continued to muse along these lines he might begin to pity Ailia, and in the conflict to come pity was an indulgence that he could ill afford. He wasted valuable time in brooding here. As the other dragons turned in their flight and tried to follow him, he warned them off with a roar and they retreated reluctantly. He had a journey to make, and allies to seek far beyond the frozen sea. Swifter than any wind of that world he flew southward, until the sun returned to the sky, and still he flew on, barely pausing to rest. He left behind the spinning stars of the pole, passing on through the tropics while the moon tilted above him, until at last it stood inverted amid the bright-burning constellations of the Antipodes.

*   *   *

IN THE LAND OF ZIMBOURA, high in the topmost tower of his old stone keep, the God-king Khalazar was at work upon a spell.

It was night and the chamber was swathed in shadow, its one narrow window showing only a few stars, its only other source of illumination a few guttering candles. Their fitful light played upon a profusion of curious objects on the shelves along the walls: black-bound volumes of gramarye, bunches of dried herbs, wooden wands, astrolabes and orreries, crystal globes of many sizes. There were bones of birds and animals, and several human skulls staring dully from dark corners. On one large oaken table were ranged all the tools of the alchemist's trade: beakers, retorts, crucibles; but all of these were now filmed with dust and strung with cobwebs. The potentate of Zimboura sat cross-legged in the center of the floor. His flowing black hair and beard were touched with gray, and deep lines of discontent were engraved on the face grown fleshy with middle age. His hand, as he traced in blood the outline of a magic circle on the floor, was far from steady. The spell was new, and much hung on its success:

"*Akhatal, azgharal, Gurushakan rhamak ta'vir . . .*" It was a spell to summon the ghost of Gurusha, ancient demon-king of Zimboura: for the task at hand no lesser spirit would suffice. If he could not succeed in this, he would know that he was not in truth the Avatar his people sought.

All was not well with his young empire. The northern plains and forests of what had once been the neighboring country of Shurkana were his, along with their vast yield of wheat and wood. But Shurkanese bandits based in the mountains continued to be-devil his troops. The Archipelagoes of Kaan were his, but to the west lay an unconquered continent, whose people had defeated his own in battle centuries before, and could well do so again. The northern island of Trynisia was his, but the oceans that divided it from Zimboura were impassable in winter, and it was populated only by hideous and hostile savages. The fledgling Zimbouran em-pire was stretched to its limit, thin and vulnerable, its few troops unable to control the restless and resentful populations of its con-quered countries.

And now, even here in the capital city of Felizia, bread riots and other minor insurrections were breaking out like wildfires among his own subjects. He badly needed allies, but in all the world there was not one to be had. So he had turned in desperation to the only other world that he knew of, the world of the spirits: day and night he had performed incantations designed to summon supernatural aid. Yet no spirit would answer his call, not the most minor imp or incubus.

It had been Khalazar's belief for many decades that he was no mere mortal, but the earthly incarnation of a god—and no minor deity, either, but that highest of all deities, his people's primary god: Valdur the Great. For years he had felt the utmost certainty concerning his godhood. As a boy he had smiled to himself whenever he heard the priests of Valdur speak of the god's coming incarnation—knowing that *he* was the one, that he was already come. He had despised his predecessor, King Zedekara, even while he served him, for that monarch had merely feigned divinity in order to impress the mobs. When Khalazar and his followers rebelled against Zedekara's rule, he took his victory for granted and was unsurprised when it came. And when news was brought to him that the location of the Star Stone—the enchanted gem preordained to be wielded by the avatar of Valdur—had at last been discovered, he took this as yet another sign that his destiny was at hand.

But then he had lost the Stone. An old woman had seized it, a witch with the power to summon terrifying winged genii out of the heavens; and one of her companions was a young girl claiming to be the Tryna Lia herself, daughter of the Queen of Night incarnate in human form. After they escaped him Khalazar had retreated to his homeland and fallen into despair, until it occurred to him at length that this too was in the prophecies—the other gods of the pantheon would do all they could to thwart Valdur's rise to power, and the Tryna Lia was their chosen champion. The avatar of Valdur must expect to confront her—so was her appearance not in fact an *affirmation* of his identity?

But if he were the Avatar, a tormenting voice now whispered in the king's mind, why could *he* not summon genii at command? Should not the incarnate Valdur also exercise authority over the spirit-world? Was he *not* Valdur, after all? The thought tortured him throughout every waking hour. He had turned to necromancy, seeking counsel from the spirits of the dead, who as all men knew were party to secrets unknown to the living. For many months he had practiced incantations on a collection of corpses (easily obtained in this violent land), but none could be induced to speak. Now in growing desperation he had turned to this alternative necromantic practice, the summoning of ghosts from beyond the grave. And as he recited the incantation, he thought that he did, in fact, hear a faint rustling sound within the chamber, though he dared not pause in midspell. Only when the incantation was properly concluded did Khalazar lower his hands and open his eyes. The chamber was empty and still as before. With an oath he sprang up, and was about to quit the magic circle when a slight movement in a far corner made him start and whirl.

A figure stood there at the dark end of the room: a tall man, or the shade of a man, clad in a hooded robe the same hue as the shadows in which he stood. The door was still barred from within; the intruder could not have entered that way. The window was open, but it was fourteen stories above the ground and the tower's smooth walls offered no purchase to a climber. As Khalazar stood gaping the figure came soundlessly forward. The beardless face within the cowl was white as death, and the eyes of the apparition burned like yellow flames. Beneath their unnatural glare the king shivered from head to toe. A spirit beyond a doubt, but this was not, could not be Gurusha: that was not a Zimbouran face within the hood.

"Avaunt!" Khalazar screamed, cowering within the circle. "Avaunt—I did not summon you!"

The specter put back its hood, letting long lion-colored hair tumble about its pale face. "Come, Khalazar," it said in a deep reverberant voice, "you are in no position to reject any help. Be sensible."

"Who are you?" rasped the king, unable to retreat any farther without leaving the protection of the circle.

"My name is Morlyn," the specter replied. "I was a prince of great renown in days of old. Surely even you in Zimboura have heard of me?"

Morlyn: the dark sorcerer-prince of Maurainia, dead now for five hundred years. Even as he sweated and trembled before the strange figure, Khalazar felt a minute flare of elation deep within his mind. He had summoned a spirit! Not the one he had sought, but a real spirit nonetheless—and a great one, the ghost of a warrior and archmage! A thin cackle of triumph escaped his shaking lips.

"Well?" the apparition said, folding his cloaked arms. "Have you nothing to say, King, now that I am here? What would you have me do?"

"Destroy—destroy my enemies," Khalazar croaked.

"A large task, that. You appear to have quite an abundance of them." The one who called himself Morlyn walked slowly around the perimeter of the magic circle, his fiery eyes fixed mockingly on Khalazar's. "Shall I start with the Shurkanese? The Western Commonwealth? Not to mention all those here in Zimboura who have designs on your throne? And then·there is that little matter of the Tryna Lia."

Khalazar pivoted fearfully, trying to keep his face always toward Morlyn. The spellbook had said that spirits were always obedient to their summoners, yet this one showed little respect or subservience. "How can you help me?" he demanded, trying to give his voice an edge of authority.

"We can help one another, Khalazar. Unite against our common foe. I bear no love for the Tryna Lia, and would gladly see her and her followers destroyed. Will you accept my offer?"

Khalazar stared at him in perplexity. With a sigh of impatience the dark figure stepped forward, and very deliberately placed his booted foot within the ring of blood. The king recoiled with a cry, but a long-fingered hand closed like a claw upon his forearm, preventing his escape. He writhed, torn between terror and outrage. This was not possible! No spirit could enter an enchanted circle— and that hand on his arm was surely flesh and blood! Peering up into the dead-white face, Khalazar saw that the "flaming" eyes were in fact reflecting the candlelight, like a cat's: they were golden in color, with slit pupils, the eyes neither of a genie nor a man, but of a beast.

"What *are* you?" he gasped.

"An ally, Khalazar of Zimboura."

For an instant Khalazar thought he must be swooning: the walls seem to reel around him. Then he blinked, dazed and disbelieving. The chamber had vanished, and with it had gone his castle and, it seemed, all of Zimboura. He and his inhuman companion drifted through an unfathomable darkness, pierced only by the silver points of stars. Stars above—and stars *beneath*!

"Where are we?" he shouted wildly.

"Have no fear, Khalazar—you are in your chamber still; at least your body is. We journey now in spirit, through the great void that lies outside the world. Look."

A long arm stretched out, and following where it pointed Khalazar saw a great blue globe suspended in the dark, half in shadow.

"That, King, is the world you know—the world you would have for your own. And now look around you! Here in the great Night, the stars lie thick as dust. They are suns, many of them greater and brighter than the sun you know, and many circled by worlds like your own. How little your ambition is, that you should be content to rule *one* world only!" The arm pointed again. "Far away, so far you cannot see it, is another, smaller sun that orbits this sun of yours, and circling that sun in turn is a world—Azar, the planet for which you were named. You have wasted your time in seeking to summon little genii of earth and air, when the great spirits, the sovereign lords of the spheres, await your bidding! Elazar, and Elombar ruler of the planet that circles the red star Utara—all the celestial thralls of Valdur dwell here in the heights. But you have foes here too."

Again a sweeping gesture of the cloaked arm. "Do you see that planet there, near the sun—the blue-white one that shines so brightly?"

"I see it, spirit."

"That is Arainia, which you of this world call the Morning Star. But it too is a world, and in it your greatest foe dwells."

Once again Khalazar felt a sense of vertigo; once again he blinked and stared about him. The stars were gone. He stood in broad daylight in a park, lush with verdure, feathery fronds waving against the sky, trees in light green leaf and slow-unfolding flower all around him. Beyond reared the towers of a city—a city such as Khalazar had never dreamed of: vast and sprawling, yet orderly, encircled by no protecting wall, filled with stately mansions and pleasure-gardens. In the sun fountains leaped, glittering.

Morlyn led him along a path to the gate of the park, and out into the city. Khalazar followed like a man in a trance; though he seemed to be walking, he felt nothing under his feet, and neither he nor the tall figure before him cast any shadow in the sun. The streets into which they entered thronged with people clad in garments of brilliant hues, tall, graceful men and women, unlike any he had ever seen.

"What city is this?" he cried as the strange people walked past him unheeding. "I have never seen the like—"

Morlyn led him to the gateway of a mansion. "Look," he said softly. "These gates are gold, Khalazar—*gold*, of which the people in this world have such an abundance that they use it even in their children's toys. And on the gateposts, embedded in the marble— do you see the many-colored patterns, the intricate floral designs? Look more closely, and you will find that each leaf and petal is in fact a gemstone: emerald, ruby, lapis lazuli. These gates alone are worth a whole Zimbouran city . . . and this is but the house of a modest merchant." The Zimbouran king tried in vain to prize a gleaming emerald leaf from its setting, swearing with frustration as his insubstantial fingers passed through it.

"Look!" Morlyn waved a white long-fingered hand toward the rooftops, and Khalazar lifted his eyes and saw a great palace with towers reaching to the sun, all alabaster and gold. It perched upon the summit of a green hill, like a sailing ship mounting the crest of a wave. "That, O King, is Halmirion, palace of the greatest sorceress in this world: the Tryna Lia. She is not that rather simple young woman whom you encountered in Trynisia: that was, I fear, a case of mistaken identity. The true Princess dwells here: Ailia Elmiria, daughter of Elarainia the Queen of Night."

Khalazar fell silent, seized with sudden dread as he gazed up at those towers, so bright and confident beneath the sun. How many times had he reassured himself that his foe was but a woman, weaker in body and mind than he. Should they ever meet face to face in mortal combat, the advantage would surely lie with him. But now his heart sank. Who could defeat a monarch of such power, such inexhaustible wealth? She need never face him at all: she could surely raise a hundred armies to his one, and defeat him utterly upon the field of battle. And she had other allies, like the fearsome genii he had beheld in Trynisia . . .

"Help me," he grated, wrenching his gaze from the hateful sight. "If you have the power, then help me defeat this evil sorceress!"

"You shall have my help," Morlyn answered. "And that of the

Valei, the servants of Valdur in other spheres, who hate this world of Arainia and its people more than you can ever know. But you have power too, Khalazar: in your armies, in the devotion you can inspire in them. Once your armies are joined with those of the Valei we will have a force that Heaven itself may fear, O Avatar of Valdur! This world is as rich and fair as Zimboura is dry and desolate. Only do as I advise, and its gold and jewels, its forests and game, its people—and its Princess—shall all be yours."

"Agreed!" the king cried.

And then the echo of that cry was ringing from the stone walls of his chamber; he had been returned to his palace, to his own corporeal form. He spun around. No dark-cloaked figure was anywhere to be seen in the room, so that he might almost have been tempted to think the visitation a delusion or a dream. But from outside the open window there came again that soft rustling sound, like a bird's wings beating in the night.

2

The Phantom
at the Feast

WHO AM I?

The girl lay motionless in her bed, staring upward with sleep blurred eyes at the white canopy. During the early days of her stay here in Halmirion, the first thing that she did on waking was always to wonder where she was, and that mental query was then followed by this second, far more unsettling one. The first question was easily answered, once full memory returned, and with time her mind ceased to pose it, but the other continued to trouble her. She was no longer Ailia Shipwright. There was no escaping that fact, though she still clung to the familiar name instead of using her true one, Elmiria. The identity that once had seemed as firm as the contours of her face had been torn away from her all in a moment, leaving her for a time bewildered and bereft. Ailia Shipwright had been raised quite literally in another world, by a family she still could not help thinking of as hers. Her "parents" Nella and Dannor, her "cousins" Jaimon and Jemma—they were all lost to her now. They lay on the far side of a void trackless as any sea and far greater in breadth: vaster than any distance she had ever before known or imagined. But more than that separated her old family from her. No bond of blood united them. All along she had been an alien in their midst.

Yet she missed them and worried about them still. Ana had told her that the community of sorcerers or Nemerei in the world of Mera would speak with Ailia's foster family and assure them that she was now safe. But they could never be made to understand where she now was, and they must be anxious about her, too— even though Dannor and Nella had known she was not theirs to keep, and might one day be reunited with her true kin. Ailia sighed. Nella and the others would be first to tell her, as practical Great Islanders, that it would do no good to lie here and fret about it. Wherever she had been fostered, this was the world of her birth, and this was the life that she must now lead. And today was the anniversary of that birth, which meant official festivities she was obliged to take part in.

She got out of the bed, parting its filmy white curtains, and stood looking around her bedchamber. It was a spacious circular room, following the shape of the tower in which it was set, with windows looking out in three directions. On a marble-topped table next to the bed was a collection of toys from the early childhood that she could not recall: a mechanized bird in a golden cage, a doll's house built by the city's craft guilds complete with tiny leaded windows and miniature furnishings. These playthings stood exactly as she had left them when her mother had taken her from the palace over twenty years ago. Ailia had not had the heart to remove them: they were, for her, a link with her lost past. She really ought to have a few faint impressions of those days. It was not extreme youth but distress of mind that had erased her earliest memories, or so the royal physicians told her. For among them there must lie buried one horrific memory of a stormy sea, a holed and sinking ship . . .

Ailia dressed, then went to one of the deep-set windows and gazed out on her palace. Its roofs filled all her view: a wilderness of towers, turrets, domes, and cupolas, of gold-plated finials and weather vanes and flagpoles from which long banners streamed. Here the sky seemed very near, and at night there were brilliant stars, and the little blue moon Miria, and the Arch of Heaven (actually a system of rings that surrounded the planet) like a pale glimmering bridge spanning the sky from end to end. Ailia had lived in this world for only three of its brief years, but even now it was becoming difficult to recall that time spent beneath another sky empty of such wondrous sights. A sky with dimmer stars and a large white moon and no shining Arch, where the sun looked smaller because it was not so near, and rose not in the west but the east. A world where she had not been the Tryna Lia, prophesied ruler of the Elei, but an ordinary girl of Great Island to whom palaces and royalty were dreams. To this day she sometimes felt like a character in a story she had once read, who as an infant was substituted by villains for the son of a lord, and lived in luxury for years before the true heir returned. "I still half-expect the *real* Tryna Lia to show up," she had confessed wryly to her friends, "and turn me out of her palace." What she did not reveal was that she often wished it could happen.

Despite her title, she was not really a *ruler* in the full sense of the word. Her title, like her father's, was honorary. The High Council that met in the Great Hall in the city, and was made up of representatives from all over Eldimia, the Territories and the Isles, formulated state policy and adjudicated disputes. The religious leaders of Arainia's numerous faiths attended to spiritual matters. In fact, Ailia realized with humility, there was really very little for her to *do*, except read the occasional speech (written by someone else), approve each action of the Council (a mere formality), and host receptions for dignitaries. The populace almost never saw her: she was for them a figure remote as the moon, a demi-goddess dwelling in her palace-fane high on its wall-encircled hill, inaccessible and otherworldly. In many ways Ailia and her retainers trod delicate ground: for prior to her mother's day the people of Eldimia had had no monarchy, and though many noble and royal families still existed, their titles were also honorary and conferred no real power. Though all Arainians had known of the Tryna Lia prophecy, some looked on it as an allegory or a fable. These had frowned when Queen Elarainia had been acclaimed as the goddess after performing some "miracles." True, her sorcerous powers had been outstanding, but such powers were not uncommon in this world, as they had been in Mera.

Those who had been opposed to Elarainia's coronation and deification had been relieved at her flight and the removal of her equally revered daughter. Ailia's reappearance and ascension to the throne had upset this faction. Their objections subsided somewhat when it became apparent that Ailia was not going to abuse her position for personal gain. If anything she had been just as frightened of the crowds' adulation. A document had been hastily drawn up, limiting her influence and ensuring that she remained little more than a figurehead. Not that any of this made a real difference. Those who believed outnumbered those who did not, and the former would have obeyed any edict she chose to issue regardless of any opposition by secular officials. That fact, she reflected with disquiet, must be troubling in certain quarters even though she did nothing to exploit it.

In the smaller turret next to hers was the guard-room; her friends Jomar and Lorelyn often frequented this room to play dice games with the off-duty guards, and when she glimpsed them in its windows Ailia would lean out of her own high casement and call across to them. But they were not there now. Beyond it was a round tower with a tall peaked window facing her own: that was Damion's room. At night she could see his lamp glowing softly through the window, and know that he was there. It was a comforting thought. Damion . . . Always she thought of him as she had first seen him in the Chapel of the Paladins, in his white priest's robe, shining in the golden light as if he and not the sacred fire on the altar were its source—a figure that at first sight had seemed to her more angelic than human. But it was the inner essence of Damion she had come to admire more and more as time passed: his kindness, his courage, his utter dependability. Once she had shyly worshiped him from afar; now he had become a friend, dearer to her than any other. And yet it was not enough.

She wondered where Damion was. In his room, in the palace

gardens, or in the city outside the walls? Damion, unlike herself, was free to go wherever he willed; Jomar and Lorelyn, too. She hoped at least one of them was in, for she was feeling sociable today. At least, "sociable" was the word she used for her present state of mind: "lonely" sounded too absurd, in this great palace with its three hundred courtiers and retainers.

She left the bedroom and wandered through the other rooms of her apartments. All were large and luxuriously appointed. Yet she paced restlessly about them as if she were a prisoner in a cell. Halmirion was a cage constructed of velvet and marble and gold, and she felt its bars more keenly with each passing day. At a full-length mirror, she paused to eye the reflection framed by its gilded scrolls. She had grown slightly taller since her arrival on Arainia— an effect of this world's lighter gravity—and the hot Arainian sun had brought out the gold in her hair, though its wispy ends (she noted with disappointment) still would not grow very far below her waist. She had dressed casually in an everyday gown, high-waisted with plain tight sleeves, but it was of sapphire-colored linen, finer by far than anything the Island girl had ever dreamed of wearing.

Her pet mimic dog, stretched out like a fur rug upon the floor, raised its head and gazed at her with great, brown, almost-human eyes. Ailia knelt beside it, hugging the massive neck with its thick tawny ruff and stroking the long, doglike muzzle. The mimic dog was a native Arainian beast, a curious blend of canine and ape, valued for its loyalty and playfulness. The creatures could perform any number of tricks and even carry out simple domestic tasks with their handlike paws. They were also ideal pets and nursemaids for small children, and this one had been Ailia's special guardian when she was small; she did not remember it, but the animal had clearly never forgotten its young mistress. "Shall we go for a walk, Bezni?" Ailia suggested. The creature leaped up at once, tail waving.

In the corridor outside two guards in blue-and-gold palace livery immediately snapped to attention, their eyes widening. "Highness," they murmured, bowing their heads as she passed. She sensed their awe at being so close to her: the Tryna Lia, titular head of all Arainian religions, figurehead of the state, believed by many to be the mortal daughter of an incarnate goddess. Ailia felt uneasily self-conscious as she walked away down the hall, feeling their eyes upon her. One of the men looked no older than she. Outside the first right-hand door she paused for a moment, before going in. This apartment was as elegantly furnished as her own, with murals and molded ceilings. Rose-colored curtains hung at the windows, and a carpet of the same tint covered the floor; the air was sweetly scented by a bouquet of fresh lilies, set in a vase on a marble table beneath a large full-length portrait.

Ailia had been born in this room: on her birthday it seemed only natural to come here.

She walked over to the portrait and stood looking up at it. The young woman in it might almost have been Ailia herself—an idealized Ailia, more beautiful, more spiritual, more serene. But this woman's eyes were as blue as the gown in which she was clad, not violet-gray like Ailia's; and the amazing ankle-length hair was a shade lighter than hers. Still, the delicate modeling of the face was like an echo of Ailia's own features, and so too were the ivory-pale complexion and long graceful neck. The portrait showed her standing in the palace gardens, with a background all misty blues and greens. Elarainia, acclaimed queen of Eldimia, named by the Elei for the goddess herself: the greatest sorceress they had ever known. Gazing at this painting, one was drawn into its tranquility; though for Ailia there would always be a poignant ache as well. Her mother had vanished in the world of Mera long years ago, and many now believed her to be dead.

This room with its contents, and one lock of blonde hair preserved in a jeweled reliquary in the chapel, were all that remained of the queen. Once, when no one else was about, Ailia had removed the holy relic from its sacred confinement, holding the silken softness against her cheek. It had briefly evoked vague images and impressions from early childhood—long, honey-colored hair that had brushed her face gently, a warm softness against which she had rested, long ago. Ailia's eyes misted at the thought.

"She was very beautiful," a voice said suddenly, behind her, "wasn't she?" Ailia turned to see her father standing in the doorway.

"I am sorry if I disturbed you," he said.

"No, no—and you needn't say any more about—about her. I know how you feel—"

Ailia and King Tiron went on apologizing awkwardly for a few moments. They still felt a slight discomfort in each other's presence, sensing the chasm of time and distance that her mother's flight had put between them. It was difficult to compensate for so much time lost.

"She was beautiful," he repeated at length, entering the room. His dark gray eyes held sorrow as he looked at the portrait. "But her real beauty came from within her: gentleness, compassion, wisdom. They—illuminated her, like a candle in a lantern. Small wonder people believed she was a goddess. They would have made this room into a holy shrine had I let them. But I needed a private place of my own, where I could be alone with her memory."

Ailia hesitated. "Father—*do* you think she could still be alive?"

He laid a hand on her shoulder. "I long to believe that she is. But my reason tells me she did not survive the wreck of her flying ship—"

"*I* shouldn't have survived it, but I did." Ailia gazed at the portrait again. "How could I have survived such a wreck alone when I was just a tiny child—not much more than an infant? If she died then how did I come to shore alive and unhurt?"

"I cannot say. It is a mystery, and it may always be."

"If only I could have known her!" she burst out. Everyone else had, it seemed—her father, the courtiers, the people—even the mimic dog had known the queen's caresses, and looked up into that lost, lovely face. The clerics in the city declared that the divine Elarainia had passed back into the realm of the Immortals, and was still with her people in spirit: so they comforted themselves and the faithful. But Ailia yearned for the mortal woman who had been her mother.

"You speak of her so seldom, Father," she said. "I haven't asked you to, because I know it hurts you to remember. But there's so much I still don't know about her."

Tiron looked at her sadly. "I have been very selfish. You lost a mother, even as I lost a wife, and you've a right to know about her. But if only you *could* remember something of her, daughter, you would understand why my grieving is still keen after all this time."

He was silent a moment, and she thought he would say no more. But presently he continued in a soft low voice. "She lived on the South Shore of Eldimia, in the wilds—as all the true Elei do."

"The forest Elei are very different from those in the city, aren't they?" Ailia asked.

"Yes: for in our part of Eldimia the Fairfolk have dwelt among Merei—true humans—for many generations, and married them and brought forth children of mixed blood like ourselves. But their kin in the forests have no dealings with the rest of humanity. They do not barter or trade, only making for themselves things of beauty that they do not sell. They do not even farm. Each takes for him- or herself whatever is needed, straight from the forest. It gives to them fruits and vegetables, roots and nuts, and many of the herbs and flowers and even the bark of certain trees possess healing properties. Their clothing they make from cottony growths, harvested from a tree: some color the fabric with natural dyes, but most simply leave it white.

"Many years ago I departed on a journey to learn more of them. I went deep into the forests, even to the shadow of Hyelanthia, the Country in the Clouds—"

"I have heard of that place. Where is it?"

"It lies near the coast, where once there was a great tableland. Over many eons the rains have swept most of it away, leaving a few vast stone columns and plateaux. The Old Ones lived there long ago, it is said, together with many strange creatures, beasts and birds that have long since vanished from the world. The Elei revere it as the dwelling-place of the goddess. Your mother lived there, at the foot of one of the mountainous columns. Her home was just a cave in the cliff, floored with moss and screened by some climbing vines. Nearby there is an inlet of the sea, bright with reefs of coral, where she used to swim in the mornings. She had no family, no friends save for the animals that gathered about her—she had a magical touch with any kind of beast, furred or feathered, finned or scaled. The woodland Elei, the forest-dwellers, held her in a kind of awe. They truly believed she was the goddess herself, and sought her out for her advice on many things. When I learned of her I was curious and decided to seek her out, too.

"I had thought to find some aged wise-woman, such as I had seen in these forest communities: learned in herb-lore from many long years of experience. Instead I saw a woman both young and lovely, with golden hair that fell to her feet. I was smitten from the very first, though I had no real hope. 'King' they may call me now, but my blood is neither royal nor noble. I am not even the most handsome of men, and she . . . when I saw her, I knew at last what the words 'divinely beautiful' meant.

"I asked her about her parents, but she did not seem to know what I meant. She did not understand 'father,' and when I asked about her mother, she only pointed skyward and said, 'She is there.' Either she meant that her mother was in Heaven, or else she believed in some celestial goddess that watched over her: I never learned which. I realize she must have been orphaned at an early age in some tragic accident of which she had no memory, for she seemed quite unconcerned to be alone. I joined her followers, sat at her feet night and day and listened to her speak. When after some weeks had passed she told me that she returned my love, I could not believe my ears. It was as though a goddess stooped to love a mere mortal." His voice had a tremor in it, and though his mouth worked for a moment he could not continue.

They were both silent for a time, her father deep in contemplation before the portrait while Bezni drowsed with her chin on his foot. Ailia was wrapped in her own thoughts.

BY SOME UNSPOKEN CONSENSUS Ailia's birthday was always treated as a national holiday. No special decree had been given: the people of Eldimia simply abandoned their work and flocked to the streets in joyous celebration each year since her return. Halmirion marked the occasion as always with a special ball and banquet in the evening.

Ailia looked in her mirror as her ladies-in-waiting bustled about her, dressing her, binding up her hair in braids, and piling it into an elaborate crown atop her head. The style made her look older, she thought with approval: more mature. Tonight, too, she did not have to wear her formal regalia, and her gown was a floating filmy thing of lavender blue, with a diaphanous capelet that hung to her hips. On her right hand was a star sapphire ring that had been her mother's, while around her neck she had placed Damion's birthday present, a silver chain from which hung a single large pearl. Damion would be at the ball tonight, she thought, and he *must* look at her for once, not as princess or friend, but as a woman. Only Damion, who had known her before ever he learned of her true identity, was capable of loving her for her own sake.

If only he would!

Her old nurse Benia came into the room and beamed at her. "Oh, my dear, that's lovely! You do look a vision." Ailia smiled. Benia still begrudged the misfortune that had taken "her" girl away from her years ago, and Ailia, knowing this, allowed Benia to fuss over her a little. She was, truth to tell, quite glad for some mothering at times.

Lady Lira, chief of her ladies-in-waiting, had also entered. In her hands was something that flashed like frost. "You must wear a tiara at least, Highness."

Three years ago Ailia would have exclaimed with delight at the jeweled thing Lira held; now she only felt irritated. "Must I? It would be so nice just to be *me* for one evening."

"You are the Tryna Lia," reproved Lady Lira. "That *is* who you are, and always shall be." She was a small, almost birdlike woman with bright eyes of a rich red-brown, masses of auburn hair, a sharp high-bridged nose, and an air of irresistible authority that fully compensated for her lack of height. She pinned the tiara firmly in place, just in front of Ailia's braided crown, while the princess submitted meekly.

"It was your mother's, Ailia dear," said Benia, her eyes touched with tears as she looked at the piece of jewelry. Ailia reached up to run her hand along the tiara, which was of gold set with pearls and little diamonds. So Elarainia had worn this, too: she felt a fleeting sense of closeness to her mother at the thought.

There was a sharp report from outside, followed by a larger explosion and then a flash of red light. Ailia went over to a window and looked down on the gardens below. The royal pyrotechnics display was underway, and the night was filled with fiery shapes: great glittering chandeliers that hung briefly from the sky as from a ceiling, and then faded away; scintillating comets, and flickers of many-colored lightning accompanied by roars of artificial thunder. Down on the ground were the set pieces, fire fountains and cascades whose every droplet was a blazing spark, and wheels of whirling flame dazzlingly mirrored in the ornamental pools. Flourishes of music accompanied them.

Ailia opened the pane and drew in deep breaths of flower-scented evening air. Miria, the little blue moon, was up: the moon whose name she bore, or rather that took its name from her. She had been told the old myth of its origin, of how the mother-goddess Elarainia had placed it in the night sky as a pleasure-garden for her beloved daughter. It was quite true that the moon had its own atmosphere, for woods and flowing waters could be seen on its surface through a spyglass. The Elei had visited Miria back in their starfaring days, it was said; now the lunar lands were unattainable. What flowers were blooming up there, what scents perfuming the air of that distant sphere?

She looked down at the earthly gardens again. Ailia always suppressed a little shiver when she gazed on one particular spot: the eastern slope of the hill where Morlyn had fallen wounded to the earth in dragon form, scarring the ground and crushing the greenery beneath him. All signs of the damage were long removed, but the memory was burned into her mind. Prince Morlyn, her most dangerous foe: he lived still, somewhere in hiding, and it had been said that she might have to face him again one day, perhaps at the head of an invading army . . .

"Are you ready, *Trynel?*" asked another lady-in-waiting, peering around the door.

She drew back from the casement and closed it. "I never feel ready for these functions. There are so many things that could go wrong. If you trip on *your* skirt, for instance, it's just embarrassing. If I trip on mine the whole world will hear of it tomorrow—"

"Ailia, dear—" began Benia.

"Councils will be held," Ailia continued in a tone of deadly calm, "to discuss the implications of the incident, the faith of believers will be shaken, my political opponents will rise up in arms, and I shall have no alternative but to flee the palace and live in the wilderness for the rest of my life, subsisting on roots and—"

"Nonsense, Your Highness," said Lady Lira, brisk as ever. "Let us go."

With her ladies in attendance Ailia set off down the hall, tottering a little in the special high-heeled shoes designed to boost her height. As she had spent most of her young life on Mera, a world of much heavier gravity, her growth was still somewhat stunted by Arainian standards. Veiled sibyls carrying silver candelabra went solemnly before her, chanting: "The Lady of Light approaches! Make way for the Daughter of Heaven, the Tryna Lia." It was a ritual that Ailia found extremely embarrassing, but she did not dare ask them to stop.

Her father was already in the ballroom, greeting the guests with his own parents and grandmother standing at his side. With them was Ana, the aged woman who had helped Ailia and her companions find the Star Stone in Mera. She looked tiny and bent next to the others, but Ailia noticed that everyone here treated her with respect—even reverence. For Ana was in fact Queen Eliana—a Nemerei, a great sorceress, who had lived for more than five hundred years. She stood holding her cat Greymalkin in her arms, stroking her silvery-gray fur absently as she watched the festivities. Beyond the receiving line was a milling mass of splendid robes and gowns, heads circled with silver or gold, white arms and necks on which bracelets and necklaces studded with real gems were displayed. It would have been a scene of almost vulgar ostentation on Mera, where jewels were the costly perquisites of the wealthy. But Arainia abounded with gemstones, some of them unknown to Mera: the sea-green *sorige*, for example, which came from the far south, and fire-yellow *reflambine*, and the wondrous pale *venudor* that shone in the dark with its own inner luminescence. All were valued simply for their beauty, though some Elei revered the "powers" said to lie within them: spirits that, lingering within the crystal lattices of natural gems, turned them into conduits between the realm of matter and the higher plane. The Star Stone itself was believed to house a spirit manifesting itself in the form of a fiery bird, the *Elmir*. Many votaries had claimed to see it rise phoenixlike from the crystalline depths.

Ailia paused before the great doors, listening to the minstrels and the murmur of conversation. After attending several of these events she had learned to combat her natural shyness by trying to isolate a few familiar faces in the crowd. Tonight that would be no difficult task: there was but one face there that she truly wished to see. She took a deep breath and swept into the ballroom, her capelet flowing back from her shoulders like gauzy wings. There was a gratifying lull in the conversation, and the eyes of all those assembled turned at once toward her. But her own eyes were only for Damion. He was standing by one of the tall windows, arrayed in court dress to honor the occasion: a sky-blue doublet with white breeches and boots. With him was Lorelyn. Her gown was *red*— bright scarlet, an unheard-of hue even for a festal gathering. The white wall she stood next to was tinted with reflected color, as though blushing at her boldness. Yet it suited her, somehow. She looked like some exotic flower that had sprung up defiantly in the midst of a garden of tame pastel-colored blooms. Damion glanced toward Ailia, and then quickly away again, turning back to Lorelyn. Stung, Ailia averted her own eyes and proceeded to greet her guests with what she hoped would pass for enthusiasm. But she kept stealing little side-glances at Damion. How handsome he was—his fairness and those fine features could turn heads even in a world where beauty was commonplace. She heaved a little inaudible sigh. Three short words, so easy to say, were it not for this impassable gulf between mouth and mind. *I love you.* In Mera young women were taught never to speak those words to a man unless he himself spoke first; Arainian girls, she knew, were less inhibited, but still she could not speak. In her mind she envisioned herself saying those words, seeing Damion's familiar features touched with surprise, embarrassment, awkwardness. He might even avoid her afterward, find excuses not to be alone with her.

I can't lose Damion's friendship, she thought in sudden panic, *I just can't.*

Then a single musician began to play upon a man-high Elei harp, the notes plucked from the strings drifting toward Ailia like petals shaken from a flowering tree. All the Elei, she knew, were musically gifted—the heritage, as they believed, of an angelic ancestry. She listened as a woman's voice was raised in song:

> Whene'er I gaze upon thy face
> To me it seemeth, more and more,
> That in another time and place
> I knew and loved thee once before.
>
> O was it in that fairer land
> That was before the worlds began
> We met, and wandered hand in hand,
> Ere grief was known to god and man?
>
> On earth thy love is not for me,
> And all my yearning is in vain.
> Yet life must end; so it may be
> In Heaven we shall love again.

It was a song of old Mera, penned by the unknown Bard of Blyssion. The court never tired of hearing Meran songs and stories: Ailia had often regaled her ladies-in-waiting with long-lost folk and faerie tales from that distant world. She had heard this particular song many times before, it was a great favorite at court, and it was simply stupid for her to have tears in her eyes as she listened. She took her seat and watched as the dances began—the dances of the Elei that were as pleasant to watch as they were to take part in, forming elaborate interweaving patterns as the dancers glided across the floor. In none of them did Damion offer to be Ailia's partner, though he danced with Lorelyn several times.

"What a lovely couple your young friends make, dear." Ailia turned to see that her great-grandmother had been following her gaze. She was more than 150 years old, for she had Elei blood: her hair was pure white, and yet she looked younger by far than would a Merei woman of four score years. And her eyes and mind were still keen. "They are both so tall, and blond!" she exclaimed, smiling. Ailia merely nodded, not trusting her voice to reply without a telltale tremor. Could it be—were the two of them . . .

A bell chimed, and the guests all drained from the room, flowing into the corridor and down the stairs to the banquet hall below. Damion and Lorelyn, she saw, walked together.

IT WAS A SPLENDID BANQUET in the Elei style, which dictated that food must feed the eye as well as the palate, so there were slices of fruit laid out to look like bright-winged butterflies and many-petaled blossoms, and melons with carved rinds, all cooled by blocks of ice sculpted to look like swans or dolphins or dancing maidens (these caused a sensation among those of the guests who had never before seen frozen water). There were blue eggs of halcyons lying in soft green nests of moss, candied flowers, and little cakes shaped like crescent moons and covered in thin layers of edible gold or silver. Ailia felt her spirits lift a little. It was a pleasure to feed people, to watch them talk and laugh as they savored the delicacies furnished by the royal kitchens.

She glanced up to see Jomar striding into the hall: she was not surprised that he was tardy, for she knew how he loathed court gatherings. Had it not been her birthday he likely wouldn't have shown up at all. He was leading a large white dog on a leash—at least, he had one end of the leash, the dog another; there seemed to be a contest under way as to which of them was leading.

"Why the dog, Jo?" asked Damion. "I didn't think you liked animals that much."

"It's for *her*," replied Jomar, gesturing brusquely at Ailia. "It's my birthday present. I want you to take this dog with you whenever you go out in the grounds," he instructed the princess. "I've trained him to attack anyone who tries to assault you or abduct you."

The hound flung itself happily on Ailia, then on Damion, greeting them with sloppy kisses. "Oh, I see—it's been trained to love people to death," Damion said, trying to fend off its enthusiastic attentions.

"Don't be stupid. It's only fierce to *assailants*," retorted Jomar. "Look—here, boy, attack!" He advanced on it in a menacing manner. With a merry yelp the faerie-hound pranced up to him, licking his face. Jomar cursed the animal with a comment on its parentage, technically correct in its case but not normally uttered in polite society. The other three laughed.

"All right, so he needs a little more training," said Jomar sheepishly.

"Do you really think there's any danger here, Jo?" Lorelyn asked. "Eldimia seems such a *safe* place."

"So far," retorted Jomar cynically.

Lorelyn was right though, Ailia reflected: this new Eldimian year was unfolding as had all the others before it, in unbroken peace and content. The world of Arainia was smaller than Mera, both in its physical size and in its population, and its events were smaller too: there were the usual minor dramas that occur wherever human beings are, but no great wars or social upheavals troubled its sphere. Yet still she felt a little shadow of unease at her heart.

"What lives we lead, don't we?" Lorelyn went on, her cheer undimmed by Jomar's scowl. "Just like those stories you tell, Ailia. Don't you feel as though you've fallen right into one?"

"Yes," said Ailia. "I have often thought that life is like a story, only the people in it are also writing it. They can help to decide what will happen, and how it will all end."

Lorelyn looked pensive. "I never thought of it that way. How would you choose to write your own story, Ailia?"

"I don't know. At the moment it seems it's being written for me." And with that Ailia fell silent again.

Jomar surveyed the festal board with distaste. "No meat. No liquor. I can't stand this!"

"Have some nectar, Jo," said Damion, offering a pitcher of clear golden liquid. "It tastes good, and it *doesn't* make you drunk."

"Where's the fun in that?" growled Jomar. But he settled into a chair and started picking at the dishes.

"What's the matter with you, Jo?" Lorelyn asked him bluntly.

Jomar glowered down at his plate, his fingers toying aimlessly with slices of fruit. "Whenever we have a party like this, I keep thinking of Zimboura, and all the slaves still in the labor camps there. Why can't we *do* something about it? Go and fight to free them?"

Ailia said nothing, her thoughts turning once more to her adoptive family in Mera. She wondered if they had remained on the western continent, or fled back to Great Island. They might not be safe for long in either place, if the king of Zimboura chose to send forth his armies.

"Remember, Jomar," said Damion, "no one in this world knows how to fight. There has been no war here in centuries."

"And then there is the question of how we're to cross the void to Mera," King Tiron added. "Only the queen succeeded in doing so. No one else knows how to construct a flying ship, not even the Nemerei. Nor have we the aid of dragons or cherubim. For the moment, any army we build can only be for our own defense, in case of an invasion."

Ailia wished they would speak of something else. It reminded her too much of the prophecy concerning herself. *Me—lead an army into Mera! As if I ever could!* she thought. *But the people here really believe that I will, one day. I feel a perfect fraud.*

The feast was followed by more entertainments. There were jugglers, singers, and, finally, a demonstration of magic by a troupe of white-robed Nemerei from the sorcerers' academy of Melnemeron. Never had anyone present seen such superb illusions. Flocks of flying rainbow-colored birds, and fireballs, and spouting fountains appeared out of nowhere, only to be banished again with a wave of the enchanter's hand. At one point the whole of the banquet hall was transformed into a forest: the frescoed roof was replaced by green foliage, while trunks of trees rose around the dining tables, and in the center of what had been the floor a stream ran bubbling. Then the illusory scene disappeared, and the revelers blinked about them at their restored surroundings.

"Well," remarked Damion as they all applauded, "this lot would put all those sleight-of-hand conjurers on Mera out of work!"

"What *is* a Nemerei, anyway?" Jomar asked in his brusque way. "Just a better and cleverer conjurer?"

"Not at all: the Nemerei do not deal only in cunning tricks." It was Master Wu, the aged and venerable court sorcerer, who answered. A small, stout man of Kaanish extraction, he sported a long silver-white beard that hung down to his belt. No one knew how old he was: he had lived in Mirimar for many years, and been an instructor at Melnemeron before coming here. As always he was flamboyantly attired, wearing for this occasion a robe of purple silk worked with silver stars and runes and a matching peaked cap. But he was a Nemerei of no mean skill, and Ailia had learned long ago to respect Wu's wisdom and advice.

"Our power is very real," the old sorcerer informed Jomar, in a tone of mild rebuke. "Nemerei are healers, augurs, warriors, ambassadors. Before priesthoods arose to mediate between gods and mortals, before the dawn of philosophy and the healing arts, the Nemerei existed. We are in all worlds, all races, all times. The ancients of Mera called our predecessors by various names: shamans, prophets, wizards, witches."

"But how do you do what you do?" asked Lorelyn, curious.

"The source of what you call *magic* is the plane of the Ether. Some of us can faintly sense it, others are fully aware of it, fewer still are able to tap its power. The Nemerei are poised on the cusp of two realities, drawing on the one to influence the other. We can use ethereal power to heal physical injuries, divine possible future events, reach out to other minds."

"But any power can be misused," observed Ana in her quiet voice.

Wu inclined his head. "That is so, Queen Eliana. Magic can hurt as easily as it can heal. Mera's King Andarion formed the Paladin Order to counter the cruelties of other armed knights; even so, the Nemerei have had to organize themselves against the abusers of magic. A sorcerer is far less likely to wield magic for evil if he knows he will be punished. The true Nemerei must be forever vigilant."

As they fell silent, snatches of conversation from the other guests at the table could be heard. ". . . fearsome visions—stars falling out of the heavens, dragons in the sky—"

Jomar turned around to face the speaker. "Visions? What is all this? You Nemerei are always seeing things," he said irritably.

It was Head Sibyl Marima who was talking. She had put back her sibyl's veil to dine, and her young-old Elei face looked into his with a solemn expression. "Many dream portents at one time or another, but for so many to dream alike is a portent in itself, and cannot be ignored. The Great Comet that entered our skies was only a forewarning. There is plainly some evil at work in our world: the influence, perhaps, of a star or planet of ill omen."

"A star *and* a planet, I think," said Wu.

Ailia stared at him. "Do you mean Azar and Azarah?" Elei lore spoke of a small, dim star accompanied by a single planet that circled the sun, far out in the void. "Master Wu, please tell us more."

But what Wu meant to say in answer they would never know. For at that moment there was a great flash, like lightning, and a figure appeared in the center of the hall. It was attired in a robe and kingly crown of strange design: its face was pale above a black beard, and its eyes glittered with savage light as it stared at the high table. "I am Khalazar of Zimboura!" thundered the apparition.

Greymalkin caterwauled and sprang from Ana's arms onto her shoulder. Tiron leaped up in anger. "What is this? Who summoned this illusion?" he demanded. But the white-robed Nemerei all stood open-mouthed, as astonished as anyone else.

"It is none of their doing," declared Wu, also rising to his feet.

"It *is* Khalazar!" Jomar leaped forward, knocking a chair aside. "Call the guards! Take him!" he shouted.

"Impossible," Ana told him calmly. Alone of them all she had remained in her seat. She stroked the bristling cat on her shoulder. "He isn't really there, Jomar. It is an ethereal double—a projection of his image."

As the dark king drew nearer they saw that he was indeed transparent and insubstantial, objects behind him showing through his red robe and golden mantle as he moved. He glared upon Ailia with his ghostly eyes. "Vile enchantress! The days of your unholy reign are ended. My armies shall descend on your world, seize and conquer it, level your cities, and slay every man down to the smallest child. Arainia shall be mine—its cities, its wealth, its women, its cattle, and all else that lies within its sphere. And you, witch, shall be cast down from your throne!" He flung his mantle aside, exposing the sword-belt its golden folds had concealed, and with a flourish he drew forth a great scimitar and brandished it.

Somehow Ailia found her voice. "Why are you doing this?" she asked, as Damion and her father moved to flank her protectively. "What have we done to you?"

The spectral figure had already begun to fade at its edges, like a mist in the sun. "I go now, witch," the harsh voice cried, "but when I return it will be in might, with many armies at my command."

And with that his ethereal form vanished from their sight, leaving them all staring at the empty air.

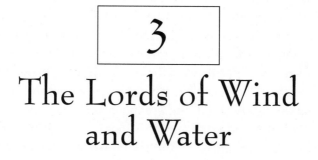

3

The Lords of Wind and Water

BY IMPERIAL COMMAND, the grand council of the Loänan gathered in its customary place of assembly, the Emperor's palace of adamant. This was the largest of many such palaces built by the Old Ones, and like all of them it sported many towers and spires, rising to majestic heights and glittering like diamond; they were carved from a crystal pure and unclouded as fine glass, which no weapon of any kind could break nor even scratch. Like a few of its sister palaces, this one had been built without any foundation, so that it might be raised aloft by sorcery. Wingless beings visiting these aerial castles found it a wonder merely to look through the floors, which being transparent were also windows: to see, there beneath their feet, vertiginous views of valleys and mountain ranges, or dimpled seas, or white canopies of cloud. The Emperor's palace was at this time suspended in the skies of Alfaran, the Motherworld. Beneath it spread a sea of blue and gold and purple cloud, with the crimson whorl of a storm visible on the far-distant horizon. No land showed through the misty gaps below, only more airy chasms floored with variegated vapors: clouds upon clouds. The planet's surface lay submerged deep at its center, and nothing lived there. On such planets as these, it was not the surface but the upper atmosphere that bore life. Alfaran's martlets and alerions and giant thunderbirds dwelt among the gyring clouds and branching bolts of its centuries-old storms, whose vortices could have engulfed many lesser planets. So did the scaly-headed safats that came here to lay their eggs in air. The pearly globes were buoyed up by the winds, light as bubbles, and from the moment the safat hatchlings' beaks broke through the shells they were able to fly. Alfaran was a world of wind-riders.

For millennia Loänan had visited this planet to play in its mantle of many-colored clouds. But within the walls of the crystal palace the mood was grave. All the dragon monarchs of the Empire were in attendance in the vast central hall, kings and queens of the four races that took their names from their preferred abodes: the cave-dwelling earth-dragons, the water-dragons that made their homes in rivers and lakes and ocean deeps, the sky-dragons that lived in lofty mountain aeries, and the ethereal dragons that spent much of their time upon the higher plane, far removed from the worlds of matter. A fifth race, the Imperial dragons, had been specially bred in ages past by the Loänan to protect their stellar realm in times of conflict. Six members of this warrior caste watched over Orbion, Emperor of the Loänan and ruler of the worlds; their own draconic attendants and guards surrounded the other monarchs.

The dragons gleamed in the heart of the crystal chamber like a rainbow within a prism, for each race sported its own distinctive hue. The sky-dragons were blue as lapis lazuli, the water-dragons jade-green, and the earth-dragons red as the molten fires of the earth; while the ethereal dragons were white, and the Imperial dragons golden. Yet when seen up close no Loänan was all one color. The scales of the sky-dragons held a sheen of violet, like the iridescence on a blue butterfly's wings; those of the green Loänan had a silver gloss like rime, and the earth-dragons bore glints of gold. Upon the white ethereal dragons, elusive pearly hues shifted and shimmered. And the eyes of the Loänan gleamed jewel-bright: irises of ruby red for the water-dragons and amethyst for the dragons of the sky, sapphire for the ethereal dragons, emerald for the guardians of the Empire, and smoldering topaz for those that dwelt within the earth. In the forehead of each was a round pale dracontias crystal, glowing with an opal's veiled fires.

The Dragon Emperor called out in his great trumpeting voice, and the other dragons fell silent. He was an ethereal Loänan of great age, his mane and beard white as fresh-fallen snow, his nacreous wings billowing high above his head like the silken canopy that surmounts a human monarch's throne. At his summons a lone Imperial dragon approached him, its golden scales flashing like a carp's when it swims up from the bottom of a pool. It took a subservient position, horned head bowed low beneath the Emperor's foreclaws. Orbion's eyes, coldly blue as mountain tarns, rested long upon the golden dragon. Then he spoke in the Loänan tongue.

"Come, Auron. You said you had something of great importance to divulge, yet dared not speak mind to mind."

"That is so, my Emperor. It was too vital a matter: an enemy in the Ether might have overheard."

"Now that you are come I shall judge whether you were right. There are no foes in this place. Speak!"

The Imperial dragon obeyed, meeting the Emperor's eyes with his own deep viridian ones. "What I wished to tell you, O Son of Heaven," he declared, "is that I am certain now. She *is* the one, without a doubt."

There was a murmur among the Loänan, and a stirring of wings that sent light breezes flowing throughout the crystal hall. But the old Emperor remained motionless. "The human female you saved in Mera?" he replied. "How can you be so sure?"

"We saved one another, Son of Heaven," the golden dragon corrected humbly. "I could never have escaped the mountain peak without her aid."

"Yes—you were bound with iron, as I recall. That was careless of you, Auron."

"It was, O my Emperor," said the other, hanging his head. "I had spent many days on the mountaintop, guarding the gate of Heaven and awaiting the travelers of whom the cherubim spoke. I was very weary. Morlyn came and chained me while I slept before the gate, leaving me unable to fly or shift my shape or even to mind-speak to the cherubim. The girl Ailia was my salvation. She did not know, then, that I was a thinking being like herself: she would have seen me as a mere beast, and one larger than any she had ever encountered. What she did required not only compassion, but uncommon courage. She *is* the one, my Emperor: I began to suspect it from that moment. I have watched her in Arainia ever since, taking various forms natural to that world. Among them is a human disguise—"

A low hiss escaped the Emperor's tusked jaws. "Dangerousss," he rasped.

Auron bowed his head again. "I have taken all possible precautions: no one there suspects my true identity."

A silence fell, broken only by the trilling cries of martlets as they darted in and out of the palace's open door and through its high-ceilinged chambers. They resembled Meran swallows, save that they lacked legs: they spent all their lives on the wing, feeding upon airborne motes, never able to alight even in sleep. Through the glassy roof above them a fierce white sun blazed. Nine hundred years ago its rays had pierced the pellucid shell of Auron's egg, calling him forth to a life of duty and service to the Celestial Empire. More than seven centuries ago Auron had left his native star, and after many wanderings had come to the world of Mera, then in its golden age. He had guarded the palace of the Elei in the land of Trynisia for generations.

But during the tumultuous Dark Age that followed, the Celestial Emperor had forbidden any further contact with humans, even with the Elei. They were a strange and troubling race, and he deemed it best to leave them to their own devices. Still, the Loänan continued to watch the worlds of Mera and Arainia, and occasional permission was given a Loänan to move among their inhabitants in sorcerous guise. Many humans forgot about the Loänan in time, and none of them knew of the dragons' secret surveillance.

A red earth-dragon stepped forward. "You bring no proof of your claim."

The Emperor and assembled monarchs watched as Auron turned and faced the red dragon, his head and wings lowered. But this deferential posture was at odds with his words. "What do you require by way of proof, King Torok? Or can it be that you prefer to follow Prince Morlyn? I saw many young dragons of your race flying with him in the skies of Mera. Has he deceived and subverted you also?"

The earth-dragon king responded with a sound like the rumble in a volcano's throat. He stretched out his neck and took an aggressive stance, spreading wide his crimson wings. "My people are free to do as they wish. We Loänan of the earth will not be ruled by others. Many among us wish to select our leaders in the old way, by their prowess in combat." He snapped his jaws shut on this last word, the crack of the mighty teeth echoing around the crystal chamber.

There was an uneasy rustle and murmur among the dragons at this unusual show of belligerence. It was primitive, atavistic, a disquieting reminder of their ancestry. A hundred million years ago their ancestors had glided over primal seas, on a small lunar world where they could fly without need for levitation. Coasting on the ocean winds, they had snatched great fish and sea-snakes from the waves, and had battled one another for territory and for mates. Nature had made the Loänan predators without peer. But their descendants had long since ceased from hunting, finding through sorcery other ways to nourish themselves: the Loänan were now an enlightened race that abhorred violence.

"You wish for a return to barbarism, King Torok?" inquired the Emperor in his calm, dry voice. "Shall we go back to slaying and eating raw flesh? Fighting over mates? Choosing our leaders from among the young and headstrong, rather than the aged and wise?"

"Perhaps what you call barbarism is in truth the way we were intended to be," returned the red king. But he lowered his wings and neck as he spoke, not wishing to challenge the Emperor—or his six guards.

"Your Majesty speaks of the way of the beasts," said Auron to

Torok. "We have long since left it behind, and turned to the realm of reason."

"You, a *warrior* of the Empire, can say this?"

Auron growled, deep in his throat. "I fight only when I must, or at the Emperor's bidding."

The red dragon showed all his teeth again. "And what of the *Meraalia*—the Star Stone? Some of us had hoped that it was merely a myth. It was said that the one who claimed it would rule the Empire. Now that it is found, would you entrust that rule to a mere human creature?"

"To this human, yes. I trust her absolutely, Majesty. It is plain that the ancients intended her to have it. I tell you she is the true heir to their realm—our realm. If the people of her world are right, her mother was not of their kind at all, but an Archon: one of the last of that race to walk the worlds. Ailia has a rightful claim to the Celestial Empire."

"Impossible!" King Torok snapped. "Our kind is older and greater than hers, whatever blood may run in her veins. The cosmos was ours before humans ever came to be. Shall we become like their captive beasts?"

There was much beating of wings and hissing among the Loänan at that. Some dragons sprang up and flapped about the chamber in agitation. "Peace!" commanded Orbion, and at his thundering voice the storm of wings subsided. "Listen to yourselves! When have Loänan sparred like this before? Only when the claw of Valdur divided us and sent us to war with one another, ages ago."

"Could not one of the cherubim take the Stone, O Son of Heaven?" asked a sky-dragon. "They too claim descent from the Archons, or so it is said. So they must have a claim to the gem, now that it is found again."

The Emperor said nothing. It was Auron who answered. "No cherub has claimed the Stone or the title of heir, Queen Kauri. They all look with eagerness for a new ruler to serve; not one of them wishes to *be* that ruler."

Torok growled. "You know well that Loänan, T'kiri, cherubim, all the old races are sworn to obey the one who bears the Stone. If you are mistaken, you may end by making us all slaves to the whim of a foolish, infantile being!"

"You have not met her, Majesty," Auron said: "How then can you judge her?" He turned back to the Emperor. "I beg you to let me continue protecting her, Son of Heaven. Our enemies also know of her, and she is in great peril."

"You may return to Arainia, Auron, and watch over this human creature," the Emperor said. "But do not reveal yourself to her, no matter what danger threatens. For I am still not satisfied that she is the one we seek. And if no proof arises that she is indeed the one expected, I shall have to look elsewhere for my successor."

It was clear from his voice and posture that Orbion would brook no argument. Auron bowed his head, and beating his golden wings upon the still air he departed the Imperial presence.

BEFORE THE DRAGON THRONE OF NEMORAH a thousand men and women stood in silent rows.

To the outward eye every one appeared to be human. But they were all of them *Loänei*, children of dragons. The hall in which they stood was decorated with many murals, now mottled with mold and age, telling in picture form the strange and ancient history of their race, and the downfall of their empire. The murals began with the dawn-time, when dragons took human form to mate with men and women (for love, some said, though the Loänei declared that their human ancestors had been selected for their superiority). Then came the first human offspring with full Loänan powers, able to control the elements at will, to travel freely between the worlds—and, most wondrous of all, to take draconic form whenever they chose. These were depicted as godlike figures, receiving homage from their human vassals. In the present age such beings had ceased to exist: only a very few Loänei, oldest of all, could still take dragon forms, and even they could do so only for brief periods of time. The Children of Wind and Water were few in number now, inbred, their magic for the most part only a faint shadow of their ancestors'. Many of the Loänan were dismayed at the thought of having human kin. They had sought in ages past to destroy the Loänei race, not by slaying them, but by scattering them throughout many worlds and so forcing them to mate with common humans. With each generation the descendants of the dragon-folk showed fewer signs of their draconic heritage, including the powers it granted. But still they believed themselves superior. Still they were the Loänei.

Those gathered here were the most powerful of their fugitive race, highly gifted and skilled in sorcery. They had come to this world of Nemorah, to the remains of one of their ancestors' proud-towered cities, to witness an execution.

Subdued light from the mist-shrouded sky outside seeped in through gaps in the vine-hung windows, gleaming dully on the gilded throne at the far end of the hall and the embroidered saffron robes of its occupant. Only the most powerful sorcerer could lay claim to the title of Great Dragon. The current claimant sat on his throne with serene confidence, gazing on the prisoner who stood facing him between two guards. The iron-shackled man was young and tall, his tawny hair sweeping broad shoulders, whereas the Lord Komora was thin and elderly, his face deeply lined, his eyes all but lost in folds of wrinkled skin. But among the Loänei age, not youth, conferred advantage. The younger a Loänei, the more his or her draconic blood was diluted and weakened by many human forebears. The Great Dragon Komora was nearly two hundred years old, closer to his Loänan ancestors, his blood more richly laden with the dragon-magic. And his mind was not enfeebled but rather fortified by wisdom and experience. He sat fingering his wispy beard—which, despite his advanced age, was still more gray than white—but said nothing. He had watched this particular dragon-sorcerer for some time from afar: the young man's powers and his growing influence were much too strong for Komora's liking.

Mandrake stood silent in his chains, returning the old one's gaze. He had longed for many an age to join with the Loänei, ever since learning that some of that ancient race had hidden from the dragons in secret places and had used their undiminished powers to contact others in whose veins the forbidden blood yet ran. But they had made no such offers to Mandrake. It seemed that these people—his people—knew nothing of his ancestry and did not suspect that he was in fact Prince Morlyn. Their cunningly concealed refuges had eluded even his centuries of search, and it had become apparent that, for reasons of their own, they did not wish him to find them. After his powers were revealed in his confrontation with the Tryna Lia in Arainia, they had begun to set traps for him, seeking to take him captive. Even the other dragon-mages viewed him as a threat.

He had avoided their first attempts at capture with ease. But now he had allowed himself to be taken, for it seemed that only in this way could he confront them at last and learn the location of their secret retreat. They had not been long in this world, he judged—no more than a century or two. For he himself had dwelt in Nemorah two hundred years ago, drawn here by rumors of Loänei still dwelling in their fallen cities. Combing through the overgrown ruins, he had found to his despair that once again rumor had played him false: though carved likenesses of his people still stared down from the broken walls, no living dragon-folk remained.

But to this place they had at last returned, and it was hard to keep elation from clouding his thoughts. It must not, for his danger was very real. With these iron bonds he could not use sorcery, and if his plans went awry he could lose his life. This, clearly, was the reason for the Loänei's earlier avoidance of him: Lord Komora and his predecessors must have feared in Mandrake a potential rival for the leadership. It was fortunate that Komora had gathered his people together, for this would give Mandrake's arguments a wider audience. But it was not yet time for him to attempt to address them. Even by a condemned captive royal protocol must be observed: the ruler must speak first.

At last Komora left off stroking the gray strands of his beard and sat up straight on his throne. "No doubt you wonder, Mandrake, for what purpose you have been brought to Nemorah. But perhaps it is better not to know."

This pronouncement sounded distinctly ominous. "Tell me, lord," Mandrake replied, keeping his voice and gaze steady.

"It is said by our people," Komora said, "that the fresh-spilled blood of a dragon can be distilled into a magical draught, conveying its power to the one who drinks it. For this potion to have effect the blood must be taken from the heart, so I fear the one providing it must be slain. We are too few in number for one of us to make such a sacrifice, even in so noble a cause. It is for this reason that I have sought you, Mandrake, and ordered you brought here to me."

Idle tales and superstition, thought Mandrake in disgust. *Is this what my people have come to?* But he chose his words with care, knowing now how great his peril was. "There, lord, is your mistake," he said, keeping his tone respectful. "I am not in dragon shape, as you can plainly see. I am a man. If you slay me while I am in this form it can do you no good."

Komora smiled. "You are cunning. Almost I wish I need not slay you, but could spare you and keep you for an ally. But it does not do to make a pet of a poisonous serpent. I know that you are a true wer-worm, able to take a dragon's form at will. That is why you name yourself Man-drake in that uncouth Meran tongue—ah! Did you think I could not decipher its meaning? I am old, and a master of tongues, among many other things.

"How it is that one so young is able to take the draconic form, I cannot say. Perhaps you have found some spell long hidden from the wise. But this matters little. As a wer-worm your blood is as potent in one form as in the other: be your heart human or dragon when the knife pierces it, the result will be the same. I will make the draught, so that your power shall pass into me, and make me the stronger, and better able to serve my people. Be comforted, therefore, that you do not die in vain." He gestured to his kneeling servants. "Bring the dagger and basin, and prepare the fire for the cauldron."

The time for courtesy was clearly past. "What have we become?" Mandrake shouted as the servants went to do their lord's bidding. "Have we Loänei not enemies enough, that we must murder one another? We should be uniting against our common foes."

"It is to fight those foes that I require the blood-draught. I am old and powerful, but our enemies are also strong."

The servants returned, bearing a huge bronze basin and a curved dagger, which they set before the lord, bowing deeply. "Do not slaughter me like an animal!" exclaimed Mandrake as Komora took up the dagger. "Let me fight for my life. You know I cannot win against you, lord."

Komora raised his silvered brows. "Why fight, then? Only a coward delays what is inevitable."

"To die fighting would give me some dignity and honor. Have the Loänei forgotten what those words mean?" Mandrake drew himself up and faced the assembly as he said this, and he could tell from their faces that they were moved at his words. Some vestige of the old proud Loänei race must remain in them yet.

The old leader, too, felt a trace of rebellion in the air, and he scowled. It would have been better, he now knew, to have had the young Loänei assassinated at a distance. He did not believe in the blood-draught. It merely provided him with a convenient excuse, so that the true motive for slaying his rival—fear—would not be too apparent to the Loänei. Now Mandrake had spoken, and the effect of his words on the dragon-folk could not be undone. Komora was once more trapped by the need to appear fearless. If he did not fight, it might seem that he did not dare to.

The old lord had not lived so long, however, by sorcery alone. Already his subtle mind had grasped and pondered the situation, and seen in it a possible advantage for himself. He would indeed pay his rival the high compliment of challenging him to single combat. It would still be an execution, after all; Mandrake was right that he could not hope to win. In the end Komora would reinforce his people's respect by triumphing in single combat—the old traditional test of Loänei leaders. The killing itself would serve, moreover, as an effective demonstration of his power. Let any other potential challengers to his reign beware! He rose without speaking, and made a curt motion to the younger man's guards to lead him outside. The Great Dragon followed, and all the Loänei flowed behind him into the outer court.

The jungle's rambling growths had been encouraged to spread over the walls and roofs of the old cities, for this made them less conspicuous to any unfriendly Loänan that might overfly them. But the creeping verdure had been cleared from the old palace's forecourt, exposing a paved area vast enough to accommodate the entire assembly of Loänei. When all were standing quietly on the moss-grown pavements, the old sorcerer commanded the guards to remove the prisoner's chains. These were taken far away from the court, so as not to hinder either combatant's power with their iron.

Komora made the first move. Raising his thin arms in their billowing saffron sleeves, he called forth power from the air. A blazing bolt of lightning arced between the cloudy sky and the prisoner. But the younger man deflected it with a quick gesture of his own, sending it crashing into the trees beyond the court. Fires sprang up, roaring. Komora jerked one hand skyward and the mist above began to roil and seethe, unleashing a fall of rain to quench the flames. But his opponent, long hair flying back in the wind of the Great Dragon's sorcery, spread his own arms and the churning vapor was stilled, the rain cut off at its source. The assembled Loänei began to murmur.

Komora heard it. He too was amazed, though he dared not show it. Could one so young command such power as this—skills that had taken *him* nearly a full century to perfect? There was only one explanation: he must have a Loänan forebear in his immediate background. That would explain his ability to take dragon shape, too. Sweat broke out on the old man's lined brow, but he knew he must not waste an instant.

He spread his arms like wings, turning instantly into a huge dragon-headed bird that flew screeching at the younger man, grasping him in its hooked claws and lifting him into the air. Mandrake immediately altered his own form. He became a horned dragon-snake, its coils binding the bird's wings to its sides so that both creatures plummeted downward, falling with a splash into the green-scummed square of an ornamental pool. The bird became a dragon-fish, its slimy body slipping with ease out of the serpent's coils. Spinning about, it attacked with teeth sharp as a shark's—but in the same instant the serpent, too, had transformed, and was now a huge dragon-headed turtle. The fish's teeth could make no dint in its armored shell. The turtle swung its head about, clamping its own steel-trap jaws upon the writhing fish's spine. Moving heavily, the turtle clambered out of the pool to deposit its gasping prey on the pavement.

The two adversaries reverted to human form. Komora was desperate now. He had already lost face, not once but three times in the space of only a few minutes. Bitterly he regretted his pride and folly in accepting the younger Loänei's challenge instead of killing him while he was still bound. He must quickly make an end of him. But even if he did, would he ever regain the fearful awe he had once commanded from his people?

He became a green-scaled dragon and flew up into the air in a clamor of beating wings, then plunged downward to the kill. But the other man as suddenly became a fire-red dragon, and rose to meet the other's attack in midair. Wildly they grappled, biting and mauling one another's armored sides. In an instant they had vanished into the ceiling of mist.

High above its gray void they flew, bursting out into the dazzling clarity of the upper atmosphere. Above them two suns shone and three moons; beneath them gray-white vapor spread in all directions, seamed with deep furrows and slow-rolling waves. Huge cumuli reared their rounded summits beyond. Like dueling hawks, the dragons repeatedly circled and lunged and disengaged, each striving to get past the other's defenses and wound an eye or wing. Occasionally they drew on the air's own latent power to supplement their own, flinging blazing bolts of lightning at one another, summoning sudden gusts of wind to disrupt the enemy's flight. The green dragon's assaults became more and more frenzied; the red dragon no longer reacted defensively, but fought with savage fury for his life.

Once more they closed in a mass of tangled limbs and wings and jaws, dropping back into the cloud layer. Lightning leaped and crackled around them, illuminating the grayness through which they fell. A vague darkness appeared far beneath them: then the jungle was there, rising to meet them. Twisting his neck around, the red dragon seized a flapping green wing in his teeth, and with all his might he tore the membrane asunder.

The wounded wing folded, and with a scream the green dragon plunged to earth, becoming an old man again even as it fell. Komora landed full upon the ancient pavement of the forecourt, his back breaking with an audible crack, as of a dry branch snapping. With a last wheezing moan the Great Dragon breathed his last, his eyes still turned up sightless to the gray sky where his victorious opponent wheeled.

Many in the crowd gasped or cried out. But they did not mourn the old one's passing. Among the Loänei there was no pity for weakness. They bowed to the victor as he alighted and returned, in an eye-wink, to his human form.

Then at last he spoke. "I am Prince Morlyn—the son of Moriana." More gasps. If this was true—and they saw no reason to disbelieve it this Loänei, despite his youthful appearance, must be at least five hundred years old. "I had no desire to do this," he continued. "But we Loänei must unite, or be destroyed. I wished only to warn your lord of the danger, but I did not know where his secret dwelling was, and so could not appear before him. In the end I had to allow myself to be captured and brought here, as it was the only way to come near him. But Lord Komora would not listen to me, and only threatened my life. Very well: he is dead now and I am free to give my warning again." His golden eyes filled with a cold light. "Our race is once more threatened with destruction. The Loänan are seeking you, and the Star Stone has been taken from its resting place on Mera and given into the hand of one who claims to be the Tryna Lia. But if we unite with the servants of Valdur, we may yet defeat her and her allies."

Something in his voice carried conviction. Even had they not seen the evidence of his powers, they could not have doubted him. "What must we do?" called one young Loänei mage, stepping forward. "Tell us what we must do to remain free!"

"To begin with," Mandrake said, with a sidelong glance at Komora's corpse, "you are in need of a new leader . . ."

IN THE THRONE ROOM OF KHALAZAR on Mera two beings of strange appearance stood gazing about them. The enormous chamber, with its gilded red walls and jeweled throne, was entirely empty apart from themselves. One was a goblin, deformed like all of his kind: so stoop-shouldered that he resembled a hunchback, with a mat of coarse hair atop his rounded head, ears with curled and pointed tips, and a nose as flat as an ape's. His fine attire of yellow robe and purple train only succeeded in making him look more grotesque. The other figure was so gnarled and wizened with age that he might have been a goblin, a human being of uncommon ugliness, or a blending of the two. He wore a plain black robe, with a heavy golden chain about his neck.

"How much longer are we to be made to wait here?" he fumed, beginning to pace.

"Impatient, Naugra? The Valei have waited thousands of years for this avatar, and you grudge him a few moments?" remarked the other with a shrug of his hunched shoulders.

The first speaker gave him a contemptuous look. "Your time may be of little consequence. You are only a leader of rabble, and merit no courtesies. But I am regent of Ombar, not a servant to wait on another's pleasure."

"Ah! That is Mandrake's little way. He respects no one, and

makes sure that we know it." The goblin ambled over to the Zimbouran monarch's throne, on whose scarlet seat-cushion the royal crown and scepter reposed. Mounting the marble steps, he took up the golden regalia and seated himself upon the cushion.

The other man's back had been toward him while he did this, but as Naugra turned again to pace in the opposite direction he stopped short and glared. "Fool! Get out of that throne!"

"Are you scowling at me, Naugra?" the goblin asked. "With that face of yours it's difficult to tell." He put the crown on his head. It was too large, tilting rakishly over one ear.

The regent advanced on him. "Get out, Roglug," he hissed. "Or I will cast you out." He raised one rheumatic hand in a threatening gesture.

The goblin king grinned. He sprang down from the throne and approached Naugra with his shambling, simian gait. "Are you sure you wouldn't rather have *me* as your avatar? I believe I would do well in the position."

"You blaspheme," snarled the regent. "Our god and master would never stoop to assume your foul carcass."

"Merely a jest," replied Roglug. "But I can't think why Mandrake is any better. I know him well: he is only taking advantage of the privileges and protections you have offered him."

"We have acclaimed him as our ruler," said the regent stiffly.

"But he doesn't *rule*," noted Roglug, toying with the scepter. "Of what use is he? Why do you not find someone better suited to the position?"

"Our augurs have spoken; we cannot say that they were mistaken!" the other growled.

"Well, say that Valdur has changed his mind! Or assassinate Mandrake, and find a replacement."

"Such as?" a new voice inquired.

They both turned quickly. A tall figure stood in the corner of the room, its scarlet robes seeming almost to blend with the walls. It watched Roglug with cold, golden eyes.

Roglug howled and flung himself down to grovel on the floor. The crown fell off his head and rolled away across the crimson carpet. "I didn't mean it! A jest—I swear it was only a—"

Mandrake interrupted him. "Never mind, Rog. I am not angry: I expect no more of you. Now tell me, what is happening in Ombar?

How goes your campaign?" He walked toward them, pausing to pick up crown and scepter and restore them to the throne.

"I won it," replied Roglug, looking somewhat relieved, but not moving from where he lay. "My rival is no more. I am the most powerful goblin in Ombar. King Ugagh got the ogres on his side, and they're brighter than my trolls. Of course, a maggot's brighter than a troll, but there it is: one takes what one can get. The ghouls don't take sides, of course—they just clean up, afterward. They love battles." Roglug chuckled and Mandrake gave an exaggerated shudder. "But Ugagh thought his cunning ogre soldiers would win the day for him."

Mandrake raised an eyebrow. "It would appear he was mistaken."

The goblin nodded. "*Because* the ogres are clever, they realized the slaughter they were heading into, and deserted in droves. The trolls, on the other hand, went into battle like the docile herd beasts they are, and so I won by sheer force of numbers."

"You Morugei—!" Mandrake laughed. "Forget this Avatar business, Rog: nothing but a common enemy is ever going to unite your squabbling races. Fortunately you've now got one."

"What?"

"The Tryna Lia, you fool," snapped the regent.

"The Tryna Lia herself is the least of our worries," replied Mandrake. "I've met her, and she is the sort of girl who spends all her time playing with children and pet animals. A sweet, gentle soul— what you'd call a weakling in your world."

"That's true," said the goblin king hopefully. "Soft heart, soft head—that's what my folk always say."

"Young Princess Ailia doesn't really matter at the moment, however. It is her followers you must fear—armies preparing for a great crusade in her name, to clear the cosmos of evil: ourselves, to wit. And when they travel to other worlds of the Empire, the ruler of the Valei realm will be their prey—especially if his followers acclaim him as the incarnation of Valdur." Roglug began to shake again. "While you Morugei have been wasting time fighting each other, I have been gathering allies. I am now the leader of the Loänei."

"What little is left of them," sniffed Naugra. "They are diminished in numbers and power."

"True," Mandrake acknowledged, unruffled, "and so I have found another source of aid for our cause: these Zimbouran people, worshipers also of Valdur. But I will *not* lead them into battle. That task must be given to another."

The regent spoke in a toneless voice. "I answered your summons, Prince, because I too seek a way to defeat the Tryna Lia. But we need the true Avatar to lead our armies to victory."

"I am not interested in doing so—pray spare me the accounts of those melodramatic prophecies made at the time of my birth," he added as the regent opened his wizened mouth, "I grow weary of hearing them. Roglug here would once have obliged you and taken on the role of Avatar, but he seems now to have lost his desire for it."

"I would never give it him," said the regent disdainfully. "He has had his uses: by defeating his rival, he has united the quarreling Morugei. I have merely taken advantage of his ambitions."

"No sane Morugei will agree to be your Avatar," continued Mandrake, "now that the Tryna Lia sits on the Moon Throne. I refuse the position, with thanks. So you are in need of another savior."

"And had you one in mind?" queried the regent dryly.

"Yes. My King!" Mandrake turned toward the entrance and called. "Will you not come in?"

They all listened to the sound of slow footsteps in the hall outside. Then King Khalazar appeared at the entrance of the chamber. At the sight of Roglug and the regent he recoiled, taking a step backward through the door. "What fiends are these you have summoned?" he cried, shrinking.

King Roglug groveled again, the picture of self-abasement. "No fiend am I, sire, but merely a humble Morugei who would do you homage."

"*Morugei*—the demon-spawn," Khalazar said, still not moving from the doorway. "So tales of these creatures are true. From whence have they come?"

"King Roglug and Lord Regent Naugra dwell in Ombar, a planet of the red star Utara in Entar—the constellation of Modrian-Valdur. My own home is in a world called Nemorah that also lies far away, among the outer stars," Mandrake told him.

"You all come from the Starry Sphere?" said Khalazar, looking from man to man in unwilling awe. "Can anyone—even an undead spirit—enter the highest heaven?"

"Of a certainty, Majesty," said Mandrake. "You yourself might do so. I have said that I can transport you to the Morning Star—why not to other stars and worlds? Are you not the Lord Valdur incarnate?"

"It is as the prophecies say," breathed Khalazar. "The God-king shall rule *all* Creation. I accept you as my vassals, spirits of the heavens. Henceforth you shall have the honor of doing my bidding."

"Your Majesty is *too* kind," mumbled Roglug. Mandrake shot him a warning glance.

Naugra gave an impatient snort and stepped forward. Raising his withered arms, he chanted briefly and then gestured toward the far end of the room where the lamplight did not reach. There was a wavering and quivering of the air, like a shimmer of heat, or like the distortion of the reflections in a pool's surface when a fish swims beneath and disturbs it. Out of the shadows two ethereal figures materialized. One was a tall, robed figure, saturnine of feature; the other was more rotund, with an almost porcine face, heavy jowls, and thick lips from which inhuman tusks protruded. They loomed threateningly before the room's occupants, larger than any living man.

Mandrake was annoyed. The regent was going too far with these childish illusions: Khalazar looked terrified.

"I am Elombar," intoned the taller figure, "servant of the star-spirit Elutara, thrall of Valdur."

Then the boar-tusked demon spoke. "I am Elazar," he rumbled, "the ruling spirit of Azar. I was present at the beginning of that world, and witnessed all its history. Once it was verdant and full of life, and it was then that I reigned there, king of a great nation of genii for whom mortal men were but the lowliest slaves. I ruled a world-kingdom greater than any Mera or Arainia has ever known: I sent armies out among the stars to war with other gods, and was worshiped by my mortal subjects. Ah, the temples of gold and silver, the sweet incense, the daily sacrifices! Those were the days of my glory. But then I watched as my world was assailed by falling stars, its mortal inhabitants perishing like flies. Now Azar is destroyed, its lands turned to deserts and its seas to dust, its cities ruined. But the sacrifice was needful. For the passage of Azarah through the cloud of comets also brought about the Great Disaster, and the end of Elei rule in Mera."

"The people perished, you say? You could not save them?" queried Khalazar.

The figure of Elazar looked at him as though with contempt. "They were but mortal creatures, and had fulfilled their purpose. Why then should I save them?"

"But now your power is lessened. What is a king or god without many slaves to serve him and work for his greater glory?"

The Elazar-image gazed long at the God-king. "I have misjudged you, Khalazar. In truth, you are the Avatar whom we have sought."

Khalazar gave a howling cry of fierce joy. "And now," he said eagerly, turning to the image of Elombar, "when shall we commence our attack upon the Tryna Lia? For it seems we have in hand such power as even she cannot repulse!"

"Patience," advised the taller apparition in its deep voice. "We must not strike ere the time is ripe. Many great powers serve the Daughter of Night." Both the figures bowed low, then vanished.

"But what am I to do?" demanded Khalazar in frustration, turning to his mortal vassals.

"Bide your time, Majesty," Mandrake interjected. "The people of Ombar and Nemorah have waited longer even than your own race to see the enemy fall. It shall not be long now. Spirits shall visit you in the days to come, and give you counsel."

"So be it." Khalazar swept from the room. Once he had gone a silence descended.

"You see?" said Mandrake presently, turning to Naugra. "This human will do what no Morugei dares: openly defy the allies of the Tryna Lia, and draw her from the safety of her own world into battle in another where her powers are not so strong. For we cannot assail her in her own sphere. I have already helped Khalazar send one challenge, to which she will surely respond. But the rest may prove difficult. Thus far, the Loänan have not meddled with the humans of Mera and Arainia. But they are watching those worlds nonetheless. If they believe Ailia truly is the figure in their own prophecies they will reveal themselves to her people and form an alliance with them. Then her forces will be more than a match for all your Morugei armies." He walked over to the gilded throne and stood gazing at it. "Not that any of this matters to me. The fate of your people is none of my concern. But if Ailia's forces come to rule all the stars, there will be no safe place left for me and my people. So we are allies, for a time at least: Valei and Loänei. But do not mistake me. I have no love for the worshipers of Valdur and never shall."

"You may deny your destiny, Prince," the regent declared, raising his voice, "but it will find you in the end. Play with this human king of yours if you will, and make a sacrifice of him. But you will come to the altar of Valdur at last, however you seek to avoid it."

Mandrake turned sharply, but the regent's words were intended as a parting shot; he was already passing out through the doorway. Roglug scuttled after him, not wanting to be left alone with the prince. On the throne room a heavy silence settled once more.

4

The Gathering Storm

"HE WAS ONLY A MOUTHPIECE, for all his boasts," said Ana, gazing at each member of the Council in turn with her gray veiled eyes. "Khalazar is not a Nemerei. He has no power to summon the armies of the Valei from their worlds. But neither should he be able to project his image across the void between Mera and Arainia."

The World Council had convened in haste to address the matter of King Khalazar's appearance and his threats to their world. Ana had been invited to speak to the high dignitaries, who were seated around the vast circular table in the center of the Hall of Governance—with the exception of Ailia, who sat apart on a carved wooden throne under a blue canopy. This arrangement had been devised both to satisfy Ailia's followers and to appease those who were against her reign: the separate chair indicated a special status, but also set her outside the circle of councillors. She sat silent on the throne, looking stiff and formal in her regalia of white gown and starred mantle, her hair bound in braids about her head. Her three friends and her father sat in chairs to either side, and they too said nothing, but only watched and listened.

Ana continued, "I see the hand of Mandrake in this."

"Mandrake!" exclaimed Chancellor Defara. "The same man whom Ailia drove out of Halmirion!"

"The same," said King Tiron, his voice grim, "if you can call him a man."

"Who is this Mandrake?" asked Governor Gwentyn of the Outer Territories.

"He is a curious creature," explained Ana, "quite unique, in many ways. He is the son of Brannar Andarion of Mera—"

"Andarion!" gasped Governor Ramonia of the Mid-sea Havens, her eyes going wide in her dusky face. "You cannot mean . . . not the Andarion of Mera who lived five centuries ago? The Maurainian king?" Ana nodded.

"This is the very same monster who appears in the annals of Mera," said Tiron. "Prince Morlyn—the wer-worm, as some call him, for his mother was of the Loänei."

Ailia shivered, as she always did when she heard that name spoken. *Morlyn*: it was a name out of the distant past, dark with terror and tragedy. Now that name had a living form and face: a nightmare come to life. She looked about the room, as though seeking escape to the world outside—but there was none, not even for the eye. The windows of the chamber were set too high to see out of: through them only the dull gold of sunset and the feathery crowns of a few tall palms showed.

"But he would be five hundred years old, then," Chancellor Defara objected. "Even the Elei do not live so long!"

"The Nemerei mages can control all the natural rhythms of their bodies, and thus many have extended their lifespans. Queen Eliana herself is more than five hundred years old," Head Sibyl Marima countered.

Governor Gwentyn lifted his grizzled brows. "I cannot accept that."

"No? How then do you explain the ancient histories, which clearly show Eliana reigned for centuries?"

"Bah! Many monarchs pass down the same names to their heirs. There were likely many queens who went by the name of Eliana, and historians have confused them as one person."

"Friends—friends!" interrupted the chancellor in distress as Marima bridled. "Let us not quarrel among ourselves."

"I know that much of what we say may appear incredible, the stuff of myths and wonder-tales," Ana said in her quiet voice. "But every word of it is true. You all take for granted the extraordinary powers of the Nemerei mages here in Arainia, clairvoyance and the rest: yet in the world of Mera these same powers would be dismissed as faerie tales. I am regarded as a myth in my home world: to Merans, Eliana the Fay is a figure out of old tales. Yet here I sit before you."

"But you at least—begging your pardon, Majesty—you at least appear to have *aged*," argued Ramonia. "Those who saw Mandrake have described him as a young man."

Ana nodded. "Mandrake owes his long life to his heredity. The Loänan can live a thousand years and more."

"I saw him," interjected Damion from his seat. "It was in a vision I had of Trynisia at the time of the Disaster: he was there, and looking no different than he does now."

Gwentyn huffed into his mustache. "You cannot expect us to believe these nursery tales, surely!" he objected.

"Will you accuse us all of speaking falsehoods?" said Marima, her dark eyes flashing. The Head Sibyl glanced around the table. "With our own eyes some of us here beheld the warlock changing from man to dragon, right before the palace gates."

"And Mandrake is unusually powerful, even for a Loänei," Ana added. "In some accounts it is said that his mother, Moriana, fled King Andarion's castle by changing to Loänan form while the child was yet within her womb, then later returned to her human form. This may have . . . affected Mandrake strangely. His eyes, for instance, are more dragonlike than human, and as a child he grew claws upon his fingers. One must remember, too, that legend says his sire was himself only half-human. Andarion was of the faerie blood—that is to say, the offspring of an Old One."

"But, Your Majesty—a moment if you will! I had thought this

Prince Morlyn was slain by Sir Ingard the Bold," ventured Ramonia. "All the tales agree on that."

"So it was thought for many centuries," said Tiron, looking grim. "It would appear that the Meran loremasters were mistaken, and Morlyn survived."

"What more can you tell us of this being, Queen Eliana?" Ramonia implored Ana.

Ana was silent for a moment, her misty eyes looking inward to ancient memories. Slowly she began to speak. "Morlyn was born in a secret place in the land of Zimboura, after his Loänei mother fled Maurainia. There, amid a small coven of surviving worshipers of Valdur, Moriana gave birth to her son. The priests delivered the infant, whom they believed to be their dark messiah, and named him Morlyn—'Night Sky,' after the starry empire he would one day rule. As for his mother, her part was to give birth: having done so she was of no further use to the thralls of Valdur. When she sickened they did nothing to save her, but allowed her to die." Ana shook her head. "That is how the Dark One rewards those who serve him.

"These priests lived in hiding, for Andarion had banned their religion and the Zimbouran people, freed from its yoke, persecuted any remaining adherents. In secret, then, Morlyn was raised. His guardians were more than a little afraid of him: the Zimbouran woman who later confessed to nursing him said that at birth he was covered in a scaly skin, which he later cast off as a snake does. Also, he was awake and aware right from the moment of his birth, and as a tiny infant learned quickly to walk and talk—only to be expected, when one thinks of it: for dragonets are fully sentient even in the egg, and active from the moment they leave it.

"The priests of Valdur moved about continually with their charge in the effort to avoid discovery, but in the end they were caught and their own people executed them. Many wanted Morlyn killed, too, for the priests had said he was born to become Valdur's new incarnation. Morlyn managed to escape however, and lived on for over a year in hiding until at last I found him."

"And you did not destroy him?" exclaimed Ramonia, appalled.

Ana's face turned pensive. "We Nemerei had thought that the child had no soul—that he was indeed nothing but a wild and mindless vessel, a body waiting for its master to enter and take command. When I saw that he did, in fact, possess a mind and free will, I could not justify slaying him." Her tone softened. "He was a pathetic little creature—a freak raised without love or understanding. He had gone from the priests' unloving hands to a life of fear and hiding, of being reviled as a monster and hunted like an animal. It was the Zimbourans' hatred, I realized, and not his own nature that made him savage. When I saw him, cowering in the cave that was his only refuge, small and half-starved and terrified—I could not find it in me to do him any harm."

"No doubt Valdur himself counted on that," observed Master Wu with a shake of his white head.

"Perhaps. Yet who can say that what I did was worse than what I might have done? To murder a child, any child, would have been to betray all that I stood for—all that the Nemerei have ever believed in. Perhaps, indeed, that was Valdur's purpose—to create this child in order to make us commit the heinous act of killing him, to stain our souls and honor with his innocent blood. Our enemy's intent is not always what we suppose.

"I took Morlyn alive, therefore, and tamed him. Though he was only ten Meran years of age at the time, I saw great potential in him. His parentage—half Elei, half Loänei—would give him tremendous powers. I brought him back to Trynisia with me and placed him in the care of the Nemerei at Liamar. When he had been properly trained in the Elei ideals of justice and mercy, I took him to his father in Maurainia. At first all went well. But deep in his soul Andarion feared his son. He could not help but see the dragon-youth as the distorted and unnatural product of an unholy union. The rest—" she added with a sigh, "is now legend."

A silence fell. Ailia glanced worriedly at Ana. How very old she looked in the wan light, her eyes faded and filmy, her face seamed with age and sorrow. There was an air of weariness about her that Ailia had not seen before. She felt a surge of panic. Despite her frail appearance, Ana was their greatest Nemerei, a tower of strength and knowledge. How could they manage if she were . . . no longer there?

The chancellor spoke at last. "If this wer-worm—this man-drake as he calls himself—still lives, then he must be slain or captured before he does any more mischief."

"But how can we seek a being who moves freely between worlds and can alter his shape at will?" argued Governor Ramonia.

"He will not come to this world again, certainly," Ana said. "In Arainia's sphere his powers are diminished. As for crossing the void between the worlds, there are many ways to do that: the mages of Melnemeron are already studying means to travel beyond this world. The cherubim and the Celestial Loänan can also be summoned to our aid. They will not intervene in human affairs as a rule, but they will protect the Star Stone and the one chosen to wield it."

The chancellor looked doubtful. "Can you not reason with this Morlyn?" he asked Ana.

Ana shook her head. "We were close once, and up until a few years ago he would still answer me if I called to him through the Ether. He had not forgotten that I once saved his life. But now that I have allied myself with the Tryna Lia he considers me an enemy. The bond between us—such as it was—is broken. And while he spared the Tryna Lia and her companions on Elendor, he did not do so out of compassion. It is possible that having other human beings to talk with at last may have given him some pleasure. But he abducted Lorelyn to make use of her all the same, and abandoned the others to the merciless Zimbourans. Living in solitude, and to such a great age, has made him cold-hearted; indeed he is now hardly *human* as we understand that word."

"But this is terrible!" said Ramonia. "How can we go to war with a being so ancient and powerful? One who has the blood of both the Old Ones and the Loänan in his veins, who can command dragons to obey him—even become one at will? What evil arts might he not have perfected over the centuries? How are we to fight him?"

"It will be difficult," Ana conceded. "There are beings in other worlds who still follow Valdur, like the Morugei; and many of them believe that Prince Morlyn is the prophesied avatar of their god. He knows this, and be certain that he will use it to his advantage. Also it is plain that he is making use of the Zimbouran people on Mera."

"It will not avail him. If he comes here he will still have to defeat the power of the mother-goddess, and that he cannot do." The one who spoke these words was the Lady Syndra Magus, chief of the Nemerei who had provided the entertainment for the feast. She had sat silent until now. Ailia noted the many jewels that hung about the woman's neck and arms: to a sorceress, of course, gemstones were no vain adornments, but the dwelling places of spirit familiars whose powers augmented her own. A huge square-cut reflambine hung at Syndra's throat, glowing with fiery yellow depths in the dying light.

"And do not forget," Syndra continued, "that though our people may know not the arts of war, yet many among them have inborn talent, and can with time and training become Nemerei."

"They may not have that time," Jomar countered. He had been fidgeting while the others spoke: now he stood up and stepped forward. "Why should we wait for the enemy to come here and attack us? Why *don't* we seek Mandrake out? If Ana's right, he's probably in Mera."

Gwentyn glared at him. "Must we tolerate these continual interruptions? The friends of the Tryna Lia have no formal right to address the assembly."

Ailia looked at the fuming Jomar. "Let him speak," she urged, leaning forward in her chair.

Had one of the carved marble caryatids adorning the chamber walls suddenly given tongue, the councillors could not have been more startled. Never before had the Tryna Lia exercised her right to advise the assembly. There was a stunned silence, and Jomar promptly seized advantage of it. "I know what I'm talking about," he declared roughly. "You've never fought in a war and I have. I know the Zimbourans, and I've met Mandrake. You can't reason with people like them. You can only fight."

"It is useless to talk of our fighting the wer-worm," said Syndra. "The prophecy is clear on this matter: only the Tryna Lia can slay the avatar of Valdur."

There was a strained silence following this pronouncement. Not all present believed in the Tryna Lia, or the prophecy. Ailia went pale at the words, shrinking back into her throne. Seeing the expression on her face, Jomar turned angrily on the sorceress. "That's a lot of rubbish," he snapped. "Leave Ailia out of it. I say we march against Mandrake with an army—I can go with the troops, to show them what to do. You Nemerei find a way to cross the void to Mera, and I'll do the rest."

"Then *we* will be the aggressor," protested the chancellor.

"Exactly. Go after your enemy in his own land, before he comes and starts ruining yours."

"We may yet sway them with words of reason," objected Ramonia. She glanced at Syndra Magus. "If they can reach through the void to speak to us, so too can our Nemerei reach them. They can offer peace to this king."

"He won't listen!" Jomar shouted, clenching his fists. "Don't you understand? If you had only seen half of the things I've seen—" His eyes smoldered, and Ailia wondered what horrors they had witnessed, atrocities beyond the imagining of any Arainian. "Let me train some men at least, teach them how to fight. Every land needs an army to defend itself."

"That would be permissible," the chancellor said after a lengthy pause, during which no voice was raised in protest. "So long as they remain in Arainia, and are only for our protection." Other heads around the circle nodded. "It is decided then," he concluded. "The Nemerei shall send their messages, and the army will be trained—though only as a precaution."

"Ailia too should be trained," said Syndra. "The mages at Melnemeron can teach her the ways of the Nemerei."

"A thought that has occurred to me also," said Master Wu. "She would be safer there, as well."

"We will gladly receive her. Will you come, Your Highness?" Syndra's dark gray eyes turned to Ailia.

Was there, perhaps, the very smallest of sardonic pauses before that "highness"—had the woman looked down her nose as she said it, as if noting Ailia's lack of height? No: Ailia decided that her worries made her oversensitive, perceiving slights where there were none. Or perhaps the woman was merely disappointed: many people expected the Tryna Lia to be taller, or more beautiful. She glanced curiously at the woman's proud, chiseled face and flowing, blue-black hair. The Lady Syndra looked to be no more than twenty-five. But for the purebred Elei, many of whom lived for two Arainian centuries, "young" was up to sixty years.

The head sibyl Marima looked askance at both Syndra and Wu. "The Tryna Lia does not require training! She is no common sorcerer, but an emissary of the Divine. The power to fulfill her appointed task is already within her. The people would be filled with confusion if she were sent away to be tutored like any other mortal."

Wu ruminated a moment. "Then we will say that she has merely gone to visit Melnemeron for a time, to share her wisdom with the Nemerei."

"That comes too near to deceit for my liking. No good can come of such a course." There was a pause, and then the head sibyl spoke again. "Do what you will," she said, her gaze sweeping the room. "But all your efforts, of war and diplomacy alike, will be to no avail. Syndra Magus is right in this: for the threat we face, there is but one solution. Only the Tryna Lia can conquer Morlyn and his armies, and only when the proper time has come."

After the council had concluded Ailia remained seated on her throne, staring listlessly into the gathering dusk of the unlit chamber. Ana went to her and laid a hand on her arm. "Ailia, my dear . . ."

Ailia looked at the old woman, searching her face. "Ana—is it true, what Marima says? About me and Mandrake?"

"It *is* in the prophecy," Ana told her. "The *Valei*, the Children of Darkness—Valdur's followers—will want Mandrake to become their ruler, and it is said that the Tryna Lia and the avatar of Valdur must confront one another." She hesitated.

"And one of us will be killed by the other," Ailia whispered.

"Not *you*, Highness, I am sure," said Marima.

"I can't do it, Ana!" said Ailia. "I'll never be able to kill him. Never!"

"Of course you cannot perform the deed now, Highness," soothed Master Wu, approaching her. "Your Nemerei powers have not yet been developed and trained. But you proved stronger than he when you confronted him at the gates of the palace. You surely have the strength to vanquish him."

"You don't understand," said Ailia. "It's not that I'm afraid to face him—I mean, I am afraid, but it isn't only that." Tears came to her eyes. "I've never killed anything, not so much as an animal. I couldn't take a human life—not even his!"

"Even if the fate of worlds hung in the balance?" asked Marima.

Ailia turned away. "I tell you it's no use—I simply can't do it!"

There was a brief pause, then Ana spoke again. "Ailia, my dear, listen to me. Mandrake is much too intelligent to serve anyone without question: so the dark Power seeks to possess him slowly, by degrees, taking him unawares. The longer this seduction continues, the less will Mandrake *be* Mandrake: in the end, he will lose what is left of his humanity and become what Valdur became—a mirror image of his Master. You are young yet, Ailia, and you still believe that death is the most terrible fate of all. But I say there are worse fates, that losing your life is better by far than losing your soul. Can you see now, my dear, how it is that I can care for Mandrake, and yet wish for his death? To see him die while he is still himself, and able to rest in peace, rather than watch him become a tool of the dark Power? It is my fault that he now lives, and presents a threat to you. For your sake I wish I had dealt with him differently when I first found him."

"Oh, no, Ana," said Ailia, horrified. "You *couldn't* have killed a child. I don't blame you at all: I would have done the same."

Ana placed her withered old hand under the girl's smooth chin. "You have a tender heart and a generous nature. May the Great Powers grant that these things prove your salvation, and not your undoing. A seeming cruelty can be kindness, Ailia, and apparent kindness great cruelty. Mandrake's life has not been a blessing to him, nor to the many others whom he has harmed. For that I must take the blame. When it comes your turn to face him, I hope you will neither suffer for my error, nor repeat it to your cost."

Ailia could not answer. There was, she knew, nothing more to be said, and misery enfolded her along with the gathering dark.

THAT EVENING WAS THE FESTIVAL of the *Elyra*, the High Gods, and the city rang with music and laughter. Tiny lamps and candleholders hung on houses, bridges, garden walls, and even trees to symbolize the stars of Heaven. Eldimia on this night mirrored the celestial realm above.

The thousands of citizens participating in the revels knew nothing of Khalazar's appearance three nights ago. The councillors had taken pains that no one else should learn of it, lest a panic ensue: all the witnesses in the banquet hall had been sworn to silence. Damion gazed pensively on the festive scenes in the streets at the beaming faces of the people around him, people who had never known war or want, or the deep divisions of Mera's faiths and nations with all their attendant strife. To the Elei, God had not one face but many. The Divine was infinite and ineffable, yet also reflected in all the things of which it was the source: rock and tree, beast and bird, human and spirit. There were thousands of temples and shrines in Eldimia, and sacred trees and springs and hills. The error of idolatry lay in identifying the Divine with one image to the exclusion of all others, and worshiping that image rather than that which it strove imperfectly to represent. The multiplicity of god-images in Arainian culture was intended to prevent idolatry, not promote it. They were hues split from a single light, facets of one many-sided jewel. In this world Damion had found his faith again. The God of his early beliefs had not diminished, but rather grown in power and majesty.

Damion was returning from a service honoring the archangel Athariel, which had been held in the cloister belonging to the Paladins. The old knightly order survived here in Arainia. At first it had been only a small group of men—and women—dedicated to good works, but since Ailia's coming their ranks had swelled with eager youths, their heads full of visions of valor. The youths liked to dress in armor and joust in real tournaments, and they revered Damion and Jomar because they had come from Mera and seen real combat. The Grand Master had engaged Jomar as a sword-trainer, and Damion had agreed to be their chaplain. He had officiated at tonight's service, and still wore the priestly robe and blue tunicle with its six-pointed silver star. The Paladin order had died out in Mera, though a few cherished dreams of restoring it: Damion's own father Arthon had been one of these, and he often thought of him when he visited the Paladins' cloister. But it was less for the idealist he longed than for the man himself. What sort of a man had Arthon been?

"I expect I was illegitimate, like most of the orphans at the monastery," he had commented to Ana once with a rueful smile.

Ana had looked amused. "Oh, I doubt that. Your mother would not concern herself with such niceties, dwelling free and wild in the mountains, but your father was very proper. Arthon would have insisted on a binding ceremony of some kind."

He gazed at the city as he passed through its broad, fair avenues. It looked both foreign and familiar, its architecture a blend of Merei and Elei styles: squat arches and thick pillars that spoke of a world of heavier gravity, contrasting with more typically Arainian spires and high-peaked roofs. Winged figures topped many of the latter: they might have been the angels and winged victories so common in Meran cities, but were more likely representations of the sorcerous Old Ones. It was as though he had been given a glimpse of an alternative Meran history, in which the Elei culture had never waned and died but instead had passed on its love of peace and beauty to all the other peoples of the world. He thought of the Elei ruins in Trynisia and Maurainia, broken and forlorn, and as he walked on to the palace he wondered with some bitterness if this civilization too was doomed.

Ailia in the meantime had retreated to the gardens of Halmirion. Usually she preferred the wilder portion of the grounds, where the trees grew in thick groves and little streams meandered where they would, and the animals of the royal menagerie roamed free. Her mother had also loved this part of the gardens; the animals, it was said, had come running to her and crowded around her whenever she walked there. Not for today the wilder groves of the park, however; Ailia needed tranquility. She had chosen a pleasance for its restful bowers, still reflecting pools and velvet-smooth lawns, its stately cypress avenues and sculpted grottoes. She walked, alone but for the faerie-hound Jomar had given her, and Bezni trotting at her heels. When she grew weary she seated herself on the rim of a small fountain, where an arc of water fell with a glittering sound from the mouth of a bronze lion's head, into the basin beneath. It was all so beautiful and so peaceful, she thought as she stroked the mimic dog's shaggy fur. It was hard to believe that an invading force from Mera could put an end to all this—destroy this harmony and serenity for all time. A breath of fresh, fragrant air wafted into her face. It was spring, and the royal gardens were a mass of billowing blossom—magnolia, gardenia, jasmine. The blossoms swung like censers on the warm breeze, filling the twilight beneath the trees with their sweet blended scents. Evergreen shrubs were clipped into whimsical shapes: coiled serpents, and birds, and cubes and spheres and pyramids. Wind harps concealed in the boughs of trees made strange, aeolian melodies, while from farther off came the aqueous strains of countless fountains, and water clocks whose wheels ground out the minutes like meal.

As night deepened the pleasance was lit by Arainia's living pyrotechnics: the little fireflylike pyrallises, which swirled in golden swarms as though sparks from a forge had come to life, and the night-flying ercines whose plumage glimmered with a ghostly pale-green radiance. The light of the stars and the Arch of Heaven grew stronger, silvering the trees. Finally Miria rose in her sapphirine splendor. There was an enchantment in her light, reflected from the hidden sun. Miria transmuted it with her blue allure, and poured it down to transform Arainia in turn.

"Ah—there you are." She turned, to see Damion standing on the path not far away.

He approached and sat down beside her. She made a pretty picture, he thought: the princess of a peaceable kingdom. How beautiful she looked, too: she had changed her regal garb for a pale-green gown all embroidered with flowers. Her hair was still up in its braided crown, but she had twined some blossoms into the braids. He found himself thinking of Ailia now as he had seen her at the ball, gliding into the room in her violet gown, her hair piled high behind her glinting tiara. He had found himself gaping at her foolishly, and looked away in sudden confusion. But she *had* been different, that night—coolly regal, graceful, even beautiful. He had always thought of her, affectionately, as the little sister he had never had; and now she was a woman—not only a woman, but a princess. He had been filled with something like awe for her on that night, something that made him hesitate to approach her or engage her in conversation. He smiled ruefully, recalling that callow reaction. What in the worlds must she have thought of him?

She gave him one of her quick, sweet smiles, and he smiled back, his heart lifting: this was the Ailia he knew, not the icy goddess of the ballroom or the monarch on her throne. "Hullo, Damion! Those robes look well on you. Blue is your color," she added teasingly.

"How are you, Ailia?" Damion probed gently. "You looked a little pale at the Council meeting. I was wondering if you were feeling unwell."

Her great, gray-purple eyes had shadows under them, making them seem larger than ever. "Oh, Damion—I think I'm going mad." But her tone was quite cheerful as she said this. "An embassy from Inner Eldimia has asked me to make it rain in their territory: they have had a drought for several weeks now. I said couldn't do that, and they said the goddess will perform the miracle—they merely

ask me to intercede on their behalf. If it *doesn't* rain I can say that
the goddess has chosen not to grant their petition. And this business with Khalazar—even if we told the people about it they
wouldn't be worried. They trust me, they believe I'm going to
make everything all right for them. I wish I could believe that too.
And I wish I could do something to *earn* this love they have for
me," she added wistfully.

"Love isn't earned, Ailia. Love is a gift."

She looked quickly up at him and then glanced away again. He
gazed at her fondly. Many young girls would have had their heads
completely turned by this sort of attention and adulation: but not
Ailia.

"I was just admiring the stars. Mera is up tonight: do you see
her?" she said.

They both looked up at the great silver-blue star, just rising beyond the trees: the star that was the world of Mera, bearing its
freight of humanity through the vast circle of another turbulent
year.

"It's hard to believe everything we used to know is *there*, inside
that little point of light," commented Ailia.

"I was just thinking how peaceful it looks. You'd not think wars
had ever been waged there."

Ailia got up, and the two of them walked on together through
the grounds. The moonlight was so bright that it seemed less a
light than an element through which the two of them moved, palpable as water. Somewhere in the gardens a peacock uttered its
shrill *hay-ow, hay-ow*. And then a soft, far-off voice was raised in
song: delicate rippling strains that rose and fell, rose and fell, from
some shadowy place high in the branches of a tree.

"What *is* that?" asked Damion. "I've heard it so often, but I've no
idea what sort of bird it is."

"It's one of the Arainian birds," replied Ailia. "They call it an attagen."

"It makes a nightingale sound like a crow. Can they be kept as
pets?"

"No—people have tried, but it's no use. An attagen won't sing if
it's caged." She sighed as she spoke, to his puzzlement: she had
sounded to him almost mournful, as though the image of the captive bird had awakened other, less pleasant thoughts.

They arrived at the large fountain that Ailia had encountered when she first came to Halmirion. Ailia sat down on its rim while Damion stood gazing up at the gleaming tiers of falling water and spouting sea monsters. For a long time neither of them spoke.

"I wish someone were staying at Melnemeron with me," she said at last. "I am being sent there in a few days, they tell me."

"Wu and Lira are staying there with you, aren't they?"

"I meant a *friend*. I know you promised to help Jo with the army—"

Damion nodded. "He and I are the only people in this world who have ever seen real combat, Ailia."

"But must Lori go as well?" she persisted. "She's a Nemerei, she ought to be trained too." *And if she attends Melnemeron I won't be tortured every minute with wondering what's happening between the two of you*, she added guiltily in her mind. She watched him closely for his reaction.

He smiled. "Lori wants to be a warrior, not a sorcerer, and Jo has decided to humor her for now. She wouldn't be happy at Melnemeron."

Neither will I—but my *happiness counts for nothing, doesn't it?* She bit her tongue to keep from saying the petulant words out loud, and was immediately appalled at herself for thinking them. It was like accusing Damion of being thoughtless, when in truth he was one of the most caring people she had ever known. He could not know what his presence meant to her, for she dared not tell him even now.

"I've heard from the Temple of Orendyl, by the way—they have granted me a dispensation from my vows of peace, so I may go to war if need be." His face was solemn as he looked about him. "The more I see of this world and its people, Ailia, the more I want to help save them. To fight for them—and for you."

Was there a special emphasis on that last sentence—a slight warmth, even a tenderness in his tone? Did he mean he wanted to defend the Tryna Lia—or someone who was dear to him? She had so often deceived herself about Damion, imagining she heard more than he really said, trying to delve beneath the surface of his words for what she wished could be there. No: she was deluding herself. If he felt anything for her, surely he would have shown it by now—by staying at Melnemeron with her, for instance. His Nemerei potential would have given him the perfect excuse. She was afraid, suddenly, to look into his honest eyes, to *not* see what she so desperately wanted in their clear blue depths. She feared his pity even more than his indifference.

"Your Highness?" They both turned to see Lady Lira standing not far away in the gardens. Marima was with her. "It is time to robe for the royal audience."

Without another word Ailia went to them, her eyes downcast, the hound and mimic dog following at her heels. Lira led her back toward the palace. Marima remained behind, eyeing Damion through her gauzy veil.

"Father Damion," she said abruptly, "I must ask you something."

He bowed. "Your Reverence?"

"What are your intentions regarding the Tryna Lia?"

"Intentions?" echoed Damion blankly. "I'm afraid I don't quite follow."

"You seem—attached to her. We have all noticed it. We know you have been close friends in the past, but—you do not by any chance hope to wed her, do you?"

"*Wed* her?" Damion burst out, startled. "I've never—what on earth put that into your mind?"

"Then you have no such intention? That is fortunate, for if you had I would be obliged to tell you to abandon it. It would not do for the Tryna Lia to marry like a common woman."

Damion stared at her. Celibacy was not required of any of the priests of this world, and he was free to marry if he chose: had Marima imagined that he was courting the Tryna Lia herself? For the Elei the joining of two lives in love was no light matter, no surrender to passing fancy nor mere domestic contract. Nor was it solely for the begetting of children. They were a long-lived race inhabiting a small world, and could not afford to increase their population by very much. They were strictly monogamous therefore, remarrying only on the death of a spouse, and often not even then. This view had been adopted by most of the Merei who shared their world. Ailia, he knew, approved of it· she had always been something of a romantic. For her not to be allowed to marry seemed cruel. "Her mother married," he said.

Marima nodded, her face inscrutable behind her veil. "That was in the prophecy, and expected. But the people have come to think of Ailia both as a mother figure and as a virgin goddess."

"Isn't that a paradox?"

"Yes—a divine paradox, which gives it great power. She is their mother *because* she is a virgin—because she has no children other than her people. Were she to wed, to love one mortal man exclusively, and—worse still—to have children of her own, it would forever alter the image she holds in the minds of the devout."

"You haven't—told her this?"

"Not yet. She is young still—by Elei reckoning, scarcely out of childhood. We would not broach such a subject to her until she came of age at fifty or so. But it would be cruel to encourage in her a desire for romance. We hope in time to reconcile her to the role that she must play."

Damion felt some irritation at that. "I don't suppose *she* has any say in the matter?" he asked coldly.

The face behind the veil was unmoved. "We must all follow the will of the Powers, Father Damion," she said; and Damion knew that her words were meant for him as well as Ailia.

THAT NIGHT, AS AILIA held her public audience in the throne hall, the city and countryside were struck by the greatest thunderstorm of the season.

It signaled its approach with angry rumors of thunder that echoed through the distant mountains, drawing ever nearer like the approaching footfalls of some tremendous beast. A great cloud mass reared up to dwarf the mountains of the Miriendori Range, dark and many-towered, rising for leagues into the sky. The storm front incandesced fitfully as it advanced, illuminated from within by lightning blasts that seemed almost to mock at the pyrotechnics display three nights before. Within moments it had swallowed the stars, moon, and Arch; a great wind came with it, shrieking around the towers of Halmirion.

Damion found a place near the front of the hall and stood watching as the crowds poured in and filled it from wall to wall. The vast chamber was dark, lit only by the luminous stars on its ceiling and the glow of the upturned crescent moon behind the crystal throne, the Meldramiria. Seated upon the throne was a figure clad in white, its mantle of midnight blue streaming across the dais; in her right hand was a star-tipped scepter, on her head a crown of argent. Above her brow the sacred Stone blazed in its setting like a point of pure light. It was a superb piece of stage setting, calculated to arouse awe in the observer. The stars in Ailia's train shone with their own soft radiance, for they were worked in luminous threads, while the glow of the moon-throne backlit her hair, lending it a halo. No one would notice her slight frame or less-than-imposing height. Her regal garb and her elevated position distracted the eye from such details. He glanced at Ana, who was standing not far away. Her features were perfectly tranquil, but he knew the old woman well enough by now to be able to sense in her an undercurrent of perturbation. Ailia herself was ill at ease, he thought: he could tell by the way she gripped her scepter with a tight-clenched hand, and he wished he could reassure her.

The Stone shone brilliantly throughout the proceedings. No one could say what exactly the gem was, what power within its translucent depths created the strange luminosity and other phenomena that surrounded it, but its seeming empathy for the young girl was one more factor that helped keep her on the throne. Everywhere Damion looked in the crowd he saw rapt, adoring faces—as always. Children loved her unreservedly, perhaps because she was so young herself; women—both maidens and matrons—saw in that virginal yet maternal figure a divine reflection of themselves; to men she was the archetypal mother-daughter-beloved. Even grim, tough, hardened men, farmers and miners from the outer territories, had been seen to burst into tears at the mere sight of her. She was a symbol of immense power.

The ethereal singing of the chorus at the back of the hall ceased. Ailia now rose from her throne and moved toward the front of the dais. She looked, with her surrounding vestals, like some great queen insect attended by its drones. Her clear voice rang out above the heads of the assembly.

"Hear me! Our ancient enemy arises to threaten us, once again. The siege of this world has begun!"

A murmur went up, and Damion and Ana exchanged sharp glances. Ailia was supposed to recite from memory a prepared speech. What in the world was she doing?

The Tryna Lia was swaying from side to side as she stood, her arms upraised. The scepter wavered in her right hand, while in her crown the Stone burned like a beacon. "Ill-omened night!" she cried in a high unnatural voice. "Eve of our doom! Call on your powers, all Nemerei! Azarah has loosed a flight of deadly arrows upon us . . ." The white-clad sibyls were swirling around her in consternation, like the surf breaking around a sea rock; as Damion watched they moved toward the door behind the throne, bearing the princess along with them: in a moment all he could see was her starry train curling around the side of the throne, passing out of sight. The crowds meanwhile were in an uproar at her words.

He ran for the dais, following the procession of women into the corridor beyond. He found them milling about in consternation while Marima and another of the sibyls propped Ailia up. She was slumping in their arms, her head bowed and her eyes closed. They had taken the scepter from her hand, but no one dared touch the crown with its holy Stone.

"She's fainted!" exclaimed Damion, starting forward.

"Impossible! The Tryna Lia cannot faint, like an ordinary mortal!" objected one of the sibyls. "She is in an ecstatic trance—"

Damion knelt at the girl's side, ignoring the protests of the sibyls, and felt her pulse. Her face was as white as her gown and thickly dewed with perspiration, her eyes darkly shadowed.

"She's in a swoon, I tell you," said Damion angrily. "Untie her mantle and take that crown off. And give her some air!"

Taken aback by his temerity, they made no effort to stop his ministrations. He freed Ailia from her heavy mantle and diadem, then slipping an arm under her legs he lifted her and carried her down the corridor. They flocked behind him as he took the unconscious girl into one of the receiving rooms and placed her on a cushioned couch. "Someone get a cup of water," he called as he set her down. "Ailia—Ailia, are you all right?"

Ailia heard. Her mind swam up from dark confusion into full awareness again, and she opened her eyes to see Damion's face above her. Other faces were there—she saw her father and grandmother and Lady Lira, but Damion's face was closest and drew all her attention. "Oh—what happened? Did I faint? It all went dark for a moment—"

"It's all right," he reassured her.

"What happened?" she asked him again.

"Don't you remember?" he asked, his brow furrowing.

"I—I was going to make my speech," she answered, frowning. "And that's when it all went dark. I didn't keel over in front of everybody, or anything embarrassing like that?" she asked anxiously.

"No, they hustled you out of there in time. You—don't recall what you said?"

Ailia stared at him in bewilderment, then at the white-clad sibyls hovering behind him. "Said?" she repeated. "I don't remember saying anything. I never made my speech. *Damion!* What did I say?" She sat up and clutched at his arm.

"Nothing much—there, don't worry about it," he soothed in his gentlest voice.

Ailia sank back, closing her eyes. Damion looked down at the slight, pale figure on the couch: it looked so terribly fragile, like a piece of finest porcelain that one scarcely dares touch for fear it will break. Had she had a fit, or nervous attack of some kind? Small wonder if she had: she had so many enemies, so many worries on her mind. Why *should* anyone want to hurt her—this innocent, delicate young girl, who had never in her life wished anyone harm? Anger stirred in him. If anyone wished to harm her, he vowed, they would have to kill him first.

Ailia was, in fact, feeling much better. Her head ached, but that was not unusual: the silver crown was heavy, and even when she took it off her temples always continued to throb for some time, as though it still weighed upon them: a phantom crown that could not be removed. Aside from this she felt perfectly all right; but it was so pleasant having Damion there watching over her that she decided not to recover *too* quickly.

"I'll just lie still for a bit," she said, and let herself sink into the cushions, listening to the wind and thunder. It was the sort of storm Ailia had always rather enjoyed, something deep inside her reveling in the drama, the utter wildness and power. But as she lay on her couch watching the rain lash against the windowpanes and hearing the storm's unrestrained fury she began to feel restless and ill at ease.

The sibyls and courtiers had all moved to an adjoining chamber. Most were clustered around the tall windows, watching the storm sweep over the grounds, bending the trees like grass and whipping the placid pools into a frenzy. The intermittent flashes made the night seem brighter than day, showing everything in unnatural detail.

"Isn't it something?" remarked Lorelyn. "I say, that lightning bolt was close! I haven't seen a storm like this since that one we ran into in Trynisia—remember, Jo? The one Ana says Mandrake conjured up, to drive us back from the mountains."

A commotion from behind them made them turn. Raimon of Lothain, one of the younger courtiers, had entered the room: his velvet cape was soaked, his hair and eyes wild. The others gazed at him with alarm. "I have never seen the like!" he gasped.

"It is a great storm, certainly," began Tiron.

"Storm!" Raimon exclaimed. "There is a wild fire loose upon the air—no thunderbolt, but rather a kind of ghostly flame that leaps from roof to roof and yet burns nothing." He collapsed into a chair. "The people in the city say it is a sign, a warning from Heaven."

Marima came into the room, her face drawn. "Nemerei from all over Eldimia and the territories have been mind-speaking with me for the past two hours. We have heard reports of prodigies throughout the realm, of people falling into oracular fits, proph-esying disaster; of animals starting and bristling at nothing—cats and Arainian beasts especially: seeing spirits, or so it's said. Some Nemerei have had visions of stars warring in the sky, of the plan-ets' orbits disordered by a fiery hell-star that drives between them."

"But what is the cause of all this?" cried King Tiron.

"It began when the Tryna Lia spoke in the chapel."

"Ailia? *Ailia* is the cause?" exclaimed Lorelyn. "But how could that be?"

"Ailia has the makings of a very powerful Nemerei," said Master Wu. "If she has inherited even a portion of her mother's talent she will one day be a force to reckon with. But those powers are sleep-ing still, unfocused and undeveloped. I think this storm is merely the first manifestation of her awakening power, a response to her inner fears and anxieties. She likely doesn't know herself that she is its source. Such power can be dangerous if it is not properly dis-ciplined."

Awe showed on all the faces present.

"What can we do, Queen Eliana?" implored the king, turning to Ana.

"She must go to the Nemerei at Melnemeron immediately," said

Master Wu. The little archmage's round, bearded face was solemn. "Not in a few days: this very night. They will protect her. No enemy could be a match for their combined sorcery. While she is there, they can also train her powers."

Ana looked thoughtful. "Mandrake is watching her, and this threat he has sent through Khalazar is likely an attempt to force her hand, make her use her powers too soon and rush to confront him. If we train her as a Nemerei, therefore, we may be endangering her life. But so long as she is no threat to him, he will make no move against her."

"But she must learn at least how to protect herself from him, and from his servants. He may yet change his mind, and seek her death," Tiron responded.

"I see little point in spending time training powers that can be canceled by a piece of cold iron. She must not come to rely on magic overmuch."

"But she cannot be left helpless either," replied Wu. "She is not a fighter. The Powers that assigned her fate did not gift her with strength of the body. She is clearly meant to be a sorceress, not a warrior."

"We do not know how her victory will be won. It may be that her gift is to inspire strength in others. And we can always give her large and strong guardians."

"So we shall," said Wu. "But there is no safer place for her in this world than Melnemeron. I only hope it is not too late. Her foe has had several centuries in which to prepare for her coming: she may have only months in which to ready herself for their contest. And she is our only champion: we stand or fall with her."

5

The Black Star

IN THE ROYAL BANQUET HALL the court of Zimboura had assembled
in a mood of hilarity, occasioned in part by the absence of King
Khalazar. A troupe of tumblers performed their routines, trying to
dodge the crusts and rinds thrown at them by the diners. As the
wine flowed more freely so did the missiles, until the floor began
to resemble a rubbish heap. Yehosi, the chief eunuch, stared
glumly at the revels from the high table and did not join in them.
Beside him sat a grizzled old warrior in Zimbouran military dress:
General Gemala, one of the northern Zimbourans who had rallied
to Khalazar's banner and helped him overthrow King Zedekara.

Gemala had also led the armies that conquered Shurkana. He
was both courageous and deeply devout, and absolutely dedicated
to his king. He was therefore, Yehosi reflected unhappily, unlikely
to survive for very much longer: his bold exploits, undertaken in
honor of his liege, drew entirely too much attention and admiration from the people for Khalazar's liking. It was only a matter of
time before the king felt threatened by his general's popularity and
put him to death on some pretext or other. Had Gemala not been
so often away from court on lengthy campaigns, he would never
have grown those gray hairs.

At the moment he was glaring at Mandrake, who was reclining
on a divan at the high table.

"Who *is* that man?" Gemala demanded of Yehosi, not troubling
to whisper.

"The new court magician, sir," replied the eunuch.

"I *know* he's the new magician, you fool! But what is all this nonsense about his being an undead spirit?"

"Lower your voice, I beg of you!"

"Bah! He's too far away to hear. Has our king been taken in by
this charlatan, then?"

"Would you suggest the avatar of a god is capable of being deceived?" asked Yehosi in a warning tone. Court was no place for an honest man: Khalazar would be furious if he learned of this. "The man *is* unusual. Those eyes of his—"

"A mere deformity. He's no more a spirit than I. More likely he's one of those repulsive Trynisian creatures, the Anthropophagi our explorers brought back with them in cages. I see there is one seated next to him"—he indicated Roglug, who was lounging at the high table and gorging on the delicacies.

"Hush! That is not an Anthropophagus, but a goblin—a very powerful being, descended from genii. He has come to us from the Starry Sphere itself."

"Or so the magician would have you believe."

Mandrake had heard every word of this exchange. His hearing was preternaturally keen, another benefit of his Loänan ancestry: he had made this discovery long ago at Andarion's court, when other courtiers had sometimes criticized him within his hearing. He had been stung at first, imagining that they did it out of spite; only later had he realized that his critics evidently thought themselves to be safely out of earshot. For this gathering, he had made some subtle alterations in his appearance with the aid of glaumerie. His thick mass of hair he left unchanged, for it easily concealed the shape of his ears with their hint of dragonlike points. But his skin was now flushed instead of pale, his features softer-edged, and these things combined with the gaudy red-and-golden robes to imply vanity and self-indulgence. He was inviting everyone present to underestimate him—always a wise move in a Zimbouran court—and he gathered from the overheard exchange that he had succeeded.

He cast a jaundiced eye over the courtiers. The never-ending parade of humanity filled him, as always, with ennui. Sometimes as he walked about the streets of modern Meran cities he would think he recognized a face in the crowd. But in the next moment he would realize that he was only recognizing types: the plump buxom matron, the lean and lanky youth, the balding scholar, the blossoming girl. He had watched so many comely maidens wither with time into aged crones that feminine beauty no longer held any attractions for him. Looking at a lovely young woman, he saw only the old one she must inevitably become: smooth cheeks seemed to sag before his eyes into flaccid jowls, wrinkles to fissure fresh skin, bright eyes to turn rheumy and dull.

The general was still scowling at him. This did not trouble Mandrake. Next to the machinations of the Loänei and Morugei the frowns of an elderly human were hardly alarming. Mandrake spoke to Roglug in his thoughts, without looking directly at the goblin. *So, Rog, what do you think of our Zimbouran friends?*

I feel right at home among them, the goblin replied cheerfully as he replenished his goblet with the contents of his neighbor's.

I doubt they would take that as a compliment, but I'm inclined to agree with you. Just don't ogle any women you may see here: the Zimbouran penalty for eyeing another man's wife is singularly unpleasant.

Roglug guzzled his wine. *A pity! I've seen some very attractive ladies: a sweet sight for eyes that have had only Morugei women to look on, all these years! Well, at least the food is good, and the entertainment.*

His thoughts were thick and blurry, and Mandrake glanced sharply at him. *Are you drunk? You'd best keep your wits about you, Rog: a Zimbouran court is a very dangerous place.*

For people with no sorcerous powers, perhaps, replied the goblin smugly.

Sorcery would be of no avail against poison. There are concoctions here that can kill a man instantly.

Poison? Roglug stopped drinking and peered into his goblet anxiously.

Poison, Mandrake repeated. *If I were you I'd be careful whose wine cup I drank from. Just in case.*

Suddenly the room went still. Turning, Mandrake saw that the door curtains had been thrown aside, and Khalazar had entered. Behind him walked his only surviving son, Prince Jari, a boy about ten years of age: his older brothers had been executed some years ago on a charge of conspiring to seize the throne from their father. Several retainers followed. There was a soft uneasy sound from the court, as of leaves stirring in a sudden wind, then silence once again. Khalazar seated himself at the high table and gestured brusquely to his retinue to follow suit. At the far end of the room, behind a filmy suspended curtain, the king's wives and concubines filed in and seated themselves upon cushions. It was a long procession. The royal harem included Zedekara's former wives and also many women supplied by the priests of Valdur, who could enter any home in the realm and take from it any attractive young maiden for their king. Each year dozens of these abducted girls were brought to the capital and paraded before Khalazar, who chose the ones that pleased him for his harem. Those who did not find favor were not released, but became slaves. Presumably the lot of the wives and concubines was better than that of the slaves, though one would never know it from their faces. They were little more than chattels of their king-husband, the mute symbols of his majesty.

In the front row, close to the curtain so that the court might at least have an idea of her beauty, sat the king's current favorite, a slender fourteen-year-old beauty named Jemina, with her personal slave at her side. Mandrake recognized the latter as Princess Marjana, daughter of the deposed king of Shurkana. She sat quietly, her eyes downcast, a slave collar around her neck. No doubt it pleased Khalazar to humiliate a royal princess so.

"Let it be known," Khalazar's voice boomed, "that Khalazar of Zimboura is the true and only God-king. In our royal person all prophecies are fulfilled: at our command genii and spirits of the Night appear"—gesturing to Mandrake and Roglug—"and at our bidding were we raised up on high, where all the secrets of the heavens were revealed to us. We did look upon the celestial body that is called the Morning Star, and beheld within its shining sphere a fair country, a veritable paradise rich in grain and timber, gold and gems, where the wild beasts are so tame that one might walk up to them and slay them with ease. As for the cities—never have I beheld such splendor, nor such iniquity. But the wickedness of the people of that world is as nothing next to that of their ruler. For this paradise of which I speak is ruled by that evil enchantress, the Tryna Lia, daughter of the Queen of Night." The God-king turned his attention to the main dish: a roasted peacock, elaborately arrayed in its feathered skin. Mandrake watched with distaste as Khalazar's fat beringed hands tore away the shell of plumage and rent the bird's carcass limb from limb. "But she shall not reign for long. Many genii and beings of great power stand ready to do our bidding. By their aid shall the witch-princess be cast down, and the riches of her sphere be given into our hands. Our armies shall enter the world of Arainia, with the aid of the chief genie of Azar—aye, even that planet whose name I bear, so you see in this the workings of fate! Azar is a rival to Arainia, and with her aid shall the cities of the Morning Star be smitten, her people slain, her ruler laid low. On that day there will be divided among our people such spoil as has never before been seen! Gold and gems, cattle and slaves, rich lands with all their yield shall be Zimboura's! I shall drive out this Tryna Lia, even as the burning sun drives away the stars of night!" He gestured to the royal crest above his chair, the golden face within a sunburst, and smote his chest with a greasy fist. "Behold us: we are the Avatar and Voice of God, the Immortal One, Valdur incarnate."

Another faint leaf-murmur ran through the court. Had not Zedekara, and others before him, made similar claims in their time? Mandrake glanced toward the high windows of the hall and concentrated. There came a collective gasp from the courtiers as a lighting bolt cracked over the battlements like a whip, so close that its glaring blue light and the ear-sundering sound were nearly simultaneous. Shouts and cries came from people in the street far below, for the sky above the battlements was clear and cloudless.

The courtiers cowered, their fear palpable as a stench of smoke. Khalazar stood somewhat shakily, regaining his composure. "You see! It is a sign. Let heralds be sent out to every quarter of the city, and to all the lands that we have conquered. Let them tell of the wonders we have wrought. Tell them that the true God-king has come! First I shall crush Maurainia and all the Commonwealth. Then when all this world is yielded to me, I shall reach into the heavens to take Arainia! The banner of the Black Star shall fly over her lands!"

The heralds would hardly be needed, Mandrake reflected as he listened to the commotion in the street below. Peasants and courtiers would spread this tale. Traders' caravans would carry word of the "sign" to all adjacent lands, and Commonwealth spies would inform the western monarch of what had taken place here. Three thousand years ago in Maurainia a lone thunderbolt had inspired a goatherd to become a prophet, and created a faith that had swept the world like flame. Who could say what his own sky-bolt might accomplish in time for this grim despot and his ravenous hordes?

Now, Ailia, he thought. *What will you do? Remain in Arainia in safety—or come to the aid of a world that once you called your home?*

* * *

"CHARGE!" JOMAR BELLOWED, holding his sword blade out in front of him as he spurred his warhorse's flanks.

With an answering roar his army plunged yelling over the stony ridge. There were hundreds of the enemy in the desert below, rank upon rank of spear-wielding foot soldiers backed by chariots and cavalry: the setting sun glowed red upon spearheads and unsheathed swords, as though the weapons were already stained with blood. But not one of Jomar's men faltered. Straight into the fray they pressed, swords and spears flashing. The air rang with the sounds of sword on shield, of yells and death-cries, of horses neighing in terror.

Jomar rode his horse apart from the battle, watching intently for several minutes. Then he raised an arm. "Enough! Stop!" he shouted.

A robed Nemerei on a nearby ridge raised his own hand in acknowledgment. At once the enemy soldiers vanished like a mirage into the desert, their armored forms thinning and fading on the air. Only Jomar's men remained. They looked at him, anxious and expectant.

"Better," said Jomar, and with this succinct appraisal he swung himself down from the saddle.

With these Arainian men, volunteers all, he had traveled to this dry and barren region of the inner continent that somewhat resembled the deserts of Zimboura, in order to train them as an invading force. The people of Eldimia, filled with alarm after Ailia's seeming oracular fit, wanted her to lead the army as foretold, but this her father and guardians would not permit. There had been some whispers that Ailia had feigned the "fit" in order to take command of her prophesied army, and though most ignored the accusations, it would not look well for her to have anything to do with it. As for the men, they had learned to tolerate the heat and arduous terrain, and Jomar's pessimistic prediction that most of them would leave within a fortnight had not come to pass. "They may not know much about fighting," he admitted to Damion as the two of them climbed back up the ridge, "but they've got spirit, I'll give them that. Lothar!" he bellowed, halting and placing his fists on his hips. "What's wrong with you?"

A young Elei knight jumped up guiltily from the boulder on which he had been sitting. "Please, sir, I'm dead, sir."

Jomar was annoyed. "Again? How many times is it this week?"

"Six, sir."

"And what happened this time?"

"Took a spear in the eye, sir. Fatal wound."

"Getting killed once might be an accident. Dying six times means you're too reckless. In a battle you're supposed to try *not* to get killed. Whatever it is you're doing, don't do it again."

"Yes, sir. I mean no, sir."

Not far away some new knights in training were practicing swordplay, moving with such a grace that they seemed to be dancing rather than fighting, even with the weights Jomar had made them strap to their legs to simulate the stronger pull of Mera's gravity. Lorelyn was with them. She fought like a mongoose battling a cobra, he thought—prancing around her opponent, darting in, darting out; inducing him to lunge at her and then dodging swiftly so that he went too far and lost his center of balance. She was turning his superior strength and weight against him, using techniques she had learned in—of all places—the Kaanish monastery where she was raised. The Kaan people, small in stature compared to the other races, had perfected a form of fighting that enabled them to take on larger and heavier adversaries. *Byn-jara* depended more on speed and agility than brute strength and was based on the movements of wild animals, birds, and wind-swayed reeds. Over time the Kaanish priests had also learned these movements, for when performed slowly and accompanied by meditation they served another purpose: to discipline body and spirit. Lorelyn had apparently made quite a study of Byn-jara when she lived with the Kaanish monks, and he had to admit that she was a better fighter for it. He cast his eye around the training field, observing the lithe armored bodies as they swung and clashed and parried. They were all good fighters, these earnest young people in their proud fighting gear.

But were they good enough? In Arainia the arts of war had become literal *arts*, like music or dance. Archers let fly their arrows at targets, not to train for killing, but in contests of skill. Swordplay was simply a sport, like fencing, and mock jousts a popular form of public entertainment. In the great Hippodrome of Mirimar, show horses were taught to rear and kick and leap sideways in a kind of graceful equine ballet; few recalled that these had originally been the battle moves of warhorses, designed to protect their riders from assailants in the field. It was almost as though the Arainians had deliberately sought over the centuries to transform violence into beauty.

All the skills of battle were present in this world, but when the time came, would Arainians be able to wound and slay their opponents? These young men had learned at last to "kill" the illusory assailants the Magi conjured for them, glaumerie warriors who made realistic yells, cries, and moans—but they still knew these to be only phantoms. Would they be as able to pass their swords through *real* bodies, strike living men?

He muttered, "They must have an instinct to kill, deep down. Perhaps not even so very deep. Scratch any man and you find a beast."

Damion remembered a firedrake skull mocking him with its grinning teeth. A man might slay such a monster—but what of the monster within himself? "True enough," he said, his tone grim. "But Jo, does it really matter whether they can kill? We're still not to do any actual fighting, by order of the Council."

"Forget the Council. The people are afraid and the Magi are studying ways to enter Mera. I'm not sending anyone there who can't defend himself. Raimon!" Jomar shouted. "You're getting careless again. Rynald doesn't really mean to kill you, but someday you may meet someone who does."

The dark-clad figure nodded, but did not answer or raise the visor of his helmet. "Raimon, stop that stupid play-acting and pay attention!" bellowed Jomar.

The knight put up his sword and turned, obediently doffing his helmet to reveal his mop of curly black hair and boyish face—indeed, Raimon of Lothain was little more than a boy. "Please, sir," he said in tones of reproach, "I told you I wished to be known as the Unknown Knight."

"I'll knight *him*," muttered Jomar under his breath as he stalked away. "On his backside with the flat of my sword. Young idiot!"

"How are those camel creatures coming along?" Damion asked as they walked along the top of the ridge. Jomar had discovered that a kind of hoofed beast known as the *ypotryll* lived in the Barrens, and that it was adept at surviving in the inhospitable environment, dromedary-fashion. They were large unwieldy creatures, with long necks, humped backs, and tapering serpentine tails. He had instructed Melnemeron to capture as many of them as possible and hand them over to animal-charming Nemerei. Training them was a slow process, however, for the beasts, though by no means savage, had a camel-like tendency toward stubbornness. They also had sharp tusks jutting from their lower jaws, which they used for piercing cactuslike desert plants to get at the stored water within, and they were not above biting people when in a cantankerous mood.

"The Nemerei tell me they've tamed a small herd," Jomar told Damion. "We'll take horses too, but ypotrylls will be more useful in the desert—which is what most of Zimboura is." He felt a thrill of anticipation. How often had he dreamed as a boy of returning to the labor camp at the head of an army—setting everyone free, and driving off the Zimbourans? It had been a boy's dream, founded on helplessness and fear: he had known this even as he dreamt it. But now Ailia had handed him a whole army of his own, and placed him at its head. *General Jomar.* It had quite a ring to it.

Lorelyn now came running up to him, her fair skin flushed with heat and victory. "Well?" she demanded.

"Well what?" he replied.

"Oh, come, Jo—you know! You've put me through much harder testing than anyone else here, and I've passed your tests again and again. So am I going to Mera with the others?"

"No."

Her blue eyes blazed indignation at him. "Why not?"

"Because it's too dangerous, that's why not."

She folded her arms across her chest. "I'm a good fighter, Jo. You can't deny that."

"I don't."

"Then what is the problem?"

"The problem," he growled, "is your attitude. You're too enthusiastic about this, and that means you're not taking it seriously enough."

"Ailia said this was supposed to be a peacekeeping mission, not an attack."

"That's right: so we don't need your fighting skills."

"Well, then it's *not* dangerous, so I can go."

Arguments with Lorelyn always seemed to have the same circular shape. Jomar glared at her in exasperation. "*You* talk to her," he grunted to Damion, and moved off along the ridge.

He gazed across the Barrens at the figures of fighting men. It was true that if they did go to Mera, it would only be to intimidate the God-king and his allies. But Jomar had no illusions about Khalazar or Mandrake obediently backing down. If only he could get at one or both of *them*, instead of having to slaughter their battalions of soldiers, many of whom were probably reluctant conscripts. In his youth Jomar had yearned to kill the Zimbouran king; when Zedekara was overthrown, he had shifted his hatred to the successor, Khalazar; now it was Mandrake who had become the chief threat. It seemed to him sometimes that there was but one enemy: some dark, lurking power that wore men's bodies like masks, taking up another guise every time one was killed.

"We *ought* to fight, Damion," he confided to his friend sometime later, when they stood watching the knights joust. He gestured to the mounted figures galloping at one another over the sere ground, raising clouds of reddish dust. "But they still aren't ready, not really. Those Paladins and their knightly names: Rynald Iron-arm, and Lothar Lion's-heart—all that rubbish! And Martan the Valiant— he's the worst of the lot. He's the kind that gets killed—the brave young warrior who asks to be put in the front line of battle, because he thinks it's going to be all glory and honor like in the stories. He believes he's indestructible—so he ends up getting slaughtered. I've seen it happen, time and time again."

But the knights *were* good. Their years of training, in the Hippodrome and at the Paladins' annual tournaments, had stood them in good stead. Several managed to unhorse all of their opponents, and young Martan was impressive—though Damion saw why Jomar was concerned about him. He took too many chances, and seemed too self-conscious. His young face under its pale halo of hair was more like a saint's than a warrior's. Raimon also acquitted himself well: he took a bad tumble early in the proceedings and had to be carried off ignominiously by the healers, but he reappeared later in the joust and managed to unseat the knight who had caused his fall.

Hope stirred in Damion's heart as he watched. Perhaps, after all, the Arainians were not as helpless as they had seemed. But it remained to be seen whether they could hold their own against the fierce warriors of Zimboura should they ever meet in battle.

AILIA TUCKED HER FUR WRAP around her, shivering. The cold would take some getting used to: she had all but forgotten what it was like to feel chilled. She felt tired, too, but that was in part the height-sickness that she had been warned about when she arrived. She had not slept well since coming here and her breathing was quick and shallow, but she had so far escaped the headaches that plagued many sufferers of the sickness. The Nemerei must be used to these things, she thought, or else they had found ways to master them. She now wore a plain white robe like all the Nemerei, for at Melnemeron she had no special status. White, she had been told, was their chosen color because it reflected all the light it received: other colors returned only a part, and black kept all, giving nothing. The robe was not very warm. At least there were the furs—taken from the bodies of animals that had died a natural death, she knew, for no one was permitted to hunt an Arainian beast.

All around her reared mountains whose jagged crowns were twice as high as any mountain of Mera, and would whiten with snow only in winter. There were many waterfalls, misting down from such stupendous heights that they looked like columns of cloud. Here, too, were the haunts of many wild Arainian creatures. A bird that Ailia took at first for an eagle soared high above the snowy crests of the range, and only when it settled upon one peak with a flap of its vast wings did she realize its vast size. A roc! She had also spied many cat-a-mountains on the crags, their luxuriant mantles of mottled fur stretching from forepaw to hind paw. When they leaped from one stony perch to another these mantles spread out on the wind, as did those of the smaller flying squirrels of Mera, making the great cats look rather comically like airborne leopard skin rugs. There was very little sound up here, for the rumor of the lands below could not reach so high. It was as though the upward-climbing land drew silence from the sky. But now and then she heard a faint, hornlike note echo down from the stony peaks above. Up there, the Nemerei told her, lived a mute beast that sported on its head a single branching antler, with hollow open-ended tubes in place of prongs. When this creature stood in a mountain pass the wind flowing through these tubes made a music that served it in place of a voice.

Ailia was reminded of the summit of Elendor in Trynisia, although this high valley held only a small cluster of connected buildings rather than a city. The structures were of the same gray granite as the mountain peak, not built of quarried blocks but rather gouged straight out of the living rock, and so seemed still to be a part of it—as though wind and water, not human hands and tools, had formed their towers and walls and arching windows. Melnemeron was truly as old as the mountain itself. One gold-plated dome stood out, shining in the sun; the rest of the complex melded perfectly with its surroundings, seeming to vanish into the granite behind it. The dome, Ailia had learned, was an observatory. For millennia the Nemerei had come here to study the stars—not as a Meran astronomer or astrologer or navigator would, as natural phenomena or portents or points of reference, but rather as the features of a celestial realm, familiar to them as the surrounding landscape. So many more stars were visible in the skies of this world than in Mera's, and here in the mountains the atmosphere was thinner still, affording excellent viewing. Many of the stars had worlds of their own, it was said, worlds to which Arainians of olden days once traveled—to which they might travel again, if today's Nemerei could but find a way to unlock the gates of the Ether. Her gaze shifted to a neighboring pinnacle, jutting from the mountain's side and divided from its summit by a plunging chasm. Atop it there stood a pair of gray stone statues: two dragons, each wound around a tall pillar. It was a spirit-gate, such as she had seen before in Mera. A slender stone bridge joined the pinnacle to the mountaintop.

She felt terribly alone here. Her father had remained behind in Mirimar, and her friends were in the Barrens. Only Wu and Lira had come here with her. As she stood and watched the light wane from gold to rose-pink on the eastward faces of towers and mountains and clouds, a voice spoke behind her and she started slightly.

"Dragons—the masters of wind and wave," said Lady Syndra in a soft voice. She was standing a few paces away, gazing at the gate. "But also the rulers of the Ether. The most ancient beings in all Creation, after the Old Ones. They hold aloft the mansions of the gods in heaven, it's said, and ride upon currents of magic that run invisibly through our physical plane. No one may enter the ethereal realm without their consent, and in their minds lies all the wisdom of the ages, which they bestow only upon those mortals they deem worthy. Few Nemerei have been so honored as to have had a Loänan for a teacher. But no Arainian has beheld a Loänan for many centuries. There are no dragons here now. Though one never knows where a dragon might be."

Ailia shuddered, recalling Mandrake's nightmarish transformation. Syndra looked at her. "I have heard it said that Your Highness and your companions have seen dragons."

"We have. I hope to see them again someday." Ailia remembered the golden dragon that had saved her. "Back then I thought they were only beasts. Tell me, Magus, is the magic gone forever from that gate? I hear the Nemerei cannot open it."

Syndra turned back to the pinnacle. "Ah, the Gate of Earth and Heaven! There is no magic in the statues themselves: they are as they appear to be, mere carved stone. The gate serves for a signpost, indicating the presence of a rift that leads from this world to a pathway in the Ether. The Loänan are the guardians and principal users of such paths, so many call them the dragon-ways, but the Old Ones made most of them. They are composed of quintessence and maintained by magic, and lead through the Ether like a system of roads to other worlds of the old Empire. But Arainia's gates were all closed long ago by the Loänan, and Mera's also, so that people from our worlds can never again enter the Ethereal Plane."

"But why?" Ailia asked.

"I do not know. No doubt the Loänan have reasons that seem good to them." But Ailia caught an eager glint in the dark gray eyes as Syndra turned away. "It is cold out here, Highness. You should go to your chamber. There is your handmaiden, looking for you."

Ailia followed Syndra back into the main entrance, where Lady Lira awaited them. The long stone passage was all carved and frescoed with scenes from Elei lore: winged beings, heroic figures riding in chariots drawn by flying horses or cherubim. Ailia noticed many stylized figures of dragons—winding in and out of painted clouds, supporting airy palaces on their scaly backs, or swimming through high-crested seas. Wavy lines emanated from their bodies: lightning bolts perhaps, or rays of magical power. Syndra paused and waved a hand at a mural depicting winged angel-like figures in a regal hall. "And these are the Old Ones in their heavenly court. The figure next to the throne of Elarainia is her daughter Elmiria: she is preparing to descend into the mortal world." The winged figure's raiment was pure white, long and flowing, she wore stars in her hair like a chaplet of flowers, and beneath her feet was a blue crescent moon. "She spoke to the great Nemerei mystic Zarthor of her coming, three thousand years ago. She told him she would challenge Valdur's Avatar." She indicated another mural, where the same figure battled a huge dragon.

Lady Lira threw a sharp glance at the Nemerei woman. "You are in the presence of the Princess Elmiria," she interrupted. "Why do you speak of her in the third person to her face?"

Syndra bowed her head. "But how foolish of me," she murmured. "It seems strange to me still that the one whom the most ancient writings speak of should now walk the earth in human form. Of course, Highness, you remember the very words you spoke to Zarthor."

Ailia, having no such recollection, felt a wave of embarrassment and was afraid Syndra expected her to repeat those words now from memory. Was this a sort of test?

"And now you have come in the flesh, Highness," Syndra commented, "the final victory over our foes is yours to win, it is written. Your powers, not ours, will save the worlds."

Ailia felt discomfited again. *Was* there an unspoken question in those words—a challenge, even? She could not meet the Elei woman's agate-gray eyes. "Excuse me," she said, turning away down a side hall. "I must go. I just remembered something—"

"Highness?" said Lira. "Will you not come to your chamber?"

"In a moment, Lady Lira. There is something I would like to see first, now that the sun has set." Ailia walked quickly down the chill stone passage to the observatory. No one else was in the vast domed space, and she sat down in front of the great gold-plated telescope. She had looked through it many times since her arrival, gazing at stars and planets, but most often she had trained its great far-seeing eye on the world of Mera. Staring at the blue seas and familiar continents of her erstwhile homeworld, she yearned to know what was happening there. Where was her foster family now, and were they all worrying about her—or had they given her up for dead?

Looking through the eyepiece now, she saw the telescope had recently been in use: the lens was fixed on a trio of stars in the Dragon constellation. She peered at the three pale round dots shining in their dark blue field, and tried to imagine them as mighty suns blazing in the skies of other worlds. This world and Mera were only the least of little kingdoms. Beyond the sky lay a vast realm of light and dark, fire and void: the Empire of the stars. Once people had actually traveled to those alien earths, walked upon them and seen all their wonders . . .

At the sound of soft footsteps she drew her gaze and her thoughts back from the heavens. Master Wu was standing there, watching her. "What are you looking at, Highness?" he asked.

"Master Wu," she said, rising and facing him, "can you teach me about the stars and worlds, and this Empire that you say unites them?"

"*Talmirennia*—the Celestial Empire. Yes, Highness. I have been meaning to tutor you in cosmology for some time," he answered. "Well, what was it you wanted to know?"

"Everything," she said simply.

"Everything! Hmm—that's a tall order, when one's dealing with the cosmos." He gestured, and suddenly the huge round chamber disappeared: she and Wu were adrift in a starlit sky. A quick glance downward showed her no ground lay beneath her feet. She knew it was only a glaumerie projected by Wu's mind into hers, but it looked very real. "Look behind you," her tutor instructed, a smile curving his lips.

She obeyed, and gasped. The point of vantage was many leagues above the world. She saw the blue globe beneath her, mottled with the familiar cloud patterns—long mare's-tails of cirrus and the curdlike clouds that presaged rain—now looking as distant from *above* as they always had from beneath. And there, only a very few leagues distant, reared the Arch of Heaven. She now saw that it was not solid after all, but was made up of many layered fragments of ice lying along the plane of the equator. From majestic blue-white bergs the size of Halmirion to little pellets no larger than hailstones, they hung weightless above the world as though some act of sorcery suspended them there. The sun blazed down on the world unveiled by cloud or air, its rays glancing from the reflecting ice surfaces as the sky-bergs rolled and tumbled in their courses. This, then, was the cause of that diamondlike glitter she had so often seen upon the Arch . . . and then, though the scene was not altered, Ailia found her perspective changed: she realized suddenly that she was looking not at a world surmounted by an Arch, but a planet enclosed within a ring. In the great Night beyond, Miria appeared as a pale blue hemisphere, but she could see its dark side dim against the stars, and the mossy sprawl of vegetation within its sunlit limb. Never again would she think of Miria as a *moon*. It was plainly a little planet in its own right.

"Your friend Welessan the Wanderer got a great many things wrong," Wu explained. "He was a man of his time, and subscribed to the erroneous Maurainian theories of concentric crystalline spheres and a planetary system that centered on his world, rather than on the sun. What he saw in his Temple vision was real enough, though: it is merely his *interpretation* of what he saw that was wrong. In the glaumerie vision given him by the sibyls he imagined himself to be traveling 'upward' into Heaven, when the vision was really of an *outward* journey, a flight into space."

Arainia was gone. In its place a fire-yellow globe appeared in the void before them. "What is that?" she asked.

"Arkurion," said Wu, "the closest planet to the sun. Not a pleasant place to visit: it rains acid there instead of water, its lakes are of sulphur and its rivers of molten stone. But the Salamanders like it."

"They're not—human, are they?" She knew the question to be foolish: no human being could live in that frightful cauldron of a world.

"No. They are curious creatures, reptilian-looking, with armored hides and a sort of fleece on their backs that protects them from the heat of the sun. Salamander wool and their shed scales were once highly prized by your people, as they are impervious even to a firedrake's flame. Also, when they are young they spin cocoons of silky stuff to shield themselves, stuff that once was woven by Elei into a light cloth that could withstand the fiercest heat without burning.

"There were, you see, Archons who had a particular affinity for certain environments. The Old Ones were skilled shapeshifters: indeed, it was they who first discovered the art. Some loved water, others liked to fly in the air, and still others preferred the deep places of the earth. The undines favored a form with a fishlike tail in place of legs. The gnomes who dwelt on Valdys took a heavy, squat form that was more comfortable on that heavier world, while sylphs, who dwelt in airy Iantha, adopted small slender bodies and great, gauzy wings. Those who mingled with Arkurion's inhabitants took their likeness and used the same name: salamander. Here in Arainia they were seraphim—bird-winged human figures. Some of these elementals brought humans with them to their worlds—except Arkurion, naturally, since no human could be expected to live *there*. The half-human offspring of the undines, gnomes, and sylphs resembled their elemental ancestors."

The yellow sphere had vanished; in its place was another globe, this one a shining white.

"Talandria, the undines' world. When Welessan made his 'journey' to it he saw a world of water, and so thought himself to be in some sort of heavenly realm composed solely of that element. But what he was seeing, of course, was actually the watery deeps of an ocean-world. That is what Talandria was like in his time, when the merfolk lived there. But the Great Disaster altered its path about the sun and caused its seas to freeze over. It may be that some life yet stirs underneath its icy shroud; or perhaps there are remains of its ancient creatures lying preserved in cold crevasses. But let us continue on our journey."

Each planet, she learned, was unique in its atmosphere and other features; and each seemed as devoid of life as the one before it. Valdys proved to be sere and desolate, a stark landscape of desert and scattered rocks under a sky of eternal night. But the gnomes and their offspring had not minded this, Wu explained, as they had lived not on the planet's surface but in deep caverns beneath its crust, warmed by the molten core. For this reason they had not suffered too greatly from the Disaster, but they had in the end chosen to abandon their world for others of the Celestial Empire whose wealth of ores and gems was yet unmined. Iantha, though a magnificent sight with its swirling golden clouds, was not habitable, nor were its five barren moons.

"The upper reaches of Iantha's atmosphere can support life," Wu told her, "but it is gaseous, a world made up mainly of cloud layers. This was the 'heaven of air and cloud' in which Welessan saw winged sylphs flying. But they went to Iantha only to play upon the winds of its upper airs. They lived on its moons, which have solid surfaces like Arainia's, and were very light, so that flying on them was easy. But the Great Disaster destroyed all these little worlds, and the sylphs too were forced to flee."

He showed her next the flight of long-tailed comets loosed by the disruptive passage of Azarah. Cast out of their places in the heavens eons ago, many were only now flying into the paths of the inner planets, and a collision with even one of them could wreak catastrophic damage on a world. "It all began long before Queen Eliana's famous prophecy in old Trynisia," he explained, "for she had not in fact made a prophecy at all, but only a statement and a warning of what was to come. We Nemerei are seeking some way to change the courses of these comets and render them harmless." Beyond the sorceries and machinations of human and Loänan, it seemed, lay a conflict far larger, more ancient and more terrible, set in motion long ago by the first rulers of the universe. He showed her the dismal planetscape of Azar, cold and empty beneath its baleful sun. Over the scene brooded the sullen face of Azarah, in a sky whose upper vault, owing to the thinness of the atmosphere, was nearly pitch-black in hue. The brown dwarf star had for billions of years granted only grudging warmth and a dim, dun-colored illumination to its sole planet; from distant Mera and Arainia it was not even visible. The great sun of Auria that warmed those worlds was but a remote yellow star in Azar's sky, its glow too distant to shed any heat on the surface. A small irregularly shaped moon tumbled across that sky like a boulder hurled by a giant, but it too afforded little light to the lands below. The plains were pocked with craters that gave them the look of a lifeless moon, yet the tumbled walls of ancient structures could be seen upon them, and the nearer surface was scattered with the bones of living things so ancient that they were now turned to stone. Ailia saw, not far away in the dull light, an ossified skeleton with skull and limbs still attached: the vertebrae of the spine were massive, forming a thick, strong column with jutting processes, and the skull was large and heavy-browed, its great jaws swelling at the front almost into a muzzle. But still it resembled, though in a grotesque and nightmarish way, the skeleton of a man.

"Is it—an animal?" she asked hesitantly. "A great ape, perhaps?"

But she knew it could not be. Strewn among the bones were weapons, large axe-heads of stone, and one of these lay not far from the creature's huge, skeletal hand.

"No," Wu answered. "Those beings were human—or at least their ancestors were. Trolls, they are called. The Morugei races are all descended from human beings who were taken to a world called Ombar long ago. Over time, the Ombarans were . . . changed. Some say they were crossbred with evil Archons, others that conditions on that world altered their forms. Many went to live on other planets, including Azar, which was then an outpost of Valdur's empire. They perished when Azar passed through the comet cloud."

Ailia could not tear her eyes from the skeletal remains. To think that such creatures could be her kin, however distant, filled her with mingled horror and fascination. Wu waved his hand, and the dreary scene faded mercifully from view. Once again they were adrift in a starry void.

"Beyond this sun's system lies the comet cloud, and beyond that nothing but the emptiness of the Great Night, until one comes to the closest star. The stars, you know, are not eternal, as the poets would have it. Stars have lifetimes, like humans and animals and trees: they simply exist for a very long time, billions of years. Their ages may be determined by their colors. Young stars are blue, then they gradually turn whiter, then become yellow, and finally red as they cool. Some shrink to glowing embers then, while others—large, swift-spinning ones with no planets of their own—burst and scatter their elements across the galaxy, and so help create new worlds in other systems. Some fade into pale ghost-stars, or . . ." He hesitated. "If you look closely at Modrian-Valdur's constellation, Entar—the Great Worm—you will see a star in it called Lotara."

"I know it. The Worm's Tail. It isn't far from the star called the Worm's Eye, because Valdur is supposed to be eating his own tail."

"If you look at Lotara in that great spyglass of yours, you will see that it is not round like other stars but has a peculiar shape."

From the field of stars ahead a pair emerged, growing larger—nearer. One was red as a coal of fire, the other a pale blue-white. It was the latter that drew her gaze, for she saw that it was stretched or warped into the shape of an egg or a teardrop, and from its point there extended a long tongue of fire that streamed through the void, then curled around upon itself at the end. "You see?" he said. "The energies of that sun are swept away from it on that side, and then . . . they vanish."

Something in his voice made her shiver and draw her fur robe close around her. "Vanish?" she said. "What do you mean? How can a star's fire vanish?"

"Because it is being consumed."

Then Ailia felt afraid, without knowing why: it was as though a shadow had fallen on her mind. "Consumed? What could do that?" she asked in a low voice, though she was not certain she wished to know the answer.

He took a moment to reply, as though he too were reluctant to say more. "You have heard of the tales of Vartara, the Black Star? It is no legend. There are such things in our cosmos. Do you recall that old Maurainian fable of the ravenous monster that ended by turning and devouring itself, until nothing but its own gaping jaws remained? Some stars, a very few, do something like that: instead of bursting at the end of their lives they collapse, shrinking into themselves. Such a star consumes itself, its own fires and light, and then the light of other stars and anything else that comes within its reach. Vartara is a star of this kind, a black star. It cannot be seen, for it no longer gives forth radiance. But as it sucks at the sphere of its companion star, Lotara, it surrounds itself with the brightness of the stolen energies, and this ring of fire reveals where it lies." Ailia looked unwillingly at the glowing circle at the end of the streamer. It had a black center, like the throat of a whirlpool, that seemed to catch her eye and draw it in. "And so," Wu said, "it is called the Worm's Mouth. There are some who say it is the Mouth of Hell."

Ailia felt as though she wavered on the edge of a pit. She had read all the mythic accounts of Modrian-Valdur, and the dark realm of Perdition he was said to have ruled. Some writers of elder days had described it as a bottomless black pit, while artists portrayed it as a monster's head with gaping jaws. The Hell-mouth. Might there really be such a place? Valdur had reigned over it first as an angel, according to the old lore, then as a hideous, monstrous dragon with a crown upon its head. That too might be myth, and it might not. She recalled what Mandrake had said of the Old

Ones and their shape-changing powers, the winged forms they had worn on Arainia and Mera, and their extraordinarily long lives. Was there truth, then, behind these nightmarish fancies? Valdur had truly existed, Mandrake said, and Ana always spoke of "the enemy" as though he lived still. But could *any* creature exist for thousands upon thousands of years?

"Is—is Valdur real, do you think?" she queried.

"I believe he was real, yes. The being we call Modrian-Valdur lived ages ago, in a past so distant that its history is long lost in myth and dream. He lived then, with the others of his kind who also became legends in time."

She asked in a faint voice, "And this black star—will it eat up everything? Our world—the whole cosmos?"

"No, Highness. It can only devour what comes within its maw. So long as we do not go near it, we are safe."

She breathed deeply, relieved: that dark hole in the heavens had begun to fill her with something like terror. She still found it hard to free her eyes from it. Wu waved a small, plump hand, banishing the image and the field of stars beyond. Once more the interior of the observatory surrounded them. "But such stars are very rare. Most are like those you see in the night sky, pouring out light upon the cosmos. Light is Life: the ancients sensed this when they saw plants wither and people grow weak without the sun. Your sun is a star, and the stars are suns, many with planetary systems that can support life. Without the stars there would not only be no light in the universe, but no planets and therefore no living creatures. For planets are birthed from the wombs of stars, and their living creatures are nursed on light. This is the nature of things: light is life and Being, and darkness death and Nonbeing. These are not poetic metaphors, but realities."

"On Mera," said Ailia, "the worshipers of Modrian used to shut themselves up in caves beneath the ground, so that they could never see the light, or the world that the light revealed."

"Yes, that is the Valei philosophy: hatred of the creation. Some of their greatest sorcerers dreamed of one day destroying the stars themselves—annihilating all light, and therefore all life, from our cosmos. But you are shivering, Highness," Wu observed with concern. "Perhaps you should go to your private chamber and warm yourself?"

"And the Star Stone," Ailia said as they walked back down the passage, "is it truly of Archonic make, do you think?"

"That would explain the legends of its origin. A treasure of the gods."

"It almost seems—alive," said Ailia.

He looked thoughtful. "Dragons possess dracontias crystals that are part of their living bodies. But the Star Stone is not alive, I think. It is an artifact, a made thing—the oldest such thing in our universe. Not only its cut facets but the lattices within it were made to a deliberate design. As to its substance, it seems to be akin to adamant, the Archon-crystal."

"And the shining light?"

"That I cannot explain. Power of some kind, from beyond this plane."

They had arrived at her room. Ailia opened the door to the bare little cell, and went to her bedside table. She opened the alabaster casket in which the gem lay. It had been removed from the royal diadem and reposed now on a blue velvet cushion. Wu entered behind her, and they both gazed at it in silence. The Stone lay glimmering like a great droplet of clear water: it held no flaw; no fissure or discoloration marred its perfect translucency. It was not glowing with its heatless light now, but seemed quiescent, withdrawn. *Stone* seemed too gross a word for this exquisite thing. Only the play of light and reflection on its facets defined it for the eye: it was like air framed in rainbows. Yet diamonds broke upon its edges. Defying analysis or explanation, it merely was. "Really, I am almost afraid of it. I can't think why it was given to me, of all people. I can't protect it, and I daren't use it."

"You are not meant to protect it: quite the opposite. It is intended to protect you. How, I do not know. I do not believe the power that lies within it could be put to evil uses, though the stuff of which it is formed is still the stuff of this material plane, and so like any other stone it is neither good nor evil in itself. The gem can be held by anyone—or Modrian-Valdur and King Gurusha of Zimboura could not have taken it for themselves. Our enemies wish to seize it from us, why we do not know, since they cannot use it. Perhaps they merely wish to keep what power it contains out of your reach."

"Strange things happen when I touch it," said Ailia.

"What things?" Wu asked.

"I have . . . peculiar feelings. There are images in my head, which slip away when I try to grasp them. Have you ever tried to recall a dream just after you've awakened, and not been quite able to? That's what it feels like. The sibyls tell me the spirits who guard it are sending me visions. If so, I wish they'd speak more plainly." But despite her words Ailia felt a lightening of the heart. As Wu spoke so calmly and matter-of-factly about it the Stone ceased to be mysterious and frightening. It could be theorized about, perhaps even explained. "The night of the great storm in Mirimar—I think the Stone took me over, somehow."

"In a sense it did. Ana and I felt that it was channeling ethereal energies through you. Energies sent from the Ether, by someone or something unknown."

"I can't seem to summon my powers at will, as the Nemerei do. Things just—happen, and I've no control over them at all. Magic frightens me, Master. What if I were to do something terrible with it?"

Wu smiled again. "If that is your first concern," he soothed, "then I think we need not worry about such a thing happening."

"But at the moment I can't do a thing, anyway," she said. "I can't even listen with my mind, like Lorelyn: and she's done it for years."

"Do you understand the Kaanish tongue, Princess?" asked Wu abruptly.

"Kaanish?" repeated Ailia, puzzled at the change of subject. "Why—no. Lorelyn speaks it, of course, and Damion knows a little—but I don't."

"That's very interesting. For you see, I'm speaking it to you now, and have been for the past twenty minutes. And you've understood every word." She turned to him, mouth open in amazement. He laughed. "You see—already you are listening with your mind, not your ears only. You can sense a thought through the shell of a spoken word. It may be that an early childhood ordeal stifled your developing gift. Or perhaps your mother used her own power in some way to suppress yours once you reached Mera, so that as a small child you would not use magic and betray yourself." He paused. "Ailia, there is . . . something else that I must tell you."

His expression was serene as ever, yet something in his tone alerted her. She looked at him in alarm. "What, Master? What is it you must say?"

"There are some Nemerei who believe that your mother was not human at all."

"You mean they believe she was a goddess, too?"

"Not precisely. They think she may have been an Archon."

"An *Archon!*" she gasped.

"Yes—the very last of her kind. There were likely still some Old Ones living in Mera right up to a few centuries ago—hence all the tales you humans have of children sired by demons or faeries or outcast angels. They were few in number by then, perhaps, but their race had not yet died out. One of them could have taken a human form and likeness: your mother's lack of any family and her extraordinary powers incline one to think that she may have been a surviving Archon—perhaps even *the* chief Archon of this world. For she used the name of Elarainia, and accepted the title of queen."

Ailia sat down on her bed and put her hands to her head. "My mother wasn't—human!" The painted portrait of the golden-haired woman seemed to float before her eyes. Her mother an Old One, an Archon. How could it be? "But—but then what am I?" Ailia cried, appalled.

Wu sat beside her and laid a plump, comforting hand on her shoulder. "There, now! I do not say it is true, and of course no one knows for certain. But I thought it best that you knew." She turned away from him.

I don't believe it. I don't . . .

6

Dragon and Phoenix

"ENTER," MANDRAKE'S VOICE CALLED.

Roglug hesitated before obeying: there was something in the prince's tone that set his flesh to crawling. He eased the heavy door open and took three steps into the chamber beyond, then halted abruptly. Mandrake was seated at the vast, claw-footed table of polished ebony that stood at the far end, apparently perusing a faded roll of vellum. The leaded panes of the window behind him were flung wide open: several were shattered, and glass shards glittered on the stone floor beneath. Blood spattered the floor.

Mandrake spoke in a mild tone, without looking up. "If you are looking for your messenger, he is not here. He had an unfortunate accident. Really, Rog, you should know better than to send some ill-trained Zimbouran to assassinate me."

"Assassinate?" Roglug sank to his knees in a genuine show of terror. "Someone attacked you? But I sent no one!" There was a dagger on the floor, he saw now, its blade gleaming among the shards of glass.

"Spare me your protests, Rog. He said you sent him." As the goblin stooped to take up the dagger Mandrake added, still without lifting his gaze, "And poison on the tip, too—I see you have learned from my lectures."

Roglug snatched his hand back from the weapon. "I tell you it wasn't I!" he wailed.

Mandrake looked up at last, his eyes sharp. "I believe you are telling the truth, for once," he said. "But if it wasn't you, then who was it?"

"Someone who knew no better, that is plain!"

Mandrake rose, frowning. "The Valei do not wish for my death. Khalazar has no desire to harm me either—and in any case he believes I am an undead spirit. One of his innumerable enemies, then? But surely if anyone could get an assassin into Yanuvan the king himself would be the first to fall?"

Roglug shuddered. "Whoever it was must hate me, too. He wanted me blamed for the attack, should you survive—"

"That may not mean he has a personal grudge against you: he could simply have viewed you as a likely scapegoat. I must make some inquiries. In the meantime, see if you can find a glazier: I want that window fixed." He sighed as the goblin scuttled from the room. So he had another, unknown enemy. It was a minor annoyance, but one that he did not need. A biting fly, when a man is dueling a deadly foe, might be a trivial thing; but it takes the edge off his concentration. He would have to do something about it. But just now he had more pressing concerns.

A new challenge had been sent to Arainia, and still nothing had happened. Ailia *must* be drawn out of Arainia, and soon—before her training at Melnemeron was completed. Nemorah, the new seat of his strength, would be the best place in which to confront her: there he would hold a clear advantage. But it was more than unlikely that she could be lured there: her guardians would never allow it, and in any case he did not want her armies in his world. The Loänei had endured enough without having to suffer an attack on their home. Mera would have to suffice, with Khalazar serving as the bait: she must be made to believe that the fated battle awaited her in this sphere, and she must enter it while her Nemerei skills were still weak. She did not really alarm him, not yet: she had at this point in time an almost touching awkwardness as she struggled to understand her powers and control them. She made him think of an eaglet, big-eyed and clumsy and covered with down, tripping over its own talons and flapping its stubby wings in a travesty of flight. She was a pathetic creature, and killing her now could bring him little satisfaction. But though he would have preferred to slay the mature eagle at the height of its strength, in a fair contest of evenly matched skills, he knew he would have to strike before then. After all these centuries it would have been intriguing to pit his powers against a truly worthy opponent. But he had not lived to this great age by taking unnecessary risks.

And he could no longer counsel himself to be patient. Time was pressing: he must know what was unfolding in Arainia. Seating himself upon a low divan, hands on knees, he drew several deep breaths—not centering himself for meditation, but rather project-ing his thoughts *outward*, out of his body and into the Ethereal Plane, where minds could meet.

And she responded, in swift obedience, for both knew that each such sending was a risk. There were many Nemerei in Arainia: any one of them might sense and intercept an ethereal message. He did not project his image into that world: she came to him instead, her ethereal form drifting before him in the still air of the chamber like a ghost. A tall feminine form, robed in red, with flowing dark hair.

Lady Syndra Magus.

"My lord prince," she said, bowing her black head.

"You have not reported in many months," said Mandrake. "How is she progressing?"

Syndra's face contorted. "I have done all I can to slow her train-ing. I have feigned to send messages and images to her mind, for instance, and expressed surprise when she heard and saw nothing. But she has a gift, and her aged tutor Wu is drawing it out. At best I can but give her the impression that her powers are inconstant, working at some times and failing at others. I have sought to stir up insurrection in the cities, to depose her, but all to no avail. The common people have been raised from the cradle on tales of the wondrous Tryna Lia"—her voice grew bitter—"and taught to re-vere her human incarnation. I myself believed that the Daughter of the Mother would be great and majestic when she took on flesh, a living goddess, full of power; not the poor, craven, stunted thing that now claims the throne of Halmirion!"

Ah, but you envy her all the same, Mandrake thought shrewdly. *You would trade your own splendid body for hers just to have a taste of the power she has, and the adulation of the mobs.*

Syndra continued: "She is not the true Daughter: how could she be? Would you not think the people could see this power-seeking little fraud for what she is? We have all been deceived, by her and by her blaspheming parents. But the people are blind! They think her the most wondrous thing they ever set eyes upon, and she thrives upon their adoration and begins to believe her own lie. Her presence in the city draws countless gawking pilgrims, so the mer-chants grow fat and flourish. Those opposed to her rule are few, and remain so for all my efforts."

"Then she must be made to leave that world. You have received the parchment from the Loänei? No one saw my dragon deliver it?"

"No one. The parchment was where you said it would be, and I have passed it on to the chiefs of the Nemerei. They now know how to open the Gate of Earth and Heaven, and send the army into Mera. But Eliana will not permit Ailia to lead the men into battle, nor has she any such inclination. She wishes to destroy you and all the Valei, but dares not make the attempt yet. Ailia is still a weakling and a coward, magic notwithstanding: she will send others to their deaths, but will not risk her own life."

"Then I have failed. My one hope was that her exalted position would go to her head, and make her incautious."

"There is hope yet, Prince. She has another weakness you might yet use to your advantage," Syndra continued. "I have spied on her and learned a secret. Indeed, the girl is utterly transparent when it comes to this one thing. She believes that no one knows it, but I can tell: she is in love with the priest, Damion Athariel. I have seen the look on her face whenever his name is mentioned. And I understand he is contemplating joining the army. If you were to seize this Damion, you would have her utterly in your power. She would do anything for him, I think."

"Very well. But the priest seems as far out of my range at the moment as Ailia herself. Continue to observe her," he instructed his spy. "But exercise great care. There are many powerful Nemerei surrounding her and one of them may guess what you are about."

The phantom figure bowed again, and vanished. Mandrake sat still for a time, gazing into space. It was well that Syndra was ambitious and power loving: it had not been hard to wake jealousy in her. Her father's Merei blood was to blame, for it doomed her to lesser powers and a shorter span of years than her purebred Elei kin. If only she had been brought up among Merei, she could at least have lorded it over them; but she had been raised in her mother's country, among Elei whose powers far surpassed her own. That in itself might have been enough to warp her character.

But then along had come the Tryna Lia, on whom the whole world's attention had been lavished. Ailia Elmiria, whose father was himself a mere half-breed. Yet mages and governors had journeyed from all over Arainia to pay homage to her when she was still a mere infant, and augurs had announced that her Nemerei powers would not be lessened by her paternal line, but grow as great as her mother's. Syndra had inevitably begun to resent this prodigy: the corrosion of envy had set in at once, and turned to seething hatred over time, hatred keen enough to make Syndra use her own powers to reach out through the Ether to Arainia's oldest foes, who alone could threaten the Tryna Lia.

The Archon Elarainia had sensed something was amiss, for she had fled her world, taking her human child with her. It must have been a great shock for Syndra when Ailia returned alive to reclaim her throne. The Magus was becoming spiteful, and therefore more dangerous to herself and Mandrake: she would end by giving herself away, and the mages of Melnemeron would discover her link with him.

"Mandrake."

He started at the mental voice, looked up to see another phantom form floating before him: a small slight figure, with hair white as her robe. He rose, staring at her in disbelief. *Eliana!*

"What do you want, old woman?" he demanded harshly, forcing back his fear. Had she somehow overheard his conversation with Syndra?

"I have come to appeal to you to reconsider your present course," she said quietly. "Mandrake, you are fast approaching the point from which there can be no return. Come back to us, to the Nemerei. It is not too late, even now."

She did not mention Syndra—she must not know of her, then. Eliana was losing her powers: there had been a time when nothing would have escaped her. He looked at the aged features, recalling a younger version of that face, and with the image came recollections dredged up from a centuries-old childhood: a soft voice, long pale hair brushing his cheek, arms that had embraced him protectively . . . Angrily he shook himself free of the memories. It had not been for love that she had saved him, he told himself, but for the sake of her precious principles, and a desire to mold and control him.

He looked coolly at the projection. "It's no use, Ana," he replied. "You have lost your claim on my soul. I will never return to you."

Ana's form seemed to fade slightly at that, but when she spoke again her voice was firm. "Mandrake, I am coming to Mera soon," she told him. "I do not want to fight you, but be sure I will if you leave me no choice. I cannot allow you to harm the Tryna Lia."

And then she was gone, leaving him with a chill of apprehension and, beneath it, an aching sense of loss. But he brushed both feelings aside.

It is done—I am free of her at last.

KHALAZAR'S FLEET WAS SET TO SAIL. Against the Armada alone the Commonwealth might have prevailed, but now the God-king had aid, in the form of armies from the Morugei worlds. These they could not hope to defeat—in fact the mere sight of such creatures, long banished to the realm of myth, would surely be enough to unman any Maurainian soldier.

On learning this Jomar had returned to the council of Arainia, this time in his official capacity as Ailia's appointed general, and argued strenuously that they could not stand idly by while their sister world suffered. It was one thing to refuse to fight for oneself, another to disregard the plight of others. From Melnemeron had come the news that the Nemerei had at long last learned how to open the airy gate leading to the Ether: Syndra Magus, it transpired, had uncovered a long-lost parchment filled with ancient lore. The Council agreed, after long discussion and with much reluctance, that the army could be transported to Mera with the Nemerei's aid, through the way that lay beyond the ethereal portal. But no fighting must be done. Their mere presence in Zimboura might, after all, cause his frightened subjects to rise against Khalazar in panic and overthrow him, all without the need for a single arrow to be fired. With this compromise Jomar had to be content. But he had secured from the Council a concession that, should the God-king's forces attack them, they had leave to fight in their own defense before retreating from that world.

Those of the men who had trained to be Paladins took their formal vows in the chapel of Melnemeron, dressed in full armor and the robelike surcoats of the Order. All that night they kept a candlelit vigil before the altar of the Elmir, praying over their weapons, and at dawn Ailia knighted them. Standing before the altar—a golden bird-figure supporting a marble slab on its wings—she took from it the ceremonial sword and touched the bowed head of each knight as he knelt before her. The sword was light,

not being made for battle, and only once were the Tryna Lia's
hands seen to tremble on its jeweled hilt. And her voice too
seemed to hold a tremor when she said, "Arise, Sir Damion
Athariel!"

After the ceremony Lady Syndra suggested that the guests all go
for a walk on the mountainside. "I can show you the Temple
Grove, where the trees are thousands of years old and tall as towers, and many other wonders," she offered. Ailia exchanged her
formal gown and circlet for a plain walking-dress, and she and her
father and friends followed Syndra and Master Wu down the
mountain to the tree line.

"The army should be here in another day or so. But do these sorcerers really think they can send me and my men all the way to
Mera?" Jomar asked as they descended the slope.

"The Nemerei have successfully reopened the rift within the
gate," Wu replied. "The void is now passable—though whether
that is a good thing remains to be seen."

King Tiron smiled. "Master Wu, I consider myself a reasonably
learned man, but I simply cannot understand these ethereal pas-
sageways of yours. You say to me they are there, and yet not there.
How can that be?"

"Hmm!" Wu frowned. "Let me try an analogy, Majesty. Imagine
that the universe is like an immense, round fruit, then picture all
the beings of the material plane as tiny ants crawling about on the
rind. They know nothing of the fruit's interior: all they know is its
outside, the rind. Then one day an ant happens upon a hole eaten
through the rind by some enterprising worm, and entering it he
finds a long tunnel gouged through the fruit's interior. He follows
this, right through the core, until presently he comes out of another hole at the tunnel end and finds himself on the far side of the
fruit. The ants there are astonished to see another of their kind appear, as it seems, out of nowhere. He explains about the wormhole,
and how he has traveled through the inside of the fruit to get to this
part of the rind. They are bewildered—there *is* nothing but the rind,
they say, no way of getting from one side of the fruit to the other
without crawling over its rounded surface. How could this strange
thing called the *inside* exist? And they will not believe the adventur-
ous insect until they have entered the hole and seen the worm-
tunnel for themselves."

"I believe I see," said Tiron after a moment. "Yes . . . the material plane is the rind, the Ether is the inner part, and that gate is the opening of the worm-hole—the dragon-way."

"With which we are able to circumvent material space, just as the ant circumvents the outer rind. Here is another question, Majesty: where is the center of the fruit?"

He looked surprised. "The center? In the core, naturally."

"Exactly! And so you see, the ants that have never been inside the fruit have never seen the center of their universe: to them, it *has* no center. And it is the same with our own universe. The material plane *has* no center, for it is only one part of reality. The core of things does not lie here, but elsewhere. You could journey through the Great Void forever without reaching it."

"Then not only can our army reach Mera, but any of us could journey to any world of Talmirennia."

Wu bowed his head by way of acknowledgment. "Still, the Ether presents many perils, and you would be well advised not to enter it without a Nemerei guide."

Ailia felt a sharp twinge at these words, knowing that she could not make any such journey. Otherworldly ambassadors might pass through the portal in years to come, but Ailia would not travel through it herself for some time—decades, perhaps. Her duty was to remain here in safety, learning to increase her powers and so give protection to Arainia's people. But to travel beyond the sky, beyond the domain of the sun to other, alien suns and worlds! To meet peoples with whom no one in Mera or Arainia had communicated for hundreds of years . . . Once again, as on Great Island long ago, she was cut off, imprisoned, deprived of the adventure and knowledge that her spirit craved.

If only I weren't what I am. Could they all be wrong about me, even now? There is nothing at all special about me, or my powers—such as they are! And as a person I'm really quite ordinary. All that about Mother being an Archon is nonsense . . .

She had done all she could to wake her slumbering talent, studying hard and imbibing the ambrosia elixir, which only gave her dreamlike visions that might or might not be true. She had learned to command her body as well as her mind, to control at will all its living rhythms from her breathing to the flow of blood in her veins. Her hair had grown, falling now almost to her thighs—a little indulgence she had half guiltily allowed herself. There were so many avenues to explore, so many newfound powers to test, that at times she was overwhelmed. Inevitably, there was temptation: how easy it would be, she thought, to spy on people. She could know exactly where Damion and Lorelyn were, for instance, whether or not they were together . . . Though she did not yield to these urges, they gave her many a restless night. She had recovered, through long sessions of supervised meditation, a few very early memories: some clear recollections of her mother's face and voice; of riding on the shaggy back of her mimic dog while a younger Benia looked on indulgently—of being lifted in her father's arms to watch her birthday fireworks display . . . long-lost scenes from her earliest childhood, more precious to her than any triumph of sorcery. Only once had she dared try to see the future, so great was her fear of it. A deep ambrosia-assisted trance had shown her the figure of Mandrake dressed in kingly robes and standing on what looked like the roof of a great tower. The sky above had been dark, with a full golden moon in it—the moon of some alien world, she thought. By its light she had seen Mandrake's face quite clearly. He was looking directly at her, hostility and hatred in his inhuman eyes.

She trembled at the recollection. Wu had tried to reassure her afterward, explaining that not all future visions came to pass: they were not foreordained, but were simply "projections of probability" that stemmed from current situations and events. She hoped fervently that he was right, that she need never come face to face with that threatening figure. But if she did, she would surely need all the strength she could summon to defeat him: far more than she now possessed.

I can't even fight, like Lorelyn . . .

Ailia shuddered. She had long since lost her own early notions of war as an exciting and heroic enterprise. Jomar's descriptions of battles he had fought in had dispelled them completely. Now the mention of war only filled her imagination with scenes of blood and turmoil: smoke and spears and confusion, screaming horses and screaming men, the bodies of the dead strewn like lifeless debris on the trampled ground. She did wish sometimes that she could have been some great Rialainish warrior-queen, rallying her troops around her chariot as she plunged boldly into the fray. The

trouble was, she realized, that she had entirely too much imagination ever to be a good warrior. She would constantly be imagining
not only her own hurts but those she would have to inflict upon
her foes. And the grief and remorse, afterward! She recalled
Damion's anguish in the forest of Trynisia after slaying the Anthropophagus. How to live with the knowledge that one had taken
a human life, even an enemy's, even in self-defense . . . ?

And these young knights and soldiers of Arainia, who had just
completed their training—did they understand what they might
one day have to do?

"Most do. Some of them still think it's all a game," Jomar said
when she gave voice to her concern.

Ailia sighed. "They're so innocent, they all think of war as a
great adventure. I *am* glad you're with us, Jo. You're the only seasoned warrior in this entire world, the only one who can teach us
what to do and to expect. It's curious, isn't it: those battle experi-
ences must have been terrible for you, but they could end by saving countless people in two worlds. You're the real savior, not I." A
lump suddenly came into her throat, and impulsively she turned
and embraced him. "Come back to us, Jo—come back safe and
sound, please!" she implored him.

"I'll try," he replied, looking awkward at her display of emotion.

"What about Lori?" Ailia asked him, quickly changing the subject. "Does she still want to be a soldier?" She waved a hand toward
the tall blonde girl, who was walking with Damion. Lorelyn had
not attended the knighting ceremony, and only turned up late for
the outing looking "mulish" as Jomar put it.

He groaned. "I think she still hopes I'm going to give in and let
her go to Mera. I won't. War may yet come of this, and war's not
for women."

"Rialainish women used to fight in battles beside their men, long
ago—and I've a feeling Lori's Rialainish by descent. It must be in
her blood."

Lorelyn noticed them looking at her. "I still think you're wrong
not to let me go," she called.

"Women don't fight," Jomar growled back.

"My whole purpose in life is to protect the Tryna Lia. Ana said
so." She turned to point at the aged queen of Mera, who was following at a distance with her gray cat padding at her heels.

"You already did that by substituting for her back on Mera. Ana said that, too."

Lorelyn stood still and crossed her arms, her pale eyes burning. "She never said it was all I would do. And I still have no idea who I am, or who my parents were. How did I come to be in that Kaanish monastery? How did I *know* that my Purpose was to save somebody else? I want to go back to Mera, and look for answers."

Jomar shrugged. "You may go there someday. But not yet, and not to fight. If you die in battle you'll never find your family. And anyway, Ailia said you'd decided to join her palace guard."

Lorelyn's face brightened a little at that. "Yes, I go back to Mirimar for my training tomorrow, and to get fitted for my livery. But it's not the same: I won't get to see any fighting. The enemy will likely never make it to Eldimia." She spoke these words in a tone of utmost pessimism before striding off.

Ana had caught up with them while they stood arguing, but remained silent throughout the conversation. Her misty eyes seemed to be trained upon faraway places and events that had nothing to do with their present situation. "I fear I must leave also," she said presently. "The Nemerei of Mera cannot fight Mandrake alone."

"Ana! *You* can't leave!" cried Ailia. "You're the wisest of us all. I was hoping you would stay here in Arainia, and help us."

"I am sorry, my dear," replied the old sorceress, gently laying a hand on her shoulder. "But Mera is my world, and it needs me. Do not fear, though: I am leaving you in the very best of hands. There are powers in this place that are a match for Mandrake and his allies."

Ailia could only gaze at her in dismay, and made no reply.

They walked on into a clearing where a cascade fell into a mountain tarn, and many wild beasts gathered to drink. It might have been a scene at some water hole in the Antipodes of Mera. But the animals were strange: mimic dogs, long-necked camelopards like attenuated giraffes, four-horned musimons, and the peculiar gnulike catoblepases whose bodies were covered like a pangolin's in scaly plates of fused hair. In the middle of the lake wallowed a family of behemoths: great gray beasts with heavy heads, blunt snouts, and jutting teeth. And there were birds: splendid purple tragopans, their heads crowned not with feathers but with hornlike projections of bone, and the lovely white caladriuses whose arching flexible necks were as graceful as any swan's. They fluttered around the beasts, even perching impudently on their backs. As the humans drew closer, one beast rose from the water's edge and came bounding toward them. It looked like a lynx—if a lynx could be the size of a lion. Jomar gave an oath while his hand, of itself, groped for the weapon he had not thought to wear.

Master Wu held up his hand. "It is but a gulon. It will do you no harm: it is not like your Meran beasts, Master Jomar. There are no eaters of flesh in this world save for carrion-scavengers." The enormous cat watched them, his amber eyes curious and unafraid. Now that their minds too were freed of fear, they saw that he was a beautiful creature: his pelt was long and luxuriant and a warm gold in color. Ana's cat approached the gulon fearlessly and raised her head to touch her small pink nose to his. He snuffed at her, waving his long plume of a tail, then turned and ambled back to the water.

Ailia and her young Meran friends watched in wonder. So the difference between that world and this lay not only in the alien forms of its beasts. The tranquility that reigned here was normal; no temporary truce brought on by common need, but an unbroken and enduring peace. As the wild beasts stooped to drink, seeming to kiss their own reflections in the water, there were no nervous side glances, nor any wary raising of heads; all drank their fill without fear. A lean pard crouched there at the water's edge, tongue lapping; had he been a Meran beast, the big cat would have worn a hide that disguised him while he stalked his prey. But here he need not hunt to live, and he was gaily arrayed in harlequin hues, rainbow spangles on a snow-white pelt. A cock and hen huppe strutted unmolested right across the path, followed by their downy brood: the hen was as colorful as her mate, with long trailing plumes. In Mera her plumage would have been drab, all brown and gray, to conceal her when she brooded on her eggs. But here in Arainia there was no need for any such protective coloration.

"But don't the animals here overbreed, and starve?" Jomar asked Wu in puzzlement when he explained this.

"Not at all. The creatures of Mera breed copiously because they know they will soon perish, and because so few of their offspring will survive. Arainian creatures do not feel that same urgency. They breed only to replace themselves, and they are longer-lived than Meran beasts. Their purpose is not mere survival, but the joy of *being*."

"In Mera, the meat-eaters kill animals that are weak or sick," argued Jomar. "That improves the herds—makes them stronger."

"I am sure it does." Wu smiled. "But here there are many plants with healing properties, and also springs with regenerative powers that can fortify the body's defenses against illness. Mera's moon, Numia, has similar springs: Ailia says she washed herself in one."

"Yes, I did," she said. "It was a sort of hot spring, and the water made me feel . . . invigorated, somehow. And—there was a strange-looking castle, too. Was that an Archon building, do you suppose?"

"No doubt," he replied. "Numia was one of their colonies. They used their powers to transform it from a dead satellite into a fertile, viable world. They did the same with your own little moon of Miria. But Numia was laid waste in the Great Disaster, and no one dwells there now."

"I almost thought I saw someone in the castle—a tall figure walking across its court; though I may have imagined it."

"It is possible some beings may visit there still. Long ago Numia was used as a sort of quarantine, where the Merans went to bathe in the healing springs before they journeyed on to Arainia. This ensured that they would not spread their ailments to this sphere. And Arainians bathed well in their own waters before venturing across the void to Mera."

It was curious, Ailia thought: as though this planet were alive, a conscious entity that actively intervened on behalf of its inhabitants. It resisted predation, disease, and all other sources of suffering in its sphere, and by some mysterious influence had even transformed its human settlers into the gentle and saintly Arainians. It was itself a living thing—vast, complex, many-selved. *The Mother*, she thought, and felt she understood the theology of the goddess-worshiping Elei at last.

She wondered what Damion thought of all this. He had been very quiet throughout the walk, she thought, scarcely speaking and appearing to be absorbed in some internal reflection or debate. She guessed what the source of this conflict must be, but did not like to approach him directly. Instead she turned to Jomar again. "And—and Damion? Is he really going to join you in Mera?"

"I hope so," Jomar remarked. "I'll want him at my side, since he's actually fought against Zimbouran soldiers before."

She shuddered at the images his words awoke in her mind. "Do you really think there will be a battle?"

"I hope so," he answered. "We have to do *something* about Khalazar. He's threatened us, after all—and even if he hadn't, we can't just stay safe here and let him take over all of Mera."

"Jo, you make me ashamed," said Ailia, staring down at her hands. "Of course we must help Mera's people, with a war if need be. I just wish . . . there were another way."

"Don't look so worried," said Jomar, misinterpreting her expression. "You won't have to go and fight, ever. That's what *we're* for."

Ailia said despairingly, "Then what use am I?" But no one answered her.

Unable to bear her thoughts any longer, she turned aside and headed off alone into the trees. Nobody followed, perhaps respecting her need for privacy. One might wander these groves in perfect safety, after all: no venomous snake or stinging scorpion lurked here, no fanged menace prowled the undergrowth. After a few minutes she slowed to a desultory walk and looked about her. The trees that grew on these wild slopes were the true trees of Arainia: the vast umbrageous perindeus, its boughs always awhir with the wings of birds attracted to its fragrant white flowers; and the tree-of-life, with fruit and flower hanging together on its dusky boughs like stars and golden suns. In Mera Ailia and her friends had seen trees of this latter kind, but in Meran soil they had grown small and stunted; here they were tall and strong as mighty oaks. She looked up wonderingly at the tremendous trunks that reared into wreathing clouds of foliage; then down again at the mighty roots that were like whole Meran trees lying on their sides. It was like a forest from a faerie-tale land where giants dwelt. Here, under their boughs, the multiple screens of leaves filtered and transmuted the sunlight into a green-golden refulgence. A droning stridulation that she at first thought came from insects of the cricket kind proved to emanate from the stiff, close-clustered leaves of certain trees, which vibrated continually in the wind. To the chorus of these singing groves were joined other sounds. The mountain stream that fed the tarn tumbled downhill not far away. Water was water no matter where it was; it made the same music here as in Mera. The thought was comforting.

And there was the birdsong. There seemed to be no fowl in this alpine forest smaller than a dove and less colorful than a parakeet, and all of them sang: each song so melodious, so resonant, so full of expression that she could almost imagine they were not merely sending messages to mates and rivals, but truly "singing" for the pleasure of it like human minstrels. One song more than any other caught her attention, emerging from the surrounding music of birds, water, and trees like a single clear-noted instrument dominating an orchestra. It was so intense, this song, so joyous, so moving in its constant repetition of a five-note refrain, that Ailia could not put aside the fancy that the singer was no mere bird but some sentient being, rejoicing in the power and beauty of its own voice. Half-unconsciously she followed the sound through the undergrowth, seeking its source.

She spied the singer at last, perched upon a mossy branch of a giant perindeus some thirty feet above the forest floor. It was the size of an eagle, but its build more closely resembled that of a pheasant, with long flowing tail-coverts that hung down behind it like a royal train. Its head and body were scarlet, with a golden crest that trailed half down its neck, the feathers fine as a woman's hair. The greater coverts on its wings were yellow, the lesser coverts and tertiary feathers bright scarlet to match the body, and the primary and secondary feathers and tail coverts a shimmering violet-blue. Beneath the coverts hung four immensely long green tail plumes, tipped with peacocklike "eyes." The plumage, like that of many tropical birds, looked almost hand-painted: lit by a single ray of sun, it blazed with the colors of every kind of fire.

Other birds perched on nearby boughs of surrounding trees, but they were quiet and motionless, as if enchanted into silence by the great bird's song.

As she stood there, gazing and listening in delight, a wind stirred the treetops above her, making the green leaf-canopy toss and roar like a sea. All the birds, including the singer, took to the air at once in a dazzling show of rainbow plumage. She gaped up at them, entranced. What could have moved them to this sudden glorious flight? *If I were in Mera,* she thought, *I'd say that something had frightened them, but of course that couldn't be the case here—*

And then, without warning, there was a rushing noise and the foliage above her burst into flame.

Ailia stumbled backward in shock, staring up at the burning boughs. The many-colored songbird swooped low above her head, its music turned to shrill, discordant cries. Something huge and dark flapped across the sky high above, and there was a rasping roar and another tree erupted in flames. Something was flying above the roof of the forest, setting it alight. As she gaped upward she saw it again: a giant shape, black against the sun, like the silhouette of a tremendous bat.

A firedrake.

It was burning the forest all around her, trying to trap her within walls of flame. Embers cascaded down from the branches high above, setting the undergrowth smoldering. She was too stunned to move for a moment; then with a cry of belated terror she caught up her skirts and fled back the way she had come, not realizing that this was in fact the monster's intent: to drive her out into the open where it could more easily reach her.

As she ran from the trees down into the alp below, Ailia thought she could hear shouts and cries of alarm, but they were faint and far away, too far for those who uttered them to be of any help . . . And though she was free of the firetrap in the wood, she was now in plain view, exposed. She struggled on, hampered by her long skirts. And then she staggered, nearly blown off her feet by a gust of hot reeking air as the creature alighted behind her, flaring its leathery wings. She could not help but turn and look, now.

The monster reared out of the mountain meadow, reeking of smoke and carrion. She had seen the skeleton of a firedrake once, in Trynisia: now, horribly, that skeleton had come to life, clothed in dark scales, gaunt and angular. It was small for a firedrake, only a little larger than an elephant. But it was hideous: unlike a Loänan, this creature had no furry mane or pointed ears, but was entirely clad in scales. Its body was jet-black above and blood-red beneath. The heat of its breath was like a furnace-blast in her face, and the air quivered before the beast's gaping jaws. The grass withered and blackened at its feet

Ailia again sought to flee, not really believing that she could outrun the monster or escape its fiery exhalations. "Help," she cried hoarsely as she ran. "Please—help me!"

There was a musical trill, high overhead: Ailia raised her eyes, to see the large many-colored bird whose song had earlier enchanted her in the forest. It swooped down upon her in a flurry of gold and red, right at her face, and she whirled and fled from its beak and claws. The mountain tarn was directly ahead of her, with its crowds of beasts who were slow to feel fear and only now starting to scatter. She swerved to avoid its brink, but the bird stooped upon her again and she fell with a cry into the water. She surfaced, choking and trying to toss wet hair out of her eyes. Above her the bird was hovering, bright wings beating the air: she flinched, but it showed no further sign of hostility.

Had it in fact been hostile? Could it have driven her into the water on purpose, to save her from the dragon-fire? As the black monster again turned her way, sending forth a jet of flame, the bird dived once more with a shrill cry, flying at her head. But she had already drawn a deep breath and ducked under the surface.

When she could hold her breath no longer she surfaced, more slowly and cautiously this time, peering through the reeds at the tarn's margin. The bird was still circling above her, ignoring its own danger. The firedrake's bellows held a harsh note of hate that made Ailia shrink back into the water. Then there was a roar and another gust of wind, and the firedrake looked up—too late—as something huge and shining dove between it and its prey.

It seemed for an instant as though the sun itself had descended into the clearing, so bright was the huge creature that dropped from the air. Ailia, in a daze, recognized the golden dragon that had saved her life in Trynisia. It hovered briefly, wings flapping, then dropped to the earth in front of the firedrake. The latter snarled in fury at the intruder, and spat a gout of orange flame.

The Imperial dragon never moved. As the fire swept toward it, the great golden beast roared as if in defiance or mockery. The flames seemed to strike an invisible barrier, parting and dissipating in the air without touching their target. The firedrake stared—it seemed a stupid creature, for all its strength and ferocity—and the golden dragon reared up and brought its clawed forelimbs down on its assailant's back, pinning it to the earth. Tail lashing wildly, the firedrake hissed and writhed in the effort to escape. It managed to twist its ghastly head around and attempted to sink its teeth into its opponent's foreleg. The golden dragon snatched the limb away and the firedrake wrenched itself free, turning to claw at its enemy's underside. As Ailia watched breathlessly her champion leaped to one side, and the firedrake spun and lunged toward her, all black jaws and blasting heat.

But the golden dragon planted its foreclaws firmly on her attacker's tail, causing it to pull up short before it had covered half the distance to Ailia's position. It whirled, screaming, to attack the Loänan again. The golden dragon dealt it a blow that sent it rolling across the turf. No fire came from its mouth this time, only a gush of dark blood; it drew a long rattling breath, beat its wings convulsively, and was still.

The Imperial dragon stood over it, panting slightly. It opened its own great jaws and gave a loud roar—whether of anger or triumph she could not tell. And then suddenly there was rain: a sun shower that drizzled down from the clouds above the mountain peak. It fell only on the forest, quenching the pockets of red flame within its verdure.

The bird craned its neck upward, and trilled again. Then it darted down and alighted on the ground beside the dragon. There was a flicker, and—Ailia blinked—the bird was no longer there. In its place stood the figure of a small, auburn-haired woman.

"Lira." Ailia whispered the name. Her lady-in-waiting was a shapeshifter!

Her eyes turned toward the dragon. Its form too was wavering, turning to a misty brightness in the air, and then it was gone and where it had stood there was a pulsing, pale light that dimmed and coalesced into the shape of a little old man in a white robe. Master Wu.

"That was too close, Auron," said Lira, pointing to the dead firedrake. "This was only a young one, thank goodness: it could have been much worse. Where it came from I can't imagine. But we shall have to be more vigilant in future."

Ailia waded ashore, walked over to the two familiar figures. There was a pause as they turned to face her.

"You," she breathed, facing Master Wu. "You were . . . the dragon, the one that saved me, on Elendor. Only—it wasn't a dragon, it was you all along. And you—" to Lady Lira. "You're a Nemerei too! I saw you shift your shape."

"I believe you are under a misapprehension, Highness," said the man she had called Wu, clearing his throat. "We are Nemerei, yes, but we are not *human* Nemerei. I am as you saw me just now, an Imperial Loänan. And it was Lira's true shape that you beheld just now, the form that she wears when she is in her own world."

Ailia stared at Lady Lira. "Her own *world*?" she whispered.

"I am of the T'kiri, the bird-people," Ailia's lady-in-waiting said, her face and voice as composed as ever. "The firebirds—or phoenixes, as your kind sometimes calls us. This absurd form I wear is only a disguise."

Wu smiled. "Only absurd because you make it so. It is quite understandable that you should think a beak is beautiful, but I must tell you most humans do not admire very long noses."

Lira swept him with a disdainful glance. "And what of you, Auron? Is there any real need for you to play the buffoon, as you do?"

"*Ailia!*" The princess turned to see her courtiers hastening toward her through the still-smoldering woods, a white-faced Tiron in the lead with Jomar and Lorelyn at his heels. Damion, Ana, and several Nemerei followed behind them. Syndra blanched and stopped short when she saw the dead firedrake.

"Oh—what *is* it?" cried Lorelyn, staring at the twisted coils of the monster.

"A firedrake," Ana told her in a calm voice, as if discussing the weather.

Tiron stepped closer to the carcass and regarded it with horror. "It has been long since one of these creatures was seen in our world. I would have sworn that none remained."

Ana nodded. "Firedrakes have been extinct in both Arainia and Mera for many hundreds of years. I think that this one came from outside—from some Valdur-blighted world." And while the others still stood gazing in horrified fascination at the dead monster, she approached Wu and Lira. Greymalkin had already reached them and was rubbing her gray sides against their ankles in apparent token of approval. "Dragon and phoenix," Ana stated. "Your celestial protectors, Ailia."

Ailia thought, *But how does she know? She wasn't here to see them transform.* Ana continued: "I have said nothing all this time, since it was plain that both of you wished to be secret. But I take it that your people are now satisfied that she is the One, Loänan?" she asked Wu.

"I am, Majesty," he concurred, bowing to her. "And I hope now to convince the others. Had I any shadow of doubt remaining after the Mirimar tempest, the attack of this creature"—gesturing to the firedrake—"has removed them. Our enemies fear Ailia, and that alone confirms what I have long believed." He turned to the princess and sank to one knee before her. "I am your servant, Highness, now and always."

"And I also," Lira added, curtseying gracefully. "If you are willing, Highness, I shall continue in your service, and Auron and I shall be your guardians from this time forth."

Ailia opened her mouth, but no words came out.

"Then I can return to Mera," said Ana, stooping to pick up her purring cat, "and the work that awaits me there."

"The Loänan will gladly convey you to your home world," the man who was not a man told her, rising to his feet again. "Have no fear for Ailia. Once the Loänan have accepted her, all the Empire will follow our lead. She will number among her followers the peoples of far-distant worlds."

Once more he bowed his head in Ailia's direction. For a time the only voices heard in the mountain meadow were those of the wild birds and the falling stream. Then Syndra Magus gave a little cry, and whirling about she fled into the trees.

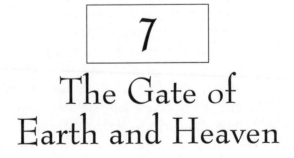

7

The Gate of Earth and Heaven

AURON PLUNGED THROUGH THE CLOUDS with a pleasant feeling of freedom regained. How good it was to take his own, natural shape again after being so long confined within a small and limiting human frame! He reveled for a moment in the sensations of flight, the roar of the wind in his ears and the headlong, fearless fall through the air. He plummeted through the base of the cloud layer into clear air, then pulled out of his dive and leveled off, spreading his wings to their full sixty-pace span as he planed low over the moon's surface.

Miria had once been an airless waste, as its innumerable craters showed. But a tremendous feat of sorcery in ancient times had made it habitable for beings that breathed, and turned its craters to circular lakes and pools, and clothed the dry ground in verdure— if "verdure" was the correct word for vegetation whose chief color was pale blue. He glided on, over a lunar forest whose titanic trees cast even longer shadows across the blue meadows beyond, and then he descended toward a crater-lake in which several Loänan were lying half-immersed. When the ground was only a wing's length below him he furled the great golden webs of his pinions and dropped, landing lightly on the very tips of his talons. The clear rare air and abrupt horizon gave him the impression of being on a high plateau. Atop a stony ridge stood the twin pillars of a dragon-gate, and on a hill further away a marble palace raised delicate towers skyward. In the blue-black sky hung Arainia, bright cerulean on her sunlit side and girded with her glittering rings: her reflection gleamed in the water of the crater-lake. How beautiful a planet looked from the void, he thought—and how terribly fragile, like a thin-shelled egg that could be shattered with a careless touch, spilling out its precious store of life.

He walked down the smooth slope of the crater wall and approached the Emperor where he lolled near the shore of the circular lake. As Orbion glanced up Auron made a draconic obeisance, forelegs outstretched and chin upon the ground. "Highness, I have the proof you sought," he announced.

Orbion Imperator splashed a little water onto his silvery flank with the multifoliate tip of his tail. "Tell me."

"The proof I offer is a young firedrake. It attacked Ailia outside the academy of Melnemeron. Had Taleera and I not been near she would surely have perished. We came close to losing her as it was. No firedrake has dwelled in Arainia for hundreds of years, nor can it be mere chance that this one chose Ailia of all people to attack.

Our enemies are behind this, I am positive of that. They fear her, and that is proof of what she is."

The blue eyes narrowed thoughtfully. "You say she came near to dying. How could that be, if this princess of yours truly was the cause of the great tempest in Eldimia? Were she in truth the Tryna Lia, should she not have been a match for any firedrake—especially a young one?"

The golden dragon gazed steadily at his ruler. "The princess is young herself, and her powers are still undeveloped. She did not create that storm by act of will: it was an unconscious response to her fear of Morlyn and his allies. When the firedrake attacked, her immediate danger overwhelmed her; her mind had no time in which to react to her peril. That is all the more reason for her to be protected. And she knows now what I am, for I could not save her without revealing my true form. There is no point in further attempts at concealment. Son of Heaven, you cannot doubt any longer that she is the one we have waited for, after all these signs! Taleera is satisfied, and has been for some time. The T'kiri now accept that Ailia is the Tryna Lia. Let us renew our ties with these human creatures, join them once more to our Imperium."

The Emperor and his guard stirred uneasily in the water, churning its blue serenity into foam with their limbs and tails. The reflection of Arainia in its surface trembled and wavered, shattering into shards of light. Auron looked away, gazing at the white palace in the distance. The Arainians had intended it as an alternative residence for their prophesied leader, a pleasant retreat on the garden-moon whose name she bore. But before the Moon Palace could be completed the Great Disaster had struck, and its human builders had been unable to return to this sphere. It was wrong, he thought, anger stirring in him. They had too much promise to be thus confined to their separate worlds, cut off from the Loänan and from each other.

"The humans still trouble me, Auron," the dragon Emperor said at last, "and what I have beheld of their doings in Mera disquiets me further. They mean to make war on one another again, until that entire world is laid waste. And now I hear that the gate at Melnemeron has been opened."

"Yes. One of the Nemerei, a Lady Syndra, discovered the means to open it. I say 'discovered,' but it appears that she may have had some aid in retrieving the old knowledge. After the attack of the firedrake failed and I revealed myself, she ran from the place. We all thought that she was only afraid, but later she was seen hurling herself into the ethereal portal, which opened to receive her. What has become of her I do not know: the Ether is perilous, and it may be that she will never again emerge from it. But I suspect that she summoned the firedrake, and told it where to find Ailia. And I do not think she could have done such a thing on her own. I feel certain Morlyn corrupted her. And so I beg you, let me protect Ailia, for he will surely strike at her again. Let me bear her away to some world of our realm, where she can be kept safe."

There was a lengthy pause as Orbion considered, and Auron waited anxiously.

"Very well," the Emperor said at last, rearing up out of the lake and shaking the water from his wings. "It shall be as you ask. There is little point in secrecy now. Guard her, and keep her safe. I will tell the other Loänan that they may reveal themselves to the people of Arainia."

"BUT LADY SYNDRA! Who would have thought she would turn traitor? A Nemerei, and Arainian-born," said King Tiron as he paced up and down Ailia's room.

"I should have thought of it," said Ana. "I knew that the Tryna Lia would be beset by every kind of evil."

"And the man Wu, not even human all this time." Tiron shuddered. "And Ailia's own handmaiden, Lira—"

"Yes. It is fortunate they were friends and not enemies. But to tell the truth, I suspected them both for some time."

"And yet you said nothing!" he cried.

Ana continued to stroke her cat, her face tranquil. "Their secret was not mine to reveal."

"It's incredible! No one here, not even the highest Magus, knows how to shape-shift," said Ailia. She had sat quietly in a chair by the window all this time, saying little, listening to her father and Ana debate.

"Yet the practice was well known once in both Mera and Arainia, as your old lore attests," Ana remarked. "Human magi learned it from the Archons."

Ailia fell silent again. She did not wish to dwell on the Archons' shape-shifting powers. Ever since Wu first spoke of the Nemerei's disturbing theory she had felt more distanced from her lost mother. She even felt a slight estrangement from herself. No longer did she wonder on waking who she was, but rather *what* she was. If the theory were true, then she had lost not only Ailia Ship-wright's old name and identity, but her very humanity. Her father, when she had mentioned it to him, declared that he did not believe it. *I don't believe it either,* her heart continued to insist. But her mind could not let the matter rest.

"Spies—spies and traitors everywhere, in every shape and form!" exclaimed her father. "How can we ever hope to keep Ailia safe?"

I am the Tryna Lia, Ailia thought. *I was supposed to keep everyone else safe.*

Presently there came a soft knock at the door. "Your Highness?" called a familiar voice.

Tiron stiffened, but Ailia called out, "Enter."

It was the voice of Master Wu—*no, not Wu,* she reminded herself. The door opened to show the small rotund figure of the mage, with Lady Lira standing beside him. Ailia looked at them both thoughtfully. Lira wore a vermilion-colored gown and a capelet of golden gulon fur. The old wizard was attired in a bright blue robe, stitched with silver runes, over which he had thrown a rainbow-spotted pard hide. On his head was a matching fur cap, perched at a jaunty angle. Did he dress and act like this in order to put her at ease, like a man playing games with a child? Ailia wondered. As he entered she looked in fascination at the fine lines fanning the corners of his eyes, the thin wisps of white hair straggling below his cap; then she looked at Lira's small neat hands and luxuriant auburn hair. Every detail told her eye that these two were human beings. But they were older than any human being that had ever lived, even an Elei, even Ana; indeed, the one in man-form was older than any living thing in Arainia save perhaps the trees in the mountain forests below, their massive trunks ringed inside with millennia of growth.

"I don't know what to call you anymore," she said, glancing away from them again.

"Your Highness may call me Lira still, if you wish," the woman said. "My true name is Taleera, which is close to it in sound." She spoke the name in a lilting voice that reminded Ailia of birdsong.

"And my name is Auron," said the man. "That, at least, is as close as the human tongue can come to it. In my own language it is a sound like a lion roaring: *Orr-onnh.*"

"Very well—Taleera, Auron." Tiron stood staring as the dragon-man settled into an empty chair. Taleera remained standing with her small hands neatly folded, the perfect picture of a dutiful lady-in-waiting. "Tell me, how long have the two of you been . . . watching my daughter?"

"I have watched her," said Auron, "ever since I first brought her here to Arainia. Taleera for not quite so long."

Ailia looked at the bird-woman. "Yes—it was two years ago that you came, wasn't it? And Auron disappeared after leaving me in the grounds of Halmirion." She turned back to him. "And when you were Wu I saw you only occasionally."

He smiled. "But I was not always Wu. I took many forms beside this human one. I was a bird in a tree above you sometimes—a carp in a pool—a spotted lizard clinging to a wall."

"You *spied* on her!" Tiron said.

"I'm afraid I did. But my motives were honorable. I believed your daughter's life was in grave danger, and you see now I was right. My ruler forbade me to show her my true form, and even as a human I could not follow her everywhere, so I took those other shapes at need."

"But I saw your true form in Mera," said Ailia.

He removed the cap of spotted fur and toyed absently with it. "Ah, yes. I could not help that: Prince Morlyn held me captive with cold iron, so I could not alter my shape."

"I thought then that he'd tamed you to ride on. I didn't know then you were a thinking being, like me. I mean no offense, but I thought you were only a beast."

He waved a plump hand. "No offense is taken. I was on Elendor to observe the arrival of your party. The cherubim who watched over Trynisia had alerted us Loänan that some humans were attempting to locate the Stone, and I knew this could mean the fulfillment of all our prophecies. So I flew to Mera at once. I also intended to ward off the rebel Loänan who had been seen flying about the Holymount—though I did not yet know it was Prince Morlyn who led them, in draconic guise. He hid himself when I came, and then caught me later resting in the temple ruin as I waited for you and your companions to turn up, imprisoning me with the iron chain as I slept. He is a cunning creature." The round face was solemn. "He knows all the lore of the Nemerei and has seduced many a follower of the White Magic, both human and Loänan, over to his side. Remember that he has lived for many hundreds of your years, and in that time gained a great deal of knowledge. My people hoped once to capture him and bind him with iron, even as he bound me on Elendor, but always he has eluded us, and now he has found strong allies among those who serve Valdur. Never underestimate him, Highness, or overestimate your own ability to resist him." He smiled then, his expression lightening. "But come! You must all have many other questions to ask us both!"

Ailia looked at her father and Ana. "I have. But I hardly know where to begin."

Auron gestured vaguely with one hand. "Begin anywhere you like, and we'll see where it leads us."

"Well . . . why did you decide to help me, back on Elendor?"

"When Morlyn chained me I was unable to escape or to reach out with my mind to the cherubim. They had elected to leave the Stone where it lay in the treasury, since this would be the perfect test for the One to whom it belonged: to pick out her sacred gem from the midst of all the other jewels. Once you freed me, of course, I was able to contact them. They said they had sensed the Stone being touched, but did not know yet who had done it. I had not seen you with the gem, but I believed you might be the one. After you freed me I would have aided you in any case, but I decided it would be best to take you to Arainia—stopping first at the moon for quarantine. The cherubim, though, were still uncertain. At last, after some debate, they decided to take the Stone to Arainia, along with your remaining companions, and let you be tested again there. Had you not proven yourself at the last, they would have returned for it and taken it back to Mera to await its true claimant."

Tiron said, "I have a question to ask. Why did the Loänan hide from humanity all this time, when we might have benefited from your knowledge?"

"We do not hide from *all* humans, sire: there are others of your kind now living out among the stars, distant relatives of yours in distant worlds, with whom we retain close ties. It is the Merei, the human beings of Mera and their kin here in Arainia, whom we are permitted only to watch from afar."

"After the Great Disaster," added Taleera, "the people of Mera rejected sorcery, fearing that its use had brought destruction upon them. In a way they were right to be afraid, for there are always abusers of magic. An argument was also made in that time that if magic use became common, people would grow lazy and indolent, no longer working for their food and so losing all the benefits of honest, hard labor."

"That is true," Ana agreed. "The dangers of magic are as great as its gifts."

"The ruler of my people also judged that we had interfered too much in Mera's history," Auron said. "That we had given its peoples knowledge for which they were not yet ready. And so we obeyed his wishes and drew apart for a time, to observe you from afar. Humanity is a curious race, and a most interesting one. You did not originate in Mera, you know, but were brought to that world from another."

"We were? What world was that?" asked Ailia, fascinated.

Auron and Taleera both shook their heads. "We do not know," the dragon-man said. "Those who took your ancestors from it sought for another planet as much like your original world as possible: a planet third in position from a lone yellow sun, with a large moon circling it. The chances of two such similar worlds being close together are small, so we guess that the world of your origins lies very far away. Mera suited the purpose of those ancient sorcerers, even though it had a harsh climate, and only a few creatures dwelt there: fierce libbards and swivel-horned yales and a few other beasts. The sorcerers made the air of Mera warmer and milder so that your race might dwell there, while the native creatures withdrew to the poles. And there the human race thrived and grew, along with many other living things taken from the original world."

"Tell me, why did you Loänan close the portals in Mera and Arainia? Do you see humans as a corrupting influence on other worlds?" Tiron asked. His manner was still accusing, and he stood close to Ailia.

"No. The Ether is not to be entered lightly even by the initiated, and sorcery is very new still to humanity. The old Merans opened far too many gates, in far too many places: the unpracticed mages of those times thought of the dragon-ways merely as a convenience, a quick way to travel from country to country. I hope to see some of these gates reopened one day, but the time for that is not yet come."

"It makes me think again of the old tales—there were all sorts of invisible doorways into the worlds of faeries and genii, if only one could find them. But the Ether—it isn't safe, you say?" Ailia asked.

"Not altogether. Your body cannot be destroyed there, for on that plane it is translated into pure quintessence. But your mind can be assaulted: deceived, or enslaved. In the Ether your only true weapon is your mind—the doughtiest warrior cannot depend on the strength of muscle and sinew there, for these he must leave behind. To enter it safely, the mind and not the body must be strong. Still, only a few of the eidolons you encounter will be hostile."

"Eidolons? What are they?"

"An *eidolon* is an image of an earthly thing. There are forms that appear in the Ether, in the likeness of living things: beasts, birds, or beings. Some say that they are gods or angels in disguise, who appear in order to test us, others that they are only images created by our minds. Some of them *seem* to possess an intelligence of their own, as those who have interacted with them can attest. Sorcerer adepts who 'summon spirits' into your world are actually bringing eidolons onto the material plane. Eidolons will obey commands, yet they also give the impression of being fully sentient in their own right. But we do not want them breaking free of our control and taking over our plane. Hence the closing of the gates."

But Ailia was intrigued at the thought of a realm where her slight body would not be a disadvantage: a realm where, for once, she could be the equal of a warrior.

"Well," said Ana, "have you spoken with your Emperor, Auron? What does he say?"

"Emperor?" echoed Tiron.

"Orbion, the Emperor of Heaven," Auron replied. "He rules over all worlds and realms of the Celestial Empire."

"What sort of being is he?" Tiron asked.

"He is a Loänan. In the beginning, when the Archons declined and disappeared from Talmirennia, it was agreed that the Emperor would be chosen from one of the four eldest races: Loänan, T'kiri, Tarnawyn, or cherub. Orbion Imperator has reigned for nearly a thousand years now." Auron returned his gaze to Ailia. "I have his leave to take the Tryna Lia through the Ether to my home world, to Temendri Alfaran in what you call the constellation of the Dragon."

"No!" Tiron faced the little man. "Ana, this cannot be allowed. You said yourself that her power is strongest in Arainia. What worse peril could await her in another world? This may be Morlyn's intent: to draw her out, make her vulnerable to attack."

"She has already nearly fallen a victim to the enemy," Ana answered. "I and many others have sought to protect her and almost failed. On Temendri Alfaran, surrounded by the greatest and oldest of dragon mages, she would be more secure, not less."

"No traitor or spy of Morlyn could reach her there," Auron agreed. "She need not stay forever, only until she is strong enough to fight her foes. As for the Arainian people, you can reassure them. For I am afraid you must remain, sire. The Loänan will make an exception for Ailia, but not for any other human of Arainia or Mera to enter their worlds—not until the Emperor and the monarchs give their leave."

Tiron sat down once more and bowed his head. "No—not again. It was like this, when *she* left—when she fled the palace with our child, leaving me—"

"Father." Ailia knelt by his side and took his hand in hers, peering up into his lowered eyes. No distance lay now between her and him. She had loved him first for his kindness and gentle ways, and later for all those things they had in common, like their desire for knowledge. Had she had any lingering doubts that he was her true father, they had vanished long ago. Now, looking up into his anguished face, she needed no Nemerei power to sense what he was suffering. He had lost her once, for many long years; then he had regained her, only to find that she had no memory of him and her love had been given to another family. They had at last begun to bridge that gap of years, and now she was to be taken away from him once more. She too felt a wrenching pain at the thought of a second separation. But she knew, too, that Auron was right. He could not protect her, and neither could Tiron. It was difficult to say what she knew she must, and she chose her words with care.

"Father, they are right. Perhaps you can come and join me, later. But I must go with them, away from here."

And now that she had her desire to see other worlds, she felt only distress and fear.

LATER THAT EVENING DAMION FOUND her sitting by herself, perched on the low stone parapet that circled the plateau. She was wrapped in a fur cloak against the cold, staring up at the sky, and her back was turned toward him so she did not see him approach. Neither, it seemed, did she hear him, for she did not turn around but remained intent on the great field of stars before her. He stood for a time watching her, reluctant to intrude on whatever thoughts were holding her rapt and motionless, and also unwilling to say what he had come to say. He felt, too, a great wave of pity and tenderness toward her, knowing what her response to his words would likely be. She was so near to him now, and yet they were soon to be parted by a distance so great that it could scarcely be imagined, and years might well pass before they saw one another again. If indeed it was their fate to meet again . . . He found himself wishing that she would turn her head and see him, so that he would be able to speak without first destroying whatever peace of mind she might have found out here. But she continued in her quiet contemplation of the heavens, unaware of him or anything in the world about her.

At last he could endure it no more. He stepped closer and cleared his throat. "Ailia? Is it safe for you out here, on your own?" he asked.

"I'm not alone." Ailia pointed to a shape like a cloud, but moving more swiftly than any cloud could, scudding across the Arch of Heaven. "A Loänan—do you see? There will be more of them scattered about, disguised as other creatures, watching over me." She stood, and turned to look at the Gate of Earth and Heaven where it loomed black against the sky. "Ana has gone. I saw her leave. She walked through the portal and then she—vanished. She told me before she went that she only stayed here in Arainia to keep an eye on me until the Loänan agreed to guard me. Somehow she knew, or guessed, that they were making up their minds about me and would decide sooner or later. So she's in Mera now, and after Jo's army goes through, the Nemerei will seal the portal again for safety. There is another rift, Auron says, high up in the air where no one but a Loänan can reach it: he and I will take that way." She looked skyward again. "I used to gaze at the stars when I was a child on Great Island, trying to imagine what it would be like to journey to them. And now I am really going to do it. I still can't quite believe it."

"I am sure you will be safe there. And you'll have another fine story to tell." Damion paused a moment before speaking again. "Ailia, I have decided to join Jo's campaign on Mera."

Ailia continued to gaze at the sky. "I was—afraid you would," she said without looking at him.

He went and stood beside her at the parapet. "Jomar is my friend, and Mera is my world. I must help them. Khalazar has to be stopped."

She turned to face him then. In the starlight, she thought, he looked more beautiful than she had ever seen him, with his pale face and nearly luminous eyes—like the archangel for whom he was named. His expression, too, held something of the serene resolve one saw on the faces of angels in paintings. "I understand," she said, "but—you're not a warrior, Damion! I saw how you looked after killing that Anthropophagus in Mera!" She hated to remind him, but she was growing desperate. "You're not meant to fight and kill people. There are other ways you can help Arainia."

Gently he tried to make her understand. "I have training and experience. I can't leave the most difficult task of all to others. I would never be able to live with myself if I let Jo and the others go into possible danger, and stayed here myself, in safety."

"How do you suppose I feel?" she cried. Her hands clenched on the edge of the parapet. "I keep thinking that if I really were the warrior queen of the prophecy, I would end this conflict myself, and not leave it to others."

"You're not strong enough yet."

"But I hope to learn a great deal from Auron's people, and become a sorceress one day. I may be able to free Mera then."

"Khalazar won't wait until you are ready—and neither will Mandrake. Many innocent lives are in danger now, and we must do something. Remember, it may not turn into a war. Mandrake won't waver, but Khalazar might become frightened and give up his ideas of conquest. But whatever *does* happen, I want to be there by Jo's side."

"I suppose nothing I say can change your mind," she said helplessly. "But I can't help saying it anyway. Damion—*please* don't go." Now was the time—to tell him she loved him, needed him, could not bear to lose him. Would even that be enough to stop him? she wondered miserably, and was suddenly afraid to speak.

He took a jeweled dagger from his belt and held the hilt out to her. "Here. I want you to have this."

Ailia recoiled from it, as if from a snake. "No, no. I could never use it. I hate weapons."

"Ailia, even roses have thorns to protect themselves. Heaven forbid, but you might someday be in a situation where sorcery won't help you. I would feel better if I knew you had this. Please."

Reluctantly she took the dagger. It felt hard and heavy in her hand. "All right then. I will call it my Thorn. When will you be—leaving?"

"The army departs tomorrow morning. I'm going with them, as Jomar's second in command. The Nemerei will open the portal for us and move us through the Ether to Mera. We will be going to the desert outside Felizia, the capital. Dragons will guard us by air and warn us at once of any attack by land."

"Mandrake will be there," she almost whispered.

"Don't worry. There are plenty of Nemerei going with us too." He looked away. "I must go and report now. We're gathering our forces on the mountainside."

"So—you came to say goodbye."

He took her hands in his, gazing down at her for a long time without speaking, and then he bent his head. She caught her breath, her cheeks flushing, but the kiss fell on her cheek and not her mouth. Releasing her without another word, he strode away toward the end of the plateau and the mountainside. Not once did he look back.

She watched him through misting eyes. As soon as he was gone from her view, she picked up her skirts and hastened indoors.

Once she was in her private cell she closed the door, then went to her bedside table. From one of its drawers she took out a little silver flask. Removing the stopper, she poured out a small amount of clear golden liquid into a goblet. As a Nemerei in training she was now permitted to take ambrosia when she pleased, but her hand shook a little as she emptied the cup. She had never before taken so much of the elixir.

But I will need a lot, to go where I am going . . .

She swallowed the last of the liquid, then lay down on her bed, her heart beating fast. She had little hope of succeeding where Melnemeron's most diplomatic efforts had already failed. But she had to make the attempt. Presently she could feel herself drifting . . . mind separating from body, slipping away . . . into the Ether. *Zimboura,* she thought. *Felizia, Yanuvan . . .*

And there was a great fortress of sand-colored stone in her mind, steep-sided, built by ancient hands. It faded from her view and was replaced by a long high-ceilinged hall, all red and gold, a foreign court filled with bright-clad courtiers. She did not see Mandrake there. On a gold-plated, jewel-encrusted throne sat Khalazar: she recognized the heavy, black-bearded face from his ethereal visitation. But now it was she, not he, who was the phantom visitor. A woman screamed shrilly from somewhere behind her, heads turned, and Ailia knew that they could see her.

"What is it? Who is she?" voices cried. She glanced down, saw her airy form clad in her white robe. "Do not be afraid," she entreated them. She raised her head again and walked forward, hands held out in a placating gesture. Through the turmoil of the throne room she walked on insubstantial feet, to stand before Khalazar's dais. She would address his court as he had hers, but her message would be very different. "People of Zimboura," she began.

One of Khalazar's bodyguards yelled and hurled his spear at her. It was hard not to flinch, but she made herself stand still as the weapon passed harmlessly through her ethereal form. Courtiers fled in many directions as the weapon fell clattering to the floor, and wails of terror went up. Khalazar's eyes seemed about to start from their sockets.

"A spirit! She's a spirit!" someone cried.

Ailia raised her voice. "I am the Tryna Lia." A collective gasp rose from the court. Ailia continued to address the man on the throne. "Why do you war with me, King? Why pursue a course that will bring only death and destruction? I have done you no harm. I want only peace for both our peoples."

"Evil enchantress!" Khalazar screamed, recoiling in his throne. "Begone—begone! Genii, I summon you—"

"King Khalazar, hear me—" Ailia began.

"Morlyn—Roglug—Elazar, I command you, come to me!" Khalazar bellowed. He was foaming at the mouth, and his face was flushed as red as his robe; he looked as though he were on the verge of a fit.

Ailia knew suddenly that it was no use: this man could not be reasoned with. She was only filling him with fear. In despair she drew her mind back, away from Yanuvan and Zimboura. The throne room faded away, and she found herself gazing up at the stark ceiling of her cell.

Oh, Damion—I tried . . .

JOMAR LOOKED UP AT THE PILLARED PORTAL rising on its tall isolated pinnacle in the light of early morning. He half-imagined he could see a curious blurring of the air between the stone dragons, like the wavering distortion of a mirage. On the far side of that gaping gate, his reason told him, was empty sky and a steep drop to the plains far, far below: yet he had been assured by the Nemerei that his men would not plunge through it to their deaths, but pass on into the Ethereal Plane, and from there into the world of Mera. He still wasn't sure about this "Ether" business, but it wasn't the worst of his worries.

The Loänan: something about them made his flesh creep. In their true, reptilian shapes they were alarming enough, but what bothered him most was their ability to masquerade in human form. If Mandrake and Auron could deceive them so easily, how many more dragons might still be hiding on this world? He had met a few more since Wu-Auron's self-revelation: tall graceful people who seemed perfectly human, though sometimes they left little details out. They forgot to put in the fine lines around the eyes, for instance, or wrinkles over their knuckles. That made him shudder. Still, they appeared to be benevolent, and had already been of great help to the Nemerei.

He drew a deep breath. "Are you ready?" he called to Damion.

"Ready, General," Damion shouted back, and rode his mount toward Jomar's. The latter turned and viewed the assembled ranks of soldiers and cavalry on the mountainside with satisfaction. What they lacked in experience they made up for in strength and spirit. Everywhere he looked he saw young faces, gleaming armor, the tossing manes of horses as eager as their riders to be off. There were over a hundred chariots, several battalions, fifty highly trained knights, cavalry, and several of the most powerful sorcerers—though Jomar was inclined to put his trust in the soldiers first. There were also many Nemerei healers. His hopes rose. Even if it did come to a battle, they might yet win the day.

"All right then!" he bawled at the troops. He could hear Nemerei speaking in the distance: they heard his words in their minds and were relaying them to all those who were too far to hear their commander's voice. "You know what it is we go to on Mera. This is *real*, you understand? Only those willing to fight must follow me." He paused, hearing the Nemerei voices repeating his words with a fractional delay, like multiple echoes flung back from a cliff: this was followed by a dead silence. Would these men truly follow him anywhere? Or would fear unman some of them at last, as they looked on the slender stone bridge and the dreadful gap of air beyond the gate? No one moved or spoke. Then a cheer broke from the ranks, ragged at first and then swelling and deepening as others took it up. Jomar grinned fiercely.

"Good! Then—forward!"

As one, the troops began to march, the chariots, knights, and cavalry leading the way. Trumpets blared, horses neighed as if in answer. The rock rang with the sound of thousands of pounding feet and hooves as they surged forward, each man feeling himself a part of some vast inexorable force—a stone in an avalanche. They marched on toward the bridge and the gate that lay beyond it. One by one they crossed the thin stone span to the portal, and one by one they vanished from the face of the earth.

8

Temendri Alfaran

THE DRAGON-WAY APPEARED as a golden-white, luminous tunnel, rounded in shape, and its course writhed like a serpent: there was always a bend ahead around which one could not see. As Auron sped through it with his small passenger, he was aware of a rising swell of emotion. Each turn of the ethereal passage brought him nearer to his home. After these years of voluntary exile he had begun to yearn for the world of his origin, and the company of his own kind. But he was aware that he was bearing Ailia to an exile of her own, and one just as lonely, for it had been agreed that she should spend most of her time with the Loänan.

Ailia said little at first, only clinging to his mane. *It feels—so strange. Why can I not recall traveling through the Ether with you before?* she said at length, speaking mind to mind. *We must have passed through it that first time, to get from Mera to Arainia.*

He rolled one great emerald eye back to look at her. *It is hard to remember this place-that-is-no-place,* he told her. *You will find the thought of it fading again once we come out the other side, though now that you are a trained Nemerei you will not forget it altogether. As for feeling strange, you have been translated. Made ethereal, your body turned to pure quintessence, like that of an eidolon.*

Ailia touched her own face, the folds of her gown. He noticed and said, *You see and feel a body because that is what your mind is used to. In fact, you and I are now merely a mass of quintessence moving through the higher plane.*

Ailia did not much like the sound of that. She settled back down into his chrysanthemum-colored mane, clinging to his great ivory horns. She noticed that his wings were folded to his sides, since he was not actually flying—perhaps, she reflected, this was the reason celestial dragons in ancient art were sometimes portrayed as wingless. *What are they like, the people of these other worlds?* she asked him presently.

Some are Merei and Elei, little different from those in Mera and Arainia, the dragon replied. *Others have a more . . . alien appearance. You see, Princess, it has been a very long time since your remote ancestors were taken out of their original world by the Archons and placed on various different planets of the old Imperium. These beings are your blood-kin, but life on other worlds and in alien climes has had an effect upon their physical forms. Still others were deliberately altered by the Archons, and their forms may seem a little—grotesque—to you at first.*

There was a burst of light, and the golden glow gave way to many more bright colors: purples and indigo blues and swathes of deep rose, all swirled together like witch-oils on water. *Behold,* Auron said, *my home!*

Ailia blinked, feeling giddy from the change. They were out of the Ether and back in her own familiar plane of matter. Yet this was not the Great Void that she had always known, that cold black vacuity thinly dusted with stars: in this place the stars were arranged in thick flurries and firefly swarms, while behind them lay a many-colored glowing light. This, Auron told her, was a great nebula, excited into radiance by the stars. Some of these were blue and fiercely bright, showing their extreme youth in sidereal reckoning; others were little more than embryos, formless luminous masses slowly condensing out of the placental dust clouds within the nebula. One small group of stars, though each was fully formed, was linked together still by hazy blue filaments. This whole region of the heavens was a stellar nursery.

It took her a moment to detect the planet against that sea of rainbow radiance. Like Arainia it was girdled with ice rings, but its mantle of cloud was opaque and varicolored. There were horizontal bands of blue and gold and violet and pale green, with here and there a red or white spot like a glaring eye. Moons surrounded it, bright as jewels, and in the sky beyond blazed the white star that was its sun. Almost she imagined she could *hear* the great planet as well as see it: a sound deep as distant thunder, continuous as a cataract, serene as a temple choir, seemed to reverberate through her mind as she looked upon it. The music of a planetary sphere, in its stately procession through space.

"What a beautiful world," she gasped. "And how huge it is." The planet filled nearly all the sky in front of them.

Yes—it is almost a star. It would have become one had it been a little larger. That is Alfaran, the mother-world, he explained. *Temendri Alfaran, our destination, is right below us. It is one of Alfaran's moons.* Auron added, *Hold on to me tightly, Highness, for there is scarcely any air to breathe up here save for the little that surrounds my body.*

She tightened her grip. The golden dragon was hurtling like a meteor through the alien sky with his wings still furled against his sides. She stared at the view below them in bewilderment. It was like a landscape painted by a child or a lunatic, with harsh bright colors in all the wrong places: blue and orange and sulphur-yellow trees, fields of red grass, lakes and rivers of luminous pink and purple water. After a moment she realized that the water was of course reflecting the glowing colors of the nebula. But those trees—! Massed together, they gave more the effect of giant gaily colored flowerbeds than forests. Beyond them lay the only touch of green—not verdure, but a range of mountains whose naked peaks were made of some emerald-green, semipellucid stone.

Perhaps they *were* emerald . . .

They were lower now, at the level of the mountaintops, and the dragon's speed had slowed. He stretched out his great golden wings, but they did not flap: he was still only gliding, using the momentum of his plunge from the heights. To the east lay water, she saw, a broad bay of one of the lunar seas of Temendri Alfaran, and it sparkled in the sun. Spread along the arms of the bay, something else gleamed: an array of crystalline and metallic shapes. It was a city—but such a city as no human being had ever built or dreamt of. The most beautiful of human-made cities is only an untidy sprawl when seen from the air; but this city had been made by beings that could fly, made to be beautiful when viewed from above. Its domes and towers and plazas were arranged in radial patterns to form floral or starlike shapes, and there were many pools and fountains in the city, shimmering with the sky's lambent hues like giant sapphires and amethysts. These were placed within ornate settings of stone, as though water was to the Loänan as gems are to a jeweler.

The wings of the dragon had at last begun to beat as his passage through the air slowed. The city flowed away beneath them, was replaced by the surface of the ocean. The Loänan planed gracefully down over a smaller bay, his reflected image following him along its surface like some golden sea-dragon. *Welcome to Temendri Alfaran, Highness,* Auron said, alighting on a carpet of soft, rose-colored moss just beyond the white shore.

AILIA SAT VERY STILL ON THE DRAGON'S NECK, gazing around her. The city's spires showed above the treetops, and beyond these in turn the mountain peaks of viridian crystal rose sharp as steeples, their slender pinnacles paling almost to translucency at the tips where the sunlight streamed through them. They might have been awe-inspiring, for they were certainly higher than any mountains she had ever seen, even on Arainia: but they were dwarfed in their turn by Temendri Alfaran's sister moons and the giant ringed planet with its bright stripes of cloud and staring storms. These hung in the sky like the suspended figures of a mobile, or like the exposed internal mechanism of a gigantic clock. No timepieces would be needed here, on clear days at least, with their waxings and wanings, and the traveling shadows they cast upon one another, marking the passing hours. Beyond lay the nebula like a colossal, unfading aurora, or a mad dream of a sunset. Within the great swirls and arabesques of violet, rose-red, and blue, many stars were plainly visible, huge and brilliant though the hot white sun still stood well above the horizon.

"What a lot of eclipses they must have here," remarked Ailia to Auron. "And how bright the sun is."

It is a younger star than your sun, the dragon told her. *It is called Anatarva.*

"Yes, I know Anatarva! It's one of the brightest stars in the sky. To think of its being a sun, as well . . ."

Ailia slipped down off Auron's back onto the moss and stood there a moment, clutching in one hand the casket containing the Star Stone. She had no other baggage: Auron had told her that all her needs would be provided for here, though she felt a bit lost without her belongings. There was a faint, sweet smell on the air, she noticed—like fruit or flowers, overlaid with some indefinable spice. "Does no one know we are here?" she asked, looking about her. The strange landscape was empty.

"I thought it best that we not announce your arrival," Auron replied. She turned to see that he had once more transformed into his human shape. "Just in case you have any enemies lurking, even here."

She shifted her gaze back to the city. There were dragons swarming about its spires: with their size diminished by distance, they gave an impression of delicacy rather than strength, their translucent wings and long slender bodies suggesting the beautiful water-flies that bore their name. Their colors were dragonfly colors, too: metallic reds and greens, blues and golds. "Are we going to that city?" she asked, pointing.

"Not yet," Auron answered. "It is not safe for you even there: many beings dwell within it, too many for us to watch. You will stay in a Loänan guest house for now."

He led the way, across the fields of rosy moss to a parklike space beyond where a path ran among the brightly colored trees. She now saw that these not only resembled but were in fact flowers, graceful plants as tall as elms with smooth greenish-white stems and many-colored blossoms the size of sunflowers. It was from these that the sweet smell came. "Your home is beautiful, Auron," she exclaimed.

He smiled. "You have seen but little of it yet."

The treelike plants overarched this section of the path and the flower scent was heavy in the warm, moist air. They passed a grove of shorter, smooth-limbed plants whose boughs bent almost to the ground. Enormous pods weighed them down, and the seams of a few had split. A white woolly substance extruded through the cracks. "It's a kind of cotton plant," said Ailia, going up to it. "But so big!" The least of the pods was larger than her torso.

"It is a barometz tree," said Auron. He looked amused.

Ailia heard a rustling sound on the far side of the tree and looked around the trunk. A white animal the size of a sheep stood a stone's throw away, grazing placidly. She had never seen anything like it: it had flat green ovals in place of eyes, and its muzzle also was pale green. Its feet were broad and flat, and it waddled on them comically. As she drew closer, curious, she saw that the creature appeared to have entangled itself on a branch. It was trying to pull free, but the smooth green stem held it like a tether. Then a closer inspection showed her that the creature was not snared on the branch: the latter appeared to be *growing* out of the animal's back. "Or the animal out of the branch," she realized suddenly, seeing the fragments of one of the huge pods littering the ground around it. She reached out, touched the thing's back. Cotton—it bore a fleece of cotton!

She laughed aloud in amazed delight. "It's a vegetable lamb!" She recited the words of Bendulus: "This beast is not born alive nor hatcheth from an egg, but groweth rather on a tree, as do fruits and nuts. It is at first attached to the tree branch whereon it grew, and grazeth upon the grass at the tree's root."

Auron smiled. "The word for the creature here is *barometz*—but yes, you behold the original of Bendulus's 'vegetable lamb.'"

Now she noticed several of the creatures wandering about eating the moss, broken stems protruding from their fleecy backs. Animals, or plants? They seemed to be both—and neither.

"These are the true inhabitants of Temendri Alfaran," Auron explained to her as they walked on. "The original world of the Loänan has long ceased to support life. We abandoned it thirty million years ago, bringing with us some of its plants and animals—but we try not to disturb the natural life of the planets that we settle."

Auron raised his hand in a greeting as three people approached them through the trees. The one in the middle of the group was recognizably an Elei: a smooth-faced, fair-haired man of middle age, clad in a simple robelike garment of white linen that reached to his ankles. But the figures flanking him had a more exotic appearance. One was an aged man with a long white beard: but so short was he that the top of his head barely reached the other man's waist. The third figure was a woman in a pale, floating gown—at least she had a woman's face and frame, but she was extraordinarily thin and slight, though still graceful. A long cape of some diaphanous, iridescent material flowed back from her shoulders, sweeping the pavement. Then as Ailia approached the "cape" twitched and fluttered, dividing into four sections that spread out, two to each side of the woman's body.

"Wings. She has wings," Ailia whispered to Auron.

"A sylph," Auron whispered back.

The three figures bowed politely as they passed, the dwarf's beard sweeping the ground. Ailia realized she was gawking foolishly and recalled what Auron had told her: human beings had developed differently on the various worlds to which they had been taken. Such extreme variations in appearance were to be expected. Her gaze turned to a woman in a white shift who was walking some way ahead of them. "Why is her hair *green?*" she asked in an undertone.

"She is a dryad. Legend has it that her people are the descendants of unions between humans and *hamadryads*—spirits that inhabit trees. However that may be, they have a powerful empathy with trees and plants. Their hair is green because a tiny plant called an alga grows in it."

"Look, there's quite an ordinary-looking person," Ailia whispered almost with relief as an elderly white-haired man came to the doorway of a low white building among the trees to the right-hand side of the path and saluted Auron.

"Appearances can be deceptive," replied Auron with a smile, leading Ailia toward the house. "Ah, Hada, my friend! Well met. This is the Princess Ailia."

Inside the doorway, the walls of the house were covered in jeweled mosaics, the pillars with gold leaf, and a fountain played in the central atrium. "It is very good to see you again," the old man wheezed, bowing stiffly.

"It's not necessary to change your shape for our sake, by the way," said Auron.

"I am grateful. I must say I find shape-shifting quite fatiguing at my age," the man replied. Suddenly his form shimmered and faded. In his place appeared a thing like a snow-white fox the size of a wolfhound.

"How goes it, Hada?"

The creature gave a long, vulpine grin. "A draconic delegation arrived here ahead of you, to accuse your Tryna Lia of agitating for war against their people and the Zimbourans of Mera. I assume this is she?"

"It is," said Auron. The fox creature bowed its head.

"The Zimbourans? It was they who threatened us," Ailia protested.

The fox creature nodded its long narrow-muzzled head. "Ah, but Morlyn's lackeys deny it, of course." Its grin widened: was it really smiling, like a human, or did the expression mean something else to its own kind? "He means to cast you as the aggressor, the builder of empires, while concealing his own aspirations in that direction."

"Has Prince Morlyn been seen?" asked Auron.

"Not here. He is using others as spies and tools, watching and biding his time. It is rumored that he has assumed leadership of the Loänei, and also revealed his true identity to those Loänan who follow him."

"Thank you, old friend. I hope you will join us when we expose his lies."

"I wouldn't miss it for all the worlds," said the creature, with a bark that sounded very much like a laugh. "I've a few things to attend to first, but I will join you presently." He turned and trotted to the back of the atrium, and disappeared inside. Ailia saw to her astonishment that the fountain and mosaics were gone and the courtyard now held a small, mossy garden with neatly placed boulders and tiny shrubs.

"Is he a Loänan too?" Ailia asked as they walked on.

"No, that is his true form," said Auron. "He is a kitsune—one of the fox people. They excel at taking human forms, and also at creating illusions. His home is really a very plain and humble place, but he likes to alter its appearance for his own amusement. He's always changing it—never the same glaumerie twice. Kitsune love variety."

"But *fox* people? How can that be? What world are they from?"

"The same as that from which your own ancestors came. The Archons did not take only humanity's forebears from the Original World. They brought many other creatures out of that unknown place, and some were introduced into alien planets. Their descendants developed differently from their Meran kin. The primitive creatures that turned into the foxes, badgers, serpents, seals, horses, cats, and wolves of Mera became kitsune, tanuki, nagas, selkies, pucas, cait-sith, and lycanthropes on other worlds. Like the human race these beings gained the ability to reason, and Nemerei powers as well. They will often take human forms for convenience's sake."

"But—but their ancestors were *animals!*" said Ailia in disbelief.

"So were yours, as a matter of fact," said Auron. "It is the same with all races. We Loänan, for example, are descended from seagoing reptiles that dwelt in our original world millions of years ago.

"The whales and dolphins that swim the seas of Mera are intelligent beings too, however animal-like you humans may find them. The Elei knew this and learned long ago to communicate with them. There are some dolphins and whales in the oceans of this world, for there were once ethereal portals beneath the waters as well as on land. I will see that you are introduced to a few of them."

Introduced to a *whale*! "It's as though all the myths of old had come to life—talking animals and so on," she remarked.

"We are all of us talking animals. All myths spring from a seed of truth," Auron told her. "The Elei and Merei still dimly remember the days when they mingled with these other peoples of the Imperium. And it may be that Nemerei-sensitives in far-off worlds may have visions of other worlds and races, and imagine themselves to be dreaming. You have not yet seen most of the races that frequent this world: many are not even distantly related to humanity."

Everyone here spoke Elensi, she had noted, though sometimes with slight differences in pronunciation. The Archons, Auron explained, had taught every young race they encountered the language, perhaps with a view to making future communication between alien races easier.

The flower forests gave way to a larger, more open space. There were some houses here, constructed out of marble and adamant: they might have been the work of human hands, but Auron told her dragons had built them. Ailia sighed. As aristocrats will play at being peasants, donning rustic garb and vacationing in picturesque country cottages, so must the Loänan play at being human: it could not be much more than an amusing pastime for them, a sublime condescension. Why did they bother taking human forms when their minds were so splendidly housed in huge, strong, graceful bodies? What must they think of the human forms they temporarily adopted? Were they amused by these naked, gangly, awkward bodies, so much smaller and weaker and less impressive than their own? She recalled sitting in a lecture hall of the Royal Academy in Mera, listening to old Magister North recite in his droning voice the words of the philosopher Elonius: "I declare Man to be no less than the Paragon of Nature: for the sovereign Beauty of his Form; for the Nobility of his Countenance and the Dignity of his Bearing; but chiefly for his faculty of Reason, which same doth elevate him to the level of an Angel." Ailia had never felt much of the pride of species, particularly when it was used to justify the mistreatment of animals. But now she could not help feeling something of a pang. "You Loänan have so much," she remarked rather bitterly. "Intelligence, magic, strength, the ability to fly. Why would you ever bother taking *our* form?"

"Because we envy you," said Auron.

"Envy *humans*! We've nothing you could possibly want."

"You have thumbs."

Ailia halted in midstep. "Did you say *thumbs*?"

"I did. The opposable thumb is a wonderful thing, that lets you grasp tools and build and make things. No other creature can do this: even we Loänan must change to your form if we wish to build. It is for that reason we call you the Makers."

"But the Archons could build—"

"They too learned the art from you. For they could see all futures, it is said, and even before you arose on your original world you already existed as a possibility waiting to become reality. The Archons often borrowed your form in the dawn-time, but it never truly belonged to them. They merely discovered it, and with it all the things that you would later make. Like that, for instance."

He was pointing at the many-colored sky. She looked up, too, and there she saw yet another vision out of legend: a ship sailing the sky as though it were a sea. There amid the clouds a gleaming golden keel was suspended, supported by winglike sails of ribbed canvas that alternately beat gently up and down and then glided motionless as the pinions of a gull. She realized now that many of the distant flying shapes she had taken for dragons were in fact flying craft like this one.

Auron chuckled. "You humans never cease to amaze. Being wingless is no obstacle to flying! No, you simply go and *make* wings to carry you aloft!"

"The Ships that Sail Over Land and Sea," breathed Ailia. "So they never lost the skill of crafting such vessels here."

"Yes—and these ships can enter the portals of the Ether also, journeying to other worlds."

"I would love to ride in one. I have always wished I could fly. Do you know, I even dream about it sometimes."

He looked at her closely. "I think, Princess, that there may be Loänan blood in you."

"In *me!*" she exclaimed, astonished.

"Yes—your longing for flight, and your ability to call up a storm, would seem to point that way. Loänan are masters of the weather-magic. And it is true that in bygone days many of our kind took human form to mingle with your ancestors. The flesh remembers what the mind cannot know. What you are, child, is written in your blood and bones. There could well be Loänan on your father's side. There were transformed dragons dwelling with humans in Arainia's early days, and many of its people may have a draconic ancestor or two. In most this would be too distant a heritage to have any effect on them, but because you are so powerful through your mother's side, any draconic blood will be amplified and carry real power."

"My mother . . . I still cannot accept what they say of her, Auron."

Auron made no reply to this. "Ah, here is someone you must meet, Princess!" he said instead.

Something was lying at rest in the shade of a flower tree: an immense animal of some kind, or so it appeared. Within a few paces she saw what it was, and her eyes, already besieged with marvels, widened in awe. She had not been with Damion and the others when they were rescued by the cherubim on Mera, and had never seen one of this remarkable race, celebrated in holy scripture, and in myths where they were known as gryphons. The cherub was a magnificent creature, with a leonine body and the beak and wings of a great bird of prey. Atop his head was a tall crest of golden plumes, rising between sharp tufted ears. Yet he was not grotesque, like a gargoyle: his avian and mammalian parts made a harmonious whole, the wings neatly folded upon the tawny-furred flanks, the shape of the pointed ears echoing the upright plumes of the crest. As he reared up, stretching and beating his wings, the white sun's light rayed through his primary feathers as though it were flowing out of him.

"That is one of the Guardians of the Stone," Auron told her. "His name, Falaar, would translate in your tongue as Sun-hunter. He has come to watch over the Stone while its bearer is occupied with her lessons."

The enormous creature came up to her with his regal leonine tread. He looked down at the small alabaster casket she carried and uttered a series of trumpeting cries that instantly translated themselves in her mind as a formal greeting. "Hail, Stone-wielder. I am sent to protect thee, and that which thou bearest."

"I am honored," she answered, bowing her head. "I have never before met with one of your kind, Falaar, but I owe your people a heavy debt for saving the lives of my dearest friends in Trynisia."

"I was of that company, Highness. I will convey thy words to those that were with me in Mera. But it was merely our duty: we were made by the Archons for such deeds. We are their creation, and not the work of nature." Pride rang in the creature's clarion voice.

"That would explain your odd appearance, certainly," remarked another voice from somewhere over their heads. They all looked up to see what looked like a child's gaily colored paper kite caught in the branches of a flower tree.

"Ah, there you are, Taleera!" said Auron. The firebird fluttered down from her perch to stand next to them.

The cherub's neck feathers and the fur along his spine bristled. "Odd! Thou wouldst call us odd!" he protested.

Auron intervened. "Ahem! I think Taleera means that your anatomical construction is observably inconsistent with any natural adaptation."

"It is true," said Falaar, mollified. "*We* did not arise from the slime like common mortals, but were made by the Archon race to combine the strongest features of many kinds of beast. And certain Archons took our form, and mated with our ancestors, so that we are of one blood with them." The great beast raised his crest until it stood erect as the plumes on a knight's helmet. "Our ancestors were *Elyra*, oldest and strongest of the Archons, who wielded power over the stars themselves. And so the star-magic is subject to us, and not we to it. Humans, dragons, even the *Elaia* may quail before cold iron, but not the cherubim: we are immune to it. I will guard thy Stone well, Highness."

"You may safely leave it with him," Auron told Ailia. She

stooped to set the little box down on the ground before Falaar. He lay down again and folded his great forepaws around it.

"Good. Now that's settled I will go to the guesthouse, and prepare Her Highness's chamber," announced Taleera, and she flew off in a whir of red and green and golden plumes.

Auron laid a hand on Ailia's arm. "Come now and meet some of the Loänan. I believe there is a hatching in progress."

They walked on into a wide, cleared area. These grounds were designed for dragonets, she realized: there were many pools, flat rocks for basking on, and taller rocks for the fledglings to try their first, experimental flights from. The water steamed, heated from beneath by some artifice that imitated natural hot springs of the earth, and the pools' surfaces glowed with the soft reflected colors of the nebula. Wallowing in these pools or stretched out along their brinks were young dragons in various stages of development, some winged, some still wingless. Of the former some were plainly but newly "fledged," the membranes between the ribs of their wings like fragile, iridescent soap films stretched between one's fingers. The older ones had more opaque, stronger-looking wings. Most were ethereal dragons, though a few had the golden coloring of Imperial Loänan. Auron stopped here and transformed to his draconic shape. He called out to the dragonets in his great booming voice, and they hastened toward him in a mass, necks outstretched and jewel-like eyes eager. They frolicked around the adult dragon, nipping him on the flanks and legs and clambering on his back, like puppies playing with a big dog.

"Enough, young ones!" Auron said at last. He gently cuffed a young ethereal dragon, the silvery creature howling with delight as he bowled it over and over. "And you, Gallada! Have you flown today?" he asked another.

"No!" the young Imperial dragon replied pertly, unfurling the amber-colored folds of her wings. "I am weary of flying practice. I wish to go to the Ether now, like you!"

"All in good time," he admonished. "One does not fly before one can walk, nor take the dragon-ways before one's wings are tutored in the ways of air. And now, you unruly creatures, be still for a moment if you can: I want to introduce you to Princess Ailia of Arainia."

"Is she a new playmate?" asked a small wingless dragon.

"She is your new classmate; she has come to learn with you about the worlds of the Empire. Now, to the hatching."

At the edge of the nearest pool there lay a mound of what looked like crystalline globes, piled pale and gleaming on the moss. Ailia was reminded of the round glass floats used by Meran fishermen to float their nets. "Those spheres you see are the eggs of my kind," Auron told her. And now she saw that there were small wriggling shapes inside the eggs. Suddenly one of the translucent spheres split, and the dragonet thrust its way through. Ailia caught her breath as it spilled out and lay in a glistening heap on the stone brink. After a moment it began to slither toward the violet-colored pool. It had neither legs nor wings at this stage, but looked something like a snake. Tiny horn-buds showed atop its head, but the dracontias crystal had not yet emerged. It also possessed gills. "I could sense this one yearning to leave the egg."

"It's an Imperial dragon," exclaimed Ailia. "It's golden, like you."

"Yes. My people wanted a special type of dragon, larger and with extra claws, to guard the Celestial Empire and its rulers. And so my kind came to be."

Ailia watched in delight as the dragonet slipped into the pool and began to swim about, its gasping gills drawing in water. "In a few centuries' time he will look just like me," said Auron. "He will have grown legs and wings, and learned to walk and fly—and to fight, if need be."

They walked on, down to the sea. Curious-looking trees grew by the shore, their winding roots immersed in the water like those of mangroves. She saw swift darting shadows among their foliage, too large for insects or hummingbirds but moving with the same whirring motion, and round coarse-rinded fruits like coconuts dropped periodically from the boughs to splash into the water. Ailia glanced at one of these nuts idly, where it floated on the surface. Suddenly it cracked open and something emerged—a downy mass like dandelion fluff, or very tiny feathers. It unfurled two wings, green and translucent as leaves, and darted upward, dragonfly-swift. As it hovered briefly above her, she saw the long, stemlike neck and almost birdlike head. The plant-creature flew upward with a leafy rustling of its green wings and vanished among the trees. "Many lives have begun today," said Auron.

The sun had set at last, so the nebula shone brighter. The

waves were all lit along their crests by the great ringed globe of Al-faran and its attendant moons. One huge wave heaved up, a con-cave cliff of water: there were dark shapes inside it, shadowed against the luminous sky like leaves in a piece of amber. Those shapes, she saw, were alive. They moved within the wave, rising as it rose, until they burst through the high foaming crest into the open air. She heard their cries as they leaped, trilling sounds halfway between birdsong and laughter. But most wonderful of all was the greeting they spoke within her mind.

It was true: what the myths and the legends, the oldest of all tales, older than home and hearth, had said. She forgot even the dragons and plant-beasts in her wonderment. They had been there all along, swimming the seas of Mera: talking beasts. She need not have traveled to the stars to find them. How often had her foster-father told her of these "animals" playing with children, and push-ing drowning sailors ashore? How could she not have understood these clear signs of thought and reason? Humanity had never been alone, save in its fearsome ignorance. It was as though she had been transported back to the dawn of her race, to the very begin-nings of time; as though humanity had never fallen into the errors that marred its history, but could start anew as part of a larger world. Suddenly she laughed aloud, and ran down to the water's edge to meet the dolphins.

DAMION STOOD GAZING across the Zimbouran desert.

It was a dreary prospect: league upon league of rolling dun-colored dunes beneath a sky blanched almost to whiteness with heat-haze. To the east a range of low brown hills sprawled, like a pride of lions sleeping in the sun, with the blue backs of mountains far beyond—though Damion found himself thinking of them merely as large hills, so conditioned was he now to the soaring grandeur, the more ambitious peaks, of Arainian mountain ranges. Behind him loomed two huge stone shapes, headless and weather-worn beasts reposing on the sand with forelegs extended. The fragmented shapes of furled wings could still be seen upon their flanks, and between their forepaws rose broken pillars built of the same tawny-colored stone. A gateway of Elei make, perhaps the oldest of the ethereal portals in Mera. Through the unseen rift within this long-neglected door the Arainians had come a few days ago, blinking and bewildered as men aroused from sleep.

To the west lay nothing but desert. He thought he could glimpse a shifting shimmer like water where the sand met the sky, but that was all.

"The Great Desert. My people called it the *Muandabi*," said Jomar, coming up behind him. "Back when these lands were ours, before the Zimbouran invaders came."

"I must admit," said Damion, "I find it hard to understand why anyone would fight over it."

"It isn't always like this," Jomar explained. "The Muandabi has cycles of dry and wet weather. The rains come here only once in a half-dozen years, but they turn this waste into a huge stretch of grasslands, with water holes where thousands of animals can graze and drink: antelopes, rhinoceri, elephants. At least, it used to be that way. The rainy season hasn't come in decades now. My people like to say the drought's a curse on the Zims. There used to be fertile areas by the river, too, but then the Zims brought their cattle and grazed the land to dust. Nothing will grow there now." Jomar moodily kicked a clod of dry earth. "That's the Zimbouran way. They move into an area, take it from its inhabitants, graze out the pastureland, and hack down the trees to make more room. Then when all the soil blows away because there aren't any trees or grasses to drain it and hold it in place, they move on—leave nothing but desolation behind. This is the result."

"*People* did this!" exclaimed Damion, appalled.

"Oh, they didn't do it out of spite. There are too many of them, that's their difficulty. There's never enough food to go around. The poor can't think beyond the next meal, let alone the next growing season."

"There won't *be* any growing season anywhere if they keep this up."

"They'll just move on—declare a war, and take someone else's land and ruin it."

Damion was silent, thinking of the verdant forests and grasslands of Arainia.

The two men walked back to their camp. It was situated near the hardscrabble farmlands that lay outside the main city. Shallow irrigation ditches carried muddy water from the nearby river Gativah to the dry fields where a few dispirited crops grew. The residents of the tumbledown farmhouses had fled at the arrival of the Arainian army, before Jomar and his men could assure them that they were in no danger. The abandoned farmsteads made the land look more desolate still. Damion was grieved to think of their poor owners fleeing in terror—*from us*, he reflected in horror. It did not matter that their fear had been unfounded. The people had felt it all the same.

Around a stagnant pool at the end of one channel were ranged the tents of the Arainian army, including the large one for Jomar and his officers. Ypotrylls stood about with insolent expressions on their long bony faces, the only living things unperturbed by the heat and dryness. Horses drank thirstily at the pond and grazed on a few tough reeds at its edges. To the east the river wound away through the hills. Somewhere beyond those hills lay Felizia, capital of Zimboura, and the stark stone bastion of Yanuvan.

He and Jomar walked on among the tents, hearing snatches of conversation, watching soldiers clean their gear and play dice games. Under the scant shade of the tents the heat was cruel. Damion saw Lothar and Raimon nearby; both had changed to loose, light clothing, but the latter still sported a helmet with closed visor. Jomar saw, too. "That's past a joke now," he said, irritated. "Raimon will be down with heatstroke next. Can't these fools think of anything but their faerie tales? We're in the enemy's territory now—anything could happen."

Damion felt a surge of excitement at those words. It all lay there, beyond the heat-browned hills: Felizia, Khalazar, Mandrake, their army. The Enemy. Danger lurked behind those hills . . . so *close!* But how much better it was to confront that danger at last, to challenge and defy it!

"Who leads their army? Your General Mazur?" That was the man who had purchased Jomar from the royal arena and forced him to become a soldier and spy.

"No, Mazur was King Zedekara's man. He was murdered when Khalazar overthrew Zedekara. Gemala, the man who helped bring Khalazar to power, is the general now."

They entered the main tent, where the leaders of the army, knights, and Nemerei were gathered. A great Elei sorcerer of Melnemeron, Ezmon Magus, looked up at them as they entered. He was an imposing figure, clad in the blue-starred robe of an astro-mancer, his grizzled hair proclaiming him to be at least a hundred Arainian years in age. Before him stood a table laden with charts and scrying crystals. "I can feel that the enemy is preparing to take action against us," he told Jomar. "But a barrier surrounds our foes like a wall of black smoke. That barrier tells me there are Nemerei on their side also. Mages of Valdur most likely, skilled in the dark arts."

Jomar shifted uneasily—even now he found it hard to accept in-telligence from a sorcerer. Plain facts were what he preferred. "What about your dragon friends? Have they seen any activity on the ground?"

"Yes—a great deal. An army is assembled, but with that sorcer-ous barrier we cannot say when—or if—they mean to attack. I have informed King Tiron and the Council of Arainia, and they ad-vise us to remain here, but to be vigilant."

Jomar said, "If they attack they'll do it soon—by night."

"Night?" repeated Damion. "Won't it be hard for them to see?"

"They'll have torches. No one fights by day in this land," ex-plained Jomar. "They'd roast inside their own armor. I don't like this," he added to Damion as they left the tent again. He gestured in the direction of the city. "There hasn't been a sign from them, even to acknowledge that we're here."

Damion glanced up to where a pair of their dragon allies circled in the reddening sky. "We can wait. With these flying friends of ours, perhaps the Zimbourans are afraid of us," he suggested hope-fully.

"Maybe. But they're more afraid of Khalazar," said Jomar. "And Mandrake. I'd give a good deal to know where *he* is right now."

The atmosphere of tension in the desert camp increased as the swift desert night closed in. Nemerei tended to make one another uneasy, moods spreading from mind to mind like a contagion. Damion looked up at the moon, its old familiar patterns of dark blotches and craters inverted here in the Antipodean sky, and thought how large it now seemed in comparison with Arainia's smaller satellite. According to Arainian lore, this moon had also been an inhabited world once: the fair green garden of Numia, be-fore the comet barrage of the Disaster reduced it to its current life-less state. He himself, in his vision of Trynisia's long-ago past, had seen that bright disc tinted viridian and streaked with white cloud. Now it was scarred and barren, like a face blotched and pocked by plague. Mera itself had only narrowly avoided the same fate.

He was turning to go back in the tent when his eye caught a movement in the sky above: a faint flare of light that came and went, like a shooting star . . . Had he imagined it? No, there it was again, a spurt of flame high over the distant hills. It could not be a meteor: it was rising, not falling. And it came from the direction of Felizia.

At the same instant a Loänan called out, high in the sky overhead. It was an inarticulate clanging cry, like the ringing of a great bell: an alert. Even his undeveloped Nemerei sense could feel the warning in it. Other dragons took up the cry as he ran back to camp, yelling to wake the sleepers and alert the guards.

"Firedrakes!"

9

The Battle in the Waste

THE ZIMBOURAN SOLDIERS STOOD GAZING fearfully across the wasteland toward the lights of the enemy camp. They spoke among themselves in whispers, as though the invaders might hear them even at that distance.

"Valdur's teeth, but there are many of them!"

"It's said they are all of them sorcerers—every one."

"We've wizards of our own, though." The soldiers looked at the figures grouped next to General Gemala's elephant. Their faces were lost in shadowy hoods, mercifully so: their grossly distorted features were enough to terrify their own side. Goblin-men these were, begotten (it was said) by fearsome genii in a far-off sphere.

Khalazar had summoned them here, from their spirit-realm beyond the mortal world.

"This is folly. How long shall we suffer these interlopers to occupy our domain? We must attack!" Gemala called impatiently from his howdah. His huge mount stirred restlessly. It was a war elephant, much larger than the more docile kind used in the cities, with a craggy brow and huge fanlike ears. Its great tusks had been sharpened, not blunted, and as it tossed its head the soldiers at either side drew back. The armored mahout held his goad at the ready in one hand and his bow in the other.

"No," returned one of the goblins. "We wait. Only if they move do we attack, and then only by the prince's order."

Gemala was incensed. "The prince!" he shouted, standing up. "Who is Morlyn to command the God-king's men? Is he the king's servant or his master?"

The goblins did not deign to reply to this. Gemala's eyes narrowed, and he seated himself again, but he gripped the battle-worn hilt of his sword as he gazed on the enemy's camp.

DAMION SAW A THIRD FLARE, off to the right. The fire-dragons were signaling their defiance to their kin. Draconic war cries rang out in answer: Loänan would not attack other Loänan, but they hated the firedrakes, mutant travesties of their race. He saw wings silhouetted against the moon and stars as they wheeled to attack. Horns brayed in the camp, echoing the dragons' cries, and there was a sudden flurry of activity. Campfires went up in sparks as they were stamped out, booted feet thudded on the sand. There was no panic, Damion was glad to see as he raced for his own armor. His heart was pounding—half in fear, and half in wild excitement.

He found Jomar, his officers, and the Nemerei in the main tent. Sir Lothar was there, looking pale by the lamplight."

"It's happening, Sir Damion—isn't it?" he asked. "They are going to attack us after all."

"Firedrakes," said another knight. "I've heard of them—"

"Get moving," barked Jomar curtly. He was clearly in his element, striding to and fro, snapping out orders. "Get as many water-holding objects as you can find—foot-basins, bathing tubs, cooking pots, your own helmets: anything that can hold water. Get to the water-ditches and douse everything in sight!" He glanced at Damion. "We always used that trick to foil attacks with burning arrows. Keeps the fire from spreading. It may not be much help though—this whole region's tinder-dry. We could have a firestorm on our hands if those shriveled crops burn."

Damion followed Jomar out of the tent. Here and there in the sky a swath of cloud was illuminated as if by a bolt of lightning, but the glow was red: a firedrake's burning exhalation. If they came down here to the camp . . . Now answering bolts of real lighting arced from cloud to cloud. The Loänan were fighting with their weather-weapons, drawing out the energies of the atmosphere to fight their foes.

Jomar sprang up on a tall outcrop of rock. In the darkness, lit only by intermittent red or blue-white flashes from above, he saw the men gathered around him.

"It's a distraction!" Jomar bellowed at them. "I know it! Keep watching the hills—there'll be an attack by land! They're keeping our Loänan busy and our eyes on the sky so we won't notice them advancing—"

Damion raced up a crumbling slope to a point of vantage. What he saw made his stomach lurch. Far out on the wasteland tiny red lights flickered, drawing nearer by the minute. "It's their army!" he yelled, running back down to Jomar. "They're coming!"

Jomar swung to face his men. "Listen, all of you—there's a force on the way, I don't know how big yet. Remember the instructions from Arainia: don't charge unless and until they do. But at the first arrow, the first cannon shot from their side, we attack—understood?" Heads nodded. "Get ready," grunted Jomar, jumping down from his rock. "All you mounted knights—you'll ride at the front, behind me. We'll form a wedge, just as we practiced on the Barrens. The Zimbourans always put their generals at the back, their seasoned soldiers farther up, and the conscripts at the front because they're least important and can be spared. It's always a mistake. Conscripts will never meet a charge: they panic and run, so you can drive right on through them."

Damion felt a pang at the thought: conscripted fighters, reluctant and fearful, poor men most likely—and husbands, and fathers. But it was too late to suffer such qualms. He lowered his visor and adjusted his armor. What good would it be against cannon fire? The balls were made of iron, too, so sorcery was useless against them. He swung himself up into his horse's saddle and took the spear handed to him by a soldier. He no longer felt either excited or afraid: in the breathless haste he was conscious only of a deepening sorrow.

"MADNESS!" SNAPPED GEMALA, glaring at the goblins. "It is I who am general. What can creatures from the spheres know of war?"

"We have fought many wars in our worlds," one goblin answered. "The heavens are not a place of peace, as you imagine."

Mounted men and foot soldiers were gathering in long ranks across the dry fields. But they did not advance. They merely stood there, as though waiting for some command or signal.

"Why do they not charge? Are they afraid?" asked one of Gemala's guards.

Afraid! Yes, it could be so, the general thought. The forces of the God-king had a reputation both formidable and well deserved. He himself had never lost a battle. And if Morlyn's reports were to be believed, the host of the Daughter of Night was but newly formed, its soldiery drawn from the indolent people of a world that had never needed to defend itself. The impassable void had kept Arainia secure—until now. Ways had been found to bridge that void, and before long the God-king's domain would stretch to encompass even that far-off star. But the alien forces had come first to Mera, and they must be taught that Zimboura brooked no rivals. "Yes—they are afraid of us! See, they dare not make the first move. They had hoped that we would all cower in terror before *them*— that they would conquer our realm without even drawing a blade!"

And before any of the goblins could reply to this the general leaned forward in his howdah and whipped his sword from its sheath, raising it high above his head. "Attack! Attack, in the name of the God-king Khalazar!" he howled into the fear-fraught silence.

At that cry the soldiers stirred as if out of a waking trance and surged forward with a roar.

"NOW!" SHOUTED JOMAR. "They're coming! Defend yourselves— and Arainia!"

The first wave of cavalry leaped forward, in the form of a spearhead with Jomar at its point. The unskilled fighters in the foe's front rank promptly broke and fled, as he had predicted, abandoning the spears with which they were meant to halt the charge. The Paladins galloped into the widening gap, followed by the foot soldiers and a detachment of Nemerei mounted on bellowing ypotrylls. The Zimbouran cavalry horses, unused to the sight of these creatures, screamed and reared in terror, throwing their riders. The ypotrylls lunged and snapped irritably, their terrible tusks flashing in the firelight.

"Onward!" Jomar yelled, raising his sword as he charged.

The knights rode on, while the wave of men behind swept the bewildered Zimbourans before it like flotsam. There was a thunderous crash and a billow of rank smoke ahead of them, and cannon shot went keening over their heads. But still they galloped on, pressing their advantage, on through the chaos that had been the front ranks of the enemy's army. The Zimbouran host was cloven in two, as if by a great knife, and in the sundered parts confusion reigned.

Suddenly a yell went up from the Zimbourans. Jomar glanced skyward as a huge shadow passed low overhead, blotting out the stars. He swore.

It was the Arainians' turn to be filled with confusion as a dragon swept right over their heads, wings stirring up dust from the dunes. It was not a firedrake but a Loänan: yet it was not one of theirs, for it was diving on their ranks. In the torchlight Jomar saw the streaming tawny mane and red-gold scales, the yellow eyes slitted like a cat's. There could be no mistaking the creature.

"It's Mandrake!" he howled. "Archers—that's no Loänan! It's Mandrake. Shoot him!"

Horses neighed shrilly as the red dragon swooped again. By the time the archers thought to loose their arrows the Loänan was out of range, circling in the sky. A cloud of dust boiled up from the sands beneath him. He was using his powers to stir up a sandstorm!

"Shoot him," Jomar yelled again, but choked on a mouthful of airborne sand.

Damion meanwhile was struggling to hold his own in the fray. It was horrible, and yet at the same time also unreal. Chaos, noise, and movement surrounded him. Through a curtain of dust and smoke shadows leaped and yelled: which were the enemy and which his side? A huge black shape loomed up out of the reddish pall. It trumpeted wildly, giant ears flapping, raising more clouds of dust with its great pounding feet. Shrieks arose as it blundered into the midst of the fighting, ignoring the commands of its mahout. *Oh, no—the elephant, the general's elephant! It's panicked, it's trampling people . . .*

He turned his horse's head and nudged its flank, making it leap sideways out of the elephant's path, and then waved his adamantine blade frantically at the shadows that sought to bar his way. The horse stumbled, tried to leap again, and toppled sideways, hurling him to the ground. He could see little, only vague shapes in the darkness. He crawled away from his own mount's thrashing hooves and found himself face down in a shallow puddle. But it was not water: when he raised his head he saw his hands and arms smeared with dark stains. Dark red . . .

Horror filled him then and he lurched to his feet, flailing wildly about him with his sword at the leaping, howling shadows, not knowing and hardly caring, now, which were enemies and which were not, only wanting to make a space between them and himself.

Jomar realized now what had happened. The terrified conscripts had been in retreat from the driving wedge of riders, but now, blinded by the flying sand, had lost all sense of direction, and many of them in their bewilderment had turned back again. These had swarmed all about the knights, and by sheer numbers had succeeded quite unintentionally in cutting off the wedge from the force behind it, leaving Jomar and his cavalry completely surrounded by panicked milling hordes. Nor could Jomar now tell in what direction the rest of his own army lay. Wherever he turned, he saw only whirling sand, armored bodies jostling and struggling, and the horses of his companions rearing as their riders strove to stay in the saddle. Then his eyes fastened on one shape that loomed above the rest. Jomar turned his horse's head and began to cut his way toward the general.

Mandrake's sandstorm had done its work. Not knowing where his own army was now positioned, he could not order either a charge or a retreat. But he could do one thing. *I'll take the general. Kill him or capture him—it doesn't matter which, as long as he's taken out of the fight.* It was with the enemy's leaders that his quarrel lay. And in any case the army of the foe might fall into further confusion without their commander to shout orders to them. Jomar pressed his heels to his horse's sides and it leaped forward, kicking out with its back legs as it did so, clearing a space in the midst of the turmoil. Then he spurred it with all his might straight at the elephant.

The general had seen him, of that Jomar was sure. The elephant swung its head around to face him, placing the great rampart of its wrinkled gray brow and its snaking trunk between him and its passenger. The mahout drew his bow. Jomar rode on, undaunted. An arrow flew at him out of the brown murk and clanged on his helmet before falling harmlessly aside. The elephant raised its head, tossing it from side to side, and he saw that the great curved lances of its tasks were too great a barrier, even were it not for the armed mahout. He turned his horse and rode around to the huge beast's side, plunging through the mounted bodyguards, meeting the blows of their scimitars with his own blade. He was too strong for them, and as he pressed on they began to give way, falling from their horses or retreating weaponless. The flank of the general's mighty mount rose before him, and he turned his horse to pace at its side. With all his might he slashed at the beast's foreleg. It bellowed and stumbled to its knees as Jomar sprang from his saddle.

The mahout fell off its neck, dropping his bow, and then leaped to his feet again. Turning, he saw Jomar and he drew his sword. But Jomar's blade bit deep beneath the other man's arm even as he raised it for the blow, and he crumpled to the ground. Jomar turned and clambered up onto the elephant's back, slashed through the howdah's curtains with his sword, and jumped onto the cushioned seat within. Then he gave a cry of rage and disappointment. The howdah was empty. His quarry was gone—where, he did not know and could not guess, but there was no use in wasting more time. The war elephant was struggling to its feet again. He ran to the front of the lurching curtained box and stared ahead of him. From his raised vantage point he could see his men, a little knot of them a bowshot away to the right, hemmed in by a bristling mass of swords and spears like a thicket of steel thorns. Already two horses were riderless—were their knights captured, dead? He must take some action before all were slain. The armed guards of the general were galloping toward them.

Bending forward over the neck of the elephant he used his sword-point as a goad, pricking the beast to make it turn. With an angry protest it obeyed. He forced it to within a few feet of his embattled friends, then made it charge the mounted assailants. Horses and men alike screamed as his vast mount plowed into them from behind, thrusting them aside with ease. Jomar continued to prod the elephant forward, sending the foot soldiers fleeing in panic, forging a path for his men through the thicket of steel. The knights followed in his wake. Arrows hissed through the air at him and the elephant, and it flung up its head and bellowed as several shafts pierced its hide. But the pain only made it quicken its pace, and ahead of him he saw men streaming back to either side, clearing his way to the open desert beyond.

They were out of the crush of battle—they were free. And peering through the flying dust, which had thinned to a light haze, Jomar could see retreating troops in the middle distance, some in Paladin armor. Loänan were diving and swooping, shepherding the Arainian army away from the heat of battle. He sheathed his sword and abandoned the elephant, jumping down off its back as the riders came up behind him. At least three were missing: he did not see Raimon or Martan. And where was Damion?

"Back there," panted Lothar when he asked, pointing at the main battle. "I cannot say what became of the other two—they may be retreating with the rest—but I saw Sir Damion. I could not get to him, though: he was surrounded. General Jomar, sir, where are you going?"

Jomar made no reply. He was running with all his might toward the press of swords and bodies, drawing his own blade as he ran.

High above both storm and battle the red dragon circled under a sky of clear stars, looking down on what he had wrought. The cloud of sand was fading and dwindling, and beyond he could see the Arainian army drawing back to the stone portal through which it had come.

Satisfied, he soared still higher and winged toward the city behind the hills.

THE SUN WAS RISING OVER THE DESERT when General Gemala strode into the throne room of Yanuvan, still attired in his dusty and bloodstained battle armor, his helmet under one arm. With his equally weary and disheveled captains in his wake, he walked unannounced into Khalazar's presence, dropped to one knee, and declared, "It is over, Majesty. A glorious victory for our side. The forces of the Tryna Lia are utterly defeated. Those not slain or taken are vanished from our land, retreating by sorcery to their own sphere."

"I must congratulate you, General," drawled Mandrake, who was leaning indolently against the back of Khalazar's throne. "You have routed an army of unskilled and unpracticed youths with uncommon panache."

"They were worthy foes—men of arms."

"Babes *in* arms, you mean!" retorted Mandrake. "The Arainians know nothing of war."

The general glowered at him. "They were true warriors: those of us who *fought* with them learned that soon enough. They also had many sorcerers with them, and winged monsters like those that serve our king. Still, we would have inflicted even greater harm upon the foe, had not that curious desert storm blown up and hindered us: more of their foul magic, perhaps. And perhaps not," he added, looking straight into Mandrake's eyes, "though why would any of our own sorcerers have hindered us in battle?"

"Why indeed?" replied Mandrake unhelpfully. Inwardly he was seething. *The old fool! How dare he strike at Ailia's forces first, and make his own side the aggressor? That was the last thing I wanted!*

At times his supposed allies seemed as troublesome as his foes. As he had feared, Syndra had betrayed herself: the sorceress had reached out with her power, touching the cold dark mind of a firedrake and sending it across the Ether in an attempt to kill the Tryna Lia. The attempt had failed, and the traitorous Arainian had since arrived in Nemorah alone, stumbling through an ethereal portal. She was no longer of any use to him, and he suspected that she would not relish her exile. Syndra had chosen to live among the Loänei, rather than among the common humans of Nemorah —an error for which she would suffer. The latter might have respected her, but not the dragon-folk: they would treat her with nothing but condescension, and he doubted her nature would sweeten during her stay. But that was of no consequence to him. Worse damage had been done. The Tryna Lia had not only failed to come to Mera with her army, she was now under strict guard in Temendri Alfaran where the greatest draconic sorcerers would watch her night and day. Mandrake hissed softly to himself in irritation. She might be there for many years, growing in knowledge and power under their protection and tutelage. However, she had at least left Arainia behind. He would have to see what he could do about getting past the Loänan's guard.

HE TURNED HIS ATTENTION BACK to Gemala's report. "I was forced to leap down from my elephant and fight on foot," the general was telling the king. "Even so, it was difficult for me to tell friend from foe. But my men won the day. The people will be heartened when they hear of my victory."

Khalazar's eyes were icy. "You mean—*my* victory."

The cropped gray head bowed. "Of course, Your Majesty."

"We are pleased," the king declared, though his voice and face did not show it. "You shall have your reward for this. But . . . do not enter our royal presence again in such a state of disarray. It does not show us the proper respect."

JOMAR TRUDGED SLOWLY OVER THE SAND, past the still bodies of men and horses. Vultures circled overhead. He had fought as hard as he could, well into the night, but he had not found Damion, and at daybreak it was clear the battle was lost. In the end he had been forced to take shelter in an abandoned shed. A scene of death and desolation had greeted him when at last he was able to venture out. In all the countryside, it seemed, no one was left alive. The sun's heat gave to the bodies he touched an illusion of living warmth, but none stirred when he shook them and they gave no sign of life. Some the sandstorm had already given burial to; others he covered up as best he could. The rest of the army had gone—they must have retreated through the portal, for there was nowhere else they could have gone to in the empty waste. Without the Loänan, he could not open up the tunnel through the Ether and return to Arainia. He was stranded here, and so were any of his men who were still left alive. The entire venture had been an utter failure. Khalazar had not been intimidated nor overthrown, but had won instead another victory, and many young Arainians had been brought here to their deaths.

My doing, he thought. *I was the one who brought them. And all for nothing . . .*

And then he found Damion.

The knight-priest was lying in the sand, surrounded by dead Zimbourans. His eyes were open and staring ahead of him, expressionless, and he took no notice of Jomar. He was breathing, and blood from a wound in the side of his head had dried in his hair.

Jomar halted. "Hello, Damion," he said quietly.

The blue eyes closed, then opened again. "Hello, Jo. There's blood on my sword," Damion murmured. "Do you see? And these men are dead. So I suppose I must have killed them. It's odd, though: I can't recall a thing . . ."

It was battle shock. Some men never recovered from it: they went mad, or suffered from fits and nightmares for the rest of their lives. Jomar leaned down and shook him, hard. "Wake up, Damion! I need you. Damion, do you hear me?"

At last the other man shuddered and rasped, "I'm all right." Color returned to his cheeks as he sat up.

"You're the first person I've seen alive," said Jomar heavily. "Come with me. Let's see if there are any more survivors."

They found Sir Martan lying not far away, his white surcoat covered with blood, his face and hair coated with sand. As they approached he stirred and looked at them without recognition, then closed his eyes and groaned. Jomar glanced at the wound in his side where the armor had been pierced, and shook his head at Damion. The priest knelt beside Martan and began to give him the Last Rites. As he prayed, the dying youth suddenly opened his eyes again, gazing skyward. "Ahh, look—look," he whispered through cracked and bloodied lips.

"What?" asked Damion, leaning forward.

But Martan was gone.

Jomar looked grim. "I knew he would die."

He and Damion looked about them. The Unknown Knight lay motionless near Martan, and he too was covered in blood. The pair of them had fought well, if all the Zimbouran dead surrounding them had fallen to their swords. Jomar bent to open Raimon's visor. Damion walked away; he had no wish to see the dead young face of the fallen knight.

The gash in his head throbbed painfully. What had happened? His memory was blank. There were not enough bodies in the sand to account for all their army. Had the Arainians retreated? Had the

Loänan taken them back to Arainia, or had they all been captured and taken to Felizia as prisoners?

A shout from behind made him turn. The Unknown Knight, apparently very far from dead, was standing up, confronting Jomar, who was yelling and gesticulating. The knight's helmet was now off; Damion froze at the sight of the face beneath the cap of short, blond hair.

"I *had* to come," Lorelyn was arguing, tossing her cropped head and waving her arms about. "I couldn't just stay behind. The army needed all the help it could get, you said so yourself. I kept thinking about that story Ailia told, about Lady Liria dressing up as a page to go into battle with her knight-prince. And then I remembered what Ailia said, about life being like a story, except that we're making it up. And I decided that this was what I wanted to happen in *my* story."

Jomar was nearly screaming. "Are you out of your mind? This is a war! You're not staying here."

"Lori?" Damion gasped.

"Damion! I'm so glad you're all right," she cried, running to him. "When I saw you had been surrounded I turned back and tried to cut my way to you. But I was pulled off my horse and had to fight—" Lorelyn fell suddenly silent: she had caught sight of Martan, lying lifeless on the ground.

Jomar saw what she was looking at. "There!" he snapped. "He's dead—do you see? Dead! This isn't a game. It's real."

Lorelyn's face was very pale. Slowly, step by step, she advanced toward the body. Slowly she knelt beside it, looking into Martan's white face. Then she kissed the boy's forehead and covered his face.

He will always be young now, Damion thought. Another thought occurred to him. "Lori—it was *you* who helped kill those Zimbourans—" he said in horror.

"I had to," she said. "I didn't want to do it, Damion, but they were going to kill you." Lorelyn walked over to the bodies and knelt beside them, her head bowed. Presently the tears that she had not shed for Martan began to stream down her cheeks.

He shook his head in amazement. "She's a true Paladin."

Jomar groaned. "She's a true imbecile. It's all pretense to her, don't you see? A kind of play-acting."

Damion watched as Lorelyn prayed over the dead soldiers. Perhaps she was a little like someone playing a role, every gesture exaggerated. As he walked up to her Lorelyn lifted brimming blue eyes to him. "Damion—I truly didn't want to kill them—I had no choice!"

He relaxed somewhat: this was real grief. No Paladin ever desired to kill, but her distress was genuine enough: he could feel it pulsing through her words. She might have proven herself a warrior, but her innocence seemed unharmed by her deeds. For himself, though, he felt no lifting of the burden. He could cleanse the stains of battle from his sword, but not from his mind. The still young faces of the dead Zimbourans would never leave it.

At last Lorelyn stood. "What are we to do, Damion? I'm afraid to call out with my mind—any sorcerer could overhear, including *him*."

"You're right. Best not to use the mind-speech, then. Perhaps our Loänan will come back to look for survivors."

"And perhaps not," said Jomar, coming up to join them. "Well, this is a mess, all right. Out in the wastelands—and no horses!"

Damion gave him a bleak look, then glanced about him. There was nothing to be seen but sand in all directions. The sandstorm had buried the pitiful fields and changed the local features of the land beyond recognition. He looked for the hills, orienting himself. "Where is the camp?" he asked.

Jomar squinted into the distance. "Due east of here."

They began to trudge along. The sun rose higher and waves of heat began to shimmer above the dunes. They were obliged to stop and remove their armor—its weight and heat were becoming unbearable.

When at last they arrived at the camp they halted in dismay.

The tents were all burned and half-buried in sand, the river and ditches choked with mud. Several sheds had blown down, adding to the destruction. All was still: there was no one in sight.

Jomar swore softly as he inspected the damage. "Here are some water bottles, at least—we'd better take them with us." He straightened. "We've got to leave. With any luck we'll run into more of our army. Some of them might have been scattered. They can't *all* be dead or captured."

A strident bellow came from behind them. Turning, they saw

the head of an ypotryll emerge from one end of a small dune. The creature rose to all fours, shedding the mound of sand that had been deposited over its humped back. It shook out its shaggy coat and grunted at them peremptorily, but did not move from the spot. It was, they saw, still hobbled at the ankles.

"We've got transportation anyway," said Damion, freeing the animal. It made at once for the shallow irrigation pond, now clogged with wet sand, and began to drink noisily.

"Can you control that brute?" asked Jomar.

"I hope so. I wish Ailia were here, she's so good with animals."

"The last thing we need is another woman on hand. Come on, let's go."

The ypotryll was willing and able to carry them, though not without some grumbling at first. They packed as many unspoiled provisions as they could onto its broad back, and there was still room for two to ride. Damion walked at the beast's head: there were no reins and no halter, as the animal was meant to be controlled by Nemerei. At last he succeeded in coaxing it to move forward by holding out a feed bag. It stretched out its long neck and followed him.

"Where to, Jomar?" asked Damion.

"There's only one place we can try. The other slaves used to say there was an oasis far out in the desert, a place that was always green whether the rains came or not. It's supposed to be where the ruins of an old Mohara city lie, with lots of natural wells. Every now and then a slave would escape and run away across the desert. We never saw them again: some said they'd died of thirst, that there never was a city. But some of the Loänan say they saw a spot of green far out in the desert. There could be a real oasis, even if there isn't any lost city. It's west of here, they said."

"It's a long way off—across all that desert."

"It's the only way. North and south are *all* desert, and east is Khalazar." They moved off slowly across the dunes.

BY NOON THE HEAT WAS UNENDURABLE.

"Tie something over your heads," said Jomar to the others. He had dismounted and Damion was taking his turn on the ypotryll's back. "That white skin of yours is going to burn to a crisp out here." He began to lecture Lorelyn again as he led the animal forward. "The idea of you coming here, endangering yourself like this. I ought to *kill* you!"

Damion couldn't help smiling at that. "Wouldn't that be self-defeating? Tell me, Lori, how did you arrange to come with us? How did you get Raimon's armor?"

"He was hurt in that fall in the Barrens—the healers said he did some damage to his back, and said it would take weeks to put it right. So I put on his armor and went and jousted in his place."

"Yes—I wondered how he was able to come back like that," said Damion. "I visited with him afterward, and he was lying flat and in a good deal of pain."

"That's right. It was I you saw in the tournament. At first I only wanted to prove to Jo that I could fight on horseback, and I meant to take the helmet off and show myself. But then I realized Jo still probably wouldn't let me go. And as I'd fooled everyone once, I thought I could again. I had to let Raimon in on the secret, though. He said he was glad someone could go in his place, he'd been feeling badly about his accident's costing Jomar one of his knights. We swore the healers to secrecy, and we told Lothar and Martan too—but no one else."

"But—" Damion felt slightly dizzy. "Lori, that must mean you were knighted too, at the ceremony in Melnemeron. You were knighted under someone else's name!"

"No, I wasn't: Ailia dubbed me 'Sir Knight Unknown,' as Raimon had asked her to do."

Jomar continued to bawl at Lorelyn. "Of all the pig-headed, lame-brained—"

"It's no use, Jo. She'll *have* to stay now," interjected Damion. "There's no way to send her back."

Jomar swore. He and Lorelyn kept on arguing for some time, and Damion soon grew heartily sick of their repartee. The ypotryll, too, had some negative feelings that it expressed volubly. Twice it halted and had to be alternately coaxed and chastised into moving again.

Their discomfort grew worse by the minute. The water had to be severely rationed, and each of them began to dream of pools and running streams and pitchers of iced water. Their mouths were dry, their throats parched, their lips and tongues seemed to swell. None of them spoke now: the only sound was the muffled thud of the ypotryll's broad hooves. The glare of sun on sand was painfully bright and harsh. Lorelyn sprawled upon the beast's hump, her eyes half-closed, her skin pink with sunburn where her makeshift turban did not protect it. Damion hunched atop the packs containing their meager supplies, squinting at the horizon.

Oasis, Damion thought, trying to picture it in his mind. *Trees. Plants. Water—water . . .* He sank slowly into a semiconscious state in which he found himself once more in the garden at Halmirion. All around were fragrant flowers, shrubbery, trees, and—tormentingly—the sound of fountains, the music of water at play. Ailia was there sitting on a fountain's rim, her face framed in flowers and her eyes large and soft and oddly hopeful as they gazed up into his . . . He tried to speak to her, but his mouth was too dry, and she faded away along with the pleasure garden, another desert mirage.

The sun began to descend by painfully slow degrees. A wind picked up, hot and dry, stirring the sand along the crests of the dunes and blowing it into their faces. Damion roused from the stupor into which he was falling as their mount gave a sudden lurch. Was it stumbling, about to collapse? He stared down. The animal was feeding.

All around them the ground was covered in tough sharp-bladed grass. Ahead of them a flat plain stretched, dotted with thorny bushes and squat gnarled trees. And in the distance was a dark blur . . .

"The oasis," he croaked. Lorelyn straightened up, blinking.

"Not far now," rasped Jomar.

The sun was sinking, huge and red beneath a bank of cloud, and as they moved on the desert night fell swiftly. A cool breeze rattled the stiff leaves and boughs of the little stunted trees. Not far, thought Damion. Not far . . .

And then the ypotryll reared up with a bellow that seemed to fill all the night around them. With a yell Lorelyn tumbled off its back onto the ground. Jomar whirled with an oath while Damion leaped down beside him and struggled to calm the beast.

It sank to its knobbed knees, shuddering, and now Damion saw the arrows protruding from its neck and side.

"Get behind it!" Jomar shouted, pulling Lorelyn toward him.

The animal's roars diminished to low groans, and it stretched out its long neck upon the sand. Even as they huddled behind its sprawled bulk the wasteland came alive with figures. Out from behind rocks and bushes they leaped, appearing almost magically out of the landscape: dark-faced men, armed with bows and spears and curved scimitars.

A voice called out: Jomar started, stood up. He yelled back in the same language, and Damion found he could understand it: it was a curious heavily accented version of Elensi. And the men were Moharas.

Jomar strode forward, conversing with them.

"It's all right," Damion heard, "all right, do you understand? We are all Moharas together." This last, Damion thought, had the ring of a ritual phrase.

"Where did you come from?" came the challenge.

"From the desert. We rode here on the back of this beast."

"What is it? We took it for another of Khalazar's demons."

"This is no Mohara!" said another. "He is a spirit, a genie. He rides upon a monster—"

"Ai! A genie—"

"Stop!" Jomar shouted. "I'm a man, the same as you!"

"Who are those with you?" the first voice demanded.

Damion and Lorelyn rose and looked cautiously at the armed men, whose spears and bows were still leveled at them.

"They're my friends," Jomar began, but was interrupted.

"Pale faces! They are Zimbourans!"

The spears advanced. "No!" Damion cried. He seized his head cloth and tore it off, exposing his fair hair. Lorelyn followed suit.

"He's no Zimbouran, and neither is the woman," Jomar said.

"Woman?" The dark-skinned warriors crowded around them: they were a fearsome sight, clad all in dark leather and sporting necklaces of animal claws and teeth. "We thought both were men."

They were interrupted by the ypotryll, which gave another loud groan and beat its long tapering tail upon the ground. The men jumped back, but the beast was dead, its blood staining the sand. Damion felt a passing sorrow for the creature, brought out of its own peaceful planet into war upon an alien world. But he turned his attention back to the Moharas.

"It is he! I know this man!" the leader shouted, pointing at Jomar. "It is Jomar of Felizia! The half-breed!"

A low muttering went up. The Mohara leader approached Jomar and deliberately spat before his feet. "Get of a dog! Serpent! You carry Zimbouran blood in your veins, you fight beneath their banner. Collaborator!" he bellowed, swinging around to face his men. "This is the half-Zimbouran lackey, the tool of Khalazar, betrayer of Moharas! He joined the Zimbouran army and fought on their side. Khalazar uses such people—spies and traitors, all of them, unworthy to be called Moharas!" He turned to face Jomar again. "So, half-breed, have you been sent back to spy on us? You've escaped, is that to be your story—you'll come with us to our hiding place, pretend to be our friend, and then run off and tell your masters where we are? But it won't happen, traitor. We will kill you now, you and your spying friends!"

A brief silence fell. Damion and Lorelyn held their breath.

"You son of a pig," said Jomar.

Damion closed his eyes, wondering how much it hurt to be killed with a spear.

"Son of a pig I call you," Jomar shouted. "All very well for you to talk—you, you're free, you've never lived in a dirty disease-ridden camp. What do you know of the suffering of slaves? I never asked to be in the army—they *took* me by force, after they had enslaved me, thrown me into the arena for their amusement. I fought for all the Mohara there—conquered all the Zimbouran gladiators they sent against me. In there I *was* the Mohara, a symbol to the Zimbouran scum of something they could never destroy. The Mohara spirit!" Jomar threw out his chest and flung back his head, defiant even in front of the spears. "When they saw they could only beat me by killing me, they decided to execute me in public. I was prepared to die. But the army bought me instead—"

"You should have refused to obey them, and died with honor," the leader snarled.

"Fool! The Zimbourans *wanted* me to die—they want us all to die. That's why I decided to live—to continue fighting them. One day, I knew, I'd get my chance—be able to desert, jump ship, run away, to my real people. Raise a rebellion and come back at the head of it. I'm a Mohara, I tell you, and we Mohara don't roll over and die. We fight—we survive."

The men exchanged glances; some appeared to be uncertain.

"And I *did* desert," Jomar continued. "And I *have* come back—

with an army, just as I promised. An army, do you hear? We fought the cursed Zims only yesterday."

"It is true—we saw signs of battle, out in the wasteland," said one warrior. "And strange lights in the sky."

"But who fights for you?" asked another. "Is it the Shurka rebels, or the peoples of the Commonwealth?"

Jomar hesitated, wondering whether to tell the truth, wondering if he would be believed. He himself had doubted all the old tales; now it was his turn to face skepticism. "I went away from Zimboura," he said slowly, "to the country in the north called Trynisia." A loud murmur went up from the men. "Yes—Trynisia!" he shouted above their voices. "It is real—and so is Eldimia, the land of the gods. I have been in both countries, come to know them and their people."

"You lie."

"Do I? Look at this beast you've killed—have you ever seen anything like it before?"

Again the mutters of uncertainty. At last the leader spoke again. "Trynisia and Eldimia we have always believed in. It is your word, half-breed, that is suspect. If you are lying, you blaspheme the gods. But we shall see. We will take you and your companions to the oasis now, and decide what your fate shall be."

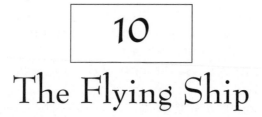

10

The Flying Ship

THE IMPERIAL PALACE, Ailia had thought on her first sight of it, would fill even a Loanan with awe. Its adamantine roof soared to such a height that small clouds formed beneath the crystal vault of the main hall, hanging overhead like thick white mists. It stood in the rolling meadows to the north of the dragons' city, but Auron had explained to her that the whole edifice could be raised aloft by levitation, and even transported to other worlds of the Empire when Orbion chose to make a processional. But now as she entered the vast crystal doorway, Ailia's head drooped and she scarcely paid any heed to her surroundings. The tidings from the Nemerei of Arainia were terrible: her peacekeeping force savagely attacked by the Zimbourans and vanquished; the surviving soldiers compelled to retreat into the Ether with the Loänan's aid; many young fighters slain and others taken prisoner. The plan to cow Khalazar had ended in calamity. The Loänan said Damion and Jomar had not been found among the slain, nor had they been paraded through the streets along with the other captives. But they had not returned to Arainia either. The Loänan could not communicate with her friends without betraying their location to the enemy. Some dragons that had tried to conduct an aerial search had seen no sign of the three near the battlefield, and finally had been forced into retreat by a flight of Morlyn's firedrakes.

Auron had told her, "The youth Raimon has come forth in Arainia, and confessed that he hid and let Lorelyn go in his stead."

"Lori is there too!" *How like her, to run off and join the men! It was a brave thing to do, a splendid thing—what I should have done, if I were really worth all this reverence people heap upon me.*

"She has not returned. She was not slain either, so she may be with Jomar and Damion. She left a note in Arainia saying that it was you who inspired her—that you told her life was a tale to be written by those who lived it."

So that is my doing, also. At least her friends lived—for now. If only she could convince other worlds of the Empire to join with her in battle against Mandrake and Khalazar! Until then her friends must wait in hiding, risking capture with each moment that they remained in enemy territory. And she could do nothing. Ailia glanced down at the casket of the Star Stone that she bore with her, and her hands tightened upon it. But she felt no stir of power within.

There was a great assemblage of creatures within the crystal hall. Ailia's mind, dulled with misery, at last began to perceive and recognize these from the old stories: dryads, sylphs, dwarfs, Fairfolk, amazons. There were animal-folk who had reverted, in this great open space, to their own natural shapes: kitsune, tanuki, pucas. The last were like small and exquisite horses, more delicately beautiful than any Arainian steed, their eyes agleam with intelligence. A great bird, larger than Taleera, roosted with its head under one bronze-feathered wing. Next to it was a figure with the body of a lion, bird's wings, and a woman's head. Ailia had seen many such images adorning the gateposts of grand estates, but this one was not of stone: it was living flesh—and feathers and fur. Its face was fiercely beautiful, with golden eyes and tumbled masses of tawny hair like a lion's mane.

Ailia and her guardians walked on up the seemingly endless aisle, Ailia striving not to stare at the creatures around her. There was a Myrmecoleon, its furred mammalian head contrasting strangely with its six many jointed legs and chitinous body armor, and a Quetzalcoatl, its serpentine body adorned with iridescent green-plumaged wings and a tall feathery crest like a ceremonial headdress. An adjacent chamber had been half-filled with seawater, and behind its crystal wall there swam many creatures from the oceanic realms, dolphins and makaras and water-dragons. There were other beings she did not recognize, ambassadors of innumerable alien worlds. They all watched Ailia intently and in complete silence as she walked with Auron, Taleera, and Falaar. They must be wondering if she were indeed the figure from their own prophecies. Or did they not believe in the old foretellings?

She raised her eyes to the dais at the far end of the hall. "Is *that* the Celestial Emperor?" she whispered to Auron, who walked at her side in his dragon form.

Upon the dais stood the Dragon Throne of Talmirennia, a great chair of stone encased in gold leaf, with the sinuous forms of celestial dragons forming its back and sides and its armrests. In it sat a man: old, wizened, the beard sweeping his chest white as a waterfall. He wore a golden robe embroidered in silver with dragons and stars, and a tall crown of beaten gold rested on his head. But his body seemed almost too frail to support these adornments. The gnarled and venous hands trembled on the carved dragon heads of the armrests, and only the eyes, blue and unclouded in the wrinkled-vellum face, seemed alive. Six Imperial dragons flanked his throne.

"It is he," said Auron. "Orbion, the ruler of the dragons and Emperor of emperors. He has taken human form as a courtesy to you, but he truly is old as he appears. He is near one thousand five hundred Meran years in age. This shape-shift is something of a strain for him."

"Then he must change back," said Ailia, distressed. "I don't want him to suffer any discomfort."

"No, it is the custom of the Emperor of Heaven to shape-shift whenever he enters a world: he takes on the likeness of the beings who dwell there, and when granting an audience he adopts the form of the being who has requested it. He will observe that custom, however weary he may be. And he does not wish to appear feeble before the Loänan dissenters. This is also a show of his power, for their benefit."

They had now reached the dais, and all—including Ailia—made the signs of obeisance traditional to their individual races.

"I bid you welcome," said the old dry voice. "It is my understanding that you would speak with these ambassadors of the worlds. Do you wish to address the assembly now, Princess?"

Ailia bowed and turned to face the creatures, cleared her throat nervously and began her prepared speech. She had grown used to addressing large assemblies on Arainia, but never had she spoken to so vast a gathering as this. Nor to so strange a collection of creatures, only a few of whom bore any resemblance to humans at all. "Peoples of the Empire, I am Ailia Elmiria of the world Arainia, which has long been cut off from your own worlds. My people wish to be reunited with you, and to see a peaceful commerce restored between our worlds."

The bronze-colored bird took its head out from under its wing, and she saw with a start that it too had a human face, female and beautiful despite its sharp features. "Why were you cut off?" the creature demanded in a shrill voice.

Ailia had not expected to depart from her memorized text, and took several moments to form her reply. "The humans of Mera cut themselves off, saying that they would have no dealings with magic or other worlds. The Loänan, in their wisdom, elected to let humanity alone for a time, and the Elei of Arainia chose to share the Merans' confinement rather than expel those Merei who dwelt still on their world. But with my coming, the Loänan declared us ready to re-enter the celestial union, if you are all agreed."

"Are you the one called the Tryna Lia?" a sylph woman asked. The crowd stirred.

"I am," said Ailia, thinking: *What now?*

The sylph approached. She was small and slender, gowned in white, and her two sets of wings shimmered like nacre. She spread them to their full span, as though in salute. "My people have long awaited your coming. If you are the one foretold, you are welcome." She curtseyed, her wingtips sweeping the ground. "I have heard it said that you will defeat Valdur's minions once and for all."

"You do not understand," said Ailia quickly. "I have come to *prevent* a war, to protect all our peoples from anyone who would destroy the peace we now enjoy. I mean no harm to those who are willing to live with others in harmony."

"You lie," rumbled a voice.

Ailia gaped at the dragon that stepped forth: its scales were red, and for a panic-stricken instant she thought it was Mandrake in his draconic form. Then she saw that this was a larger dragon, and its mane was dark rather than russet-colored. "That is Torok, king of the earth-dragons," Auron told her in a whisper. Ailia inclined her head courteously, as one monarch greets another.

The red dragon approached with a smooth gliding gait, like a cat stalking its prey. Its sulphur-yellow eyes were narrowed, intent. "So this is the creature of whom you spoke?" it demanded of Auron. "Does it expect me to bow down before it?"

"No; and if Your Majesty cannot be courteous enough to address Ailia directly, at least refer to her as *she*, not *it*," said Auron sharply.

"She is human. My people will not be ruled by a human!"

"You appear to hold humans in great disdain, and yet you have also argued that we should accept the Loänei," noted Auron.

The red dragon growled. "They carry our ancestors' blood. That blood must be respected, however base the vessel. Ailia and her kind have no such link with us."

"How can you know she is not of Loänan descent? I think it quite possible that she is."

"Can you furnish proof of that?"

"Naturally not; and what does it matter, in any case? The prophecies do not say that the Stone's wielder must have dragon blood."

Torok said, "There is another claimant to the title, one in whom lies not only the blood of Archons but that of Loänan also."

Auron hissed. "Morlyn."

"Do you deny his Archonic ancestry?"

"I do not; it is his own personal history that troubles me. He is an outlaw and renegade of the worst sort."

"Still, I and many others of my people would choose him to wield the Stone, for the sake of his dragon blood. The Valei have chosen him already for their leader, and would be at peace with us too if we accepted him." The dragon king's yellow stare returned to Ailia. "But *this* is such a little thing to rule a stellar empire."

Auron took up a protective stance in front of Ailia, head lowered. "You speak like a dragonet, Torok, not like a king. Size has no importance."

"Is it wisdom to let such a one rule all the Celestial Empire? You have seen how the human creatures govern themselves! They make ceaseless war on one another."

Ailia could bear this no longer. "I do not wish to rule," she cried, "nor go to war, but only to see us all live in peace."

"We have always desired to live in peace with other beings. That is why we always shared our knowledge with humans. If they turned our knowledge to folly we are not to blame."

"They were too young as a race for the teachings that your people gave them," retorted Auron. "The fault was yours, not theirs. They have grown in wisdom since."

"Have they?" The red dragon snorted. "They are flawed as ever. That is why we of the earth blended our blood with theirs long ago, to breed a better race. Even so did the Archons, before us. But you other Loänan turned against us and the Loänei. You scattered them among the stars, beings that were our own kin. You let the weaker humans triumph over their wisdom and might."

"You bred a race of monsters," countered Auron, "who were cruel and contemptuous to other humans. We merely corrected your error, and freed the Loanei's human slaves."

The red dragon growled low in his throat. "If this Tryna Lia of yours was a true leader, she would duel Morlyn to the death in proper Loänei fashion, to determine the succession. Do not the humans' prophecies speak of such a conflict? Tell them why you are come, human. You wish to go to war against Morlyn and the Loänei!"

"No! Son of Heaven," Ailia turned and addressed the Emperor by his ceremonial title, "I am come only to ask your people to aid mine in our struggle against the Avatar of Valdur. I ask you to help us *prevent* a war."

The aged face gazed down at her impassively. "The answer is not mine to give, Princess," the old, dust-dry voice replied. "It is for these beings, the emissaries of their various worlds and star-states, to determine. If we intervene in human affairs, if we take sides, then the followers of Valdur have sworn to rise up against us and make war."

A tall armor-clad woman stepped forward from the crowd and dropped to one knee. "Son of Heaven, all the races with human blood are in agreement on this: we accept this woman as the one foretold in our prophecies. And we accept the people of Mera as our blood-kin, who require our aid."

Hada the kitsune also stepped forward from the crowd. He had set aside his true form for his human one: a sign of support for Ailia. "My people too see the humans as kin, since our ancestors long ago shared one world and their blood has mixed with ours since we learned to take their form. It is the same with the nagas and lycanthropes, the tanuki and cait-sith, the pucas and the selkies. But we know not the arts of war, and could not hope to defeat all of Morlyn's allies. It is the older races of the Imperium who recall the battles against the Valei: we must have their aid if we are to succeed."

The king of the earth-dragons now leaped forward, challenging. "I will speak for Morlyn and his people!" Torok faced Ailia, his yellow eyes narrowed to slits. "This human creature has no right to command us!" She sensed a mental undercurrent of hostility beneath his words, a message meant for her alone.

"I do not command you," Ailia replied, distressed. "I only ask you for your help."

"You ask us to set peace aside, and go to war with our own kin!"

There was another murmur from the crowd of ambassadors. A manticore stepped forward, a great russet-furred creature with a coarse-featured, almost human face and barbed segmented tail. "We will not make war, even against those who are not our kin!" he bellowed, opening his jaws wide so Ailia could see all his pointed teeth, arranged like a shark's in many rows. "Why should we rise up against this Prince Morlyn? What has he done?"

"Much," returned Taleera. She flew upward, hovering over the assembly's heads. "But it is what he means to do that troubles us most. He wishes to rule the Valei, and breed more Loänei like himself. To challenge our Empire and take Orbion's place."

"And why should he not," demanded Torok, "rather than this small frail creature here?"

"But I do not wish to rule," Ailia said again. "That has never been my desire."

The Emperor looked at her. "It is the Stone-wielder's destiny to rule after me. I shall not reign forever. I have awaited your coming for centuries: the Archons clearly intended that you should rule. In their wisdom they foresaw it, ages ago. The Tryna Lia shall become the princess of the stars: the Celestial Empress. It is for that reason I had this throne made, carved with the likenesses of my people but shaped for one of your kind. A human throne for a human ruler."

"How do you know that she is the One to fill it, O Emperor?" roared Torok, and the earth dragons that were with him all showed their great teeth. The Imperial dragons upon the dais hissed in reply, and their wings snapped like banners in a sudden wind.

"Peace," said the Emperor. And though his human voice was weak, the undiminished power of his mind reached out to silence them all. "Princess, perhaps you should present the proof of your identity before the Assembly. Show them that which has come into your keeping."

The sun had gone behind Alfaran's great disc, and a blue gloom like the shade of evening filled the hall. Ailia held out the small alabaster casket. "Behold," she said, "the Stone of the Stars." She lifted the lid and took the gem from its resting place.

A ray of light sprang up from the stone, piercing the thin gauze of a captive cloud to rise through the crystal vault high above. Within it there rose a radiant form that resembled a flying bird—a bird of fire, soaring up from the Stone's depths. It too soared up to the cloudy roof and vanished from their sight. It was the very same sign that the Arainians had beheld when Ailia took her throne, the Stone's acknowledgment of its chosen wielder. The ambassadors were moved: the rumor of their awe went up like the voice of a sea, rebounding from the adamantine walls. In the watery chamber a makara raised his elephantine head above the surface and trumpeted.

"It is a sign," exclaimed one of the dragon monarchs. "A sign! An eidolon out of the Ether—the Elmir itself!"

The earth-dragons' king snarled. "That, or a conjuring trick. How can we know? And even if she is the one prophesied, what of it? That proves only that you have indeed come to bring war, as the prophecy said. I will have none of it, or you!" Torok declared, rearing up on his haunches and spreading his crimson wings wide. "Morlyn wants us to be free, as he is free."

"Free!" exclaimed Taleera. "Can you call any being free who has sold his soul to the dark one? If you do not beware, you will fall into the same trap! There will be no more talk of freedom then!"

"Morlyn does not wish to make war," the red dragon replied. "I am come to convey a message from him. He asks that the Tryna Lia go to him on his home world of Nemorah, to parley. He will not come to her, as his life has too often been threatened by her allies, but he assures her safety if only she will go to him."

"That is out of the question," said Taleera decidedly, before Ailia could speak.

"You see?" Torok said, turning to the rest of the creatures. "His offer is rejected. If war follows, it will not be the prince's fault."

The Emperor of Heaven arose. "We will think on these matters," he announced, "and all come together again tomorrow eventide, to see if an accord can be reached." And with that he descended the throne, accompanied by the Imperial dragons, signaling that the audience was at an end.

"WELL, I FAILED," said Ailia to Auron and Taleera, as they sat in the garden of the dragons' guesthouse.

"At least you tried," said the dragon. "That is important. No one can say you did not try for peace."

The garden was filled with people, all of such unearthly beauty that they seemed more like animated statuary than human beings: the women all young with skin like flawless porcelain, the men like idealized heroes cast in marble. Most Loänan preferred to assume young, strong bodies when they took the shapes of other species.

But she had grown used to this by now, and her eyes barely dwelled on them. Only Auron continued to take the form of a plump and diminutive old man—to put her at ease, perhaps. The firebird in her own shape perched on the back of the stone bench where he and Ailia sat. Hada the kitsune was there, too, in his true form. There were also two serpents larger than pythons, with necks that they could flatten and spread in the manner of a cobra, and a black furred creature that looked not unlike a domestic cat, only the size of a leopard.

"Well!" exclaimed Taleera, cocking a ruby-red eye at Auron. "There's one that will bear watching—King Torok! He is clearly Morlyn's creature."

"He does not speak for all the Loänan, Princess," the golden dragon assured Ailia. "Not even for all dragons of earth."

She looked at him. "Mandrake and I are dividing your people, aren't we? Auron, I'm so sorry."

"No, Princess, this schism is very old. It dates to the time when my people first lived and mingled with yours."

"Then I must try to convince Torok that I mean no harm."

"Small chance of that, I fear," said Taleera.

"Falaar, is there nothing your people can do?" Ailia implored the cherub. He was reposing sphinx-fashion on the mossy ground, head raised.

The cherub's voice was solemn as he replied. "When last my people went to war the very face of Heaven was marred. We fear what may happen should we confront Valdur's hosts again. We do not fear our own fates—it is an honor undreamed-of for one of us to die in battle—but the human worlds would be laid waste by the sorceries we unleashed."

"You mean, another Disaster?" asked Ailia.

"That is our fear. And so we watch and wait, and the votaries of Valdur watch and wait, and the wars in your little worlds go on. Yet they are as nothing compared to the destruction that would occur, should our hosts join in this fray."

She turned desperately to Auron again. "Is there anything that can be done? Can the Emperor do nothing?"

"He has lived more than a thousand of your years, remember, and his strength and authority are not what they once were. His body weakens, and I think it will not be long before he seeks the

Ether and dies. And our enemies know it. He will do what he can, but he is not the master of the people, rather their servant."

"All races that bear human blood will support Ailia in whatever she wishes to do," said Hada, looking at the cait-sith and the two nagas. "And Chukala, queen of the myrmecoleons, has declared she is on Ailia's side: though being a hive-creature she naturally favors a female ruler. Her people will all follow her lead, of course. And the cherubim are with us, and the firebirds. But the manticores do not favor our cause, and the rest are undecided. I am afraid a war is inevitable," he stated, shaking his head. "Now not only the Loänan are divided but all the Celestial Empire."

"Curse that Mandrake creature!" said Taleera angrily. "What does he hope to gain from all of this?"

"If only I could go to his own world and talk to him, as he asked," said Ailia. "Perhaps—perhaps I could reason with him."

"Far too dangerous," said Taleera.

"Then I could go there by ethereal projection, as I did for Khalazar."

"No, child. You do not understand yet how dangerous Mandrake is, how subtle and persuasive he can be. It is not so much his powers that I fear. He is cunning and filled with deceit. He traps his victims in webs of words—not lies, but half-truths. Do not speak to him!"

"What if he and I met here?" Ailia suggested.

"He would not come," said Taleera. "He would say that the Loänan have threatened him in the past, and he would not be safe here. I know him! He made you that offer on purpose, knowing that you must refuse it. Thus he appears to be the conciliatory one, you the haughty leader bent on war. We might as well begin to prepare for battle."

"But a stellar conflict!" said Auron, aghast. "It could turn into another War of Heaven."

Ailia rose. "I beg your pardon, but I must retire. This has been a long day, and a frightening one. I feel very weary."

Taleera agreed. "Yes, it grows late and you need your rest. There will be much to do tomorrow."

Ailia left them and walked slowly toward the guesthouse. She was filled with anguish for the losses in the battle. Even if Jomar had thought of it, she had given her approval to the plan, and the responsibility for it lay with her. There must be no more such battles. Above her the stars were big and bright and alien: the old familiar constellations that had accompanied her on all her previous travels were nowhere to be seen. Those strange stars blazed down upon her—like eyes, she thought: watching, judging, taking her measure. Whatever decision the Empire's peoples came to, pain and suffering on an unimaginable scale would be the inevitable result. *It must not happen*, Ailia thought, filled with horror. *I am the cause of all this, I started it just by being who I am.* She bent her head beneath their luminous gaze.

A plan had begun to form within her mind even as she listened to the others talk. But to act on it would require all the courage she could summon, and what wisdom she had as well, for from this time on her deeds would affect not only her own life but the lives of countless others. Her own words came back to her, the same words that had inspired Lorelyn: *Life is a story, except that the people in it are also writing it. They can help to decide what will happen, and how it will end.*

Ailia glanced around her as she entered the front hall of the house. No one was there. She would have watchers, guardians shape-shifted to innocuous forms. But she too could play that trick: not with shape-shifting, not yet; but she could disguise herself. She quickly and quietly summoned a glaumerie: the likeness of an Elei woman, tall and fair, and clad in raiment finer than the simple apricot-colored chiton Ailia wore, a woman whose beauty would have turned heads on Mera, but whose appearance in this world was commonplace.

No one stopped her as she walked back out the door. Her deception had worked, she knew, for the Loänan would never have let her leave alone.

She walked on through the grounds. Ephemeri fluttered among the trees, their leaf-wings rustling stiffly like paper fans. Fountains, lit from beneath by many-colored underwater lights, flung up plumes of luminous blue, or gold, or crimson spray against the gathering darkness.

She continued on, through the orderly parks, to the edge of the city. It might have been Mirimar on a carnival day, she thought as she looked at the teeming streets. All around her were wondrous figures, furred, feathered, scaled, strangely bedizened. But these were not costumed revelers, they were living beings: visitors from every world of the Imperium, come to sample the wares and wonders of the dragon-world. On the far side of the street strolled a group of men and women who were literally covered in hair— thick shaggy fur that coated even their faces and hands. It took Ailia some time to realize they were human at all, and not some species of ape. Woodwoses, they must be: the Wild Men of Meran legend. A group of satyrs capered to the music of a flutelike instrument, horned heads tossing, naked swaying torsos changing strangely into the shaggy and backward-curving legs of goats. Brazen automata shaped like horses clopped along the streets, bearing their riders all about the city without tiring. No, the mythmakers of old had not been idle dreamers. They had merely recorded what they had actually seen here, and in other distant worlds of Talmirennia.

She continued to walk purposefully along the city's broad avenues, until she came to the wharfs. And here were many sky-ships resting quietly at anchor, just as ordinary seagoing vessels might, their wing-sails folded upright like the wings of butterflies. Some were small, no larger than a skiff, others were immense and many-winged, with heavily ornamented fore- and aftercastles.

"May I be of assistance?" asked a voice in her ear as she gazed.

She turned. Beside her stood a tengu, a singular-looking creature. He resembled a great bird, with leaf-green plumage and a hooked bill, but there was something oddly anthropomorphic about him, too: his head was rounded, with large dark eyes, and at the "wrists" of his wings were handlike claws. He was speaking Elensi too, in a croaking parroty voice. He winked at her, mimicking the human gesture roguishly, and waved a pinion toward the winged vessels. "Are you a Nemerei, my lady? If so, all these elegant flying conveyances are for hire."

"Don't you listen to him!" shouted another voice, this one speaking an unknown tongue that she had to translate mentally. "Tengus can't be trusted, lady. Hire your conveyance from me." Another curious creature came forward, running on short stubby legs: he was a kappa, something like an ape but with the hard shell-armor of a turtle encasing his body. "Don't you believe that *petask*. Tengus are full of trickery! And that one is the worst of them all. He's got all the scruples of—"

"A kappa?" suggested the tengu.

"A goblin, crossbred with a—"

The tengu reached out, placed a wing-claw atop the kappa's head, and thrust it down inside his turtle shell. Noises of muffled outrage came from within and the hairy arms waved wildly. "Pay no heed, mistress," the bird-man said. "Kappas are tiresome creatures. Stupid, too. It's said their brains are mostly water," he explained in a penetrating stage whisper. "That's why they never bend over—else their brains would dribble out their noses." He pointed with a pinion at a vessel. "I can see you are a lady of means and—if I may say so—good character. You needn't pay right away! Pay me only on your return, if you wish."

The ship had no bowsprit: instead its prow was carved in the shape of a dragon's horned head, with eyes that were pale gems, glittering cold as rime. Prow and hulls were clad in lapping scales that shone like beaten gold. Its wings were broad sheets of yellow canvas supported by ribs of gilded wood. Another pole thrust out horizontally from the stern like an elongated rudder, ending in a flat fan shape: it reminded Ailia of the toy windmills with wooden blades that Island villagers whittled for their children.

An inner voice shrilled at her. There was still a chance: she could decline his generous offer and return to the guesthouse at once. "I would like to see the inside first," she said instead.

"Of course, my lady." They crossed the wooden gangway and stepped onto the ship's deck. It was tiled like the hull with thousands of golden salamander-scales, hard as metal under her slippered feet. The windows were panes of unbreakable adamant, carefully caulked around the edges to prevent any air from escaping should the ship be forced to drop out of the Ethereal Plane and into the vacuum of the void.

"Here is the entrance," said the tengu, pushing a lever. It opened a low rectangular door in the stern cabin. "It is designed to be an airtight seal, and there is an antechamber within." They passed through the small cubicle and descended a metal stair into a long, low-roofed room with padded walls—"To prevent injury once one is outside the sphere of gravity." There was a table on which several maps lay: star charts, and maps of the continents of alien worlds. A console was set into the front wall under a window. Many strange knobs and projections arose from it, and mounted in its center was a crystal globe about the size of her head. "Now, however great a Nemerei you may be, your power alone could not lift the ship far or fast enough to make it an effective vehicle for travel. That is where the mechanism comes in, to make it an ornithopter—a vessel that flies like a bird." The tengu pulled on a brass knob shaped like a flying eagle. There was a clanking of gears and Ailia saw, out the port window, a great silken pinion lower itself until it was at right angles to the hull. Its twin on the starboard side did the same. "To fly, you simply put two powers, magical and mechanical, together. This is how dragons are able to fly, by combining sorcery with physical flight."

Ailia turned to examine the crystalline globe. It was clear as glass, but she thought she saw a flickering of pale light within its depths. "That is an oracle, my lady, such as all our star-ships have. There is a power within it that comes from the Ethereal Plane, and can reveal to you the portals leading to that realm. It will augment your own powers as well, and it can warn you of dangers, and display things on command. Spirit of the crystal, show us another world," commanded the tengu, stroking the globe with his wingtip.

The quivering luminescence was gone; in its place an image filled the crystal's depths. Peering at it, she saw it was a scene in some strange land. There was a forest unlike any she had ever seen: the foliage of its trees was red and gold and vermilion, the harsh brilliant hues of autumn, yet the leaves showed no signs of decay, and none had fallen to the ground. It seemed these were their normal colors. The sun above was huge and red-golden, like a setting sun—only it stood at the zenith; its beams fanned down red as firelight through the boughs. In and out among the trees firebirds were gliding on their jewel-bright wings. Their nests were not untidy heaps of twigs, but elaborate bowers adorned with flowers and spices and brightly colored stones. They sang as they flew, the same joyous song that Taleera had sung in the alpine forest.

"I can *hear* them!" she exclaimed.

Then the scene changed to a vista from another world: its colors were as cool and restful as those of Taleera's world had been hot and vibrant, shades of blue and pale purple melting one into the other. Through hanging veils of mist she saw a forest of pale azure and lavender color; a purple shore sloping down to a dim blue sea;

an amethyst sky in which an immense moon hung, three-quarters full. Blue and green fronds stirred. Out of the wood there stepped a lithe, graceful creature, ivory-white, in size between a horse and a deer. The tail was long and ended in a plumy tuft, while a mane like a horse's, only softer and more luxuriant, fell like foam along the crest of the neck. She gazed at it in open-mouthed wonderment. Among her foster father's exotic south-sea treasures had been the dried body of a seahorse, and Ailia had often marveled at how closely its arching neck and head mimicked those of a real horse. She saw here that same miracle, that same blend of familiar and alien. But it was the horn that held her gaze: that wondrous, single horn, with no stump or socket to show where a second horn might once have been. It was shaped like a spiral seashell, softly shining with its own nacreous luster, as though its coils enclosed a shaft of light. For a brief moment the creature stood there, poised on the points of its cloven hooves, holding her still with its horn, its seahorse strangeness, the beneficence of its lamblike smile. Then with a single light and airy bound it was away, not galloping like a horse but moving in graceful leaps like a gazelle. "A *Tarnawyn*," she whispered. "A unicorn—I have never seen one before—"

"You see! This vessel can take you anywhere in the Imperium—anywhere at all," said the voice of the tengu behind her. "The power within the stone will reveal to you the doorways in the Ether, and the way that leads you to the world you desire to see. Come, lady! One trial flight, and no payment afterward if you are not satisfied. I know you Elei are an honorable race."

Ailia clutched the edge of the console. The aperture of Possibility beckoned, but it was closing, like a gap between clouds. It was now, or never: an opportunity to be grasped at once, or lost for all time. Ignoring the inner voice that still desperately counseled retreat, she made herself answer, "I will take it. Thank you."

His round black eyes gleamed. "Very good, my lady . . ." Suddenly he fell silent. Puzzled, she looked at him and then realized he was staring at the window next to which she stood. The night was dark behind it, and in its surface was mirrored her true form, clad in the apricot-colored chiton. Ailia drew in a sharp breath.

She had forgotten all about reflections.

It was too late now to extend her glaumerie to the window. The tengu's eyes widened in surprise and puzzlement and he backed away slightly as she turned toward him.

"Yes, I concealed my true form from you. I am the Tryna Lia, Ailia Elarainia," she told him. "And I am on a—an urgent mission. Do you understand? If you tell no one of my flight until after I have gone, I give you my word you will be paid for my passage—you may demand it from the royal treasury of Arainia itself. If . . ." she looked away again. ". . . if I should fail to return, they will make good to you the cost of your ship. Is that agreeable to you?"

He hesitated; he would not agree to such a bargain; he would refuse, and she would be able to return to the guesthouse, her moment of madness over. But he did not refuse. "Highness . . ." the bird-man murmured. He seemed about to ask a question, then apparently thought better of it, picturing the riches of a royal treasury. He bowed his green-plumed head and backed out of the cabin, and the door closed upon him. It might have been the door of a prison slamming shut upon her. She felt herself locked into this course of action now.

Ailia twisted the eagle-shaped knob, then laid her hands upon the sphere of crystal. It was cool beneath her hands, but she felt a surge of power in her mind as she touched it. There was a force within it, something strong and alive that was not of this plane, that could move between matter and Ether as it willed—and take her along with it, once she joined her power to its own. A tremor ran through the little ship. Then it rose, spinning slightly as it ascended, and she saw the lights of the city beyond the window begin to drop away. The wing-sails beat the air, the dragon's-head prow pointed toward the stars like a compass needle swinging to the north. Within minutes sea and land had vanished from her view.

So *fast!*

Clouds wisped past the windows like steam: bulbous cumuli, then a flat layer of cirrus like thin ice. Alfaran and its moons loomed huge before her, and the nebula grew brighter as the sky between them deepened. She watched as it darkened, within minutes, from blue to black. Her flight no longer seemed to her like an escape, but had become an adventure: her heart raced with exhilaration as she gazed on the blackening heights. More stars appeared: not in slow-blooming groups as at nightfall, but springing into view even as she watched. Whole stellar hosts came crowding out of spaces that had been dark and empty before. A part of her— the draconic side, perhaps—knew a heady moment of fierce joy that swept aside all her fears. She was flying by her own will for the first time, soaring where she wished to go and not where another chose to take her.

Ailia reached out to the pulsing force within the globe. "Take me to the portal in the sky," she said, "and show me the way through the Ether to Nemorah."

Part Two

THE GAMES OF GODS

11

The Zayim

ROGLUG HASTENED ALONG A CORRIDOR in Khalazar's palace.

Murky gray light fell in long beams from the tall windows, but rather than illuminating the gloom of the halls the subdued and isolated shafts seemed only to emphasize it. Live snakes coiled and slithered on the floors, causing the goblin to take care where he stepped. He could stop a striking snake with sorcery, but if one bit him before he saw it the venom would spread through his veins too quickly for any remedy. Mandrake's new pets were all venomous—indeed, he had obtained them for that very reason: their presence discouraged spies and assassins. It seemed to Roglug that the snakes were restless today, hissing and lunging peevishly at one another. Mandrake's odd menagerie was almost an extension of his mind: they reflected, like so many empathetic familiars, the mood of their master. Roglug felt a stab of dread at the thought of facing the prince. Mandrake, by the look of things, was in no humor for bad news.

He paused before the door that led to the prince's tower room. It was ajar. He knocked softly: still no answer. The goblin opened the door, and peered in.

The chamber within was also poorly lit. He entered and looked along its gloomy length with trepidation. He saw no sign of the prince, but Mandrake did not always take a human form, and if he wanted to cow his servants he would appear as a beast: a giant serpent perhaps, or a dragon. As Roglug walked forward something moved with a dry rustle in the prince's great thronelike chair: he glimpsed a scaly coil gleaming dully in the light from the doorway and shuddered.

He scuttled forward and knelt before the throne. The serpent in the chair lifted its head with a hiss, its neck flaring into a wide hood. Yes, the prince was in an ill temper. "Forgive the interruption, Highness, but I've just had word—" he began, choosing an even humbler posture and a quavering tone in order to stave off more anger.

"Who are you talking to, Roglug?" It was Mandrake's voice— coming from *behind* him! The goblin jumped and whirled.

"I thought that was you in the chair!" he gasped, the tremor in his voice now quite unfeigned.

Mandrake laughed. "No, that is my latest acquisition—a king cobra. Magnificent, isn't he? I found him down by the river."

"Is he—it—poisonous?"

"Extremely. You are lucky you weren't bitten: you would have died almost at once. But tell me why you are here." Mandrake picked the serpent up carelessly, and it grew calm and flaccid as a piece of rope in his hands. Hanging its scaly length about his neck, he took his seat in the throne.

Roglug began his report, trembling as Mandrake's fingers began to beat an ominous tattoo on the armrests of his chair.

"And that is the last that was seen of her," Roglug finished.

Mandrake's hands clenched on the armrests. "What!" The goblin cringed as Mandrake rose to his full towering height. The cobra spread its hood again, striking at the air. "She has truly fled her keepers? For the life of me, I can't say if this be good news, or bad."

"I think it's good news," said the goblin nervously. "I expect she's lost her nerve and run away."

"Or else she has grown impatient at her confinement, and seized her freedom. But what does she mean to do now? She knows she has not the power to challenge me directly, not yet. Does she think she can raise an army on her own?" Mandrake spoke as if to himself; then he turned to the goblin king again. "Send out your goblins and some firedrakes to search all the worlds where she might have gone. And let me know *immediately* if they find her."

KING TIRON LOOKED OUT from the highest balcony of Halmirion, at the varicolored, granular-looking mass of innumerable bodies massed together on the hillside. The crowds anxiously awaited word of the Tryna Lia. In her absence he was the figure to whom they looked for solace, and he tried hard to throw himself into the role. But the terrifying news of his daughter's disappearance, at first feared to be an abduction, had left him sleepless and haggard. And now it transpired that she had not been captured, but had run away.

He raised his arms in a benediction gesture, then went back inside and went to his daughter's room. The sight of her possessions and the girlish innocence that still clung to them brought tears to his eyes. *My daughter, my Ailia—what existence have your mother and I cursed you with? To what life—or what death—have we doomed you?*

"Poor lamb, poor lamb!" the nurse Benia had sobbed on hearing the news, until he at last sent her off to bed with a soothing draught. *Lamb indeed*, he thought grimly. It was a fitting word, with echoes of ancient Meran custom. *The sacrificial lamb . . .*

And what was *his* part in all this? Merely to love his wife and daughter, and then to lose them? Only that, and no more?

"You stand for all of us," Marima had told him, "the symbol of every mortal: you are the Beloved of the Goddess."

"A limited role, that."

"The noblest role of all. For without you, Elarainia would not have descended from the heavens. Without you, the Daughter of the Mother would not have become enfleshed, to walk in our midst as one of us. You are the door by which both Mother and Daughter entered our human world. When you stand forth on the balcony, we are all present and reflected in you."

But Tiron wanted no glory and never had: he wanted only the two women he loved.

Ela . . . in his mind he saw her again: not the queen and goddess of Mirimar's adoring masses, but his wife, the woman he had loved. He saw again the blue sun-sequined bay, the lush green forest that grew almost to the water's edge, the towering rock plateaux of Hyelanthia with their cloud-hung summits. The sea was a pale turquoise color this close to shore, and transparent as glass: one saw through it to the smooth sand and the colorful fish that idled to and fro, each accompanied by a black distinct shadow like its dark twin. Ela was sitting on a rock combing out the golden cascade of her hair. It was half-dry, rippled with damp, waving in the sea breeze. She looked like a mermaid. Later she would wear silk and satin and cloth of gold, with jeweled diadems upon her head: transformed into a living idol, she would be paraded through city streets. But here she had been a wild goddess of the woods, and he her sole votary. He strove to hold the moment in his mind.

She had turned to him, he remembered, and told him of the child.

"You're with child?" he had exclaimed, sitting up on the sand.

Her laughter rippled, like her hair. "Not yet! One day. It will be a daughter."

"How do you know this?" he asked.

"For me, knowing is like seeing. You see these waves approaching the shore, one after the other breaking on the sands. You cannot say *how* it is that you see: you merely open your eyes and do it. That is how it is with me and the things that are to come."

"Then is our fate fixed?" he asked frowning. "Are there no real choices, is everything we do predestined? Were we fated to meet, Ela, and fall in love?"

"Fated?" she repeated, as though the word were unknown to her. "You chose to seek me out, did you not? And I saw you coming, from far off—like the wave. But one may walk away from shore, away from the wave; or one may go gladly to meet it. Our child is born of choice, my love. We met like the swimmer and the wave, and from that meeting she springs forth, like spray." She leaped lightly from her rock and ran over to entwine him with her arms and sea-washed hair. "And now we have this time, my love, this moment of happiness. Cherish it!"

She had not meant merely to live for the moment, as he had then thought. She had wanted him to treasure this scene in memory, he realized now, so that he might call upon it again for comfort. Had she foreseen her flight and death then, he wondered, as well as Ailia's birth? And their daughter's ultimate fate—had Ela known that also?

His thoughts turned again to sacrifices, and the tales he had heard of old Zimbouran ways. It was said that they had once chosen young men and women of unblemished beauty, and given them lives of luxury for one year, clothing them in finery and feeding them delicacies. But when the year was out the young people were led in procession to the temple, like fattened calves, there to yield up their lives on the altar of Valdur. And Ailia—was she also a victim like them, pampered and cosseted at first in this palace of Halmirion, only to go on from here to some terrible foreordained contest in which she was likely to perish? Bitterness filled him. She was no mere tool of the gods: she was his daughter, flesh of his flesh. Even if it were true that she was some sort of divine being incarnate, yet by that very incarnation he had a claim on her.

"Ailia," he said aloud, "if your guardians do not find you soon, I swear I will go myself and search every world for you."

JOMAR PEERED OUT THE OPEN DOORWAY of the hut in which he and his friends had been confined.

All around the Mohara village, here in the heart of the oasis, stood ruins covered in fearsome-looking stone figures. In one ornate alcove the form of a man sat cross-legged with his hands resting on his knees. A small fire burned before it—a votive fire, Jomar had thought last night when he first glimpsed the figure, imagining it to be an image of stone. But by daylight he saw that it was a living man who sat there, elderly and emaciated, clad only in a loincloth. His eyes were half-open, but he had not stirred, not even to stretch a limb. Every handspan of the ancient facade above him was carved, so that the stone seemed to writhe and dance with life. The features of the statues were Moharan: proud wide nostrils and pursed lips, hair arranged in tight stylized curls.

So it's true, Jomar thought.

He remembered the elders in the work camp telling of the Lost Cities of the Mohara: as a child he had been entranced by the tales, but once he had grown to manhood he dismissed them as wishful thinking. Vanished cities and realms—buildings filled with the treasure of long-gone kings—surely, he had thought, these were fables to comfort the wretched slaves, to make them feel that their race and lineage were honorable even if they were not free. Yet here were the stone faces, gazing back at him with a fierce and breathtaking dignity. *It's true. We had all this once, long ago.*

"Can you still not hear any voices in your head, Lori?" he heard Damion ask behind him.

"No—not a thing. It's as though the back of my mind is empty. And when I try to send a thought out, there's no answer. There is something very strange about this place," said Lorelyn. "If there are

Nemerei here I can't reach any of them." She moved to stand at Jomar's side. "Did *your* ancestors build all of that?" she asked, gesturing at the ruins.

"Of course. Do you think a Zimbouran could make something that magnificent?" returned Jomar passionately.

Lorelyn stared at him in surprise. She had never heard him speak like this before, with such pride and intensity. For a moment he looked almost like one of the carved stone warrior-kings. She stood silent for a moment, pondering this new Jomar.

He remained facing the doorway and the city. "The Mohara had a great kingdom here once. The old people used to tell me about it. Valdur put a curse on my people, they said, dividing the tribes and making them fight one another, to make it easier for the Zimbourans to come up from the southern steppes and enslave them. When King Andarion declared war on the Zimbourans thousands of Mohara slaves rose up, and Zimboura was conquered. But our cities had fallen into ruin, and we never went back to them: they still had a curse on them, people said. The Mohara tried to live off the land, the way we did before the time of the cities. Then Zimboura rose again. Now all my people build are roads and bridges for the God-king. Slave-work."

"What was it like in the labor camp, Jo?" asked Lorelyn. "You've never talked about it much."

"I can't describe it. You would have to live it yourself to understand." But Jomar realized he wanted to tell them: about his mother dying of the fever while the witch doctor stood over her, gravely shaking his head despite Jomar's tearful pleas; of the old man who had cared for him after her death falling ill in his turn, and being left to die in the dirt; of the flies and the heat and the beatings, and hungry children crying through the night. He told them of these things now, and they listened quietly.

"They worked the people to death—literally. Anyone who got too old or too sick to work was abandoned to die. Sometimes the soldiers would just kill someone, at random, to keep everyone else afraid and obedient. I just—endured it, as everyone else did. And then—"

"And then the lion came," said Damion, his voice gentle.

Jomar touched the trophy claw dangling from his earring. "The lion—yes, I had to go and kill that blasted marauding lion." And he had been hauled off to the arena to fight more lions, and other beasts, and men; and afterward he was taken into the army and forced to be a spy. He had dared to hope, then, that he might escape. But Zefron Shezzek had been assigned to keep a close eye on Jomar: Shezzek the half-breed, the perfect spy with his ruddy complexion and his pale greenish eyes that were unlike any true-bred Zimbouran's. Shezzek was dead now, but in his dreams Jomar still sometimes saw that face, those eyes watching his every move.

"Jo, how could you bear to come back here?" exclaimed Lorelyn.

Jomar set his jaw. "Because I wanted to stop it: the camps and the slavery. Forever."

Damion looked at him: the Mohara man's face was becoming hard and closed-in, as it had looked when they first met him. Now at last he understood why. "Who are the figures on those ruins?" he asked, changing the subject. "Do you know?"

"I don't know all of them. That one near the top is the *Zayim*— the one with the spear in his hand. He's supposed to be a kind of warrior who'll come some day and save Mohar. They used to talk about him a lot in the camps: it gave the slaves hope, I guess. All I can say is, he's taking his sweet time coming." To each side of the statue of the Zayim stood a winged figure, guarding him. "Angels," said Jomar, nodding at the two images. "My people believe in them too. The other statues are Mohara gods, I think. Akkar and Nayah, and Kaliman, and the old kings."

Lorelyn looked at him, incredulous. "Your kings were worshiped, just like Khalazar?"

"No!" Jomar's tone was scornful. "Only the Zims worship living kings! Mohara kings were supposed to become gods *after* they died. It's a lot of rubbish, but no Mohara has ever been revered while he was still alive." His eyes turned to the huts again, looking long and hungrily at the community beyond the open door, at the women carrying clay pots filled with spring water, their babies in pouches at their backs; at the children laughing and playing with sticks, pretending to be warriors; at the young men sharpening their swords and spears and talking together. Moharas as they should be: free, happy, bowing to no one. This should have been his home.

Damion fell silent too, gazing on the stone ruins. Only the Trynisian realm was older than this, and for much of its early history it had been kept separate from the rest of the world. The true civilization of Mera had begun *here*, long before the ancestors of the Elei sought out their Merei kin in other lands. The Mohara were the first to build, before the Kaans or Shurkanese or the peoples of the west. He felt that he looked back through some enchanted window on an earlier time, the very morning of the human world.

Time passed, and began to weigh upon the prisoners. What were their captors planning to do with them? To calm her thoughts, Lorelyn began to do Byn-jara exercises, standing on one foot with her arms spread to either side like wings. The "bird in flight" exercise was supposed to train the body's sense of balance and compose the mind, but Jomar thought it looked ridiculous. He turned away moodily and went to the door. The sentry outside, a tall man with a necklace of warthog teeth over his white linen robe, stopped him with his spear. "Any farther and you die."

Jomar bristled. "I'm a Mohara! I belong here, with my people."

"Are you sure you would not prefer the company of Zimbourans?"

Jomar clenched his fists. "You say that again, and you'll be wearing your *own* teeth on that necklace."

For a moment Damion feared the two men were going to come to blows, but the other just contented himself with a glare. Presently another warrior came striding up to the hut, with several men behind him. It was Unguru, the leader of the men who had captured them. "Take them to the elders now," he ordered. "It is time for the judging."

They were forced to walk in front of the warriors' leveled spears and scimitars, toward the center of the village. They walked slowly, despite the prodding spearheads. All of them were hurt and weary, and Damion held his hand often to his temple as he walked: the sword gash in it had begun to throb painfully. In the open area at the center of the huts stood a row of Mohara elders. They were unexpectedly magnificent, clad in long robes over billowing trousers of some soft material, dyed in rich ochre and bronze and wine-purple. On their heads were turbans, also dyed in bright hues: the chief's had a large jewel over the forehead, and a pair of ostrich plumes. At their sides their guards stood, wearing great

curved scimitars. Younger men, women, and children gathered behind them, watching with wide eyes.

"Hear our judgment," one of the elders intoned, a tall man wearing a leopard skin cloak over his robe. "We hold that you, Jomar,
are a spy and informer, in the pay of Khalazar—"

"That's a lie!" Jomar shouted. "Who accuses me? I demand to
know. I challenge him to a duel!"

Unguru's lip curled. "You are not Mohara. You have no right to
challenge anyone."

Damion could feel the fear and anger radiating from Unguru
and the others. He could not blame them, for they lived each day
in fear of a Zimbouran invasion. Warriors' spears surrounded Jomar
now, as he stood desperate and furious as a beast at bay.

Then one of the women cried out, pointing toward the ruin.
"The shaman, the shaman!" Others took up her cry. The seated figure was stirring in its alcove: perhaps the commotion had roused
the old man from his trance. Gasps arose from the villagers as he
stood, climbed slowly and stiffly down from his stone seat, and approached the gathering. In addition to the goatskin loincloth he
wore a string of animal claws and teeth, his only ornament. The
old man walked up to the prisoners with his halting gait, then
stood still in front of them and spoke. "I knew that you would
come," he said in a wheezing voice. "I asked for help to come to us
here, help to fight our enemy, and I received a dream in answer. In
it I saw you."

"You are a Nemerei?" Damion said.

"That is the Elei word. Yes." The old man nodded. "Speak to me
of your errand: I will understand. I am Wakunga: I dream for this
tribe, and the gods talk to me."

"You know why we are here?" asked Damion.

The old man nodded. "I know," he answered in his own tongue.
"I have dreamt it. You and the warrior and the woman, but chiefly
you. It is your presence here that will decide the later course of
events: how, I cannot say yet, but I feel it. And you have all walked
the Dream-place. This, too, I can tell."

"You mean the Ethereal Plane?" asked Lorelyn. "We passed
through it to come here."

"Yes. You come from the Morning Star's daughter." Wakunga
gestured skyward with one arm. "It is she who sent you."

"What do you know of her?" asked Damion.

"We have tales in our tribe, that the star of morning and evening would at times descend to the earth in a woman's form. That she would one day take a mortal mate and bring forth a woman-child. And that this being will one day save, not only Mohar, but all the world."

Damion recognized the strands of Elei lore. They had brought their tales and traditions to this place in ages past. Wakunga was gazing at him with deep, dark eyes. "And you have dwelt on high with her; she has sent you down from the sky to aid us in our struggle."

"Yes," said Damion. It was near enough to the truth, after all.

The shaman turned and addressed the people in the old Mohara tongue. A hush fell over them all as he spoke. Unguru and a few other young men looked displeased.

"What is he saying, Jo?" asked Lorelyn.

"He says we were sent here by the gods," said Jomar, listening intently. "He says—he says that *I'm* the Zayim!"

"But you're not," she objected. "And we *aren't* sent from the gods. We must tell them they're wrong about that."

"Not if it keeps them from sticking spears in our backs," replied Jomar. "It won't hurt them or us—look!"

A group of women had come forward, their hands full of flowers. They laid these shyly at the travelers' feet, looking up with wondering eyes. The chief stepped forward, his face for a moment impassive beneath his plumed headdress as he gazed at them. Then he bowed his proud head.

"Lorelyn is right, Jo," said Damion, disturbed. "We can't allow this to continue."

"I doubt you could stop it now if you tried," Jomar told him. "These people are desperate for hope. So they think we're servants of a goddess: what of it? It's much better than being killed."

A FEAST WAS HELD THAT NIGHT in the village. The three visitors from the stars were enthroned on chairs of woven cane, and garlands were placed about their necks, while the Mohara performed a dance of gratitude to the Evening Star, raising their hands to Arainia where she shone in the clear sky, praising her and the emissaries she had sent.

Jomar clearly reveled in his new status. Now sporting elaborate war paint all over his face and torso, he spoke with his fellow Moharas in their own ancient native tongue and joined in their celebrations. Damion and Lorelyn felt rather abandoned as they sat watching the leaping flames of the bonfires and the dancing flame-lit figures. Jomar seemed to be moving away from them, becoming incorporated into this alien tribe of which they still knew so little.

"At least he has returned to his own people," said Damion. "He wanted that very badly."

"I know, but—it's as though he's not *our* Jo, anymore," said Lorelyn, trying to distinguish the painted figure of her friend as it blended with all the others in the night. The thought saddened her somehow.

But as the light of dawn seeped out of the east he came back to them at last, bounding over the ashen remains of the fires to stand before them in triumph. "There's talk of getting up a raid on the Zimbouran farmsteads," he told them, "instead of just defending this old city. These people are tired of hiding and skulking around; they want to *do* something."

"They wouldn't attack the farmers?" said Damion. "Those people can't help their lot, you said."

Jomar looked stern. "They still stole our land."

Damion noted the *our*, and said: "Their forefathers did. And they've nowhere else to go. It's Khalazar who is the real enemy, remember. He is the one we came to deal with."

"Yes. Well, there's some talk of freeing slaves from the camps. But there aren't many of us, we can hardly take on the God-king's troops. The whole Arainian army couldn't defeat them! All we can hope to do is conduct a few forays."

"I'll help," offered Lorelyn eagerly. "He's right, Damion, we should do whatever we can, even if it's only a little. Otherwise the whole mission to Mera will have been a failure. We can't go back home, so we might as well fight on, as best we can."

"I don't know what the Moharas will make of a woman warrior," said Jomar doubtfully.

"If any of them wants to challenge me, he's welcome," she declared, tossing her cropped head defiantly. "I *won't* be left out of this, Jo."

Damion sighed. "All right, I'll join you. I promised I'd help, Jo, and I will."

Glancing up, Damion suddenly noticed Wakunga standing not far off. The old man, he realized with some discomfort, was gazing not at Jomar but at *him*, and his expression was oddly intent.

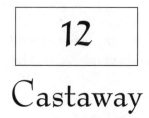

12

Castaway

"IT IS MY FAULT!" moaned Auron. The dragon paced to and fro like a fretting dog in the gardens of the guesthouse. "My fault . . . I have failed utterly in my sacred duty."

"I, too," said Taleera, her crest and pinions drooping. "I am not worthy to be her guardian."

Falaar raised his head from his forepaws and fixed them both with a golden eye. "Thou sayest sooth, but deeds are needed now, not words."

"What!" screeched Taleera, rising from the ground in a many-colored flurry and hovering in front of the cherub. "I have never been so insulted in my life!"

"The words were thine," said Falaar, tilting his eagle's head in puzzlement.

"Lummox! You did not have to *agree* with me." Taleera flew over to Auron and settled to the ground in front of him. "Don't you worry, Auron, we will find her."

"But where to seek her?" Falaar queried. "She hath at her command a flying vessel, and may have fled through the Mid-Heaven to any world."

"She has not fled." There was a curious note of pride in Auron's voice. "I know my pupil's character. She has not run from danger, but *toward* it. She has gone to Mandrake—to face him, to parley. You heard how she asked, again and again, to be allowed to do so."

"Merciful heavens!" exclaimed the firebird, holding up her pinions in horror. "He'll not parley with her. He will kill her!"

"Then we must needs seek for her in Mera or in Nemorah," the cherub said. "For if thy presumption is correct, Loänan, it is to one of those worlds that she has gone."

"You will come with us?" said Taleera in surprise. "Should you not guard the Star Stone?"

"The Archons' gem is safe here," the cherub answered. "My people will take charge of it. I would aid thee and Auron in the search. And we must not delay in seeking her. It is not good for Ailia to be so long separated from the Star Stone." He looked down at the alabaster casket lying between his paws. "It is lodestar and lodestone to her, guiding her toward her true purpose. Without its influence she may go astray, and be lost to us."

"The parley was to take place in Nemorah," Auron said. He reared up and spread his golden wings. "We must go there, I think. Even if it is too late to stop their confrontation, we can at least lend her our aid."

AILIA WOKE TO THE SIGHT of a window filled with stars.

It might have been the night sky as she had seen it so often before, from windows in houses, dormitories, and palaces. But as she gazed at it a blazing blue star rose before her eyes, larger than any star save a sun ever looks from a planet's surface; and after it there came another that was smaller and yellow in color. Many stars, Auron had told her, were partnered in their cosmic dance as these two were: Meraur and Merilia, the suns of Nemorah. Her craft was suspended in the void not far from that world, and she was suspended within it. For the planet was not near enough to draw upon Ailia with its binding force: she hung in midair as though levitating, her limbs afloat and her hair billowing about her like a cloud, along with the star charts and various small objects she had not thought to store away in the ship's cabinets. It had been rather pleasant to fall asleep in that position, and every muscle in her body was utterly relaxed. But now that she was awake, she was once more uneasily aware of her situation. She had fled those whose duty it was to protect her from harm. Her star-ship was adrift within the domain of the alien suns: beyond her little vessel stretched black unimaginable abysses that she shared with no other creature, not the merest mote of living matter. A pale moon shone high above: she stared at its gray face, at the nameless mountains and night-filled valleys, the arid airless wastes. Nothing lived there—had ever lived there, and nothing ever would. There was no atmosphere, no body of water, no green and growing thing in its sphere. No mortal had ever walked the slopes of those barren vales, climbed those stony peaks, sat and contemplated the luminous beauty of the dust-gray deserts. She gave a little shiver. She was *alone* as no Arainian or Meran had ever been in living memory. Like the stars and planets themselves—for they were lonelier by far than islands, which were rooted at least in the same seabed, and joined together in chains. There was nothing at all to connect these flying spheres, these fragile havens of life and warmth, with one another: each spun and circled in absolute solitude, surrounded only by emptiness. The thought filled her with a kind of dread.

But she had a mission to fulfill, and she must follow it through. She must meet with Mandrake, accept his offer of parley, and attempt to reason with him. And if she failed, if she were lost— "The others can carry on without me," she said to herself. "I am not that important, whatever they say." And she forced down her fear.

Beating her limbs as though she were swimming, Ailia made her way to the window and gazed in silence at the world below: a world green as an emerald, robed with seas and sprawling continents. She reached down to touch the crystal ball. She must leave this exalted orbit, re-enter the Ether by some other portal and emerge within the air of the green planet. Presently she felt the surge of power, and the vessel shifted from its course as a seagoing ship does when a wind takes its sails. The blazing chasm of the Ether opened before her, then vanished again, and she saw that she was in the atmosphere. At once the celestial body's pull asserted itself: Ailia dropped to the cabin's floor with a painful thud, while the loose objects showered down around her.

The ship was falling freely. A red glow flickered outside the windows as her passage burned the air. She was not afraid: a shield of quintessence surrounded the dragon-ship, and even were it to give way she knew the hull could withstand the fiercest temperatures. The sails too were of purest salamander silk. *I must look like a falling star to those below,* Ailia thought. The red glow increased, and then faded away again, and she guessed that the invisible shield had gone, too. She was among the clouds now. Beneath them, and patched with their doubled shadows, lay a green ocean scattered with a few irregularly shaped islands. A larger land mass lay to the east, its edge scalloped with many bays. Land, sea, and sky were all green—the land darker than the sea, while the sky above was lighter in hue than either. Sea and sky owed their tint to the blended light of the suns, no doubt, but as the ship descended she saw that the land's greenness came from dense jungles clothing it.

She went to the console, rubbing a bruised elbow, and seized the knob that made the wings beat. "Crystal," she said, shifting her hands to the globe, "show me the chief city of this world." It displayed for her an aerial view of a great river, with many buildings surrounding it. "Take me there," she commanded it, and again the ship altered its course like an obedient mount. A few hours passed before she looked down and recognized the river, a long red-brown one with countless venous tributaries, a great artery in the planet's flesh. To either side of it were many curious mounds rising from the green canopy: they were like small steep-sided hills, completely enveloped in verdure. She could also see ranges of mountains with conical summits to the east, some belching forth fumes like immense chimneys.

The crystal globe suddenly flared with a bright red light, like a warning. Ailia glanced out the window and recoiled in alarm. A flight of dragons was approaching her vessel, flying at great speed through the clouds: but they were not Loänan. Their scales were black as night. Firedrakes! With them were other, smaller creatures like two-legged and long-necked dragons, with the tiny figures of riders clinging to their backs. So Mandrake had set a guard on his city. She called to the creatures with her mind, but received no reply.

Wildly she reached for the crystal. But the swift-flying firedrakes were already nearly upon her, spouting flame.

Not far away lay a chain of volcanic islands, heavy plumes of ashen smoke hanging above their peaks to form one tremendous cloud. *What if I were to go through that smoke? They couldn't follow me through it.* The inside was likely pitch-dark, the smokes poisonous and heavy with suspended ash. Surely nothing that breathed, even a firedrake, could enter that cloud and live. *But I would be safe. This ship was made to be impervious to all outer atmospheres.*

The *wyverns* and their riders fell back as soon as it became apparent where she was heading, but the firedrakes continued to close on the ornithopter, their wings drawn in tight against their flanks as they dived: swift deadly shapes like javelins in flight. They could not burn the salamander silk of the sails, but they could easily tear them asunder with their claws and teeth. And magic alone would not hold the ornithopter aloft . . .

Quickly Ailia spun the little wheel next to the eagle knob, bringing the craft about and at the same time working the lever that increased the frequency of the wing beats. The heavy gray-black crag of smoke and ash lay directly ahead of her now. Behind her the firedrakes opened their jaws, but the speed of their flight did not permit them to spout fire: the flames would merely have streamed back around their own bodies.

The ornithopter plunged into the smoke. At once the windows were enveloped in pitch-black darkness, so that she could not tell if she moved up or down. But presently she became aware of a dull red glow as of firelight, coming from beneath. It seemed to grow stronger by the minute. She glanced sharply through the side window and there beheld a vision out of hell: only a short distance below her lay a lake of fire, from whose seething surface jetted red fountains of molten stone.

"Rise! Rise!" she screamed, grabbing at the knob, and the ship obeyed. But there was a splintering crash as it ascended, like the sound of a great bough splitting off from the trunk of a tree. As she burst out with startling suddenness into sunlight again she saw that one of the wing-sails had been sheared away, and half the supporting mast with it. The little craft shuddered and dropped like a wounded bird.

It struck the surface of the sea with a deafening roar, and an explosion of steam and spray.

IT WAS DARK AND THERE WAS WATER, cold water soaking her to the skin. Her mother was somewhere in the darkness, but Ailia could not find her. "Mamma!" she wailed in terror, splashing helplessly about in the ship's flooded and lightless cabin. "Mamma, where are you . . . ?"

She reached out—and woke, choking and spluttering. It was night no longer: bright light blazed in the ship's windows. *I remember—the flying ship. The firedrakes, the volcanoes* . . . She was lying on the cabin's padded wall: the ship was wallowing on its side and water was gurgling through a gaping hole in the bow. She sat upright, feeling dazed, waded toward the doorway—the door had been torn off its hinges by the impact—and scrambled out onto the hull.

Green ocean lay all around her. There was a little islet not far away, a low green hill in the sea with clumps of plumose vegetation at its summit. It looked more inviting than the only other land within sight, the barren isle with its fuming fire mountains. She slipped off her shoes and tied them about her neck by their laces. Then she jumped into the water. It was pleasantly warm, like the sea of southern Arainia, and its surface was calm. Some fifteen minutes of steady swimming brought her to the shore of the island. Its beach was not sandy like an atoll's, she saw, but made of some hard gray stone like basalt. Once safely ashore she stood and turned around to look for the wreck.

It was gone. No trace of the little dragon-headed ship remained, save for a few fragments of gilded wood bobbing on the waves, and a foamy swirl to show where it had gone down. Ailia's legs gave way and she collapsed upon the shore. She lay huddled in her sodden gown as the delayed shock at last set in, and the desperation of her present situation was driven home to her. She was marooned without any hope of escape or rescue.

At length she made herself stand again, put her damp shoes on, and began to walk about the island, for lack of anything better to do. It was truly small: within a few minutes she had made a complete circuit of it. It was shaped something like a teardrop, thinner at one end than the other, and was higher in the center than at the sides, with a grassy ridge running along its length. There were fruit-bearing plants growing on it, with dark purple or red berries, but as she reached out to pick them it occurred to her in a flash of alarm that they might be poisonous. And then she realized that there was no pool or stream or spring of fresh water. Ailia swallowed, trying to remember just how long it was that people could go without water before dying of thirst. The heat of two suns beat down on the island: already her mouth and throat were parched. She didn't dare call out through the Ether, for fear Mandrake and his dragons would hear and determine where she was. Waves lapped at the island with a soft watery sound, making her feel even worse.

She walked down to the shore. The gray rock continued under the water for about a stone's throw, then shelved away sharply. Ailia ventured out into the shallows and peered down into the depths, getting the impression of a steep drop. There was no other land anywhere on the horizon: she wasn't even certain in which direction the large continent lay.

It occurred to her that this tiny islet offered few hiding places should the firedrakes come back to search for her, as they most likely would. Might a glaumerie work, or would the use of magic only alert other, sorcerous beings to her presence? She looked down at the star sapphire ring on her right hand. It was an "inspirited gem," a conduit to the power of the Ether. If she drew on that power, Auron had said, she could summon pure quintessence onto this plane in the form of a fiery bolt. But could she repulse an attack by several firedrakes at once? "Call yourself a Nemerei!" she mocked herself bitterly. Why had she not listened to her guardians? Mandrake obviously had no intention of parleying with her. He had only been trying to lure her into a trap. And like a fool she had played into his hands.

Hunger gnawed at her. Her last meal in Temendri Alfaran seemed a distant memory, and all her stores of food had gone down with the ship. She chewed timidly on a plant leaf, but found it bitter, then in desperation she tried a fruit. Just a nibble, she decided. Not enough to be poisoned. The taste was very sweet, like a wild berry. "It doesn't *taste* poisonous," she murmured, knowing that she was growing tired and losing her judgment. But the sweet wild taste was seductive, the cool fruit flesh satisfying hunger and thirst together. "After all, it's no worse than starving to death," she reasoned aloud. The juice was like balm to her dry throat. She plucked and ate until she was sated. As the double shadows around her lengthened and she felt no warning pangs, she was certain that she was safe.

The knowledge that the island supplied food and, in a manner of speaking, drink, calmed her considerably. With the worst of her physical sufferings abated she could now take stock of her situation in a more levelheaded fashion. But as she stood pondering there came a curious gurgling sound, and a steaming geyser burst up through the bushes at the rounded end of the islet, showering warm spray upon the leaves before subsiding once more.

So it *was* a volcano island, after all. She hoped it wasn't signaling its intention to erupt.

Even as she thought this there was a sudden disturbance of the surface about a bowshot from the islet's opposite end, a patch of frothy unrest in contrast with the tranquil swell elsewhere. Perhaps some volcanic vent lay there, its submarine exhalations breaking the rhythm of the waves? As she watched the disturbance became a bubbling, churning upsurge with fountains of foam at the center. To her alarm there was at the same instant a sharp jolt beneath her feet, followed by a long tremor. She lost her balance and tumbled to her knees. *Was* it an eruption? Or—

A fantastic thought came to her. Ailia went stumbling and scrambling up to the top of the ridge and stared about her.

She could see now, extending from the narrow end of the islet, a long V-shaped furrow of foam like the wake left by a ship, only larger. There could be no doubt about it. The "island" was moving. Two gigantic fins, stone gray and covered in clinging shellfish, rose and fell to either side, and beyond the tapered end beat the flukes of a colossal tail. There was a deep breathing sound, and another geyserlike spout from the rounded end: she could see, now, that it was not one jet but two, set close together, and she could see also the two moist dark orifices from which they issued.

This was no island: she was perched, improbably, upon the carapace of a gigantic sea creature and it was bearing her, along with the parasitic plants upon its back, to some unknown destination.

YEHOSI THE STEWARD WAS UNEASY as he paced about the council chamber. Yanuvan had always been a dangerous place, full of plots and intrigues, but now a greater shadow of fear lay upon it, a sense of lurking evil. It had all begun with the coming of the mysterious Morlyn—Mandrake, as he preferred to be called—and his goblin-men. Courtiers huddled in corners whispering fearfully, while the slaves told frightful tales about the castle's new inhabitants, rumors that found their way into the court itself. The goblins—those strange, half-human beings—were the offspring of evil genii, or else they were themselves genii incarnate. They observed vile rituals, it was said, in the privacy of their quarters. It was they who had replaced all the palace guard dogs with *barguests*: terrifying creatures from their own world that were twice the size of a Zimbouran hound, red-eyed and black as pitch. There were tales, too, of winged monsters that flew through the skies at night, breathing fire. But Mandrake was feared most of all, for the king's familiar could see into the minds of men, and cast spells on them, and summon evil spirits with whom he could be heard talking, late into the night, in his tower room.

Only yesterday night a terrifying shape, a great red beast with horns on its head and wings like a giant bat's, had been seen flying above the castle—flapping about the towers, and then perching like some huge and malevolent gargoyle on the very roof of the throne hall. Some said it was an ill omen; others declared the creature was none other than Mandrake himself, magically transformed. Who could say what was true and what was invention anymore?

"Well, Yehosi, where is everyone?"

Yehosi started and turned at the voice. Mandrake stood there behind him, having appeared it seemed out of nowhere: a common trick of his. Yanuvan was full of secret passages, long ago designed for the safety of royal families in case of war or uprising, but Yehosi knew where all the hidden entrances were, and Mandrake it seemed never used them. Either the dark figure was noiseless as a shadow when he walked the halls, or he had the power to become invisible at will.

"I understood there was to be a council meeting here," the prince said.

Yehosi nodded. "Our work is not done yet: the war with the daughter of the Queen of Night did not end with the battle in the desert. The king will not be satisfied until Ailia is cast down from her throne in the heavens. It is she, he says, who has brought ruin on Zimboura—the influence of her evil star has caused the drought and desolation of the land, the hunger of our people."

"Indeed?" Mandrake raised an eyebrow. "Was it not Khalazar who ordered his people to make farms out on the barrens, and have many more children than they could feed?"

"Oh, hush! Do not say such things, wizard though you be. Remember, the Tryna Lia herself appeared before our court and threatened us. It's said that she was taller than a man, with eyes of fire, and she swore to destroy us all."

Mandrake frowned. "Did she really say that?"

"Your humble servant," said Yehosi bowing, "was hiding underneath a table at that point, but I distinctly heard her speak of death and destruction coming to our people. I did not hear all—the courtiers were terrified, you understand, shouting and running about—but that I did hear."

"Power did not take long to corrupt her."

"It never does, Highness," said Yehosi.

Mandrake looked with interest at the head eunuch. The secret of success in a Zimbouran court, it appeared, was to make oneself useful, but only in a self-effacing way. One must never set one's sights on the throne itself, nor appear to be seeking power or influence. In Zimboura women and eunuchs were forbidden to take any kind of office, so Yehosi, though his services were indispensable, could never be viewed by his master as a threat. Perhaps he felt his sacrifice was worth the virtual guarantee of safety?

The door opened and both men glanced up, but it was only the boy Jari. The little prince sauntered into the chamber, sucking on a sweetmeat and eyeing them both in a way that made Yehosi blanch.

"Fat one!" he laughed, pointing at the eunuch. "Jump up and down, fat one! You have to do as I say! I'm the son of immortal Khalazar. Now jump!"

Quaking, Yehosi obliged, though the exertion made sweat pour in rivulets down his plump face.

"Don't stop, or I'll have you executed," the boy taunted, dancing about the hopping eunuch. "Old fat-belly! I'm the prince, I could have you hanged if I wanted to. And you"—pointing at Mandrake—"you have to do as I tell you, too."

"Be quiet, you abominable child," said Mandrake.

Yehosi tripped and fell sprawling on the carpet. The boy swallowed his sweet in his surprise, then stuck his lower lip out truculently. "I'm the crown prince. You can't talk to *me* like that!"

"Crown prince? How can you be heir to the throne if your father's immortal?" asked Mandrake.

Jari glared, but there was uncertainty in his stance. "I could have you executed for talking to me like that."

"Hardly. I am a ghost. You can't kill someone who's dead already, now can you?" Mandrake replied in an admonishing avuncular tone.

"You're no spirit!" Jari shouted in fury, clenching his fists. "General Gemala says you're just a man! He says you're a wicked wizard with evil powers, but you're only human all the same. He says you should be killed."

Mandrake's golden eyes grew cold. "Does he indeed."

"Do not be angry, Prince," Yehosi begged from the floor. "I am sure it is not true. The palace is full of false rumors these days."

"It is too true," insisted Jari. "I was there, I heard him say it. He didn't see me, but I heard."

Gemala, thought Mandrake. *But of course: it was he who sent the assassin to kill me. Gemala's followers are as loyal to him as he is to his king: that is why the man risked his life, why he lied about Roglug being the one who sent him. To protect his general, and also divide the enemy.*

"He'll kill you," Jari taunted. "Gemala will kill you! I heard him say so."

Mandrake glanced down at him. "The king will be here soon to hold council with his advisors. Now run along and play, or have someone flogged, or whatever you find amusing. We adults have business to discuss."

The boy wandered off sulkily, to Yehosi's relief. "He's a monster—a monster!" the eunuch wheezed as he struggled to his feet.

"No. He's a child." Mandrake never had been sentimental about children. The memory of being bullied and stoned by other boys in Zimbouran villages was still vivid in his mind, even after hundreds of years. Children were human, after all, cruelty merely one of many unpleasant traits they shared with their elders. And a child spoiled and indulged from infancy, bowed to and given his own way in everything—what else *could* he be like? "Khalazar is not a monster either," Mandrake added. "The problem with a tyrant, Yehosi, is not that he is an evil being but simply that he is a *human* being in the wrong place. It is his humanity, not his supposed inhumanity, that makes him what he is. If Khalazar were not the God-king, if he were living in the slums rather than the palace, he would simply be the irascible old gentleman whom no one can bear, who beats his wives and shouts at the street urchins for making too much noise when he is napping. It is the fact of his being here, on a throne where he has no business to be, that is monstrous. Princess Ailia is not a monster either: back when she believed herself to be no one in particular, she was rather a pleasant young girl. Power is the real enemy, Yehosi, and it began with what you like to call civilization: there were no tyrants in the days when humans lived in caves and foraged for their food."

He fell silent, for Khalazar was now approaching the council chamber. They heard the monarch long before they saw him: wild shouts and curses rang through the passages beyond. The doors were flung open and Khalazar, literally frothing at the mouth and bellowing incoherently, came in surrounded by terrified aides and councillors and attended by the regent of Ombar and Berengazi, the high priest of Valdur.

"Have you need of counsel, O King?" Mandrake asked. The angry potentate growled in his throat like an animal, but made no reply. It was Berengazi who spoke.

"It's said there were a few survivors of the witch-princess's army, and that they fled to the ruined city. The slaves have learned this and are making heroes of them. The Moharas say that one of the foreign fighters is their Zayim."

"I am not familiar with that title," the regent said. Berengazi explained, "The Zayim is the messiah of the Mohara legends, a man sent by the gods who will come and liberate them all from our rule—"

"They dare!" Khalazar burst out.

"And the other two who escaped are said to be angels in human guise, sent to serve the Zayim. They are fair-haired and pale, like the angels painted by western barbarians. Not only the Moharas, but some Zimbourans out in the farm country are turning to them and to the worship of their Morning Star goddess."

"I will not tolerate this!" the God-king raged. "I am the true and only god of Zimboura! I will not be supplanted by this goddess and her lying prophet! Gemala"—turning to the general—"why have you not captured these villains?"

"My men fear to enter the old city, Majesty," the general replied. "They say there is a curse on it, and no one who enters it comes out alive again. And it is true that the scouts we send there never return."

"They would do better to fear *me!*" snapped the king. "I will have their heads if they do not obey me. Tell them that!"

"Has this false prophet, this Zayim, a name like other men?" asked Mandrake abruptly.

Again the high priest answered, as Khalazar was too angry to reply. "Our spies say that the Zayim is called Jomar, and the two angels are Lorelyn and Damion."

"Those three!" exclaimed Mandrake. "So they came with the Arainian force. They have survived—and been left behind. Khalazar"—turning to God-king—"you do not realize what a boon has fallen into your grasp. Capture these three by all means, but do not harm them—yet. They are the close friends of the Tryna Lia herself!"

The God-king looked back at him blankly. The word "friend" conveyed nothing to him. Mandrake sighed. "They are her allies, her close companions—the one named Damion especially, or so I am told. I heard once of a she-wolf who was caught when hunters lay in wait for her with a special bait: her own mate, tethered to a tree. Find those dear to her, and you will have Ailia in your power."

"I will set a bounty for them," the king said. "I will tell all the citizenry a reward will go to the one who captures these three." He scowled. "I may have won a great victory against her forces, but I spend every day in torment knowing that the Daughter of Night still lives, and may march against me again."

"Unlikely, Majesty," said Mandrake. "The Tryna Lia will be reluctant to send again fighters who have already proven so hopeless in battle. And it is even less likely that she will fight you personally. So be comforted."

"I *must* fight her personally! I alone can slay the daughter of the Queen of Night: no mortal hand could accomplish such a task. Yet my godhood is but newly awakened. What if she should strike before my powers are strong enough? I cannot—*must* not be defeated by her. It is disgrace beyond imagining for any man to die by the hand of a woman. Such a man would be a laughingstock for generations to come."

"You are no mere man, O Voice of Valdur," said Berengazi with an obsequious bow.

"True, I am not, but neither is she a common woman."

"Do you doubt yourself, King?" asked Mandrake.

Khalazar straightened. "No; in my heart of hearts I know that I am king and god. But I had not reckoned with a struggle such as this. When gods war with one another, it is said, the very stars are shaken: now I know that saying is true."

Mandrake reflected that the loss of lives should have turned the Arainians against Ailia, the direct cause of the first war to trouble their world in centuries. But they were too blind in their devotion to her: he must seek to bring her down in other ways. He still had not learned where the Tryna Lia had gone; but her own allies did not know either. To have her friends as hostages could prove very useful. There was only one possible way to control a being as powerful as Ailia: capture weaker ones that she loved.

The regent of Ombar spoke in a low voice to Mandrake as they left the room together. "Even if the Tryna Lia does not come to Mera, it is well that we have a firm foothold in this world."

"Thanks to *my* efforts," Mandrake reminded him.

Naugra smiled. "Yours? Surely it was Valdur who told you to do these things. You thought only to set Khalazar in your place, confusing the enemy and sparing yourself from attack; and now you see what has happened: a Valei reign is established on Mera! You have heard that Marakor has signed a pact with Zimboura? And that their crown prince has wed the heir to Maurainia's throne? Soon all of this world will be ours, and our hosts shall gather here to mount their assault upon Arainia. Now *you* would not have thought of that, Prince, not alone: you never cared what became of that world."

"As a matter of fact, I did," replied Mandrake, heading for the stair that led to his tower room. "I have always opposed the lingering taint of Archonic interference wherever I found it, and Arainia was one of their chief worlds. But I am unconvinced that your Valdur was any better than his rivals."

"He sought to end their dominance of the worlds—"

"Merely to substitute his own particular brand of tyranny."

The regent's thin lip curled. "You understand nothing."

"You're very disrespectful," said Mandrake. "Have you no fear that I might pay you back for your insolence should I ever accept this throne you offer me?"

The curve of the withered lips widened. "But when you take the kingship of Ombar you will no longer be *yourself*, Prince. On that day Valdur will remove your spirit from your mortal frame, and replace it with his own."

I wouldn't count too much on that, my friend, Mandrake thought as he climbed the stairs to his private chamber. *And I will remember those words.*

But the conversation had left a disagreeable aftertaste.

He had scarcely entered the chamber when the air in one corner quivered and Roglug's ethereal form stood there. "Well?" asked Mandrake curtly.

"We have found Ailia."

Mandrake seated himself. "You don't say. Well, where is she?"

"At the bottom of the sea."

"What?"

"She tried to enter Nemorah in her star-ship—wishing to find and fight you, no doubt. But one of your wing-patrols pursued the craft, and it struck an island mountain and went down over the Eastern Ocean."

Mandrake let out a long breath. Ailia—lost in the Nemoran sea! *Could* it be true? "The last time I believed her drowned, she turned out to be very much alive," he pointed out dryly.

"But she has not been seen since. There have been no sorcerous manifestations, and no calls through the Ether for help," the goblin told him.

"Which proves nothing: she could be lying low somewhere. Tell the Loänei to conduct a search for her body. How many know of this?"

"Just the patrol riders and the drakes. And they don't know yet it was the Tryna Lia's ship: they just considered it an intruder, and brought it down. I recognized the description of the vessel she fled Temendri Alfaran in, but I did not tell them."

"Good. Then conduct the search yourself, and take with you one of the Loänan that are loyal to me. If you do find her remains, tell me. But I suspect that she lives, and I will continue to do so until it is proven otherwise."

But despite these words, he yearned to believe that it *could* end so easily for both of them.

*   *   *

AILIA WAS DREAMING: of emerald deeps and watery abysses, of great beds of kelplike plants towering to many times the height of the tallest tree, casting beneath them a green shade and sun-stipple like a terrestrial forest. Here was the haunt of the serpent, and the many-armed kraken; here too was her home, and the dwelling place of all her kind. She glided slowly and ponderously through the depths, beating giant fins, until a rumbling tremor brought her back to herself.

Ailia rubbed her eyes and sat up, to find that she was lying on the grassy slope of the island-beast, under the glare of the twinned suns.

What a strange dream that was. And what a mess you've gotten yourself into, Ailia scolded herself. *You and your absurd notions of being brave! You will probably end up perishing of heatstroke: a fine heroic end* that *would be!*

The giant sea creature was still swimming steadily. Her greatest fear was that it would decide to dive into the depths, bearing her down with it to a watery death. According to Bendulus's *Bestiary* aspidochelones had been known to do this to sailors who were unfortunate enough to set campfires on what they thought was an island. That might only be a fable, but Ailia was very glad she had not made any magical attempts to start a fire. The tortoiselike shell armor seemed as impervious as the rock it resembled, but one never knew . . .

Aside from the great flailing fins and whalelike tail, she saw very little of the beast; most of it remained below the surface, like an iceberg. Certainly it evinced not the slightest interest in the tiny human parasite now riding upon its back. She thought of the monsters she had seen in her dream-vision: the great sea serpents, the orcs like huge reptilian fish with their finned and streamlined bodies. No doubt the aspidochelone's armor was a natural defense from their attacks. She shuddered now to recall how she herself had swum, unprotected, through this very sea to reach the "island." There were creatures in the deeps below that could have eaten her in one bite.

None of these aquatic hunters came to menace her mount, fortunately. In the early morning, before the suns had set fire to the Eastern Sea, it crossed paths with a scolopendra, which Ailia in the gray light took at first for a trireme oaring through the waves. She was close to hailing it when it drew nearer and she saw the seg-

mented chitinous carapace and the long waving antennae, and recognized the gigantic crustacean of legend rowing along at the surface with its multiple legs, like an immense water beetle. She held
her breath, fearing it might engage the aspidochelone in a titanic
battle that would prove disastrous to her, but the two monsters only
swam past one another, indifferent as passing ships.

She sat down again and returned her gaze to the horizon, chin
in hands. Hours passed, and the day grew bright. Her eyes were so
dazzled by the play of sea and double sunlight to the east that she
did not at first take in what she saw.

Then she shot to her feet and ran to the shore of shell at the
sea's edge.

There was a long dark strip on the eastern horizon. Land! In desperation she flung herself on the mossy back of the aspidochelone
and pounded it with her fists, crying, "The land—go to the land!"
But of course it wouldn't, she knew—it was a creature of the deeps,
and would only strand itself in the shallows.

Yet after a while she was certain that the land was drawing
slowly nearer. Dare she try and swim for it? Who knew what monsters might lurk in the water between her and the shore? She could
see vegetation now, lush and green, and behind it some cloud-clad
mountains. The aspidochelone was definitely heading toward it.
The water level gradually dropped, exposing the beast's gray shell-
plated sides and its enormous scaly flippers. She could see the rest
of the huge head now, all covered in weeds and shellfish, like a
boulder exposed by low tide.

It will beach itself and die if it goes any closer, thought Ailia. What if she
had been influencing the huge animal? That curious vision of the
deeps—perhaps while she slept she had formed a mental link with
the primitive mind of the aspidochelone. She had been told her
powers were stronger than she knew: what if, in sharing its
thoughts of the deep, she had somehow passed on to it her own
desire for the land? In sudden dismay at the creature's plight, she
ran impulsively to the side of its shell, behind the fin, and leaped
into the clear green water. It had saved her life, albeit unintentionally: she must return the favor. As she swam landward the pale
sandy bottom grew more distinct. Soon she was splashing and
wading rather than swimming, and then with a gasp she fell her
length on the smooth sand of the shore.

There was a rushing sound behind her, and great waves swept up the beach, nearly sucking her out to sea again. Turning, she saw an awesome sight: the aspidochelone bulked behind her, stone-gray and colossal beyond belief, the "island" only a small patch of green on its back, like a saddle. In shape it resembled a monstrous whale, and yet it was reptilian, too: the shell armor and curving fore flippers reminded her of a sea turtle's. For a moment the giant eye, large as a temple window and green as the deeps from whence it had come, seemed to stare directly at her. Then the creature turned itself laboriously about and headed for the open ocean. Far out amid the waves she saw its mighty fluked tail lift briefly against the sky as the gigantic animal, together with the unlucky trees upon its back, plunged back into the depths and was gone.

Ailia was alone upon an alien shore.

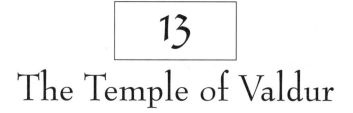

The Temple of Valdur

"WHAT IS ALL THAT COMMOTION?" asked Lorelyn, setting down the sword she had been sharpening and standing up.

The calm of evening had settled upon the village in the oasis, along with a rich wine-colored light; a few half-naked children still played in the square of earth before the chieftain's hut, but most had withdrawn to their homes. Women sat together in doorways, chattering as they strung beads or sewed torn garments, and the smallest children leaned against their sides or slept in their laps. Most of the men had gone out on patrol, and a few were starting to trickle back in small groups. Now Unguru and his scouts came into the village, dragging a young man with them and shattering the peace. "We found this Zim pig trying to approach the oasis," said Unguru, dumping the man unceremoniously on the ground. "Shall we kill him?"

"Was he alone?" asked Makitu, the Mohara chieftain, emerging from his hut.

"Yes—on horseback. We shot his mount out from under him."

"Waste of a good animal," gasped the young man, speaking in coarse, halting Elensi. "A pity—even though it wasn't mine."

"He surely wouldn't have come all by himself if he were trying to harm us," Lorelyn argued as Unguru stood over the prisoner, his fingers tightening around the hilt of his sword. "Why, he's not even armed."

"That is right," the Zimbouran said. "I am here with—with peaceful intent—"

"Spy," hissed Unguru, and raised the sword. "You came here to find us, and get the reward from your king!"

"No." Lorelyn stepped between the Zimbouran and the blade, looking steadily into the Mohara warrior's dark eyes. "He should be taken to Jomar. To the Zayim—remember? It's for him to say what shall be done. Somebody find Jomar and Damion."

Unguru's eyes smoldered as she had seen Jomar's do so many times before, and some of the other warriors began muttering among themselves. But a few also looked uneasy. This angel with her strange sky-colored eyes served the Zayim, whose authority came directly from the Morning Star. Feeling their mood, Unguru reluctantly lowered the sword and looked at Makitu, who nodded his turbaned head. "The prisoner shall be shown to Jomar first."

Once Jomar and Damion had arrived the Zimbouran defended himself against all charges of spying and assassination. "I came to join you," he said, over and over again. "See, I have no weapon. I am only a farmer, Kiran Jariss by name, not a servant of the king. I would gladly help his enemies, and there are many in the country-side who feel the same."

"Zimbourans join with the Mohara?" Unguru retorted. "Your kind hates us. You care only for your God-king." He spat in the sand.

"Care for him!" The other's eyes flashed. "I hate Khalazar! He has made our lives a misery, he and his clerics. They keep us poor and hungry by punishing us if we have fewer than three wives and if those wives do not all bear children. They do not care if the children have bread to eat or not. I only want a decent life for my family, and food on the table. Khalazar is a fraud, like all the other God-kings before him. Any enemy of his is a friend of ours. And the Elei people liberated Zimboura once before." He looked hopefully toward Damion, who stood close by.

"How can we believe this Zimbouran?" Jomar asked Damion. "Unguru's right. He might be a spy, sent to fool us and trap us."

"He risked his life to come here, didn't he?" argued Damion. "I can't believe anyone would do that unless he were truly desperate."

Jomar sniffed. "Or if he were a crazy zealot obeying his God-king."

"But those Valdur zealots in the city are the exception, aren't they? From what I have heard most Zimbourans are more interested in surviving than in serving Khalazar. They're a very practical people, really. This man doesn't seem insane or fanatical. And when sane people do mad things it's usually because they are pushed into them by circumstances outside their control." Something about the young man's angry denunciations, he thought, rang true.

Some Moharas put up considerable resistance to Damion's arguments, be he an angel or not: old hatreds died hard in this land. But eventually most saw the logic of including at least some Zimbourans in their plans. "We need spies," Damion pointed out. "And only Zimbourans would be able to move freely in the city. They could tell us what's happening there."

"Pah! They'll betray us as soon as they're offered money by their soldiers," said Unguru. "The Pale Ones are loyal only to their own kind—though they will never fight for anything unless they are forced."

Kiran Jariss looked up at that and said, with a sudden glint in his brown eyes, "We are fighters. We fight to live. We have done so ever since we dwelt on the steppes of the Southern Peninsula, where all is barren and cold. Our will to thrive caused us to leave that place at last, moving north to warmer climes. Nothing could stand before us. We conquered the old empire of Kaana, took the Kaans' lands and drove them across the sea to their island colonies, from which they have never returned. We are warriors, we Zimbourans, because we love life despite its harshness—else we never would have survived our long ages in the bitter South."

"Children of Valdur," Unguru spat.

"So you call us. But long ago," the other replied, "ages before the clerics of Valdur ever arose and demanded that we worship him, we revered the same gods as you Moharas. It was from you that we first learned of Nayah the sky-goddess, and Akkar her consort who dwells in the earth. Now their worship is banned in our country, but the Zimbouran people have not forgotten the old beliefs."

"Liar!" snarled the warrior, and swung toward Jomar. "Why do you not silence him?"

Jomar hesitated. He sympathized with Unguru, but his time away from Mera had dulled the sharp edge of his hatred and given him perspective. Certainly some Zimbourans had as much reason as the Moharas to hate the God-king under whose tyranny they lived. Better still, their disaffection might spread. To turn Khalazar's own people against him would be a great achievement.

"All right, Jariss," he agreed reluctantly. "We'll try it for a while— but if you betray us, Zimbouran, you'll pay a heavy price. I'll hunt you down myself—and that's a promise."

Jariss smiled broadly. "I will not fail you," he swore. "I do this for my family. I have two wives now, one of them my sister-in-law who was widowed in the battle. I had to take her in, and her children. I have four children of my own by my first wife. Now our farm is ruined by the battle and I have had to move my family to the city to live. I tell you, the people there have no hatred for the Moharas or the peoples of the west: it is Khalazar they murmur against, though they dare say nothing in public. They would gladly serve the son of Jemosa."

"Who's he?" grunted Jomar.

"You."

Jomar stared. "What are you saying?"

"You don't know who your parents were, do you, Jomar? But I think I do. General Jemosa was a great warrior and a well-born man of my race, much loved in the city, for he used his wealth and position to help the poor. Both Khalazar and King Zedekara grew to hate him for his popularity. They feared the people would want him for their ruler. But Zedekara was afraid to do anything against him, and Khalazar could not make any charge against him stick. Then the family of the general's first wife denounced him publicly. He had shamed them, they said. There was a slave in the household, a Mohara woman, whom Jemosa had been in love with ever since he was a boy. They had grown up together in his father's house. Jemosa did not see a slave when he looked at Nehari, but only a beautiful girl. She secretly returned his love, and he freed her of all her slave's duties and vowed to make her his wife in name. When Khalazar heard this, he knew he finally had his excuse to execute the general, and send Nehari and her child to the slave camps. I think you are that child, Jomar."

Jomar stared. "You say your Jemosa *loved* this woman? He used her—she was just a slave in his household. And you say he married other women." But he remembered the sorrow in his mother's face, the tears that would slip silently down her cheeks when she thought he was not watching. The weary, daily anguish of a slave? Or something more?

"He married only because his father had forced him to: they were the daughters of rich and influential men, and he felt nothing for any of them. He used a slave, you say? At the risk of arrest and execution? He *must* have loved her, and she him. It's the only explanation. Your father was a good man, Jomar, whatever you may think," said Jariss. "If you hate him, then you hate a part of yourself."

"I do," said Jomar shortly. "The Zimbouran part."

"That is a pity. For the city people would love you, too, if they knew that you were his son. Jemosa is remembered with increasing fondness as the times worsen."

"Tell us what is happening in the city now," said Damion, seeing that Jomar's face was working.

Kiran Jariss answered at length, and they listened with keen interest. Many Arainians had been taken prisoner by Gemala's troops. They were alive, but were being held in the dungeons of Yanuvan. Others were not so fortunate. Some Zimbouran conscripts who had tried to escape from the army were to be executed at the great temple of Valdur that very night. The youngest was a boy of fourteen who had been hidden by his mother from the recruiting officers, but who had been betrayed by a neighbor in exchange for money. The young farmer's voice shook with anger as he spoke. "The prisoners are being sent to the Temple to receive the formal condemnation of the high priest, and be executed in the paved forecourt that fronts it. Khalazar does not yet dare to kill human victims on the sacrificial altar, but we all know this must soon come to pass. He *must* be toppled from power."

"We have to save them!" exclaimed Lorelyn. They all stared at her, Jariss included.

"Save those prisoners? You're not serious. What could *we* do?" returned Jomar. "They're being held in the dungeons."

"They are now. But they'll have to be taken through the streets to get to the Temple, won't they? There are only half a dozen of them, he says. Why couldn't we snatch them away from their guards?"

Unguru looked incredulous. "Rescue *Zimbourans*! Madness!"

"No," said Damion. "These people are dying because of us, and the invasion of our army. Ailia would want us to save them if we could."

Jariss was watching them closely. "It would be a good thing," he said, "if you were to do this. It would get the citizens of Zimboura on your side. God-kings have been overthrown before, and it can happen again. People do not resist Khalazar now because he seems all-powerful and they have lost their courage. Save those prisoners and you will be loved for it, and they will remember that they too have the power to act."

Damion went to the ruin where Wakunga was meditating alone, as was his wont at day's end. The old man appeared to be deep in a trance, but at the sound of Damion's footfalls he looked up, then nodded as if at the confirmation of something he had long suspected. "Come," he said, his manner succinct as always. "Tell me."

Damion sat down in the alcove beside him and told him about the farmer and his news. The shaman was thoughtful. "All that you say is true. To go to the aid of the helpless is a noble thing, and will win you admiration. But I fear this wizard, this one you call Mandrake." He gazed up through the carved frame of the alcove at the darkening sky. "There was once a Mohara shaman—what you would call a Nemerei—who long ago became adept at shifting his shape. He took the form of a black leopard most often, for it was the beast he most admired, owing to its beauty and agility; and before long he came to scorn his own human body, with all its weaknesses and imperfections. Eventually he would take no shape other than the leopard's, and his disdain for the human form became disdain for all human beings. He saw himself as superior to the villagers, and as the years passed by he grew to hate them, and preyed upon them as a beast would—but with a cruelty and malice no beast ever showed. The people did not know what to make of this leopard that slew, but never consumed, his prey; this strange black leopard that hunted only by night, and was somehow too cunning to fall for any trap or ambush they could devise. They began to fear that he was an evil spirit, unleashed by some curse to make war on all men. But one young warrior of the tribe was wise as well as brave. He journeyed to this old city, where he knew a great treasure lay: a black stone, larger than a man, that fell from the sky."

"A shooting star?" said Damion.

"Yes. A great sorcerer of the Mohara saw it fall, long and long ago. His tribe feared to go near it, and when he did so he found that his powers waned the closer he came to the sky-stone. Then he knew it was a potent thing, a gift from the gods, and he had it buried deep in the earth and this city built over it. And that is why no magic can be done here, and no evil genie or wizard can come near."

"Cold iron," said Damion. "The stone is iron, and that overpowers all sorcery."

"Even so. I can still receive my visions, for they are sent me from the high gods of the stars, those you call the Elyra, who fear no iron. But to continue my tale: this warrior knew of the buried sky-stone, and he found where it lay and broke off a piece of it to forge into a weapon. With this he was able to force the leopard-shaman back into his own shape, and slay him."

There was a silence, broken only by the sound of a few raised voices in the village below. Another argument had broken out, it seemed. But Damion's mind was still bound up in the old man's tale. "What a terrible story," he said. "Is it true?"

"Yes, it is true. Every shaman is told that tale when he is young, to caution him." Wakunga's face was solemn. "That is the danger in becoming an animal: the spirit follows the body, and in the end one combines in oneself the worst of both man and beast. This Mandrake, you say, is often in a dragon's shape: that is bad, very bad indeed."

"Why? Dragons are not beasts, nor are they evil."

"That is so: I have often heard it said that they are both wise and good. But dragons are also accustomed to their large and strong bodies, and think nothing of them. For a man to be suddenly gifted, through magic, with such a mighty form is perilous: like the shaman, he will come to despise his humanity and believe he has become a superior being. A dragon does not see *itself* as large, any more than you see yourself as a giant—although you are, in comparison to lesser creatures. But a man who takes a dragon's form glories in its unaccustomed size and power. Therein lies the difference. I think Mandrake desires not the wisdom of the dragon, but only its greater strength and size: he wishes not to be an enlightened being, but only a bigger and better animal. That is the false path, and others have trod it before him to their ruin."

"How do you know these things?" Damion asked, fascinated.

"My totem tells me, and he is never wrong."

"Your what?"

"My spirit-helper. Those who enter the Great Dreaming usually encounter their totem there: a spirit who will lead them through their life's quest. Mine comes to me in the shape of a desert fox. I have met him many times in my visions, and he has shared much wisdom with me over the years. I have learned to listen well to what he has to say. He is a wise old fox." The shaman smiled. "If you would be a true Nemerei you must re-enter the Dreaming, and have speech with your totem."

Damion looked up and saw Jomar approaching. He could still hear distant voices raised in an uproar. "What is it, Jo? What's happened?"

"That girl is a menace," observed Jomar, coming up to them. But there was an odd note to his voice, as though annoyance struggled with amusement. "We were discussing how to free the prisoners. Lorelyn insisted on putting her word in, as usual, and some of the men started taunting her, saying no woman could ever be a warrior. She said she'd prove it by taking them on—all of them, at once. Three accepted the challenge."

"And—?"

"Two are still unconscious. The other can't walk on his right foot." Jomar flung up his hands. "Three men down, and the raid's tonight!"

"If she can do that, she's worth three men. Let her come with us, Jomar."

"I just hate the thought of a woman in battle." Jomar flung himself down beside Damion, resting his arms on his knees.

"So do I. It goes against all I have ever been taught. I can't bear the thought of any woman being hurt. But wherever did we men get the idea that we can bear pain, and women can't? Women give birth, after all, and that must be more painful than we can imagine. Yet they seem to come through it all right. They're not made out of spun glass, you know."

Jomar nodded reluctantly. "In the camp, it was often the women who endured the most suffering, and lived longest."

"So have you come up with a plan?"

Jomar looked glum. "Of a sort. We're talking it over now."

Damion went with him to the village's central space, where the Mohara warriors were deep in discussion. Lorelyn was there too, kneeling apart and praying in silent penance. The men, Damion noticed, now kept a respectful distance from her. He had a feeling that there would be no more trouble from that quarter: it was in their own best interests, now, to acknowledge her as an angel. They would rather admit to being beaten by a spirit than by a woman.

After some heated debate the warriors had rejected several possible plans of action. The only plan not to be shot down was also the most outrageous: it was, simply, to send a number of fighters into the city with Kiran Jariss, disguised as his wives. They could throw off their disguises as the prisoners were led past, fell the guards, and free the captives. With the guards out of the way no one would stop them from fleeing the city: certainly the Zimbouran citizens would not intervene, if anger at the proposed executions were running as high as Jariss claimed.

Unguru objected to this. "I will not slink about disguised in woman's clothing! It would dishonor me."

"I agree," said Lorelyn, who was also disappointed in the plan. "I won't do it either."

Jomar stared at her in exasperation. "But you *are* a woman!"

"I am no coward to conceal my face from my foe," snapped Unguru. "That is not the warrior's way."

"All right," said Jomar throwing up his hands. "Please yourselves. Gallop up to the Zimbourans on your desert stallions giving heroic war cries. You'll be stuck full of arrows, but at least you'll have died honorably."

The old shaman, on learning of the plan, raised no objections. He merely presented them all with some little bone charms and scraps of hide. "These are sacred gifts, Mohara luck charms," the tribal chief explained to Damion and Lorelyn as they looked in puzzlement at the bits of skin they were given. Some were rodent or lizard pelts, others were taken from larger animals. "The spirit of an animal lingers with its bones and pelt, or so we believe, and will enter into anyone who possesses them. A man who wears a lion's skin next to his own will become strong and fearless, and one who wears a gazelle's hide will become fleet of foot. The asp strikes with the speed of lightning; and the lizard always escapes his foe, for he leaves his tail in his enemy's grasp and runs free."

Jomar held up one tiny pelt by its tail, looking at it with distaste. "The skin of a jumping mouse," the shaman said. "These mice are very difficult to catch, so they are a potent luck charm."

"I don't think I want *this* one's luck," remarked Jomar, putting the pelt down again.

Unguru glared. "You speak like a Zimbouran, mocking our ways."

"He is the Zayim." The shaman spoke in his quiet voice, stepping forward.

His look of serene trust only made Jomar feel irritable. "You don't really believe that, do you? That I'm fated to do this?" he growled when Unguru and the others had moved off.

Wakunga smiled. "I do not say you are predestined to lead, Jomar. Perhaps this tale of the Zayim is but a dream of our people, as you have said. What of it? You have the power to make that dream become reality."

"All right, then! Now let's get going, or all the luck in the world won't help those prisoners."

"One more thing," Wakunga said, holding out a bundle of leopard hide.

"What is it now? I'm not supposed to wear that, too, am I?"

"Not this—no." The old shaman unfolded the hide from around the object it had concealed. Damion and Lorelyn leaned close, and gasped as one.

It was a sword: a plain unadorned scimitar of gray metal. In its very simplicity there was a harsh beauty. "This is the Star Sword," Wakunga told them. "Forged from the star that fell into the desert. Its power will turn back any sorcery: even a genie cannot stand before it, and it has already been the bane of one evil shaman. I give it to you, Zayim, to use against the dragon wizard and his sorcerers. It is the only weapon that can prevail against them."

"It's iron!" exclaimed Lorelyn. "Pure iron. He's right, Jo: no magic can touch you when you wield that blade!"

Jomar silently took the scimitar and held it up. A weapon to banish magic! For the first time his heart swelled with a fierce hope.

JARISS LED THE RAIDING PARTY to an abandoned farm not far from the city walls. He kept there a decrepit wagon and a mismatched pair of dray horses, one gray and one chestnut. Both looked equally dispirited. Dismounting, the warriors left their own horses tethered in the farmyard and climbed into the wagon.

"Here are some clothes," he told them. "Not much, but they are the best I can find." There were some loose shapeless robes of what looked like sacking, some thin scarves and a number of voluminous shawls in neutral colors: brown, gray, and black. From their tattered state they looked to have been gleaned from rubbish heaps, but had in fact been left by fleeing owners.

"What dreary clothes," commented Lorelyn, trying on a shawl. "I can't say I think much of Zimbouran fashion!"

"They are not meant to be attractive," Jariss explained. "In Zimboura it is considered vulgar for a woman to draw attention to herself in public. In fact, Khalazar has decreed that no woman must ever again be seen on a public street—on pain of death. The highborn ladies get around this by having themselves transported in curtained litters, but the poorer women have to improvise. The scarves are to put over your faces: they are fine enough to see through, but not enough to show your features clearly. The shawls are to be wrapped around your heads, and you must tuck your hands inside them. So long as you obey the letter of the law, and no part of you is actually *seen* by anyone, you may go wherever you will."

"Well, it makes for a good disguise anyway," remarked Lorelyn as she disappeared under the shawl.

"And remember that you are wives: you must walk respectfully behind me, one after the other. The first wife leads, followed by the second and third wives and so on, with concubines coming last. Don't clump together: you must walk in a neat line, so that passersby can count how many wives I have. It is the custom. And don't ever get in front of me or you will be charged with unseemly conduct. Once we are mingling with the crowds at the temple you can move apart without being noticed."

They drove into the city by the West Gate, moving on into dreary neighborhoods that seemed not so much inhabited as haunted, by shades that peered surreptitiously from broken windows or cowered back in alleyways—the living ghosts that were the poor.

"I thought we would take the scenic route," said Jariss.

Damion and Lorelyn had never seen such poverty, not even in the meanest alleys of Raimar or Jardjana. They passed through a reeking meat market, whose pens were crammed to capacity with live poultry, pigs, goats, and—to Damion and Lorelyn's distress—rats and reptiles, and even insects of various kinds. To the vast and voracious Zimbouran population anything remotely edible was food. But after a time they noticed that the houses had become larger and more affluent in appearance. People thronged the inner courtyard of one house whose gate was briefly opened as they passed by. At the center of the gathering stood a little girl in a red-and-gold robe, her slight frame heavily loaded with flower garlands and jewelry.

"What's all that about?" Damion asked their guide.

"It's a wedding."

"Wedding! Why, she can't be more than twelve!"

"It's Zimbouran law to marry young. More children that way."

Lorelyn looked at the crowded streets. "Why would they want *more* children? They've too many people as it is."

"It's the mandate of Khalazar—we must fill all the earth, and conquer its other peoples. More people means more soldiers. A Zimbouran man may now have as many wives—and children—as he pleases."

"But how does he feed them all?"

"He can't, of course. Many families end up destitute, and the children starve. Most girl children are killed, though, before they get a chance to starve. Girls aren't valued as much as boys here, and their dowries can beggar a family. That little girl-bride is very lucky to be alive."

"Why not get rid of the dowries?" asked Lorelyn. "If every man *must* marry by law, then he hardly needs a dowry to attract him!"

"Dowries are traditional. As for killing girl babies," said Jariss bleakly, "when I think of my own daughter and the life she will probably have, I wonder sometimes if she would have been better off dead."

"Kiran, you make me feel like an absolute pig," said Lorelyn quietly. "Your people have suffered, too—far more than the Arainians could ever know."

They passed the huge arena, where statues atop towering pedestals depicted gladiators battling bulls and lions. The gates were closed, but from within the circular walls came the noises of the crowd. Jomar stiffened, remembering horrors, and Lorelyn put a hand on his shawled shoulder. He said nothing.

"You can smell the blood from here," said Damion softly.

Kiran Jariss raised his head as they turned down another lane. "No, that is the temple—we are near it now. The daily animal sacrifices make every temple of Valdur stink like an abattoir."

Soon they could see the great building—or what was left of it. The high temple was half in ruins, heavily damaged by both the Elei forces and the liberated Zimbouran peasants centuries ago. There were slaves of many races at work upon the ruined portion: Shurkas, Moharas, Kaans, and a tribe Lorelyn and Damion had never seen before, pale-skinned and very muscular with sloping foreheads, heavy jaws, and pronounced brow ridges. Even their women had well-muscled arms and shoulders. Jariss called them the *Dogoda*: they were a very ancient race from the barren regions of the far south, he said, their numbers now greatly dwindled. They made popular slaves because of their superior strength and their capacity to endure all manner of hardship.

Within the broken mud-brick walls there stood an idol, lit by the flickering sacrificial fires beneath: a stone colossus that dwarfed the human figures milling below. It had wings like an angel's, spreading to either side: the feathers at their outer edges curved and undulated like flames. Royal robes flowed about the gargantuan figure, and robes and wings were plated with gold.

Atop the head was a kingly crown, with more gold leaf adorning it and a rime of glittering gems. But the face of the statue was gone, its features blackened and blasted away as if by a great fire.

Damion stared up. "You remember Ailia's story about the old Holy War, and the idol of Valdur?" he whispered to Lorelyn. "This must be the very same statue! Look, you can see there's a little depression carved into the front of its crown. The Star Stone must have been set there."

"Some say the Stone destroyed the idol's face with its magic power, others that the city people themselves defaced the statue after the Holy War. Khalazar intends to have the face repaired, but with his own features, of course," said Jariss.

"Of all the nerve!" burst out Lorelyn. "How dare he think he's a god, the nasty, conceited, stupid little man—"

"Will you all *shut up*," hissed an exasperated Jomar. "They'll hear you. We're almost at the door."

Jariss stopped the wagon and tethered the horses to a ring in the stone wall. "Leave the spears and any other weapons you can't carry in with you, and cover them up with these bits of sacking," he instructed. He led them into the thronging mob at the main entrance, then quietly slipped away again. "No one will notice you're unaccompanied now," he whispered. "I'll wait for you in the wagon, so we can make a quick getaway."

They filed into the vast inner space within the broken pillars and drew near to the colossus. There was a low square door between its great stone feet: the entrance to the inner sanctum. Here the holy sacrifices were made, and only priests could pass within: it was a dark, fearsome place with, it was said, an altar and a well-like shaft into which the carcasses of the sacrificial animals were cast after they were slain—for no mortal must ever eat of their sanctified flesh. Damion stared at the dark door, seized with horror and another emotion that was strange to him, neither fear nor fascination but some blend of both. With an effort he tore his eyes away.

The intruders knew that in their female garb they dared not approach within a bowshot of that sacred door, or they would be beaten for their impertinence. But they had the advantage of invisibility. No man here would deign to notice their somber swathed forms waiting quietly in the shadows, so they would not call unwanted attention to themselves. They moved along the walls and stationed themselves behind pillars, moving slowly and silently.

As they watched, the high priest emerged from the sanctum. Berengazi had been sacrificing beasts: his hands glistened red in the torchlight as he held them aloft, gloved with blood. "Bring the prisoners!" he bellowed, as more priests appeared and stood at his side.

Damion and the others quickly separated and dispersed themselves throughout the crowd. Drums beat, approaching: the procession was drawing near. The six prisoners from the farmlands were flanked by twice as many soldiers. Half were quite old men, others mere youths. In the crowd women sobbed and men cursed; the soldiers gripped their weapons.

"How can you do this? They are your own people!" one man in the crowd called out, anguish overcoming his fear. "The invaders you took prisoner have not been slain!"

"Not *yet*. And those who die tonight have defied their own God-king," returned the captain harshly. "Indeed they are more guilty than the enemy, for it was their sacred *duty* to serve Khalazar."

Jomar watched, hardly able to contain his anger. *"Execution" in the temple—bah! It's the return of human sacrifices, and the people know it. Today they use prisoners; tomorrow they'll not bother with such excuses. It will be innocent victims—women, children . . .* He elbowed Damion and Lorelyn in the ribs, and the three of them began to move slowly forward.

Damion's mouth was dry and his heart pounding. He regretted, now, his decision not to go to Melnemeron: there were plenty of good fighting men here; it was a sorcerer who was needed most. Ailia had been right after all.

The black-robed high priest saw them approaching and scowled. "Now," whispered Jomar. The rebels all moved to surround the prisoners. Berengazi glared at the cloaked forms in righteous indignation. "You women—get back! I told you there would be no appeals for clemency."

"But Your Reverence," said Jomar in a falsetto whine, sidling up to the high priest.

"No! How dare you address me, woman!" thundered the cleric. "Leave the temple! Where is your husband? If he cannot better control you he must go, too. Leave the holy place at once." He turned his back, gesturing to the other clerics.

"I will—and you can come with me!" roared Jomar in his own voice. Flinging off shawl and cloak, he drew his sword in a blur of iron and pinioned the astounded Berengazi from behind, holding the blade to his throat. "You're coming with us now, Reverend, and the prisoners, too. Back," he added to the soldiers, "get back, or your high priest dies!"

The crowd surged back in confusion, and the soldiers after a moment's stupefaction drew their weapons. But they were too late: already Damion, Lorelyn, Unguru, and the others had thrown off their concealing garments and leaped forward, swords flashing in their hands. The captain fell first, then the soldiers one by one dropped their swords and fell to the floor, clutching deadly wounds.

Damion and Lorelyn hacked away the ropes that bound the captives together. "You can still be free!" Lorelyn shouted. "Turn away from Khalazar!" The people milled and murmured, like frightened herd animals. The hammers of the slaves were stilled.

"All right—run!" yelled Jomar, and they fled back down the temple aisle, dragging the high priest with them.

"Now, if only Kiran is there with the wagon—" panted Lorelyn.

They scanned the street in anxiety, but saw no sign of the wagon or its driver. Jariss had gone.

"I told you," Jomar shouted wildly over the struggling priest's head. "I *told* you he couldn't be trusted! He's betrayed us all!"

They tore down the steps, urging the dazed prisoners along. "Get back!" Jomar shouted at the pursuing priests, his sword at Berengazi's throat. "Back, or your master dies!" *It'll be just my luck if one of them wants his job*, he thought sourly. But the clerics halted in dismay.

"Jo—there he is!" cried Lorelyn pointing.

Jariss was driving toward them at top speed, whipping his foaming horses, a small company of mounted watchmen in hot pursuit. He drew up so sharply that the lead rider's horse collided with the rear of the wagon and fell to its knees. At once Unguru sprang at the rider, hauled him out of the saddle, and mounted. The horse, still neighing in fear, struggled to its feet again and Unguru gave a fierce yell of exultation, drawing his sword. The watchmen saw at

once that their knives and truncheons were no match for the warriors and pulled back in alarm.

"Everyone into the wagon!" Damion shouted, shoving the bewildered captives toward it. "Quickly! They'll have more soldiers
here in an instant."

They all piled into the wagon, Jomar still gripping the high
priest. "Where were *you*?" he demanded, looking over his shoulder
at Jariss.

"Had an argument with some of the Watch," Jariss panted. "And
they tried to search the wagon. If they'd found the weapons I
would have been arrested. I took off, and I've been driving around
and around in circles ever since, hoping you'd come out before
they managed to catch me—" He shook the reins with a cry of,
"Hah-hahh!" and plied the whip with vigor.

The horses galloped forward madly. Unguru rode alongside, his
eyes flashing with savage joy as he brandished his sword and
howled. One watchman had seized hold of the left horse's harness
and leaped onto its back. Jariss lashed him with the whip, but the
blows fell on his armor and helmet and he clung on. He had his
dagger out now, and seemed to be trying to cut the traces. Again
and again the desperate farmer struck him with the whip.

Unguru saw. Urging his horse forward until it was neck-and-
neck with the cart-horse, he swung at the watchman with his
sword. The man ducked and jabbed at the horse's dappled flanks
with his knife. The big animal screamed and reared, bringing the
wagon to a halt.

Unguru vaulted from his own mount's saddle. Then he drew his
sword and the man fell, his arm slashed open from shoulder to
elbow.

"*Get in the wagon!*" Jomar bawled at Unguru. The Mohara warrior
looked around for his stolen horse, but it had fled the scene in terror. He raced for the wagon and sprang over the side even as it
lurched forward again.

The watchman rolled, arms raised, as his pursuing colleagues
trampled him beneath their own horses' hooves.

Berengazi had taken advantage of the momentary distraction to
struggle out of Jomar's grasp. Damion and Lorelyn tackled him together, pulled him down, and sat on him.

"Faster—faster!" yelled Jomar.

"They're going as fast as they can," Jariss shouted back. "The gray's hurt."

They tore on through the marketplace, scattering bewildered vendors together with their stalls. Everywhere were piles of vegetables, flapping fowl, and startled faces. Pieces of rotting wood flew off the wagon's sides as they thundered on through the main streets. The horses were foaming at their mouths.

Lorelyn flung the last of her concealing rags off and fitted an arrow to her bow, trying vainly to nock it as the disintegrating wagon careened from side to side. Some of the pursuers, seeing an archer aiming at them, began to drop behind. But there were soldiers at the city gate ahead, and these had spears and arrows.

Lorelyn fired, missed, and turned to Jomar. "Now what?" she yelled.

He hauled Berengazi up into a kneeling position and held the man in front of him with his sword at his throat. "Everyone in the back lie down! They won't risk killing their high priest." *I hope.* "Keep driving, farmer. Don't stop now!"

Jariss, ashen-faced, obeyed. As the armed men, seeing that this speeding wagon had no intention of stopping, leveled their spears and bows, Jomar thrust Berengazi in front of him as a living shield. Their eyes bulged as they recognized him and their weapons wavered.

"Tell them to let us pass," hissed Jomar into Berengazi's ear. "Tell them or I'll run you through right now."

"Then they will kill you," gasped the priest.

"Probably. But you won't get to see it." Jomar pressed the point of his sword into the man's plump side and he squealed like a terrified pig.

"Let us pass! Let us pass!" he implored the soldiers.

In Zimboura all fighting men were conditioned to obedience. The soldiers at the gate stepped back immediately.

"On—on!" Jomar yelled.

An arrow struck the wagon's side as it rumbled through the gate, but the soldiers dared not follow. To cause the high priest's death would surely mean their own.

"We've done it," Lorelyn whooped, throwing down her bow. "Oh, we've done it!" Jomar shook his head in disbelief.

They drove on in a cloud of dust, toward their waiting mounts.

The Jungle and the City

AILIA SPENT THE NIGHT in the broad boughs of a giant banyanlike tree. She had been forced to leave the beach for the jungle, afraid that the enemy might catch sight of her on its wide white expanse of sand: she had glimpsed firedrakes in the distance, flying high through the clouds, and realized that the dense tree canopy would give her better shelter. Once beneath its green concealment she breathed more easily. But still she dared not summon help through the Ether.

It was not comfortable in the tree, but she felt far safer there than on the ground. A Nemerei in sleep is as vulnerable as any other being, and this alien jungle seemed a hostile place. Sorcery might reveal the living aura of one of its denizens, but she would not be able to tell whether the creature it belonged to was harmful in any way. She dozed fitfully, huddled in a narrow niche between two branches, waking several times before the dawn lightened the sky. Each waking moment was filled with fear.

Never again would she think of Night and Day as two equal but opposite things, like the two sides of a coin. She knew now that what she had called "Day" was merely a phenomenon peculiar to planets with atmospheres: a sun's light diffused through an envelope of air. Beyond sun and atmosphere lay the Great Night with its unfading stars and its fathomless dark, an abyss deep and vast beyond imagining. Nor was this the tranquil and harmonious forest of Arainia. Here continuous war was waged, as the creatures slew and devoured one another down to the minutest insect; here even the trees and vines fought each other for the light, entwining and strangling each other with limb and tendril as they thrust up toward the sky, shutting out the suns from those below: and the mold and fungoid growths of the jungle's dank floor fed on the resulting rot. She listened as the shadowed groves filled with the roars, screeches, bellows, and growls of their night-dwelling denizens, and she shuddered. It was the howl of Chaos itself she heard through these primeval voices: brutish, mindless, pitiless. She envisioned a time before her own race began, when the original world was home only to beasts: a world without philosophy, without religion or science, without consciousness; a world whose only law was the grim and savage struggle for life. She huddled in her tree, trying hard not to imagine the beasts that were making those sounds.

At long last the sunrise came. It was spectacular, unlike any she had ever yet seen. The rising limb of the yellow sun climbing above the banks of jungle mist turned them and the whole of the eastern sky to lambent gold, and then as it climbed she saw the second sun rise behind it, and its own fierce, blue light blended with that of the first to tint the whole sky jade-green. A whole chorus of cries, low, shrill, harsh, sonorous, greeted that double sunrise. What had been a tenebrous gloom slowly became a jungle, shaping itself out of the shadows: gaunt threatening forms turned into trees with mossy writhing limbs while the darkness drained away from the understory beneath.

She began to make her way carefully down the trunk, clutching at the vines that wound about it. As she passed the lower limbs of the tree something flew past her head, uttering piercing cries. At first she thought it was a bat, then a bird. It swooped down upon her again, then perched on a branch above her and scolded. It was a strange creature, more reptile than bird: it had a beak and a fleshy crest rather like a cockerel's, but its wings were naked and leathery and it had a long, scaly tail. Of course—it was a cockatrice. Bendulus had written about these creatures in his bestiary.

The cockatrice screeched and darted down at her again.

"Shoo—shoo!" she cried, ducking and waving her free hand. "I don't want your eggs!" For she now saw the thick clump of twigs on the branch above. She tried to empathize with the creature, reaching out to its mind, but the dull reptile brain was slow to respond, and she was finally forced to hasten on down the vine to the tree's roots and break into a run.

When at last she had left the flapping fury behind she slowed to a walk. With the dense upper layers of foliage screening out much of the suns' light the jungle was a dim, dusky place. Nor did the leaf barrier above relieve the relentless heat. The air around her was stiflingly humid—she half-expected it to steam, like a boiling kettle. After an hour's walk she was bathed in perspiration, her breath coming in short gasps. Even the chiton seemed unbearably hot, clinging to her damp skin: she was forced to strip to her undergarment and carry the dress rolled under one arm. And still the humidity pressed down upon her. Very soon her situation would become desperate, she knew. She needed food, clean water, shelter, and then a way off this world. Somehow, with little hope of any of these, she managed to force herself onward. So unbearable was the climate that even the slight chance of escaping it enabled her to toil on.

The trees seemed to go on forever, but surely there must be a stream or pool somewhere. She listened longingly for the sound of water, but there was nothing—only the calls of more wild creatures.

Then as she approached a little clearing in the jungle—clear yet sunless still, due to the gloomy vaults formed by the interweaving boughs of the trees surrounding it—a high-pitched cry of fear arose from somewhere near at hand, and something came fleeing out of the jungle.

Knowing herself to be in an alien world, Ailia had tried to prepare herself for things outside her experience, things that were strange beyond imagining. But her eyes could make no sense of what she saw. This thing looked like a hubless and spokeless wheel—a round gray hoop-shape, rolling rapidly along apparently of its own volition. She could only gape foolishly at it as it bowled through the clearing. What on this foreign earth could it be?

The gray hoop vanished into the bushes to her left. Their leaves stirred and rustled, and then a head looked out. It was about the size of a cat's, hairless and scaly, and it was attached to a very long, flexible neck, also covered in scales. Then a second head appeared, just in front of the first. This one was a little larger, about the size of a dog's, with a longer muzzle. Yet the two heads were similar, with the same round dark eyes and pointed ears. She surmised that the first animal was the offspring of the second.

The head of the larger animal moved cautiously forward, with the other following it closely. Then it moved out of the bushes, and Ailia gaped at it in disbelief. The creature's long neck was attached to a two-legged body like a bird's, with clawed feet and a pair of stubby, vestigial wings. But strangest of all, the head she had thought belonged to a second animal was attached to the end of the creature's long tapering tail. As she watched, the tail—or was it a neck?—rose erect, and the second head swept its gaze about the clearing.

There was another crashing sound in the underbrush. At once *both* heads uttered croaking cries of alarm, and the odd little biped dropped onto its back, as if playing dead. The larger front head clamped its jaws on those of the hind head, the two necks curving and the back arching until the whole body formed a circular shape. One clawed leg shoved hard against the ground, propelling it forward, and the creature began to roll away like a hoop.

But it was too late. The crashing noise drew nearer, and out of the greenery many dark winding shapes came coiling like tentacles—only each had at its tip a long wicked head with a darting tongue. *A hydra!* Ailia froze where she stood.

Hydras were found in many worlds, she knew: long ago Valdur had released great numbers of them on the planets of his Archon enemies, to poison the air and water and terrorize the inhabitants. But whether they were natural animals or magically altered creatures was not known. The two-headed beast screamed and wheeled right into a tree trunk in its haste to escape, crumpling into a heap. It cowered as the long necks advanced, followed by a squat body with four short, clawed legs. The hydra could not move very quickly on those bowed limbs, but it would not have to: its breath was venomous, and could reach its victim more than a dozen paces away. The two-headed beast cried out again, not a scream this time but a twittering, chittering sound. Ailia sensed patterns behind the sounds, distorted with fear but still recognizable as thought. *No, no, no, oh no—please no!*

This little oddity was an intelligent, thinking being.

Awareness of her own physical weaknesses had made Ailia deeply sympathetic to all defenseless things. Emotion thrust aside thought. She sprang forward, forgetting her own danger and the exposure any use of sorcery would bring, drawing on all her Nemerei power to cast a glaumerie before the hydra's many eyes. A firedrake seemed to appear out of the misty air, a mass of black

scales and claws and horns filling all the clearing, red flames licking forth from its jaws.

The hydra recoiled, every one of its heads hissing in alarm.
Then, whipping its great bulk around with surprising speed, it
scuttled back into the undergrowth. The thrashing sounds of its
hurried retreat faded into the distance. Ailia was left alone in the
clearing with the small creature, which lay prostrated in terror at
this new and still more deadly menace.

"No, no—it's not real!" she called, stepping forward so that she
stood before the illusory monster's forefeet. With a wave of her
hand she banished it. "It was only my magic. You're safe now."

Very cautiously the head at the creature's tail-end peered at her.
Then the front head came up and also fixed its eyes on her. "You
are sorceress! Great Nemerei!" twittered the being, approaching
her with a cringing posture. Both its heads were held low: the hind
one, she noticed, still had its eyes trained nervously on the bushes
where the hydra had vanished. "You save us! We grateful, your servant always, beautiful sorceress-lady!"

"That's all right," Ailia replied, gazing anxiously about her. Too
late, now, she realized the great risk she had taken. Were there any
other sorcerers in the vicinity, and had they felt that burst of power
she drew from the Ether? "Think nothing of it. I must go now,
but—tell me, do you happen to know where the ruler of this world
lives? It's not near here, is it?" She hoped it was not, or Mandrake
would surely have felt her use of magic.

"Ruler! Yes, yes, we know!" it replied, fawning. "Is not far, in
great city. Loänanmar. We show you way there, sorceress-lady." It
was clear that the creature, having found itself a powerful and
benevolent protector, had no intention of ever being parted from
her again.

Ailia was about to say she had no interest in actually going to
Mandrake's home. She wanted only to leave this terrible world and
return to her guardians. But she could never do so on her own, she
reflected, while in a city there might just be a portal or other
means of transport that could carry her back into the Ether. In any
case, she could not hide in the jungle forever. She was beginning
to feel faint with heat and hunger and loss of sleep. She must dare
the city, then, hide and disguise herself in the hope of finding a
way to escape.

The creature hopped closer to her and spoke again. "Let us introduce ourself: we are called—" It made a chattering sound that might have been "Twidjik."

"I am pleased to make your acquaintance, ahh—Twidjik," she said. "Will you please lead me to this city of yours, then?"

She was eager to leave the area. That surge of power *must* certainly have betrayed her location, and the watchers of this world would soon be hunting her again.

"Yes, yes, we lead. This way, lady."

SHE WOULD HAVE BEEN GRATEFUL for almost any company after her prolonged solitude, but Twidjik proved to be an unexpectedly valuable guide. Ailia could not make out whether the creature was male or female: since it referred to itself in the plural, it might easily be both—a sort of hermaphrodite, like an earthworm; or perhaps it was just an *it*, and its kind reproduced in some way unimaginable to her. Not wishing to broach the delicate subject, she did not ask. But as they journeyed together she soon learned that he (or she, or it, or they) knew all about surviving in the jungles of Nemorah. Twidjik showed her the fruits that were safe to eat as well as those that were poisonous (there were many more of these than of the former), and instructed her on other dangers to avoid. She began to see that her seemingly rash act of mercy had been rewarded, after all. There were far more perils here than she had realized.

"Beware," Twidjik cautioned her as it led her through one dense grove where the suns' light was muted to a green dusk by the overhanging branches. "Are jaculi in trees here."

"Jaculi?"

"Tree snakes, with scaly flaps like wings." The creature's front head swept from side to side, watching for danger, while its hind head gazed at her. "A jaculus will wait on branch, very quiet, then leap down fast on those who pass beneath." And Ailia, looking up into the shadowy canopy, saw that what she had taken for hanging vines twined throughout the trees were in fact large green snakes coiled around the boughs.

There were many other dangerous creatures here, Twidjik told her as they hastened away from the grove. There were scitales, snakes that could change the color of their scales with dazzling effect, fascinating their prey into immobility, while their relatives the hypnales relied on a form of mesmerism, swaying to and fro in a languorous dance. The cerastes or "hornsnake" used the sharp curving horns on its head as weapons in place of fangs. Then there were the guivres, giant serpentine creatures that lived in the rivers and seized animals that came down to drink; and the horrible lindworms, which had powerful hind legs on which they loped along at great speed, but no forelimbs at all: they scooped up their living prey in their huge jaws, swallowing it whole. Worst of all was the basilisk, a many-legged reptile that breathed out poison like a hydra. It was very much smaller than a hydra, but that made it more deadly, not less: it could creep right up close to you before you had realized your danger.

"How can you bear to live in such a dreadful place?" she asked, appalled.

"We have no choice, no other place to live. All here learn of poisonous beasts, learn to fear them. There are sauras—little lizards, that smell venom of other reptiles, and leap about in alarm. Humans carry these in cages, get warning of serpents that way."

"There wouldn't be any of those lizards hereabouts?" Ailia asked.

"We do not know. But is not much farther to place where humans are."

Ailia reflected that humans were as dangerous in their own way as any beast. She was beginning to feel worried about this unknown city and its inhabitants. Would they welcome a stranger, or not? "And what are your people called, Twidjik?" she asked, trying to distract herself from her thoughts.

"*Amphisbaena* your word for us," Twidjik replied. "We live in jungle, very careful, always looking around us, always moving fast." To demonstrate, the amphisbaena swung both necks to and fro, looking both behind it and ahead, then rolled on its back and formed a hoop again. In this fashion, she saw, it could progress with surprising rapidity.

"Wait!" she called out, breaking into a run. "I can't keep up with you!" Employing its feet as brakes, digging its claws into the earth, Twidjik resumed its upright position with both necks raised.

"We go slow for you," the amphisbaena said.

About midafternoon clouds began to cover the sky, changing it from green to gray-green. A murky underwater light lay all around them, and soon it was pouring. The amphisbaena was of course quite unconcerned by the rain pouring down its scaly sides. Ailia held up her tattered skirts and trudged on grimly through the mud. Already the chiton she carried was badly torn from her passage through the thick undergrowth. She looked at the jungle stretching in dull shades of green and gray about her, the seemingly interminable aisles of tree trunks. The rain soon ceased, as quickly as it had begun, but a dense steam took its place. She felt as though she were suffocating.

Something moved at the corner of her vision, and she whirled and gave a yell, echoed by a double shriek from her guide.

"What is it?" the amphisbaena gasped, staring wildly about it with both sets of eyes.

But Ailia only repeated its words. "Heavens—what *is* it?"

What she had taken at first for the leafy limb of a huge tree was moving—bending, swinging to and fro without any wind to blow it. And now other boughs behind it were also in motion, dipping and swaying. As she gaped at the nearer one she saw that the clump of leaves and twigs at its end did not sprout from it, but rather from a torn tree branch that was clenched in a pair of long toothy jaws. The giant reptile's head had small dark eyes and scaly gray-green skin, rough as bark. There was a row of spiky upright scales along the back of the neck.

"Stop! Stop!" Twidjik called as she turned to flee. "These not dangerous!"

"Not—dangerous!" she cried.

"No—see, they eat only leaves."

Ailia stared. The enormous serpentine creatures were grazing on the foliage of the trees, like camelopards. And then she saw that they were not serpents at all; the long scaly necks were attached to vast gray-green bodies, with tapering tails behind. She had taken their massive legs for tree trunks, while the foliage had hidden their bodies. As she and Twidjik walked on she saw more of the monsters—whole herds of them, some with their young at their sides: colossal infants the size of full-grown behemoths. "What are they?" she asked.

"Creatures from other place. Are not from Nemorah, but brought here from another world by First Ones." Twidjik gestured with its front head at the giant grazing beasts. "Those who lived here long ago, before Loänei. Many, many years ago they came, placed these creatures here. *Tanathon* they named them—tree-eaters."

Ailia was again filled with awe at the power of the Archons. What beings would have kept such huge creatures as *pets?*

They walked on, leaving the giant reptiles to their grazing. At long last the great river appeared through the trees, a swift red-brown torrent. They followed its bank for about an hour, and presently came upon a small wooden jetty with a roofed shelter attached. Ailia was gladdened at the sight of it. It was a very ramshackle affair and the wood of planks and roof were rotting; but it was of human make, humble and modest in size, constructed by creatures akin to herself.

"Now we follow river," said Twidjik. "It go near city."

"Thank you," said Ailia. "But not just now, if you don't mind. It's starting to rain again."

They waited, huddling under the shelter. Twidjik curled up with his front head resting on his paws—when exactly had she begun to think of "it" as "he"? She was not certain, but there had been a shift in her thoughts regarding him. He was a personality to her now, not merely an alien curiosity. As she watched he fell fast asleep—his front end at least; the eyes of the hind head, she noticed with fascination, remained wide open and watchful, and the tail-neck turned from side to side in slow sweeps as if searching for any signs of danger. Once more she saw that her impetuous intervention on the amphisbaena's behalf was not without benefit to herself: with such a companion she need not worry again about being attacked while she slept. She was grateful, for she was exhausted. Stretching out on the floor, she made a pillow of her gown and laid her head on it. The invisible suns went down, and darkness dropped again like a muffling curtain.

At morning light she rose, stretching painfully stiff muscles, and looked about the inside of the shed. There was no food anywhere to be seen, but a cupboard set into one wall held some other supplies, belonging no doubt to those who used the jetty. There were straw hats with wide sheltering brims, and several long wooden staves: the latter, Twidjik told her, were used to defend against snakes as one walked. Ailia took one of each, and also a loose, coarse garment that somewhat resembled a burlap sack. Then after some hesitation she removed a thin gold necklace that she was wearing still, and left it in the cupboard as payment. It would not be wise to begin her stay among the people of this world as a thief.

They moved on up the river. All around them reared the strangely shaped hills, very narrow at the base and pointed at the top, that Ailia had seen from the air. The rugged outcroppings spoke of the tumultuous powers of the earth, of upwelling extrusions from the planet's fiery heart, and they loomed above the river swathed in green cloaks of foliage, exuding an eerie presence. And some, indeed, had faces. Huge human faces, and smaller figures of people and animals, and flat-topped doorways were carved into the dark gray rock that showed here and there through the clinging vegetation.

"That is old city," said Twidjik, seeing her stare. "No one live there now. We go to newer city, where many people are. Hills were carved in olden days. Great city stood here once, city of Loänei people. Are many like it, but no one living in them now. No Loänei. Jungle swallowed cities up." They walked closer to the nearest hill, and she gazed at the surviving images of the old city's rulers: majestic robed people, with proudly chiseled and fierce-looking faces, looking back at her from under the layers of moss and winding tree-roots. "*Loänei*—children of dragons," said Twidjik.

So these were Mandrake's people. She saw the resemblance now: the elegant, arrogant features, the tall lean bodies. Ailia turned away from the staring stone faces, not relishing the reminder of her strong and treacherous foe. Once more she reproached herself for falling so easily into his trap, and wondered if she would ever find a way to flee this world without confronting him.

A league or so farther up the river the jungle gave way with surprising suddenness to cleared areas, wastes of stumps; and cultivated fields sown with vegetables and grain. The crops looked healthy and abundant: volcanic soil, she had once heard, was very fertile. And this region, like the islands, was certainly prone to volcanism. Steaming hot springs sent up white plumes here and there, like the smoke of great fires.

They were drawing near to the city of Loänanmar. Ailia hurriedly cast a glaumerie that would make her look to any observer like a nondescript young woman with a plain broad face, braid of straight brown hair, and dark eyes. Her star sapphire ring, her last remaining item of jewelry, was also concealed by the illusion. Twidjik showed no surprise at her sudden transformation, apparently taking in stride this latest manifestation of powers that he had already accepted as godlike and illimitable. They passed on together under a stone gate formed by the figures of two rearing, snarling dragons. There were two guards by the gate, dressed in old and rusty armor, with long snoutlike visors to their helmets and halberds clenched in their gauntleted hands. They resembled men in size and shape, but when one raised its visor to look more closely at Ailia she saw the face within was not human, but canine: it had a long muzzle covered in brown fur, and a black nose twitched as it drew in her scent. *Cynocephali*: one of the Morugei races, bred by Valdur to be sentinels and watchdogs in one. Neither of the dog-guards prevented her from entering, to her relief.

As Ailia walked through into the city, she looked about her curiously. Loänanmar was a thriving, crowded metropolis: the streets thronged with pedestrians, with peddlers hawking their wares from baskets borne on poles atop their shoulders—fresh fish, breads, strange-looking gourds and vegetables. Some were driving goats or geese; one young man had a large striped snake draped about his shoulders, though whether this was a pet, or his dinner, or part of a snake-charming act, she never learned. Large pools were filled with live carp, but they were not for ornamental purposes: people were dipping small nets into them and scooping up the struggling fish.

There was, she saw, only one temple in this city: a grand structure covered in decorative gilding, with a cluster of onion-shaped domes and fearsome fanged beasts cast in bronze guarding its door. Ailia peered inside the temple as she passed it and saw that the floor was strewn with dead leaves and litter. In the sanctuary was a pool, and behind it the gigantic figure of a crowned Loänan carved of some green stone. It had once been plated with gold leaf: bright yellow traces still clung to the crown and edged some of its scales. But the fane was empty, and had a sad, abandoned air.

It was growing dark again, and the surroundings were becoming sinister. Most of the "houses" near the river were mere wooden shacks, with leaning walls and sagging roofs. Humans and various kinds of Morugei lazed about their front doors, half-clad in ragged garments. Small children fought and screamed in the dirty streets. A young woman with glazed eyes and filthy matted hair was sitting on a street corner in a sort of stupor, an emaciated infant lying limp in her arms. She stared blankly ahead of her, showing no reaction to passersby or even to her own child. Flies crawled upon its face. Beggars held out leathery palms in mute supplication, but Ailia had nothing to give. A couple of shabby-looking men eyed her speculatively as she passed. Perhaps, she reflected, she should have made her glaumerie self male instead of female. But it was too late to change now: too many eyes were upon her. She gripped the wooden stave and quickened her pace, but to her relief the men made no effort to follow her and she had no need to defend herself. She had no training in the use of either the stave or the dagger that she still carried with her, and it would not do to make a conspicuous display of sorcery in the city. Even if Mandrake were not here, his spies and cohorts might well be everywhere, awaiting his return.

She halted in a grimy little square, where a bronze statue of a robed man stood on a tall plinth. The sides of the plinth were scrawled with obscenities, and some wag had climbed up and placed a cracked clay pipe between the bearded bronze lips. There was an inn nearby, with smoky torches burning outside its door. As she watched, two men were forcibly ejected from the door, cursing and raving. She halted at the sight, and began to wonder if perhaps it had been safer in the jungle. Even as she thought this another group of men sauntered down the steps of the inn.

"What's this! What's this!" bellowed one of them, running up and seizing Ailia by the arm before she could flee. With his other arm he knocked the stave from her hand.

"I saw her first, Rad," complained another man.

"Shouldn't be out after dark, my lass," the first continued, paying no attention. "Dangerous men about at this hour. Like me," he leered into her face, his breath foul. Ailia looked about her desperately, but the passersby showed no interest in her plight. A few even turned their faces away and quickened their pace as they walked past.

"And what's this bit of vermin?" One of her persecutor's companions snatched up the amphisbaena by his fore-neck. Twidjik writhed in his grip and bawled at both ends like a pair of ill-played trumpets. It was no use, Ailia thought in resignation: she would have to use sorcery, and give herself away yet again. But even as she drew upon her power another figure came bounding out of the inn door.

"Just you let her alone, Rad!" shouted the new arrival, a small wiry woman in a red dress. She wore a red and gold head scarf under which grizzled black hair streamed, and hoops of gold swung from her earlobes. Standing in the street, hands on hips, she glared at the man who held Ailia's arm.

Rad shrugged. "Why? She's just an ugly little street wench."

"That's still too good for the likes of you, Radmon Targ."

"D'you want your tongue cut out, woman!" snarled Rad, releasing Ailia and advancing on the small woman.

"You just try it, Rat-face Rad," she retorted, holding her ground. "I'll put a hex on you, I will: a real witch's curse that'll turn your food to mud in your mouth, and your drink to bog water, and fill every bed you lie in with bugs. And that'll be the least of it." She took a step toward him. "Do you want to know when you're going to die, Rad?" she asked softly.

To Ailia's astonishment and vast relief Rad and his followers backed sullenly off, seemingly cowed by these colorful threats. Twidjik's captor set the wailing amphisbaena down, and he scuttled behind Ailia's skirts again.

"Pond scum," observed the woman with contempt, watching them go. "Don't you mind them, lass. You and your little pet just go on your way now."

Ailia looked into the dark flashing eyes and felt she saw a kindred spirit there. "We've nowhere to go," she ventured. "We don't know these parts very well."

"New in town, are you?" The woman cocked her scarfed head, earrings swaying, and gave her a thoughtful look. "Ah, you country folk will keep coming here, but you'll find things are no better in the city—worse, I'd say. Well, never mind: you can bide the night at my inn, dear."

"I've no money." Ailia had parted with her necklace, but was not about to give up her mother's star sapphire ring. "Might I do some work for you in place of payment—wash dishes for instance—"

"No need for that. I've a room or two free. You're welcome to stay in one. Come along! It's getting dark, and you'll not find any other place to stay hereabouts that's safe."

Ailia stared at her, much moved by the simple generosity of the offer. "Thank you so much. But—couldn't I help somehow? Cook, or clean?"

"Eh now, there must be something else you can do," the woman suggested in an encouraging manner. "Sing a bit, perhaps?"

"Well—I can tell stories," Ailia offered after a moment's thought. "Tales no one here has likely ever heard."

"Ah, that'd be grand," the woman said. "That'll keep 'em all entertained: they're that fed up with the flute player, I was hard put to stop 'em throwing food at him. Come you in and make yourself at home. The name is Mag, by the bye—just plain Mag, I've no other."

"My name is—Lia." If Mag noticed the brief hesitation she gave no sign of it. "And this is Twidjik. Are you really a witch?" Ailia asked.

Mag shrugged. "Folk say I am, and I don't contradict 'em. If it makes 'em scared of me, well, hereabouts that's a good thing. They do say my grandma was a witch, and I've an old book of hers that's supposed to be full of spells and charms, though they mostly look like ordinary poultices and such-like to me. And I do get pictures in my head sometimes, like dreams in the daytime. But I can't go putting curses on nobody. I once told a man who used to come here that he was going to drop dead if he didn't watch himself. A heavy drinker he was, and not young: anybody might have told him the same thing. But it so happened that he died the very same night—he was so drunk he fell in the fish pond and drowned—and a rumor got started that I'd foreseen it, or even made it happen. Load of nonsense! But that's how I got my reputation, and it's a great help to me when louts like Rad come by trying to throw their weight around."

Pictures in her head! thought Ailia. Here, in the malodorous murk of this strange and terrible city, was a Nemerei. It was like finding a precious jewel in a trash heap. She felt a sudden kinship with this shabby plain-spoken woman. "Can the authorities do nothing about that man Rad?" she asked sympathetically as she and Twidjik followed Mag to the inn door.

The woman snorted derisively. "What authorities? You mean the Overseer?"

"Overseer?"

"You've not heard of the Overseer? Him as won the Great Revolt twenty years ago, and cast down the theocrats? That's his statue, there in the square. An image of him has been placed in every quarter of the city, so that the people can pay him homage."

Ailia realized her ignorance was probably too great even for some backwoods peasant. "I've heard some of the story, but not all," she said cautiously.

"Well, in the old days there was some in this city as claimed they had dragon blood, you see, and whether 'twas true or no they demanded special treatment and privileges, saying they was children of the dragon-gods. And they worshipped a Dragon King, who they said lived here once and would again some day, and they started up a priesthood for him. And they lorded it over the rest of us, and took the best of everything, and left us poor. Then one fellow—Brannion Duron—he said enough of this, from now on all folk are to be equal, and share and share alike. He raised a secret army, he and his friends, and they rose against the oppressors, as he called 'em. And everyone that claimed dragon blood was killed, and the priests were all driven out and the Dragon King's temple ransacked. And Duron said there was no Dragon King, nor never was—nor no gods nor spirits of any sort rulin' over us: 'twas all a lot o' nonsense. And he made himself Overseer, and said from now on we was to live in peace and plenty. Though I can't say as I've seen much of either, and neither has anyone else here."

"May I meet with him? Your Overseer?" Ailia asked, hope rising in her. It seemed Mandrake was *not* the city's ruler after all. Perhaps this Overseer could help her escape this world.

"I'm afraid not, dear. He sees no one."

"But isn't he your leader? Don't you go to him when you need help? Perhaps he could do something about Rad and his crew."

"That lot? They works for him! Collectors, they're called: they comes around to collect goods and money as their price for 'protecting' us—though what we're being protected from they never say. Seems to me we could all use some protection from *them*. Most of what we have ends up in their pockets." She said this last sentence in a hushed voice, as though afraid she might be overheard.

"So Rad comes to my inn whenever he wants a drink, and I must give it him even though I can't abide the man. He's killed people as got in his way."

"Then you risked a great deal to help me just now," said Ailia. "I hope you won't suffer for it, Mag."

The woman only shrugged again. "It's high time someone stood up to him," she remarked. "I should have done it long before."

Ailia and the amphisbaena followed her inside. The main room was noisy and noisome, full of large unkempt patrons who hunched over tankards of the local brew or snuffed at handfuls of what looked like crushed flower petals, the cloying sweet aroma blending sickeningly with the smoky air. A troll bulked beside the door, his small eyes under their massive ridged brows watching the people in the room. "This is Gorg," Mag said, nodding to him. She clapped the huge creature on the shoulder as she passed and he grunted back at her. "I hired him to keep the peace in here, and I pay him in food. He's worth every crumb, too. He's not a bad sort, for a troll: just wants to sleep and eat and live, same as anyone else."

When they reached the front of the room Mag waved her to a vacant table. Ailia perched upon it, cleared her throat nervously, and then began to tell her stories, tailoring them for her audience: amusing animal fables and folktales full of magic and adventure. She told them the tale of the "Magic Ring," and "The Horse of Brass," and "The King and the Shepherdess." They gradually fell silent and listened to her, some even laughing in the right places.

When she had finished the third tale Mag reappeared and led Ailia into the small kitchen for her promised meal: roasted eggs of some creature or other and two slabs of rather greasy fried bread. "That's the best we can do," Mag apologized. But Ailia fell to hungrily, passing half the food to Twidjik, who hid under her chair for safety.

A young girl was helping Mag with the serving. Ailia watched her as she set dishes down and took orders from the rowdy patrons. "What a beautiful girl," she remarked. It was no idle compliment, but a statement of fact: the girl was unquestionably lovely, with the slender grace and huge, dark eyes of a gazelle. She also had a gazellelike shyness: her great long-lashed eyes were nearly always turned down, as if fearfully aware of their own devastating effect.

Mag smiled. "That's my daughter, Mai. Oh, I know what you're thinking: she should be out of the home by now, and making her own way."

"Her own way? But she can't be more than fifteen."

"She's fourteen, this year. Do youngsters stay home longer in the country, then?"

"Where I live they do," replied Ailia truthfully.

"Here in the city they're treated as adults. Throw her into the street, everyone said. Let her sink or swim, that's the way it's done. But my Mai's timid. And she's not ready to be with a man yet. I won't force her into anything until she's ready." She sighed. "It's been hard. We've had to make it on our own, Mai and me."

"Is her father dead?"

"Him? Not for all my wishing." Mag scowled as she kneaded dough. "I lived with him for years, the scoundrel, and not a finger did he lift in honest labor: I did all the work, made clay pots and wove hangings to sell for food. Then he up and brought home another woman: his new lady-love, already with child. We'll all live happily together, he says, be one big loving family. It'll work out fine, you'll see . . . except that My Lady and her baby boy always got the best of everything, and Mai and I had to work all the harder to feed their mouths."

"Does this sort of thing happen often?" asked Ailia, astounded.

"In the city it does. It's a man's world here, and it has been for a good long while. The Overseer don't approve of marriage—says people didn't ought to belong to each other, no more than wild beasts do. So the men do pretty much as they please, take a woman and then move on, and we women must either put up with their ways or leave. The last straw for me was when one of his no-good friends began to get designs on Mai—with *his* encouragement, of course. Trying to get her alone, making advances, that sort of thing. She was frightened, poor love, and that finally opened my eyes. I snatched her out of there at once, and we set up this place on our own. We've been here a couple of years now. I should have left sooner, fool that I am. But so help me, I loved him—the good-for-nothing lout!" She gave the dough a hearty thwack with her floury hands. Seeing that she had broached a sensitive subject,

Ailia said no more and discreetly returned her attention to her meal.

Presently she became aware that Mag was no longer working the dough or performing any other tasks, but standing quietly and watching her as she ate. "You're an odd one," the woman remarked suddenly. "Don't look like much, if you don't mind my saying so—and you don't put on any airs. Yet somehow I feel as if I should be giving you finer provender, and plates of gold to eat it on."

Ailia, who was sopping up the last of the egg yolk with a crust, stopped and laughed uneasily. "Whatever can you mean?"

Mag's eyes were dreamy, unfocussed. "There's another woman within you: a beautiful lady like a princess in a story, gowned in white. She shines through you, like a moon through a cloud . . . Eh now! What am I saying? I must be wandering in my wits." Mag shook her head, the gold hoops in her ears glinting in the torchlight. "Don't you mind me, love, I get odd spells at times. Now, tell me where you're from, and why you're all on your own."

It was awkward, as Ailia did not like lying and in any case she did not know enough about this world to pretend that she lived here. But it transpired that Mag knew very little about it either: she had never left the city in her entire life. So Ailia spun a tale about growing up in a small rural settlement and being orphaned young, so that she had to learn to live on her own. She passed hastily over this part of the narrative, focusing more on the trip to the city, to which she could append any number of details from her actual journey through the jungle. "Mag, can you tell me any more about this Dragon King?" she asked when she had finished. A suspicion had grown in her mind from the first mention of him.

"Not much. He hasn't been seen by anyone for hundreds of years. I know only what my mother told me—what her mother told her before. He lived inside the big hill just outside the city, the one what's always got steam and mist around it. It's he who brings the rain, they used to say, and sends the thunder and lightning when he's angry. And he can be any shape he wants, bird or beast—or man. My mother said her great-grandma told her that his name is Morlyn, but no one else seems to remember that."

So Ailia had guessed correctly: these people had once worshiped Mandrake as a god. And well they might. He seemed not to age, and commanded the weather at will; they were not to know that the rain would still fall without him. To their eyes he must seem immortal—and invulnerable. He had evidently ruled over this city in days long gone, letting its inhabitants revere him; then for some reason he had abandoned the place, leaving them all to fend for themselves. Perhaps he had simply grown bored with his role, or perhaps the Loänan had driven him out. Whatever the reason, if he returned he would no doubt mean to stay, and order things again as he willed.

Mag continued: "But the Dragon King, he's not really a man but a dragon—one of the Celestial Ones, the greatest of them all. There's an image of him in the old temple—the dragon with a crown. It was all golden once, that statue, with jewels for eyes, but the Collectors took all the valuable stuff from the temple when they closed it down. They said he couldn't be a real god, or he'd have stopped them doing it. But some of the folk still continues his cult in secret, all the same. The Overseer tried to ban his worship, but he could never quite stamp it out and now he mostly turns a blind eye. We're not supposed to talk about him, leastways not in public. Me, I'm just afeared of the Dragon King. Not many may believe in him nowadays, but I'm thinking maybe he just went away for a while, and he'll come back one day—and he won't be too pleased with what he finds here when he does."

Thunder rumbled softly in the distance, and Mag started. "There now, what am I saying? I'll be giving us both bad luck with such talk." She rose abruptly. "All through? Then I'll show you to your room."

Ailia followed her hostess up the creaking wooden staircase, Twidjik trailing behind them. Glancing out a window, she saw that the inn had been built around a square courtyard, with a hot spring at its center. Several people were bathing in the steaming pool.

"This one's yours, dear," said Mag, opening a door. "Right next to mine, so if anyone gives you trouble you just bang on the wall."

Ailia entered the narrow little room, which held a bed and a clothes chest and nothing much else. She looked out the window, which gave a view of the city. High over the sharp volcanic hills beyond the roofs a bright light was shining through the night like a star. But the light was a pale ghostly green, and as she stood there watching, it moved, progressing swiftly across the sky until it passed out of sight behind the mists that enveloped the highest hill. It moved too slowly to be a meteor, and left no shining tail behind.

"What was that?" she asked. "Did you see, Mag?"

"You've never spied one of those before? 'Tis a dragon-lantern. At least, that's what we call 'em hereabouts. They rise out of the sea and float inland, usually at this time of the year when the weather's calm, and hang about the towers of the Forbidden Palace and the spires of the old temple, glowing like lamps. The old-timers say they're magical tokens sent by the dragons that live under the sea, to honor their sacred places."

"What are they really?" Ailia gazed at the hills, intrigued by this new mystery, but the enigmatic light did not reappear.

"No one knows. The Overseer and his lot say they're naught but a sort of marsh gas or sailor's-fire, and they just hang about those towers because they're the tallest points in the city. But there do seem to be more of 'em these days. I used to watch for dragon-lanterns when I was a little girl, and I don't ever recall seeing so many. Some come from the sky, and they do say one was seen rising from the ocean and vanishing into the clouds. Look, the weather's changing."

The wind had picked up, shredding the steams that had hung like a cloud about the hilltops. On the highest summit the wisping vapor swirled aside to reveal the pointed towers of a huge castle.

Ailia gave a little involuntary cry. "*He* lives there?" she exclaimed. "The Dragon King?"

"His priests used to, up to twenty years ago. 'Twas they built the palace for themselves, or rather their slaves built it, there on the hill that was sacred to him. No one's allowed to live there now, by order of the Overseer: it's kept as a museum. Nigh on three hundred years it's been since the Dragon King last revealed himself, but if he ever does come back that's surely the place he will go to."

Ailia stared in fascination at the fortress on the hill. She recognized that tall central tower rising from its inner citadel, with the four tall pinnacles stabbing at the sky. It was the one she had glimpsed in her vision of the confrontation with Mandrake.

15

A Snare Is Set

THE HAREM OF YANUVAN filled one entire wing of the castle, housing the two hundred or so women who were Khalazar's wives and concubines. It had been built to accommodate guests long ago, and retained its luxurious appointments: it boasted a courtyard pleasance, hand-painted tiles and murals, sunken marble baths the size of fishponds. So many were the women, and so often did the king's wandering fancy alight on some particular favorite, that a royal wife or concubine might wait many months before being summoned to his chamber. Some he never called—peasant girls, chosen by the clerics from among the villagers and brought here by force, tearful and trembling: Khalazar would often forget all about these, and they went on to become the pariahs of the harem, humiliated and used by the others as slaves. Their parents, already impoverished, were ruined by the dowries they were forced to pay to the king. Those women who enjoyed Khalazar's favor lived a life of relative comfort and indolence, their royal children and their pets playing about them. But they were prisoners all the same. The enclosed garden was all they ever saw of the outside world.

The eunuchs presided over the harem wing, and could be bribed to bring news from the court and the world beyond. No man ever entered this place on pain of death. But Mandrake was not considered a mortal man, and he visited the harem as he pleased. He found the gossip interesting: the eunuch network was highly efficient at information gathering, and the harem was the hub of rumor at the court.

Today he sat on a marble bench, strumming on a Zimbouran sitar. He had no particular interest in music: it was merely one of the many pursuits to which he had turned to stave off boredom as the centuries of his protracted life wore on. There was no instru-

ment he could not play, and he played them all well. The harem
women, who in his presence need not veil themselves, cast on him
many lingering glances and then quickly withdrew them—for
even those completely ignored by Khalazar were forbidden to take
lovers of their own.

Today their talk was all of the rescue of the deserters by the Mohara rebels. "The people tell such wondrous tales of these warriors," one royal wife said. "One is a sort of prophet, who used to
fight gladiators in the arena before he escaped. They say that no
living thing, man nor beast, could defeat him. And he is assisted in
his battles by two angels. One wears armor of silver, they say, and
carries a sword with a diamond blade. He is like a fair northern
barbarian to look upon, with hair of gold and eyes blue as the sky.
The other appears as an otherworldly being, neither man nor
woman—"

"But where do these rebels hide themselves?" interrupted another woman skeptically.

"Have you heard of the lost city, built by the Moharas long ago?
It lies in the deep desert, an enchanted city surrounded by trees
and water, with roofs of gold and pillars of silver. In it there is a
great palace, where Mohara kings and queens of ages past lie in
sarcophagi carved from diamond, so perfectly embalmed that they
seem merely to be sleeping. Frightful spirits guard the palace door,
genii with lions' feet and the wings of eagles, and should anyone
get past these guardians worse evil awaits: for the kings and queens
laid mighty curses on all who would dare disturb their rest. Those
few thieves who escape do not live long enough to enjoy their
plunder . . ."

Faerie tales, Mandrake thought. He had flown more than once
above those ruins in dragon form and knew they were little more
than rubble, though the watery oasis that surrounded them was
real enough. The escaped Mohara slaves who dwelt there lived
only in rude huts of wood and reeds, and seemed to pose little
threat to the armed might of Zimboura. More disturbing to him
had been the silent howl of pure iron coming from somewhere
within the ruin. The Mohara, like the Elei, had made little use of
this metal until late in their history, and then usually only in its al-
loyed form. They would not likely wield cold iron against Khalazar's armies. Were they perhaps crafting weapons to use against

Mandrake? Or merely using the metal as a shield against his sorcery? He had flown above the place afterward only at a great height, and cautioned his Loänan and goblin allies against approaching it. Let the soldiers of the God-king storm the place in their stead! They might be weaker beings, but they at least had little to dread from cold iron save for a blade's biting edge.

"Prince Morlyn." He looked up to see Ashvari, eldest of Khalazar's wives—once a royal wife of Zedekara—eyeing him. "Why do you come here to the harem, yet again? A spirit is immune to the charms of mortal women, or so they say."

He continued to play. "That is true."

She reached out, silencing the strings with her hand. "Come! You know that you are no spirit! Who are you really—and what are you doing here? If Khalazar guessed you were only a mortal man you would be denied the harem—and likely lose your head as well. You are playing a dangerous game."

His eyes met hers over the sitar. "I assure you, I do not play games."

"We all know you seek to become king in his place, even as he overthrew King Zedekara! You play augur to him, as he did with Zedekara. It has not escaped our notice, Prince, that by increasing the king's power and his confidence you have made the people hate him more than ever before. It is his downfall you are contriving, not his triumph." Her kohl-rimmed eyes searched his. "When he seized the throne Khalazar chose to take Zedekara's women and keep us for himself—meaning to dishonor him thereby. Will you do as he did, in your turn—add us to your harem?"

Mandrake sighed. How weary he was of humanity, and Zimbourans in particular! "For the last time, I am not seeking the throne. Only a madman would want to reign over this sinkhole of intrigue! And I will thank you not to spread any such rumors. The last thing I need is to have Khalazar panicking and sending paid assassins after me!"

"So you *are* mortal!" Ashvari's face turned grave. "Prince, I must warn you. If you *do* seek the throne, beware. General Gemala swears he will kill you first."

It was not hard to understand the woman's wish to preserve Mandrake from harm. He was the only hope for her and all the harem. Should Khalazar die a natural death and pass on the throne to his son, the laws of succession demanded that every adult who dwelt here in the harem be slain and interred in the dead monarch's tomb. This was not because he required their services in the afterlife, but simply because it would dishonor his name should any of his chattels survive to become the property of another man. His women had no purpose beyond pleasing him, and without him they had no reason to be; as for his slaves, they had been made to swear oaths of lifelong fealty to him alone, so it would be unseemly for them to serve another. They lived each day in that knowledge, these wives and slaves: from the wise and mature Ashvari to the child-bride Jemina, from the chief eunuch to the captive princess of Shurkana, all dreaded to hear that their aging master had succumbed to some fit or perished in his sleep. But a usurper might yet spare them for his own use. Disgust at the barbarism, and a stirring of pity for the doomed prisoners within these walls, arose within him and must have shown in his face, for Ashvari made as if to speak again. But she was interrupted by the entrance of Yehosi, who was wringing his hands and wailing. "He is mad—mad!"

"You mean the king?" said Mandrake.

The chief eunuch mopped his perspiring forehead. "Yesterday some poor women of the city came to the castle gates, to plead for their hungry children who had accompanied them—Zimboura's children, they called them. You would think a heart of stone would relent, but he had them executed for their impudence, and hung their bodies from the battlements. And he has slain Captain Jofi of the palace guard, not for any crime or failing, but because he wants a spirit-servant to report to him from the Netherworld, and it must be someone whom he can trust! And last week in the arena—you will not believe this, but it is true—a bear mauled two cheetahs that had been set on it. Khalazar wanted the cheetahs to win— they were hunting cheetahs from his own royal stables. You will hardly believe me, I say, but he had the bear formally charged with treason, and held a trial for it, and the royal executioner publicly beheaded it! He has gone mad, I tell you!"

Mandrake shook his head. "No, not mad. He is merely showing the populace that he is king and god, and can do anything he pleases. It is a warning to anyone who would dare oppose him."

"But how much longer will the people endure it? There will be a riot next, and the castle will be sacked and all of us slain. Unless there is a revolt from within—a palace revolt . . ." He looked at Mandrake hopefully.

The prince went back to his strumming, indifferent. "Nothing will ever change that way, Yehosi. You will just end up with another despot."

"Better than have the mob rule! *Too* much will change then!"

"Why do you not overthrow him yourselves? Here in the harem he is vulnerable as he is nowhere else. It would be the work of a moment to slip a dagger between his ribs while he sleeps. Yet none of you does anything."

"We are afraid." Yehosi avoided his eye, and Ashvari laid her head in her hands.

"Yes. It is not your king that holds you all prisoner, but your own fear."

They all glanced up as another eunuch entered and bowed. "Yehosi, Prince Morlyn: your presence in the throne room is required immediately."

Yehosi blanched. Mandrake set the sitar down and rose from the bench, his face calm. "Well, let us see what he wants."

KHALAZAR WAS IN AN ILL HUMOR.

Crown Prince Jari had been taken to the arena that afternoon, where a large crowd had watched him kill a tethered antelope with half a dozen arrows. The boy had come into the throne room flushed with excitement, clutching the animal's decapitated head by its horns. His first kill. From ancient times a Zimbouran male had been considered to be fully adult only after his first kill—usually a wild beast, though the poor had to be content with slaughtering a pig or chicken for their sons' manhood ceremonies. But Khalazar had felt no pride in his son's achievement: he was, rather, disturbed by the rite of passage.

If Jari was a child no longer, then did that not mean he, Khalazar, was growing old? His own angry visage peered at him from his bedroom mirror. There, in his beard—yet another gray hair, amid the black! They continued to appear, ruthless reminders of mortality, despite all the promises of the genii.

"How can this be?" he raged. "I am a god! How can I age like any mortal? Have they lied to me?" Cold fear washed over his anger, momentarily quenching it. He yearned to kill his son, to stop him from growing older.

"I am immortal!" he told the puffy, flushed face in the mirror. But there was doubt in his mind now. Where were his divine powers, said to be awakening soon? Were the spirits deceiving him for their own ends?

He stormed out of the bedchamber and down the stone stair to the council room. Mandrake, Gemala, Yehosi, and the replacement for Berengazi awaited him.

"Let me guess," said Mandrake. "Is it Jomar and the others again?"

At the name of Jomar Khalazar turned beet-red and slammed his fist down upon the table, making Yehosi jump. "They must be captured and killed—killed! I have set a bounty on their heads—and raised it—where does it stand now, Yehosi?"

"Ten thousand silvers, Majesty," Yehosi quavered.

"Yet still no one brings me these villains, alive or dead!" Khalazar tore at his own hair. "I am sick of them, do you hear! They have attacked my caravan in the desert, stolen the goods, and taken away the slaves!"

"Majesty, this is a war unlike any you have ever fought before. These three intruders are fighting you, not for your land, but for the hearts of your people. The Zimbourans will not betray their helpers," Mandrake said.

"What? Because of a few pathetic deserters? Do my own subjects oppose me now? I will send my soldiers to burn down a few houses, cut off a few heads, and we will see how sympathetic they remain to the rebels! But my soldiers—why do they not bring me the heads of my enemies?"

"The rebels are concealed in the desert ruin," Gemala informed him. "It serves them well as a fortress, and they have springs of fresh water to draw on. They fire arrows and cast spears at my men, who must also endure the heat of the desert when they seek to besiege the oasis."

"Excuses, always excuses! Is there no one in Zimboura loyal enough to do my bidding? Where is the captain of my guard?"

Yehosi trembled. "Dead, Majesty—by your order."

"Then why has he not yet been replaced?"

"Perhaps they are having difficulty finding an aspirant for the position," suggested Mandrake, straight-faced.

Khalazar glared at him. "And you, spirit—why can you not locate these criminals, for all your powers?"

"Remember they too have supernatural allies, Majesty, and can call on those powers to conceal them." Mandrake decided to say nothing of the iron he had sensed within the ruin. "But I have a plan," he added, stepping forward. "You will prepare another sacrifice, but this time you will *anticipate* a rescue attempt by these warriors. There must be no more Zimbouran executions for a while: the people will not stand for it. Princess Marjana will do instead. She is a foreigner, and a slave. Send her to the Valley of the Tombs, supposedly for sacrifice to the firedrake that now dwells there. But you will prepare an ambush."

Gemala scowled. "And if the monster attacks my men?"

Mandrake had to admit that was a possibility: firedrakes were notoriously stupid and vicious, and not infrequently ignored or forgot the instructions of their masters. "I will send the drake out of the valley. By night, so no one will know it has gone from its lair."

"A true warrior does not use trickery in order to obtain a victory," said Gemala with disdain.

Mandrake raised both eyebrows. "Then you would have me leave the drake in the valley? As you please."

"Silence, Gemala! *You* have not succeeded in taking the rebels, for all your vaunted warrior skills," snapped Khalazar. "Make the necessary preparations. It shall be done as Prince Morlyn says."

How I weary of these games! Mandrake thought as he left the room. There was little point in capturing Ailia's friends now, if she were truly dead. But there was no way to know for certain. He had heard nothing yet from the searchers on Nemorah, but the longer her body went unfound, the more he began to suspect that she lived still.

I must go there and seek for her myself, he thought. *In Nemorah my powers are the stronger: in seeking to find and destroy me where I live, the poor fool has put herself at a disadvantage. But I cannot go now, not until this business is concluded. It may yet prove useful to have hostages. For then I need not fight the Tryna Lia at all . . .*

*   *   *

THE VILLAGE IN THE OASIS was growing. Many forays had been made against the work camps in the desert, freeing Moharas and Zimbourans to join them and swell their ranks. Every night there were campfires glowing openly throughout the oasis, and the sound of singing in the air. The rebels had set up some elaborate traps, covered pits and tripwires and nets rigged to fall on those below, and archers were always hiding in the ruins. Several scouts and one Zimbouran platoon had entered, their fear of Khalazar worse than their fear of the rebels. They had all been captured before they got halfway to the village. Some of the Mohara men had wanted to kill them, but Damion and the shaman insisted they be kept as prisoners. Some of them offered to join forces with the Moharas, as Kiran Jariss had done. When none of the men returned to the city, their fellow soldiers balked at following them. Kiran reported that the conscripted men were close to mutiny.

The few zealots among the captured soldiers were not grateful to be spared; rather, they thought the Moharas cruel for taking live prisoners. "I wish nothing more than to die for my God-king!" one objected as he was brought in. Lorelyn stared at him. Something burned in this man like a fever, giving his eyes a hard gleam and his cheeks an unhealthy flush.

"If Khalazar really was a god," she declared, folding her arms, "he'd love your people, wouldn't he? Not draw them into a war, where many of them will die."

The soldier stared back at her. "But Khalazar-Valdur is making us into a great and populous nation," he argued, "and he offers us the world. For that we owe him payment, even our lives. Our priests say the Maurainians' god must be very weak, for he has given his followers nothing."

"Well, yours hasn't given you the world yet, you know. You've still not won this war you've begun. Can't you see you're just his tools—his means of getting revenge on the world?"

"Revenge? I don't know what you mean. Our god punishes the wicked and ungodly. He destroyed the Elei kingdom centuries ago, with fire from the sky."

"And what harm had they ever done *him*, I'd like to know?" returned Lorelyn angrily.

"He is a god. Who are we mortals to question the gods? Valdur gives out life and bounty with one hand, death and destruction with the other. It is his right."

"Well, where I come from 'two-faced' isn't a compliment," muttered Lorelyn.

Berengazi looked over at her and smiled. "You are all doomed, every one of you. The Avatar of Valdur will have his vengeance on you yet," he declared.

Jomar, who was passing by, glared at him. "Quiet, you, or we'll send you back home by installments." Berengazi glowered, but said no more. Clearly he did not share his compatriot's zeal for martyrdom.

"Has anyone seen Damion?" asked Jomar, glancing about.

"He's gone to the ruin, to see Wakunga," Lorelyn told him.

"Again? He seems to spend all his time with the shaman these days."

"Why not? He wants to find out more about his Nemerei power—how to summon it at will, like the magi. He thinks he can be of more use to us as a mage than a fighter, and perhaps he's right. He's already learned to understand any language, like me."

Jomar could not say why Damion's new fascination with sorcery troubled him so. He knew well that his own reputation as the Zayim had grown in part because of his two wonderful golden-haired "angels." Lorelyn in particular filled both the Moharas and the Zimbourans with awe—this curious, otherworldly being who was neither woman nor man, and could fight without even needing to use a weapon. But Damion intrigued them too. They imagined that, being divine, he must be imparting some heavenly wisdom to Wakunga, and little knew that the teaching was mainly in the opposite direction. Only Unguru and a few of his close friends remained skeptical. Unease filled Jomar, together with a sudden weariness of the role he himself played—weariness of the constant pretense and the burden of their expectations. For the first time he understood how Ailia must have felt when she faced the crowds of adoring Arainians.

He left the village and headed for the ruin, where he found the priest and the shaman sitting together under an ancient wall. Damion's eyes were closed, his hands lying loose in his lap as Wakunga spoke softly in his ear.

"Damion! Damion, wake up!" called Jomar, striding up to the

meditating priest and leaning over him. Damion's eyelids fluttered open.

"You should not interrupt," reproved Wakunga mildly as Damion rose, stretching stiffened muscles and groaning.

"What is he doing? What are you doing to him?" demanded Jomar.

"Helping him find his way. The path that is set out for him."

"It's all right, Jo," put in Damion. "He really is helping me. I understand now what Lorelyn means when she speaks of having a Purpose. I didn't come here to fight and kill, but to discover what that Purpose is."

"Don't talk like that, Damion," said Jomar. "Just because these people think you're an angel—"

Damion smiled at him. "Jo, it was you who told me to go along with this."

"But that was only at the beginning, when our lives were in danger! And I didn't tell you to go and believe in it yourself!"

The priest's face turned serious. "Jo, I may not be an angel, but I do believe I've a power I can learn to use and—a mission of some kind. Something that I am *meant* to do."

"You're mad," Jomar said. Damion made no reply. He continued to stare into space, his expression tranquil. The Mohara felt a stab of anxiety. Was it the battle shock again? Some soldiers appeared to recover from the illness, only to be stricken again when they attempted to return to daily life. Some died, not at once but by slow degrees, mind and body fading together. The same thing had happened in the slave camps, to people who had suffered until they could endure no more. They were beyond help as a mortally wounded person was beyond the aid of healers. He had watched them in anguish until he learned to armor himself against sorrow and look the other way. And he had sworn that he himself would never surrender in that pitiful way, but would die fighting when it came to be his turn. So it was that he had flung himself in mindless fury upon the lion that invaded his work camp, daring its terrible claws and fangs. For in his mind it had not been a lion at all, but King Zedekara, and the slave drivers, and the desert itself in all its inexorable cruelty. In later years his act seemed to him one of madness rather than courage. It had not been the lion's fault that its hunting grounds and prey had been destroyed by men. Slaying it was like striking down the conscripts in Khalazar's army: the true enemy was never the one you actually killed. And after you had bloodied your sword, this enemy seemed to mock you from its unassailable retreat—to jeer at your petty and futile victories.

Damion's eyes were shut: he had retreated once more to that place where Jomar could not follow. The warrior shuddered as he turned away, and walked back to the village.

Lorelyn had retired to the lean-to of animal hide that had been set up for her, and he stood for a moment gazing at her as she lay on her bed of furs. She was asleep, giving to this activity the same single-minded concentration she gave to everything else: lying with limbs asprawl and body utterly relaxed, sleeping with all her might and main. He pondered her lean grace. At any moment, he felt, she would leap up and be instantly alert, like a tigress roused from slumber. But he sensed something beyond her physical strengths: a flawless purity like some rare crystal's. Hers was a spirit incapable of any kind of duplicity or falsehood, on whom one could rely with absolute sureness, to trust with one's life. An ideal comrade in arms who would be at one's side in the battle charge and hold the line, never retreat and never fail in her duty, unless she was slain. She was well able to look out for herself, yet somehow he found himself wanting to protect her. Was that not in fact why he had been so opposed to her fighting, he suddenly wondered—because he could not bear to see her come to harm?

I love her, he thought in amazement. It was a bolt from the Ether—a revelation.

As he gazed at her she stirred, yawned, opened her eyes, and when she saw him she smiled. He suddenly yearned to tell her what he had been thinking about her, but the words would not come, and he thought in helpless self-reproach that he never had known how to translate thoughts to words. It was a skill that his warrior's life had never required of him. Damion, now, would have known what to say. But he, Jomar, could only stand there awkwardly as the moment passed him by.

As Lorelyn looked up at Jomar she felt a warmth toward him, stronger than any she had known before. Despite their not-infrequent spats, there was something about him that was as firm and solid and reassuring as the ground beneath her feet. Such bonds, she knew, often formed between comrades-in-arms: those who faced danger together could not help but forge strong ties of heart and mind, overcoming any minor differences. She sat up and smiled again, and for an instant there seemed an answering warmth in his dark eyes, and he looked as though he was on the verge of speaking. But what he meant to say she never learned. A loud shout shattered the quiet evening, and the moment was lost.

"News! There is news!" Hoofbeats accompanied the cry.

Jomar swung around looking irritable. "What is it now?" he snapped.

Kiran Jariss came riding into camp on the desert horse that they had given him. "What's all the noise about?" asked Jomar again.

"News from the city," Kiran gasped, scrambling down off the horse. "It is announced that, since no one can capture you, the God-king will slaughter people until you surrender."

"How are they to die, Kiran?" demanded Lorelyn, springing to her feet. "Is it the temple again?"

"Not this time. They are to be given to one of the fire-breathing monsters that lair in the Valley of the Tombs. A sacrifice is to be offered each day. The first victim is a prisoner of noble blood— Marjana, daughter of the Shurka king whom Khalazar slew. She has been kept as a slave in the castle, but now she is to die."

"No! We can't allow this!" said Lorelyn. "When is she to die, Kiran?"

"At sunset today. At the Tomb of Zedekara."

"Then we still have time to get up a raiding party."

"I don't like the sound of this at all," said Jomar. "Why the Valley? It's so far from the city. Why not the arena or the temple? It sounds like a trap to me: they're baiting us, drawing us out."

"Jo, we can't let that girl die," protested Damion, who, along with Wakunga, had been drawn to the village by the disturbance.

"Do not go," said the shaman to Damion.

"My friends need me. And Khalazar—"

"You do not understand. This is nothing to do with Khalazar. It is the dragon-wizard who seeks you—you, in particular. If he captures you, it may bring ruin on us all—the daughter of the Morning Star included."

Damion wavered. "I'm not that important, surely?"

"Everything is important. A flood begins with one drop, a sandstorm with one grain. You are like that, Damion: at this moment in time at least. Everything now depends on you. Go on this mission, and you walk the wrong path," the old man warned. "You will lose your way. You must remain, and learn, not ride out with a weapon like any other man."

"Perhaps Damion *should* stay behind," suggested Lorelyn. "The rest of us can go."

"Listen to her," said the shaman to Damion. "She and the others go into danger, but for you it will be worse. It will be the ruin of another's life."

Reluctantly the priest acquiesced. "Take my sword, Lorelyn. The adamant blade is stronger than yours. I will remain here."

Just as well, Jomar thought. *If he is losing his mind, it's better for him to stay here.*

As the warriors readied their mounts and weapons, Damion came and watched their preparations with a wistful eye. "Be careful, won't you?" he urged. "If Jo is right, and it is a trap . . ."

"We'll be on our guard, don't worry," promised Lorelyn, fastening his sword at her side.

They had prepared every day for more raids, practicing sword-thrusts and parries, testing their bows and spears. As the sun dipped lower and the wind dropped they saddled and harnessed their horses and pulled on their armor. The Mohara women gathered, uttering the shrill ringing cries with which they traditionally sent their warriors off to battle. At last the small force set off across the wasteland, Damion watching anxiously.

"Good luck to you!" he called. And watched until they vanished into the darkening distance.

THE OXEN THAT DREW THE CART were pure white, the color of sacrifice. Lambs and doves and other white animals were slaughtered on holy days, and in olden times human sacrifices had once been led to the altar of Valdur garbed in white linen and mounted on white steeds. Marjana knew these things: while she dwelt still in her father's house she had studied many books of travelers' tales, curious about the ways and customs of foreign lands. So it was that, although no one told the reason for her unexpected journey, she knew well what it must mean as soon as they clad her in white and set flowers in her unbound hair. And the ox-team, with their white hides and garlanded horns, had confirmed her fear.

The cart, with its company of mounted guards, moved slowly

through a wide dry wadi, occasionally halting as one of its wheels struck a large stone or one of the cracks that gaped in the ground like parched mouths. Presently the wadi dipped, then opened onto a broad valley, the bed of a river in ancient days. Its long-vanished waters had carved strange shapes out of the earth: tall upright forms like trees turned to stone, or like statues on pedestals. But there were other shapes in the red walls of the gorge that were not the work of nature: lowering facades of temples, pillared porticoes carved into the living rock, and the ornate fronts of tombs also, with friezes depicting the glorious deeds of the kings interred within. Fearsome colossi, stone giants with the heads of jackals or crocodiles, guarded the doors. Here, in days of old, every Zimbouran king had been entombed upon his death with his entire household—wives, concubines, slaves: all except his children. In this valley hundreds of men and women, at swordpoint, had drunk poison and perished beside the royal sarcophagi.

It was a desolate place, and now more so than ever: great patches of the already sere earth were blasted and blackened as if by fire, and the few hardy desert shrubs had been reduced to charred sticks. And scattered all about were the gnawed and burnt bones of animals: cattle, goats, horses, even the massive skeletons of elephants, all offered to feed the huge hunger of the beast that had made its dwelling place here. The small procession that now made its way along the dry bed of the river was aware of that forbidding presence. The faces of the soldiers were ashen, while their horses tossed their heads and snorted at the brimstone-and-carrion stench that lay heavy on the air. One of them reared, its frightened neigh echoing off the walls of the gorge. Its rider cursed, his own nerves as brittle as his mount's. The oxen bellowed and balked until they had to be goaded forward.

As for the young woman lying bound in the cart, she had long since gone beyond fear into a stupor in which her surroundings seemed scarcely real. She had been a princess once, pampered and protected and loved by her doting widowed father and four elder brothers—all of them dead now, murdered by Khalazar's troops. The fall in her fortunes had been so swift and irrevocable that Marjana had moved through her capture and subsequent enslavement in a trancelike state. This final ordeal at least promised to end those sufferings forever. She wept only a little, therefore, as she realized that she neared the end of her journey and of her life. In her mind she prayed that she be reunited with her parents and her brothers after death.

But oh, to enter Paradise by so terrible a door!

She tried to imagine a different scene: to pretend that she was on the path leading to her home, returning from a pleasure outing. Marjana shut her eyes, exchanging in her imagination the crude cart for one of her royal father's open carriages. She could almost hear the tinkling of the little tin bells on the yaks' harnesses as they drew the carriage steadily uphill. Many more of the longhaired mountain cattle grazed in the alps far above. For the yak was to the Shurka as the llama to the Marakite, the reindeer to the Rialainish: giver of milk and meat and hide, burden bearer and bride price, the oldest currency of the realm. Her father, being king, had herds numbering in the thousands. Farther away lay those wild mountain valleys where herds of wild mastodons and woolly rhinoceri roamed, but these sheltered slopes had been terraced and culti-vated since ancient times. Above them loomed old ruins, carved into the living rock of the mountains—cliff cities built by the van-ished Elei. She could see them clearly—and see, too, the mountain palace with its high protecting walls and watchtowers, and the kindly, kingly face of her father, and her brothers with their teas-ing eyes. She must indeed be near her end, for their faces to be so clear to her inward vision.

They await me in my final home . . .

The cart jolted against a stone again, and her eyes fluttered open unwillingly. Up ahead was a great frowning facade of pillars and statues cut into living rock, its doorless entrance utterly dark. Mar-jana averted her eyes, and a tremor shook her slender frame. Only a little longer now . . .

"Yonder is its lair," the captain said. "In the largest of the tombs."

"You are sure the monster will not attack us?" asked a soldier.

The captain shook his head. "The goblin-men swore it would not. It is no mere brute, they say, but reasons like a man."

"Still, we could leave the sacrifice here."

"Are you mad? If she somehow managed to escape, Khalazar would have our heads! Tie her to a pillar, and then let us withdraw."

They obeyed, and then made as if to leave, but as they did so there came a clanging noise and the captain staggered: an arrow had struck his helmet. The soldiers started and reached for their weapons, but to no avail: their enemies were hiding within the entranceway of another tomb on the opposite side of the valley. As more arrows flew, the soldiers fled in haste, howling, leaving the princess still bound to the stone pillar at the tomb's mouth.

The raiders flowed out from the shadowed entrance and crossed the valley floor, some riding on horseback. Marjana looked up, her head clearing as she gazed great-eyed at her rescuers. A tall golden-haired figure dismounted to slash at Marjana's bonds with a sword. The princess gave a cry as she was freed.

"Sir Damion!" And she flung herself at the figure's feet, weeping, kissing the gauntleted hands of her deliverer. "I have heard the women tell tales of you—"

Lorelyn, startled, realized suddenly that in the silver armor, she might easily be taken for Damion. "I'm not—" she began. But Marjana sobbed with joy and pent-up anguish, clutching at the other woman's hand, and crying out again and again.

"Sir Damion! How can I thank you?"

Lorelyn tried again to correct her, but at that moment they all fell silent as a low rumble came, like the voice of the earth itself, from the depths of the tomb before them. In the gloom within its yawning portal two lights appeared, like lamps borne by unseen hands, and with them came a sound of rasping breaths. The dragon had come.

Marjana rose with a scream. "Run! Run!"

"Retreat!" yelled Jomar to the men.

"No!" cried Lorelyn. "It'll follow, and kill us all. It will spit fire on us from the air! We must kill it here, on the ground." And she remounted and spurred her snorting stallion toward the entrance of the tomb, toward the waiting eyes.

The desert horse of the Mohara had the blood of Elei steeds in its veins, and it obeyed her command, though its ears were laid back on its skull and its eyes rolled. Lorelyn gripped her sword. There was a chance, if she could get in a mortal blow before the beast could draw its breath to expel a flame . . . Then there was a roar, and with the speed of a striking snake a huge shape sprang out of the entrance. Lorelyn pulled up, staring. This was no ebon-armored firedrake, but a Loänan, its wings and scales red as the rock on which it stood.

"Mandrake!" she cried, brandishing the adamantine blade. It flickered with blue flame. "It's you, isn't it—Mandrake! Come on and fight us then!"

Jomar shouted, "Lori! You can't fight *him*!"

But she only waved the burning blade again, and urged her horse directly toward the red dragon.

He crouched, then hurled himself into the air even as she charged. Seeing this, she tried to pull her horse up, but her speed was too great. As she plunged on into his shadow he furled his wings and dropped. One foreclaw raked the stallion's hindquarters, making him rear; then the tail swept forward, knocking his hind legs out from under him. Lorelyn leaped clear as the stallion fell screaming onto his side, hooves beating at the air. At once Jomar was there, charging in so that she might be protected by the iron sword's sphere of power. Again the dragon lunged skyward, evading the iron, then circled within the walls of the gorge before diving low. Jomar swung up at him as he swept over their heads, but he was beyond the blade's reach.

And now the enemy was upon them, as they were ambushed in turn. Scores of fighters poured out from the entrance of the great tomb. Several of the figures who stepped forward had strange, misshapen features: goblins who flung fiery bolts toward Jomar. But the sorcerous fires died away as he raised the Star Sword. Then one of the other Moharas yelled and threw himself in front of Jomar as a Zimbouran soldier unloosed an arrow at him. The man fell, pierced through the upper chest. It was Unguru.

"No!" Lorelyn screamed. She ran to the fallen man, throwing down her weapon, cradling his head. His own sword was still clenched in his hand. His eyes opened, focused on Jomar, who had dropped to his knees beside him.

"Zayim," he rasped. Then his head fell back, heavy against Lorelyn's arm.

"Unguru!" she whispered, staring down into the dark eyes that gazed upward, yet did not now see her. She was dazed, unbelieving at the speed with which the spark of his life had been extinguished.

The red dragon roared, high in the sky. Passing low overhead once more, he banked on one wing and flew off in the direction of Yanuvan.

"Which of you is Damion Athariel?" demanded one of the Zimbouran soldiers, pulling his sword from its sheath.

"He isn't with us—" Jomar began, when another soldier gave a shout.

"He lies! There, that one—that is he! The slave girl knew him, and spoke his name! I heard."

Jomar turned to stare. The soldier was pointing at Lorelyn. "That is Damion," the man declared. "The warrior with hair like gold."

"Are you blind?" shouted Jomar. "That isn't—"

"No, Jo!" interrupted Lorelyn. She stood, faced the soldier. "It's true. I'm Damion."

The Zimbouran grinned. "Not much of a warrior after all, are you? You're nothing but a boy."

Jomar watched in desperation. These Zimbouran soldiers had never seen a woman like Lorelyn before: she was as different from the little, timid, shawl-shrouded Zimbouran women as day from night. Nor would the goblin-creatures likely know the difference. And her coloring *was* the same as Damion's. Now Lorelyn was actually encouraging them in their error—but why? How long did she think she could keep up such a charade? Was she hoping they would kill her on the spot, and so save the real Damion?

"That isn't Damion," he argued, stepping forward. "I tell you he's not with us."

"Are you Damion or not?" demanded the soldier of Lorelyn.

Her eyes never wavered. "Yes."

"No!" Jomar bellowed, at the same time.

He staggered as the soldier turned and struck him across the face. "Liar! Try to protect him, would you?"

"Enough," said another voice. It was General Gemala, striding forward through the ranks of his men. "Bind them all, and take them to the king. As for the dead man, let him be buried here. He is of the enemy, but he served his master well. And he did us this favor: he named that master with his last breath, so that we know who he is." His eyes settled on Jomar. "We have caught the leader. The *Zuyim*."

INTO THE THRONE HALL they were all led in chains, Lorelyn and Jomar grim, Marjana sobbing, the rebel Moharas subdued. On his throne Khalazar sat with his eyes black and expressionless as an adder's. Mandrake stood at his side, clad in a red robe.

Gemala glowered at him. "Since you could not be troubled to join us in battle, Prince, it was left to me and my troops to take the prize. We have the Zayim, and also the one on whom you say the Tryna Lia dotes: Sir Damion."

"My congratulations to you and your men, General," said Mandrake. "I am sure it took all of your courage and daring to capture that girl."

Gemala blinked. "Girl? What do you mean?"

"That is a woman, you fool, not a man. Can't you tell the difference?"

"Sir Damion is a *woman*?" gasped a soldier.

Mandrake raised his golden eyes to the ceiling. "No! Damion *is not here.*"

"What!" Khalazar roared, his face flushing with wrath. He flung himself on the luckless guards, beating and berating them. "Brainless curs—witless dolts! Always you fail me!" He swung around to face Lorelyn and Jomar, breathing hard. "I *will* have this Damion—do you hear? I will have him if I must execute every man, woman, and child in the city! As for you two"—he paced close to them, black eyes glaring—"I will have your heads for my gateposts!"

Marjana gasped, then burst into tears. He struck her savagely and she sank to the floor in a swoon. "Take her back to the harem, and put all the captives in the dungeons—all but these two. They die *now!*"

"No," said Mandrake.

"What do you mean, no?"

"Your Majesty needs them alive. They know where Damion is. Find him and you will have Ailia, too, in your grasp. As for you, Jomar and Lorelyn, I advise you to tell them where Damion is."

Lorelyn met his eyes with her own clear blue ones. "I will not."

"They will torture you, you young fool."

"I don't care."

"You'll get nothing out of us," added Jomar. His guard hit him, with such force that he staggered sideways and fell to the floor. He fell heavily, unable to catch himself with his shackled hands, and Lorelyn rushed to kneel at his side.

Mandrake turned to go. "Keep these two alive, King, and keep them from harming themselves, even if you have to bind them hand and foot. They must live to tell what they know."

"You dare to tell me what I must do!" Khalazar raged. "I, who am your master!"

Mandrake looked at him coldly, filled with a disgust so strong that he knew he could no longer conceal it. Gods above, but he was weary of this! "Follow my advice, King, or you will surely live to regret it," he said curtly. "I will return now to my own place." He swung around in midsentence and swept from the room.

Khalazar glared after him, and for a moment he considered calling for the executions to show his power. Then, seeing that the goblin-mages had surrounded the huddled figures of Lorelyn and the Zayim, he thought better of it, and ordered both the prisoners to be taken to the dungeons with their fellow rebels.

MANDRAKE WALKED SWIFTLY along the grand entrance hall. The shadows of evening were beginning to settle in its corners and behind its mighty pillars, and servants were lighting the oil lamps on their long chains. Sentries stood on guard, the iron of their weapons throbbing sickeningly, yet he barely registered their presence, his mind a welter of conflicting emotions.

What pathetic figures those two were: Jomar so unrelentingly stubborn, Lorelyn wrapped in her dreams of chivalry. Not even the threat of death would make them talk, Mandrake knew. Lorelyn in particular had plainly decided to be a martyr: the Paladins were always so pitifully certain of their reward in Heaven. No Zimbouran could imagine facing Valdur the Terrible without fear; but the Paladins believed their god to be good and loving, and death held no terrors for them. Mandrake suddenly felt depression settle over him. Why was he still affected by the fates of humans, after all this time? Their lives—and deaths—must run their own course, and had nothing to do with him . . . why was his mind so full of death, all of a sudden?

Absorbed in his thoughts, he did not sense the danger soon enough. The figure that sprang from behind caught him almost off-guard. An arm came up across his throat, and as he grabbed at it with both hands the dagger that sought his heart glanced off a rib. The blade roared with iron in his mind: a mental sound that might have warned him of its wielder's approach, had it not been masked by that of the other iron weapons. He wrenched himself free, his cry of mingled pain and fury and alarm bringing the palace guards running, and even Khalazar and his courtiers emerged from the throne hall.

General Gemala stood motionless, the iron-bladed dagger still in his hand. Mandrake stood with one hand clasped to the ragged wound in his chest, the red robe torn around it: the other hand was raised and crooked like a claw as he confronted his failed assassin.

"You!" cried Khalazar. "I should have known!"

"Your Majesty," the grizzled old warrior began, "I had my reasons. When have I not served you well? I have been with you from the beginning. Hear me. This man is no spirit, but only an evil sorcerer—he is here to serve not you but his own ends. I saw how he dared to dismiss your command, just now! He means to murder you and take your place. I procured this dagger of cold iron days ago, waiting my chance. I intended to lay his lifeless body at your feet as proof of my claim. I have failed to slay him, but, Majesty, look!" He held out the bloodstained blade. "Did you ever hear of a spirit that *bled?*"

"General, I admire your courage and devotion to your king," hissed Mandrake through his teeth. "But I'm going to kill you nonetheless," he added, stepping forward.

"No, his fate is mine to decide!" snarled the king. "Guards, take the general to the dungeon! He dies tonight—slowly, in torment. No, Mandrake, unhand him! I say he dies *slowly!*"

"Majesty, I entreat you," Gemala shouted as he was dragged off.

Mandrake strode away. Through the throbbing pain that clouded his mind he felt a rising disgust. Assassinations and machinations! He was sick of it all. And now he had come near to losing his life, and would bear this iron-inflicted wound even if he shifted shape.

Had he courted danger on purpose, he wondered, warding off boredom with its heady spice? If so, he would do so no more: he had grown careless, and it had nearly proved fatal. What worse intrigues might await him in this accursed land? Let the goblins watch over Jomar and Lorelyn, and seek for Damion in the wastelands. He had a realm and a people of his own to deal with, and an even more dangerous foe who had not yet been found.

It was long past time for him to return to Nemorah.

16

The Forbidden Palace

AILIA HAD NOW SPENT TWO NIGHTS at the inn and, she reflected, had slept better in the tree. The din from the common room below seeped up through the cracks in the warped and knotty floorboards, along with chinks of lamplight and the reek of smoke and ale. The troll guard was evidently kept very busy, from all the shouts and the sound of bodies being hurled down the front steps. She felt herself grow tense every time a heavy tread ascended the stairs and went past her door. Twidjik was as edgy as she, one set of eyes watching the door and the other the window.

In the evenings she helped Mai to serve food to patrons in the main room, or joined Mag in the kitchen while Twidjik followed her about like a dog, frequently getting underfoot. At last Ailia convinced him to withdraw underneath the table.

"I can't understand it," said Mag. "Those little two-heads are supposed to be the most timorous creatures alive. I never heard of one hanging about with humans before. They're usually terrified of anything bigger than themselves."

"I suppose I'm not very frightening," Ailia said. Privately she felt grateful that no one here could understand amphisbaena speech. Twidjik might have let slip the fact that he clung to her because of the magical protection she offered.

As she worked Ailia pondered her next move. There were clearly no sky-faring vessels here: she had asked, discreetly, and received only blank stares from those she questioned. Only the dragon-folk, she was told, knew of such things, and they had not been seen for years and would have nothing to do with ordinary humans in any case. Could she find and confront Mandrake's minions, perhaps, and somehow compel them to help her? But what if the prince himself were with them? The Loänei she might hope to defeat, but Mandrake was another matter. He had centuries of experience in fighting any number of formidable enemies, and she had never been trained in any sort of combat. No doubt she would have been, eventually. Had the Loänan had their way, she would probably not have faced Mandrake for many more years. What should she do? Flee him, or fight him?

I defeated him once before, she told herself on the evening of the third day.

Not you, an inner voice replied. *You were on your own world then, and its power and the Stone's drove him away. You've no Stone with you this time, and you're on his ground, his world.*

I couldn't have brought the Stone with me. I couldn't risk it falling into his hands. He would use it for a symbol, to pretend to the Valei that he really is their god.

True—but now you haven't got its power. You are alone.

Alone . . . The word reverberated through her mind. Auron and Taleera did not know where she was, and poor Twidjik was not much of an ally now that he had fulfilled his role in bringing her to Loänanmar. Ailia drew on her magic, tried to feel its presence within her, a vast reservoir of untapped energy. She had power, even without the Stone—but not the practical skills she needed to fight for her life.

She walked out into the courtyard, where Mag was cooking food over a small earthen pit near the hot spring. It steamed just like a boiling pot, and next to it was a smaller, bubbling pool in which dishes and pans were scouring. The glare of both suns filled the courtyard, but it no longer seemed so hot. A breeze was blowing, stirring the ferny fronds of the little trees, and clouds scudded across a sky the clear green shade of spring leaves.

"Lovely weather, isn't it?" said Mag. "It changed so suddenly last night."

Ailia murmured a reply. Her gaze was fixed on the fortress atop the volcanic hill, looming above the roofs of the city. No road climbed the sheer rock face below it, and no gate pierced its walls. It could be reached only from the air, according to Mag, though a cave in the hillside was believed to be an entrance to its cellars. The opening sent forth a continuous steam, like smoke from a firedrake's mouth, and no one dared enter it.

"By the way," Mag went on, "I've aired your bedding for you, and put another old gown of mine in your room. It's a mercy we're nearly the same size: however did you manage to leave home with only the clothes on your back? I'm afraid I can't repair that yellow undergarment of yours, though; it's in tatters. A pity. Such lovely weaving, fine as mist: I've never seen anything like it."

Undergarment? Ailia suddenly recalled the Alfaranian chiton: she had not been able to hide it in the bare little room, and now Mag had gone in and found it. The older woman's face looked too curious for her liking. She forced a smile and a nonchalant tone. "Oh, thank you, Mag, but it can be thrown out."

"Throw it away! It's too fine for that, even torn. You'll find nothing like it here in the city. Give it to me, I'll make something out of it."

"Well—you might turn it into cleaning rags, I suppose." She tried to keep her voice light and careless, afraid to excite Mag's interest. She really should have discarded the garment . . .

The woman's eyes lit up. "Oh, thank you! But if I'm not mistaken, it's much too good for rags. You can keep my old gown, if you like. But you'll need to get more clothing, somehow."

"Thank you," said Ailia. "But I don't think I shall be staying in the city after all. I think I'll return home." At the word *home* she felt a sharp twinge of yearning—for her father, for Halmirion, for her friends, to whom anything might now have happened. And how could she hope to leave this planet? She could not keep a little tremor out of her voice as she spoke, and felt a sudden mad longing to tell this sympathetic woman everything—the whole truth, rather than elaborate lies. Oh, to share her real burdens with someone!

"Now how about a bite to eat?" Mag continued, getting up and brushing the dirt from her knees.

Before Ailia could reply there was a swift movement in the sky overhead, and she glanced up sharply, shielding her eyes. To her relief she saw only a bright-plumaged bird circling hawklike against the green. Its wings shone bright as beaten gold in the sunlight, flashing on each downstroke. To her surprise Mag had gone as pale as her bronze-colored skin would allow. "Did you see that? Did you see?"

"I saw a bird," said Ailia, puzzled.

"That was no bird, it was *he*. One of the many forms that he takes is a gold-plumed bird. There's no other like it in all the world."

"He?" asked Ailia with a little stab of fear.

"The Dragon King. Once in a while he flies out of that steaming cave in the side of the hill, transformed into that shape: the golden bird. My mother told me about it, long ago when I was a little girl. It's a sort of sign, his way of saying that he's watching us. If I ever saw such a bird, she said, I should show it reverence—for it would be he. This means he has come back!"

Ailia's mind was awhirl. She too stared with widened eyes as the bird flew up away over the roofs, out of sight. Could it really be Mandrake? Or was this merely a local superstition?

"This Dragon King, Mag," she explained urgently as they returned to the kitchen, "I think I may know what he is. There is a story where I come from, of a sorcerer—a man of great power, who has lived many hundreds of years. He could easily convince people he was a god, using his powers of shape-shifting and illusion. If I am right, your Dragon King is no myth: he is very real, and I am afraid he really may have come back here to Loänanmar. He lived here once, I think, and after he departed the memory of him remained, so your people continued to revere him. I must warn your leader. It is one thing to overthrow a sorcerer's acolytes: you cannot hope to fight *him*, if he really has come to retake this city. If your Overseer tries to oppose Morlyn—the sorcerer—his life will be in danger—"

"No!" Mag looked more frightened still. "You must say nothing to him! Brannion Duron—the Overseer—does not permit discussion of such things. Magic and such-like. I can tell Rad and his no-good ruffians that I am a witch, but to say such things to Duron . . . People have been arrested for saying they believed in sorcery or gods or dragons or lost countries in the stars. It would be no use to plead that you're a girl of the country, unaware of our laws. He would say you were seeking to cow him with old wives' tales, and he'd put you in prison."

"Still, your people must be warned. If Morlyn has come back here, you must all flee this place at once."

"Duron will say you are spreading lies, and must be stopped." Mag's voice dropped to a rasping whisper. "The truth is the Overseer is a tyrant bad as any that came before him. He killed everyone who dared oppose him years ago, and anyone who speaks out against his rule is taken by his Collectors and never seen again. They come for you in the dead of night, in your home. They carry you off, and no one ever knows what's happened to you. And the Collectors know where you are staying, Lia."

Ailia was puzzled. "But I'm only one person."

"You might give voice to the dissatisfaction of others. He'll not brook any dissent at all, I tell you. If you ask me, I think he is afraid that the cult of the dragon god didn't die, but lives on in secret. That the old priesthood will rise again, and cast him down."

Here was one more reason for Ailia to leave Loänanmar. "Then, Mag, I will be sure to be gone from here as soon as I give my warning," she said.

They spoke no more of the matter. Mag fried some carp and brewed a pot of bitter green tea while Ailia took her turn serving the customers, and then when Mai took her place Ailia had her supper. She ate hungrily, and was surprised to find that the hot drink left her feeling cool and refreshed. As she sat in the kitchen the suns set, in a flood of crimson and vermilion clouds followed by a turquoise-colored dusk. Glancing out the back window, she saw that the castle on the hill had turned to a threatening shadow, and around its towers there played luminous orbs of many colors. No doubt these were more "dragon lanterns," like the one she had glimpsed earlier. They looked to be made of light, or quintessence: like the bright formless eidolons called will o' the wisps, which skilled Nemerei could summon out of the Ether when in need of illumination. Could they perhaps be tokens of the Dragon King's return? There were other lights within the dark mass of the castle, opening like fiery eyes to the night: lamplit windows, scores of them. One red light burned high in the main tower, just below its crown of pinnacles.

Mag saw. "You see!" she said, gripping Ailia's shoulder. "Someone is living in the Forbidden Palace again."

But Ailia's attention had shifted to a noise that was coming from the streets: drums, it sounded like, and a babel of voices. It swelled like a river in spate as she listened. The procession, if that was what it was, was drawing nearer. "Whatever is it?" she asked Mag. The woman's face was drawn with fear.

"They have seen the dragon lanterns—the ones who still believe. They will make a sacrifice next, to stay his wrath for all the years of neglect. It was done in the olden days. The temple priests selected a virgin—the Bride of the Dragon. She was brought to the castle hill, to the Dragon King, and if he was pleased with her he sent the rains for the crops. Lia, don't you see?" Mag sprang up. "He's *here*—he's come back! They would never dare this otherwise. The Overseer's rule is finished!"

Ailia ran to the door. Torches were burning through the dusk, drums pounding. Many curious onlookers were gathering, and more peered down from windows and rickety balconies above. Then as Ailia watched, a dragon came around the corner and into their street.

It was only an image, made of cloth and gilded paper, its wooden framework supported by more than a dozen men moving in a line. The long cylindrical body was covered in red and golden scales, with a pair of fan-shaped wings made of wood and paper, and a mass of multicolored ribbons for a mane. Its eyes were painted wooden balls that rolled in their sockets. A child squealed as the head oscillated from side to side, snapping its wooden jaws. Then it danced forward, propelled by the men underneath. A procession of young girls trailed after it. All wore veils or wreaths of lilylike flowers on their heads, and long white gowns.

"The virgin brides," Mag said, peering over Ailia's shoulder. "Oh, mercy—my daughter—they will want my daughter, Mai! She's beautiful and young, and a maiden still. She will have to go with them, and offer herself. I daren't refuse, now that I know *he* is back. I should have made her take up with that cursed scoundrel after all! Then at least she would have been safe from *this*." Mag twisted her calloused hands together and groaned. "*He* is back, he has come to reclaim his realm. And those poor girls—how could they know? They all think this is just a new festival, a bit of fun—but now *he* is here and will take what is offered him. And he will punish all the unbelievers—and if I withhold my daughter from him he will punish me—" She trembled, and put her hands to her mouth.

"Mag." Ailia turned to face her. "I will go and see what is happening. Don't be afraid! There are other powers than the Dragon King's in the world, powers for good. Believe me, you won't be left at his mercy." Even as she spoke she wondered, unhappily, if she ought to be making such promises to this distraught woman.

Mag shook her head. "No one can fight a *god*, Lia."

Ailia drew a deep breath. "But I swear to you, he isn't a god. He is just a living, mortal creature, who came to your world long ago from another one."

"How can you know that?" the older woman asked, staring.

"I *know*. There are—things I haven't told you, Mag. Things no one else here knows about. This wizard must be fought." Saying it aloud helped harden her resolve. "Listen to me, Mag. I can disguise myself, make people think I am your daughter. I can go to the Dragon King in her place—"

"No." The voice came from the room behind them. Young Mai was standing there, her expression rapt, her beautiful dark eyes shining in the torchlight. "I want to go with them—those other girls. I'm not afraid! I believe the Dragon King is good and kind. He's come back, to save us from our hardship, and punish people like Rad and the Overseer." There was love and trust in the girl's face. "When I was little I used to think how wonderful it would be if he were to come back, and set everything back in order again."

Mag tried to talk, then gave a little sob and buried her face in her hands. Ailia said, "I will go with you then, Mai. I'm a maiden too. At least she'll not be alone, Mag." The woman made no answer. Mai went to her mother, kissed her lightly on the forehead, and slipped away into the crowded street.

Mag gave a cry and caught at Ailia's hand. "Yes, Lia—go with her! You've a sort of power, haven't you—a gift, like mine? I've felt it before now. I don't know who you are, or why you've come, but if there's anything at all you can do—"

Ailia patted the work-roughened fingers clinging to her own. "I will do what I can, I promise. Will you please look after Twidjik for me? He will need another caregiver now." Then she gently withdrew her hand, and ran out into the street after Mai.

THE TEMPLE WAS DESOLATE no more: it was aglow with lights within, and full of young girls of all ages between twelve and twenty, veiled and clad in the white garments of vestals. Ailia doubted, given what she had learnt of Loänanmar, that all were maidens: from the smiles and titters the girls exchanged she suspected that Mag was right, and the people thought this was nothing but a sort of harmless street festival. She looked around for Mai and saw her standing by herself near the sacred pool, gazing up at the idol. She looked very young and fragile in her white shift. Several old men in dirty, dragon-embroidered robes were anointing the statue's stone feet with oils and muttering a chant in which she distinctly heard the name of Morlyn repeated, over and over. Ailia turned and followed a gaggle of laughing girls into a robing room to the left of the sanctum, where some elderly women were distributing white gowns and veils. The Overseer had been right in his suspicion that the cult of the dragon was not dead. It appeared that much secret preparation had preceded this night. Ailia joined the other girls in stripping to her undergarments, then took the long loose shift offered her and obediently pulled it over her head.

A gong sounded in the main temple and the young girls, now gowned and veiled, were led out the door by another group of priests, and Ailia slipped into the rear of the procession. Through the streets they went, past crowds of gawking city dwellers, until they joined with the group following the paper dragon. Some of the girls began to laugh and dance. On and on the strange parade wound, through the main thoroughfares and then out of the city, into the steaming region of hot springs and bubbling muddy pools that lay beyond. To the very foot of the high volcanic hill they went, looking up at the now brightly lit castle on its summit, and there the priests called a halt. The laughing and chattering ceased. The girls in their shroud-white attire stood uneasily, clumping together in tight little groups. Mai, despite her earlier words, had begun to quake visibly and the soft glow had gone from her eyes. She stood quietly at Ailia's side, and reached out to hold her hand.

"What will they do now?" she whispered. "Will—*he*—come?"

"I don't know," Ailia said softly. "Stay close to me."

"Hear me!" An elderly priest in a dragon-patterned robe came forward, looking over the girls. "Our master has returned from the heavens, to throw down the unbelievers and impose his rule on the world again. One of you will become the bride of the Dragon this night," he intoned. "Bound to him for all time, never to be the bride of mortal man. Have no doubt, it is an honor: an honor beyond the lot of most women." There were a few muffled giggles, but most of the girls had fallen silent.

Ailia listened, sickened. What horrific ritual was about to be enacted here? She looked at the steaming cave mouth in the hillside: was Mandrake concealed there in his dragon's shape, perhaps, awaiting the arrival of this sacrificial offering? What would he do?

Then there was a piercing scream in her ear, and the hand in hers was pulled away.

The priests had gathered around Mai, laid their heavy beringed hands on her slender arms. As Ailia watched they tore the veil from the girl's head. Mai panicked, writhing wildly in the effort to free herself. "Lia—Lia!" she cried.

Ailia shouted: "No—wait! Take *me* instead!"

The high priest looked her up and down with a sneer on his thick features. "You? You're nothing to look at. He will not want *you*. Go back to your home with the others. Our choice is made." The girls were all streaming away like a flock of frightened sheep, their pale figures dispersing into the gloom beyond the torches. Mai now stood motionless in the men's grip, her breast heaving like a trapped bird's. Her eyes were fixed on Ailia's.

"Let me go with her then," Ailia offered. "What is wrong with making *two* offerings in place of one?"

The men looked at one another and shrugged. "As you wish," the high priest said, and gave her a paper lantern. "Go. He awaits you in the cave."

Slowly Ailia and Mai mounted the narrow stony path that led to the cave entrance. It truly was as if they walked into a firedrake's mouth, Ailia thought, and could not keep down her rising dread. She glanced up at the fortress on the summit. The great stronghold looked even more formidable at close range, seeming almost to lean over them. It had crenellated battlements and barbicans, and as if to frighten any attackers, there were also stone dragons along its walls, silently roaring with open jaws. They reminded her of the dragon statues on the ruined walls of Haldarion back on Mera.

The cave gaped before them, and Mai hung back. Taking her hand, Ailia stepped forward. The steam misted her face, and the light was feeble, fading farther down to darkness. Holding the lantern high, Ailia led the way down the glistening rough-walled tunnel into the core of the dead volcano, Mai trailing behind her. It grew stiflingly warm as they descended—perhaps this volcano was *not* completely extinct after all? It was a disturbing thought, summoning images of seas of molten stone rolling and bubbling far down beneath her feet . . . Presently the tunnel ceased its steep plunge and grew almost level. They emerged into a wide space, a natural cavern. Its interior was very warm and damp, the rock faces glittering in the light of her lantern with more than moisture: it was all covered in crystals, like the inside of an immense geode. Were these crystals an aid to Mandrake's sorcerous powers?

A second tunnel opened out of the opposite wall.

The steam rose from a body of water that half-filled the cave. It was a sort of cist, then—and the water was warmed by natural heat from deep down in the volcano's bowels. Though it steamed it did not bubble—she guessed it to be hot but not scalding, bath temperature. Dragons, she knew, were fond of such natural cauldrons and would lie immersed in them for hours or even days on end. Was the Dragon King in this one, lurking just below the surface like an immense crocodile, hidden from view by the dense vapor?

Suddenly Mai clutched at her and gasped. Someone was coming down the opposite tunnel. A glow of lamplight bloomed within its dark door, and as they watched a man appeared. He wore a dragon-patterned robe like the priest's, but his was clean and well-kept and embroidered with thread of gold. He was very tall, and his long black hair was held back from his face by a gold clasp, so that his elegant patrician features clearly showed. He reminded Ailia all at once of the statues on the jungle ruins: a slightly debased version, perhaps, but still recognizable as a Loänei.

The man looked appraisingly at Mai, a little smile curling his full lips. She trembled as he approached them, skirting the edge of the fuming pool.

He smiled more broadly. "Welcome! This tribute is long overdue, as is the punishment for those who did not believe. And what a lovely creature you are, my dear." He reached out with his free hand, touched Mai's cheek. The girl flinched and shrank back, her eyes widening, but made no sound. Then the man turned, and frowned at Ailia. "But who might you be?"

"I am called Lia. And this is my friend Mai. I asked to come with her," Ailia explained as he continued to stare with raised black brows.

"You don't say! Well, you can always do for a servant, I suppose. You had both better come with me now."

He made a peremptory gesture, which Mai moved to obey, but Ailia stood still. "With you? I don't understand. We were sent as brides for the Dragon King. Will he not claim us?"

"Brides!" He laughed. "So they call you—but it is merely a formality. I doubt he will have any time for you. I will take you both to the royal court. If none of the courtiers wants either of you, then you'll go back to the city temple to become vestals."

He had no very great Nemerei powers: a sorcerer adept would have seen through Ailia's guise by now. She took a deep breath, drawing on all her power, and followed him and Mai.

The tunnel up which he led them was very like the first, rough-hewn and narrow. But at its top was a wooden door bound with brass, and beyond this a stone passageway, large and lamplit. Crimson carpets ran along the floor. Ailia and Mai followed the robed man through a number of corridors. Presently a sound of music and laughter came from up ahead: it flowed from a set of high carved doors.

Across from the doors and whatever great chamber lay behind them was a furnished receiving room not unlike those at Halmirion. Here the two girls were met by attendants and made to don long red over-robes with voluminous hanging sleeves, while their veils were removed and replaced with heavy headdresses from which hung lengths of red fabric, embroidered like the robes with golden dragons.

"But we cannot see through these," protested Ailia as hers was fitted on her head. The red cloth hung before her face, and was completely opaque. "How can we find our way?"

"You will be led by the hand. You are not to look on the divine presence before it is time," one of the women told her.

It was just as well, she decided: with her face covered she would not have to expend any more energy on glaumerie. Mandrake would sense no sorcery as she was led to him—until it was too late.

They were ushered from the receiving room by the attendants holding their wrists and elbows. Ailia heard the sound of a door being opened. "Go in, and approach the Dragon Throne," the Loänei man instructed their attendants curtly.

The girls walked on, feeling the moss-thick piles of a carpet under their feet. Glancing down, Ailia saw that it was bright scarlet like her robe, worked with gold designs. This room must be huge: they walked for some time down what must be a central aisle, and she could hear the voices of what sounded like hundreds of people.

Then their attendants hissed at them to stop and stand still. They obeyed, Ailia with growing tension. Was Mandrake here? Should she try to sense him, or would that give him too much warning of her presence?

"The new bride, Majesty," the Loänei said behind them, in his smooth obsequious voice.

A deep voice spoke from the dais, sending a shiver of recognition through Ailia. "It would appear I am seeing double," it said. "Are my eyes at fault, Erron, or do I see *two* women where you announce one?"

The man stooped and drew up the girls' veils from their faces. Quickly Ailia reemployed her glaumerie. "The chosen bride is this maiden, by name Mai; her companion, Lia, also seeks the honor of being brought before you. If you do not want her, Majesty, she can be a servant."

Ailia and Mai looked about them. The throne hall was all of dark green marble, and lit by huge lamps that hung on gold chains from the ceiling. Gold-plated dragons were twined about the pillars that supported the roof, their eyes of glowing red venudor seeming to glare upon the people below. The crimson carpet ran down the central aisle and ascended the dais at the far end. Upon this dais was a throne, also of gold, fashioned in the likeness of four dragons—two formed the armrests, and two reared up to make the back of the throne. It was made in imitation of the Emperor's Dragon Throne—a sign, perhaps, that the Loänei considered themselves the Empire's rightful heirs. Behind it a doorway was set in the wall, with heavy red curtains to conceal what lay beyond. The splendidly robed people assembled all around turned and stared at the two girls. Like the Loänei man they were tall and graceful, with finely sculpted features.

But Ailia's eyes were riveted on the occupant of the throne.

Mandrake was resplendent in regal attire, a wide-sleeved black silk robe under a red mantle that hung down and pooled like blood upon the dais. Both robe and mantle were richly embroidered with dragons in thread-of-gold, and on his head was a circlet of gold in the form of a ruby-eyed serpent biting its own tail.

Mandrake ignored Mai. His eyes were on Ailia, and their golden gaze was piercing: she felt it penetrate her hastily imposed glaumerie as a sunbeam lances through a mist. Swiftly he rose, and for an instant stood tall and straight, facing her. The ruby flashed its fire at her, like a challenge. Then without a word he turned and swept through the red curtains behind the dais.

Dropping her illusory disguise, brushing aside the protesting attendants with a single burst of power, Ailia sprang onto the dais and rushed after him.

17

The Dragon's Lair

"O GOD OF THE GLASS," intoned the high priest of the fisher-folk, "hear our petitions!" The young man bent his sun-bronzed torso in reverence, his necklace of jungle flowers swinging low. Before him the magical crystal, still attached to a fragment of console from the downed star-ship, gleamed dully in the light of the tall standing torches erected in a circle about it. "Will we catch many fish, Spirit of the Glass? Will the Dragon King, who rules the world's waters, give to us of his bounty? Will we be in any danger from sea serpents or orcs?" There was a flicker, and scenes of nets filled with fish appeared within the crystal's depths. The priest prostrated himself upon the sandy shore.

The other villagers, in their various attitudes of abasement, paid no heed to Auron and Taleera standing quietly behind them. The Loänan and T'kiri wore their human forms, plainly clad so as not to draw attention. They watched as the priest bowed once more, and all the people stood: the women, along with the children and the elderly, streaming toward their lamplit huts while the men gathered their nets and headed for the little slant-sailed fishing boats.

"Now, Auron!" whispered Taleera as soon as the boats had passed beyond the outer reef. "They're all gone."

The two guardians approached the globe. "Tell me!" said Taleera urgently. "What became of your passenger, oracle? Is she alive, did she survive the wreck of the flying ship?"

There was no response from the sphere. "It is no use," said Auron. "The power that is within the crystal obeys the laws of the Archons. It may not spy on one being for another—for any reason."

Taleera exploded. "It's not spying! It's a matter of life and death! She might have drowned, or been captured." She turned to face Auron. "Well, what are we to do? We cannot reach out to her ourselves, by calling mind to mind. He, or one of his servants, would overhear us. And if she is in hiding we might betray her location to Mandrake. She would respond when she felt our presence, and call out to us, and then he would have her."

"We shall just have to hunt for her then. We might look along the shore, and try to find her track or scent-trail. She must have come ashore not far from the wreckage."

"Auron." A little quaver had entered Taleera's voice. "We don't even know if she did come ashore."

Auron turned toward the globe. "Can you at least say that, eidolon? Can you tell us whether she lives? Light the crystal if she still lives!"

There was another flicker in the globe, a pause in which both their hearts seemed to stop, then a pure white radiance filled its depths.

They left the shore and village and rejoined Falaar, who was waiting for them deep within the jungle. Taleera shifted back to her own avian form. In the dusk her feathers glowed like an ercine's with a fiery luminescence. "We must hurry!" she shrilled, raising her wings. "I feel certain that she's in terrible danger!"

Falaar's great aquiline head tilted to one side. "I would not have her come to harm. The Stone is of little use without the wielder."

"The Stone!" Taleera screeched. "Is that all you care about? Where are your feelings, you great ungainly thing?"

"Friends, please! Enough of this, we must find Ailia quickly!" Auron remonstrated. "This world is fraught with danger, and our transformations may have alerted Mandrake. He is very sensitive to sorcery. We must go on to that city at once!"

"It is thy belief, then, that Her Highness is there?" Falaar said, ignoring the still-fuming firebird.

"It is my hope. For she lives yet, and being human—at least in part—she would naturally seek out the safety of her kind rather than remain in the jungle."

"That means taking human forms again," declared Taleera. "How tired I am of it! But I daren't let them see me in my own shape: they would shoot me for the pot, most likely, or for my plumes."

"I cannot alter my form at all," confessed the cherub with reluctance. "I have not the art."

"Then you must remain here in the jungle for the present," said Auron. "We will call on you if we need your aid."

AILIA RAN UP THE SPIRALING FLIGHTS of a narrow stone stairwell. She could not see Mandrake, but the sound of his footsteps came from high above her. He was not fleeing—she felt no panic from him; he could surely escape her with ease by using his sorcery. It was almost as though he wanted her to follow him. But where? Was he leading her into a trap of some kind?

At this thought she slowed her ascent. But even as she debated the wisdom of going on, there came a last turn to the stone steps, then the cold light of moons and stars above her. She emerged from the coils of the stairwell onto a broad platform atop a tower, surrounded by four jutting pinnacles. *The* tower from her vision. He was there, at the far end. He had not taken dragon form, not tried to flee by air. He stood with his back to the parapet, watching her, and waited until she had approached to within ten paces before he spoke. "I grow weary of retreating from the Nemerei. This is my home, and I intend to defend it this time."

Ailia stood still. She had forgotten the extraordinary power of Mandrake's voice, the deep rich resonance that reminded her of a bronze gong. *He must not know I am afraid,* she told herself. *However afraid I am, he must not sense it . . .*

"So fight me if you wish. I hear your powers have been well honed and trained by the Loänan. A good thing for you, if you are still as squeamish as I recall. You can kill, now, without bloodying your hands, or risking any injury to yourself."

He was trying to taunt her into attacking first. She felt anger from him now, and fear too: under his calm exterior seethed a volatile admixture of emotion that the slightest provocation would ignite into violence. He had come here in order to fight for his life, choosing the place for their duel. The scene before her was very close to the one in her vision. Had he had a similar vision, perhaps?

"I don't want to fight you, Mandrake," she answered. Did her apprehension show in her own face or voice? She thought of Damion and her other friends, and her voice grew firmer. "But I don't want any more people to die because of this prophecy—if it *is* a prophecy. If there must be a fight, then let us limit it to our own two persons, and not sacrifice whole armies and thousands of innocent lives."

He was silent for a moment, and she sensed uncertainty from him, as though her words were not what he had expected. And she felt something else: a familiar, jarring note of discord. Was he in pain? And then all at once she realized what it was. Iron. Somehow, someone had recently injured him with iron. It had weakened him, taken the edge off his powers. In any contest of sorcery she would hold a slight advantage, even though she was out of her own sphere. She could defeat him: it was possible. She had her ring, and the magical skill to use it: to force from the depths of its blue gem the energies that slept there, tear asunder the wall that divided matter and Ether and turn the resulting burst of power on him. As she thought this she knew a thrilling moment of pride and potency. Then she banished the exultation, suddenly repelled by it. This was not what she had come to do.

It was too late, though: he had read her thoughts in her face, and his own expression became colder still. "I should perhaps mention that your friends are now in my hands—or rather in Khalazar's, which is the same thing. To order their deaths would be the work of a moment. Can you kill me quickly enough to prevent it? Shall we see?"

She nearly reeled, steadying herself with an effort. Damion and the others—captured! Was this true? Or only another of his lies?

Again he watched her reaction. "So: we are at an impasse," he said. "Unless your friends' lives are an acceptable price to pay for destroying me?"

"Why, Mandrake?" she asked at last. "What have we ever done to you?"

"I might ask the same question of the Loänan, and of all the Nemerei," he said. "What did I do to deserve being hounded by them across the void? And when at last I found a home, far from their precious empire and its peoples—why did they still persecute me?"

Righteous indignation came to Ailia's aid. "You deceived the people here—made them believe you are a god! And after they rejected you, you came back to enslave them again! Did you think the Nemerei would allow that to happen?"

He raised his hand. "One moment. I believe you are under a misapprehension, Princess. I came back here because it is my home. I want nothing to do with the people of Loänanmar: I didn't invent that absurd religion, *they* did."

"But you let them worship you as a god—they built a temple to you—"

"What if they did? Human beings must worship something: it is their nature. This castle is built upon a volcano, a former sacred site. When I first came here—long before the castle was constructed—I took to living in the cave deep within. The people caught glimpses of my dragon-form, and it reminded them of their former Loänei masters, and also took the old volcano goddess's place in their imagination. Their adulation was no idea of mine."

"But the Brides—"

"A different version of an old ritual: the volcano virgins, the human sacrifices these people's ancestors used to throw alive into calderas as an offering to the goddess Elnemorah. Only rather than giving their lives, the Brides were simply presented to me—once every year, in the old days, to ensure rains and healthy crops. Though in this case, of course, the god could actually grant the mortals' requests."

They were circling one another now, eyes fixed on one another's faces. "And those poor girls? What did you do with them?" she demanded.

If he would only give her a reason to hate him—confess to some hideous cruelty or barbarism, so that she might be able to summon the will to hurt him, to kill him . . . But he only shrugged. "It was a symbolic union, no more. The ritual over, the maidens became holy vestals serving in my temple. I saw no reason to interfere. I am not so very different from a god, after all: remote, indifferent, observing but not taking part in their lives. Let them worship that, if they wish. It is not as evil as volcano worship. And is it any worse than that Arainian cult that's centered on yourself? You don't believe in that lunacy about being a goddess's daughter, do you?"

She could not look him in the face and deny it. He had thrown her charge back at her. "But I don't demand any sacrifices," she said, and even to her the protest sounded feeble and defensive.

He laughed without humor. "Now you split hairs. You have been playing god too, Tryna Lia. Though, to be just, you had no more say in your deification than I. You are no natural being, but rather the result of Archonic schemes—like me. Did your Archon mother truly love your father, or did she merely make use of him in order to create you? The truth is, even the Morugei are more human than you are, Tryna Lia. Perhaps I am a monster, but you are one too."

She fell silent; seeing that his barb had gone home he added, "As for that cursed Archon gem of yours—don't you realize what the Star Stone is? You know who owned it before you: the dark god himself!"

Ailia shivered, but kept her gaze steady. "I thought you didn't believe Valdur was a god."

"No more I do. But I am sure the tale of Valdur's fall contains some seed of truth. Hasn't your pretty Archon bauble already bound you to a life you never chose? I must say, when I heard you had fled your guardians I hoped you had finally rebelled and taken your freedom. But no, you have merely come here to do your duty"—his voice grew harsh, bitter—"and once that is accomplished you will fly back to your prison-palace and to the Stone, yearning to be enslaved again."

She should have set aside her distaste for violence, she realized, and attacked him right away. It was too late now. His words seemed to penetrate her soul, reflect her innermost thoughts: she could not help but hear.

"Do you remember the glaumerie I cast for you?" he pursued. "I meant to return you to Mera in truth. You would have gone into the convent as you had planned, spent a happy useful life in library and scriptorium. But now it is too late. You are not the same Ailia, and you can never return to your former existence. Is that not so?" He made it sound like an irrevocable loss. "Yes—I know all about these things, thanks to the efforts of Lady Syndra, who overheard more than you ever knew."

"If you know all, then why do you ask?" was all she could find to say.

"I want you to admit your feelings to yourself, out loud. Ailia, I cannot send you back to your Island home. That life is ended forever. But I can make you another offer. Stay here with me and the other Loänei. We will accept you as one of us, allow you to be yourself." His golden eyes held hers. "Three days. Give me that long to convince you. And you, in turn, can attempt to convince me that it is you who are right. We will be very civilized to one another, and then"—he took a step toward her—"at the end of your stay, if neither one of us has converted the other, we will return to this tower and conclude what we left unfinished."

He would be slightly stronger in three days, she knew, more able to fight her. But he was also offering her what she had come to Nemorah for: a chance to plead, to argue, to parley. She might yet avoid having to use her newfound powers to wound and kill. Ailia saw Ana's sad aged face in her mind, heard again the sorrow in her voice as she spoke of the child she had saved. She had urged Ailia not to be weakened, as she was, by compassion; but how could one receive an offer of peace, and not take it? And there were her friends in Zimboura to be considered, too . . .

She held his feral golden eyes with her own. "Agreed," she said. "But on one condition."

The eyes narrowed in suspicion. "What would that be?"

"The young girl who was brought here with me—Mai. I want her sent back to her home."

He looked indifferent. "The Bride? I don't want her. She is free to go. And so are you, for that matter. No one here can hold you against your will. Call on your keepers, if you like, and return home with them. We can always fight another day."

"I will stay here," she said.

"Very well." His tone suddenly became courteous. "But it is late, and you must be tired. I will have the Loänei prepare a room for you."

*   *   *

SHE WAS SHOWN BY HUMAN servants into a large, luxurious apartment, with intricate moldings on the ceiling and gilded furnishings. The Loänei must have been secretly restoring their old palace to its former state of luxury. Her aching soles sank into the soft pile of a crimson carpet. Through an open door she glimpsed the bedroom, the bed draped with fine curtains to keep insects out. Another door opened on a bathroom with a sunken marble bath. There were tapestries upon the walls, and vases so full of flowers that the air was heavy with their scent. An alabaster statue of a nymph danced motionlessly in a wall niche. There were bottles of fragrant unguents, perfumes, oils, gilded combs and brushes, a jewel box brimming with brooches and necklaces.

The windows looked down on the inner court, a pleasure garden filled with both ferny and blossoming trees.

Despite her luxurious surroundings Ailia was wary and afraid. If at the end of her stay she had not succeeded in turning him back to her side, they would duel to the death. The vision she had had could still come to pass: she had not managed to circumvent it. She took Damion's silver dagger from its sheath at her thigh and sat gazing down at the blade. She would sleep with it tonight.

There was a pattering sound at the windows, making her look up nervously. The panes were streaked and glistening, the sky gray beyond. Mandrake, it appeared, had chosen to reward the bridal offering with rain.

"INCREDIBLE. IT SEEMS THAT SHE came not to challenge me, but to answer my request to parley. She knows now it was not a sincere offer, but all the same she hopes to strike a pact. To appeal to my better nature!"

The prince had returned to his throne room and summoned his councillors. The ethereal forms of King Roglug and the regent of Ombar also floated on the air before him: both had now returned to their home world. Roglug guffawed loudly at Mandrake's last words, then hastily subsided as the wer-worm's golden eyes turned to him.

"How could you let her live?" snapped the black-haired Loänei who had brought the Brides. "The Tryna Lia herself! Was it not you, Prince, who told us she was perilous? It is mad—heedless. She will destroy us all."

"She cares nothing about you—and, Erron Komora, it was you brought her into the fortress—into my very presence!" Mandrake spoke harshly, with a reptilian hiss on each sibilant, as he only did when really angry. "Shall we speak of *your* heedlessness? Unless, perhaps, you suspected who she was all along, and intended that she slay me?"

Erron paled. "I swear I did not know who she was, Highness! She was too well disguised."

"It is not too late to kill her," said a voice from the doorway. Lady Syndra stood there, clad in a long green gown of Loänei make, her dark hair loose about her shoulders. "Reconsider, Prince, and rid yourself of this threat once and for all."

Naugra's spectral eyes were also fixed on Mandrake. "Hear her, Prince. This is an opportunity, a gift of fate. You must slay the Tryna Lia if you wish to continue as our Avatar, and enjoy Ombar's protection."

Mandrake rose abruptly from his throne. "I will consider the matter, and let you know my decision."

Naugra's image dimmed and faded, though Roglug's remained. Mandrake went to the nearest of the tall windows. The lower pane was designed to swing outward: he opened it and stood for a moment staring out.

"What are you going to do?" asked Roglug.

The prince made no reply. Drawing on his magic, he began to transform. A moment later a bright-plumed bird whirred up from the carpet and swooped out of the window into the night.

The golden bird was an old familiar form, not based on any real fowl but invented by him on a whim when first he became adept at shape-shifting. In flight it was fast as a falcon, and the cry it uttered was piercing and powerful, rising and falling like the howl of a wolf: hearing that warning note, few other winged creatures dared approach it. He flew up to the battlements with a few strokes of his golden wings, riding a column of heated air from the boiling springs below. The city lay spread out before him, its lights shining even at this late hour. His temple glowed at the center, like a great lantern of stone.

He recalled a time when there had been no lights on the land below, save for a few flickering tallow candles in mud huts along the river's edge. The Loänei had left behind their human slaves when the Loänan drove them from this world, and over time the descendants of the freed thralls had thrived and spread. He found them when he came here to seek their vanished masters, and claim the cavern in the hill for his new home. Slowly and inevitably the human population had grown as he watched, driving back the jungle and tainting the river. When at last it grew too large for his liking, Mandrake attacked the settlement in dragon form, frightening away the herd animals, disrupting the local weather so that the villagers' crops were alternately battered with hail and parched by drought. But the humans had come back over time, lured by the gold-bearing river and the rich volcanic soil. Again and again he had assailed them, and always they had returned in time.

One day a small group of them carried a slaughtered goat up to the very mouth of his cave. Disguised as a lizard clinging to the rock nearby, he watched them with contempt. They killed wyverns in this way, he knew, setting out carcasses laced with poison. Did they think him a mere beast, to fall for such tricks? But a few hours later he noticed that some cockatrices gorging on the carrion were unharmed. Was the goat meat an honest gift, then? Or possibly a bribe? Or . . . Then he realized in a flash what it was: a sacrificial offering, brought here to placate him. They must have some dim recollection of the fearsome dragon-people their ancestors revered. There was something pathetic about their gesture of appeasement, and though he attacked the settlement again that night he did it halfheartedly, inflicting only minor damage this time.

But in his long years of exile from his kind he had forgotten about human tenacity. The people, finding their meat offering spurned, sent a second delegation, this one carrying many trinkets of beaten gold and precious gems. These attracted him as the meat had not, calling to him with their seductive and radiant power. He left his cave at last, tempted beyond bearing, gathered the treasures up, and carried them back to his lair. From that moment on he made no more forays against the settlers, and the town flourished and grew into a great city.

And so the curious cult had developed. The tributes continued, and in time he lost his resentment of the humans and even found their presence diverting. He watched as their settlement expanded, and sometimes he even visited it in his human form. But this nearly proved fatal. He became infatuated with a human woman, a young vestal in his own temple, and revealed himself to her. Unknown to Mandrake, a Loänan was then visiting the city in human guise, observing this cult and suspecting its originator to be a Loänei. It was the Imperial dragon Auron, sent by Orbion to seek news of Prince Morlyn in all the worlds. Even then he had been striving to protect the Tryna Lia, who would not be born yet for centuries, by searching out her prophesied adversary. He had challenged Mandrake, who was forced to flee, and from that day forward the prince had cherished a bitter hatred of Auron for driving him from his chosen home. He had sought refuge, in desperation, among the followers of Valdur in the world of Ombar where the Loänan never went. And there for many years he had been forced to remain.

The golden bird glided down to Ailia's window, just as he had flown to Khalazar's tower window on that first night in Zimboura. He alighted on the sill and perched there a moment, staring in. The window was open, as were all windows in the castle on this hot night. Mandrake fluttered down onto the floor, and returned to his human shape. His feet made no sound upon the soft carpet as he approached the bed. With one hand he pushed back the diaphanous netting, gazing down at the sleeper within.

Ailia lay half under the satin sheet, her face turned up and defenseless. Her slender arms and neck were bared by the filmy white nightgown the servants had given her, and with her eyes closed she looked suddenly vulnerable. Her breast rose and fell slowly beneath the thin sheet. It would be the work of an instant to kill her. She had even given him a weapon. A silver dagger lay on the pillow where it had tumbled from her fingers. He took it up carefully, weighing it in his hand. Poor Ailia. She had committed the fatal mistake of listening to her enemy, of desiring a truce. Had she been wiser she would have tried to kill him immediately.

He looked down at her sleeping form again, willing her to move, to flutter her eyelids, to utter a murmur: to appear to be on the verge of waking. How easy, then, it would be to use the knife. If she saw him standing there she would surely attack, defend herself with all the awesome power at her disposal. He would be entitled to protect himself. But Ailia slept the impenetrable sleep of one exhausted in body and mind, drained of all animation but for the slow rise and fall of her breast beneath the covers. Her breathing was regular, soft, peaceful, and she did not stir. Her face was pale and still, emptied of expression, with not even a flutter of her long dark eyelashes to hint at some passing dream. All at once she looked to him like a child—as if sleep had given back to her the innocence she had lost. He stood rooted to the spot, gazing down at her.

Then he set the dagger down again and walked softly back to the window. *She has made victory too easy! She has thrown it in my lap. And why, after all, should I kill this girl? She is not what I feared she was. I listened to Syndra's accounts of her, and never stopped to think that the image she painted of the Tryna Lia was distorted with her own hate and envy. Ailia has no desire for power and dominance: she is only a hapless pawn in the games of the Archons and the Loänan and the Nemerei. They are the true enemy.*

He could have hoped to fight any other foes without recourse to sorcery. His mother's race was exceptionally tall and strong, and he had worked for uncounted years to push the limits of his physical frame. He could wield a bow or broadsword as tall as himself, jump a wall as high as a man's head, break a plank with a blow from his bare hand. Yet it was not enough. These skills might give him the advantage over a human assailant, but his worst adversaries were creatures many times his size and immeasurably stronger. In a physical contest with the least of these he would not stand a chance, and there were many situations in which his sorcery could fail him. If only he could exchange this body for another . . .

There was a sudden sharp pain in the side of his neck, as though a red-hot blade were biting into the flesh. It was there that his father's sword, wielded by the knight Ingard, had struck him long ago. It was not uncommon for a wound from a magical weapon to remanifest as a *stigma*: such wounds could even fester and bleed. And now there was another stab of agony, this one in his left side: for that same sword had pierced him again, in his fight with Ailia's companions on Arainia.

He staggered against the window frame, clutching at his neck. Yes, there were two angry welts rising from the skin. The manifestations were caused by stress and fear: he had but to eliminate those emotions, and the wounds would vanish with them. He took several deep, calming breaths, *willing* the pain away. After a moment it eased, subsiding to a dull ache. With an effort, Mandrake stood upright again. He climbed onto the sill, stooping, and then flung himself over the edge as he called upon the power of the Ether to shift from human to dragon-form.

His human skin he exchanged for a mail of metallic scales; his hands curled into claws; his blood pulsed through mazy veins powered by the vast engine of a draconic heart. He had the eyes and claws of an eagle now, and the wings and ears of a bat; his teeth were tusks that could shear through steel as if through paper. With his altered eyes he was able to see minute details on the ground far below, while his ears were open to a wide range of sounds unknown to the human ear. Two long whip-shaped vibrissae extended from the end of his muzzle, waving gently as they sensed the air currents. His consciousness expanded with his cranium, spreading like a thrown net to encompass centuries of memory a human brain could not hold—instincts and reflexes foreign to his man-self, strange dark hungers, hoards of ancient knowledge, lodes of power.

Fire-red wings arched into the air as he plummeted from the battlements. In this form the sheer drop that would have been death to a human was of no consequence. And very few weapons could harm him. This was the form in which he felt safest: if only he could maintain it for longer periods of time! Some day he would learn to take this dragon-shape permanently, discard his human body forever. He would live as a Loänan, his former human existence all but forgotten. True dragons began their lives as tiny, helpless larvae: even so would the man he was evolve into something greater and stronger. For now he must devise other means to protect himself.

I planned once to make use of the Tryna Lia: perhaps I can still do so. One can knock the sword from the hand of the opponent and snatch it up to use against him. The weapon itself is not the enemy, but rather the one who wields it. The servants of the Imperium are my enemies, not this sorry creature. If I could win her to my side, all her sorcerous powers would be at my disposal. I could take up this prized weapon of theirs—on which they have so clumsily lost their grip—and turn it against them. With Ailia's power joined to mine, I would not need the Valei—would never need, nor fear, anyone or anything else again.

It was a tempting vision. But how could he seduce the Tryna Lia into becoming his ally and turning on her former protectors?

18

The Duelers' Dance

WHEN SHE WOKE, AILIA looked about her in blank bewilderment: she had awakened so often of late in strange surroundings that she felt completely at a loss. Then she remembered. The audience hall—the tower—Mandrake.

She sat up, and then she saw that her dagger had been moved. She had set her Thorn with its handle toward her so that she could grab it quickly at need. Now it was the tip of the blade that faced her. She knew at once whose hand had taken it up. He had been here in the room—right beside her, while she slept! She shivered.

But he had done her no harm. She was alive still.

It was a little triumph in its own right. She had trusted him, and he had not betrayed her trust. Her instincts had been right. Thanks to Ana and the Paladins there remained in him some vestige of virtue, a memory of the code of honor he had once served. And if that were so, then he might yet be redeemed.

She threw off the silken covers and pulled the filmy netting aside. The suns were up, and the room in their harsh brilliant light still looked elegant, but had lost its faerie-tale glamor. She washed in the marble bathroom, and combed and braided her hair, then had another look around the apartments. There were many fine gowns in a wardrobe, the property no doubt of one who had intended to use this room before the unexpected guest took her place. Ailia did not touch them, but dressed in her white shift from the temple.

Presently she heard a knock at the door, and cautiously she opened it a crack and peered out. There stood an aged stoop-shouldered woman, her hair wrapped in a scarf. She carried a tray with a domed silver cover. "I have brought you something to break your fast, my lady," she said.

Ailia opened the door wide, and the maidservant shuffled in and set the tray down on a table near the window. "Your pardon, Highness," said the elderly woman as she lifted the cover, "but His Highness ordered us to taste the dishes first, lest you should fear any poison in them." Ailia nodded, but thought it highly unlikely that Mandrake would spare her while she slept only to kill her by poisoning. What would be the point? She watched as the servant sampled the dish of rice, eggs, and boiled fish. Then, the tasting over, she asked the old woman to sit with her and talk to her while she ate. Surprised and a little flustered, the servant obeyed.

"How did you come to be here, may I ask?" Ailia said.

"Offered up, I was, sixty years ago. Bridal offerings was often made then. My mother couldn't afford to feed me, so to the temple I went. I was only seventeen then: my, but I was frightened! But it was just a place like any other—except grander. They made me a vestal, and put a roof over my head, and gave me bread each day, but I wasn't ever to leave. Still, it was more'n I ever had at home, where there were so many of us, and so little food. When the Overseer came all we vestals was thrown into the streets, except for the ones his friends carried off for themselves—I can still hear their screams, poor things. But I wasn't took, praise be, for I was long past my youth—though I was left to make my own way in the world, and I've been poor and hungry ever since. When I heard the Golden Bird had been seen in the city, and that people was coming back to live at the castle like in the old days, I offered my services again. They don't want me for no temple maiden, o' course, but they brought me up here to be a maidservant."

Ailia listened, moved. This poor woman had never known true kindness in her life—of course to her the theocrats had been benefactors. She had been used, taken advantage of by them and now by the Loänei. It was an outrage—but for the moment there was nothing she could do.

She picked at the rice dish, but found she had little appetite.

The next few days she spent wandering about the castle on her own. "They always do sleep in the daytime here," the old woman had explained, "and come out at nightfall—creatures of the night, that's what the dragon-folk are. I'm afraid you'll have to amuse yourself, mistress, until the evening. There is to be a ball tonight, in your honor I understand." It was a truly magnificent place, very reminiscent of Halmirion: there were rooms of marble in many different colors, splendid statues in niches, gold candelabra the size of saplings everywhere she looked. In addition to a banquet hall and the great throne room there was a ballroom with gilded and muraled walls, and a conservatory so large it had graveled paths winding in and out of its potted trees, all under a dome of glass. She found a door leading out into the courtyard her room looked down on, with its fish pool and rose bowers and trees. The suns' heat smote the back of her neck like the blast of a forge as she stepped out on the grass, and nothing stirred in the garden. Even the carp hung motionless in the shade of the lily pads. Perhaps this was the reason the Loänei preferred to be active at night: no sinister preference for darkness, but merely a desire to avoid the oppressive heat.

By late afternoon the silence and emptiness of the place had become unsettling. She retreated to her guest room, and found that someone had been there: a cold meal stood on the table, and a red silk kimono and a magnificent formal gown were lying on the bed. The latter was rose-colored, sewn with silk rosettes on skirts and sleeves, and trimmed at neck and cuffs and hem with lace as fine as frost. She held it up against her body: it was lower in the neck than she liked. Its original owner, whoever she might be, was broader in the shoulders and had longer arms, and the hem had been raised. But all in all it was not a bad fit. And the color was flattering. Looking around, she saw a pair of pink slippers also adorned with rosettes and tried them on. These fit her exactly: of course, it would have been easy for them to measure her shoes while she slept. But there was still something almost magical about it, and to her own alarm she felt a foolish flutter. Hastily she put the things away and headed for the bathroom. She had not had a proper bath in days.

The room was as magnificent and luxurious as the other chambers, with its large sunken bath of marble and taps that gave hot water on demand: she wondered if this came from the hot springs in the caverns below. There were aromatic soaps and bath oils such as the Arainians liked to use—indeed, every luxury had been provided. Only the room's mirrored walls gave her pause. People here were plainly not troubled by nudity: she had been amazed to see scores of unclad bathers of both sexes lolling in Mag's hot spring every morning. It was true that she had been raised on Mera, in a

society with a long tradition of shame and modesty. Only on
Arainia had she begun to feel, when dressing alone in her bedchamber, the innocent animal pleasure of possessing a body—of
being *embodied*. At such times the sheath of her skin seemed to
come alive as it never did under clothing, and her mind in turn
knew a thrill of guiltless pleasure. But this room with its abundance
of mirrors—this went beyond mere enjoyment of one's own flesh-
liness. She felt as though she were being manipulated into self-
admiration, and she averted her eyes from the reflected images as
she stepped into the foaming bath.

She had a long soak and washed her hair. Then she toweled herself dry, put on the kimono, and had her meal. She must wait for
night to fall, and the Loänei to emerge.

THE BALLROOM WAS A VERY DIFFERENT place when it was occupied:
alive, filled with light and color and sound. Ailia hesitated as she
stood in the doorway, looking at the dancers spinning to swift-
paced music, the couples entwined on the cushioned divans and
standing behind huge potted ferns. The women had elaborately
dressed hair, great curls and rolls piled high upon their heads, and
voluminous flowing gowns. Whenever they moved, jewels winked
slyly in the depths of their hair or glittered on their clothing. Flowers were everywhere—bursting from slender vases, twined about
the candelabra, scattered across the refreshment table. A fountain
of crystal had been set up in the middle of the room, a lantern at
its center illuminating the droplets that showered around it. The
scene looked deceptively pleasant and even familiar: it might have
been any of the state occasions she had attended as princess of
Arainia. No doubt the entertainment had been devised with just
that goal in mind, to put her at her ease—and off her guard. She
must not succumb to those designs. This was no light and pleasing
diversion, but an encounter fraught with danger, orchestrated by a
powerful and capricious adversary.

She looked about her warily, but could not see Mandrake anywhere.

She entered the room, holding her head high so as not to betray
her unease. She had no diadem to wear, but she had bound the
braids of her hair in a coronet about her head as a reminder of her

rank. Still, she did not quite like the way the other revelers looked at her as she passed them.

"Good evening," said a voice in her ear as she turned to inspect the fountain. She jumped violently, to her chagrin, and spun to face the speaker. Mandrake was splendidly attired in a doublet of black velvet, dark leggings, and boots. He wore no crown tonight, his mass of tawny hair falling freely to his shoulders. A medallion hung upon his breast: a dragon of red enamel, rampant within a circle of gold. The emblem of Morlyn, the Dragon Prince. Perhaps it was the very pendant he had worn at court in Mera, five centuries ago . . .

"Well, what do you think?" he inquired politely, waving a hand at the room.

"It's—splendid," she replied, regaining her composure. She eyed the elaborate floral displays, the cascades of many-colored blooms that gave the grand chamber the look of an arbor. "You have gone to a great deal of effort."

"The occasion warrants it," Mandrake said. He offered his black velvet arm. "This ball is in your honor, did you know? Come, Princess," he reproved as she made no move to approach him, "can it be that you still don't trust me? You have been under my roof for a night and a day and I have done you no harm. But perhaps you would rather be back in your court, with dozens of enamored suitors attending you and writing you bad poetry."

"I have no suitors," she said, taking his arm with some reluctance.

"No?" he raised an eyebrow, and she realized he knew perfectly well that she had none.

She glanced away. "Who is that man with the long black hair, the one who first brought me to you? Why does he glare at you so?"

"That is Erron Komora. He glares because he hates me," said Mandrake. "I killed his grandfather, the former Great Dragon." He did not speak boastfully, but with a cool indifference that was somehow more appalling.

"So he wants to avenge him," Ailia said.

"Avenge? Not at all. He was hoping to kill the old man himself, as soon as his powers were strong enough. His father had already tried and failed—with fatal results. Erron's powers are weak, but he knew the Great Dragon would one day become too old and feeble to fight. Then he would have an easy kill—and the throne would be his for the taking. But I beat him to it, and for that he cannot forgive me. I suppose I should eliminate him," added the prince without so much as glancing at his rival, "but I don't wish to alienate the Loänei too much at first. He bears watching, though. He may not have great powers, but he has a nasty cunning mind."

"But that is horrible!" Ailia exclaimed. "How can you live with such people?"

"You're sounding more like Ana all the time," he said with disapproval. Then he swung around sharply. Everywhere in the hall heads turned away, and a buzz of hastily improvised conversation arose. "What a prying, inquisitive lot they are," he said without rancor. "What are you smiling at, Princess? No—don't stop. It's a pleasure for once to see a smile that has no malice or mockery in it. Shall we find a more private place to talk?"

He offered his arm again and she allowed him to lead her out of the room and down the corridor. He stopped in front of a closed door and pushed it open. "Here," he said. "We can talk in here."

Ailia looked around the room curiously as she entered: it looked almost like a museum, full of peculiar objects.

"My private collection of curiosities," he told her. "I gathered some of them as a dragon. Stole, you would say, though the men I stole from were thieves too: robber barons and tyrant kings. Even as a child I always kept a hoard of shiny objects about me—I didn't know why then, of course. I have always surrounded myself with beautiful things." He was looking at her as he spoke. "It's good to see you wearing a color for once, instead of that everlasting white. Don't you ever get tired of it?" He gestured at the rose garden.

Ailia was more interested in examining the objects. She recognized a Kaanish vase, a Shurkanese hanging, an Elei bard-harp. There was a model of a man's head made apparently of brass, atop a pedestal of the same material. The jaw, she noticed, was hinged as though it were designed to move.

"It is a kind of automaton called a Cogitator," Mandrake said in answer to her unspoken query. "If you ask it a question it will compute an answer, and respond."

"The twelfth king of Shurkana had a brazen head like this. A gift from the Elei, or so the story went."

"This is the same one."

"However did you come by it?" she asked, fascinated in spite of herself.

"That is a story I must tell you, one of these days."

Ailia turned to a glass aquarium containing water, some odd-looking aquatic plants, and—"Good Heavens! Whatever is it?" she exclaimed. The creature was like an eel, a silvery ribbon-shaped creature, but it had several round dark eyes spaced along the length of its body, and no discernible head.

"I don't know: I found it in a world that lies outside Talmirennia."

"You've traveled *beyond* the Empire?" she asked, not knowing whether to believe him or not.

"I have. Ah, the things I could show you! You, who have lived all your life on Mera and Arainia! It is as though you had spent all your life in a couple of backwoods villages, never going outside, never seeing the world with its forests, mountains, oceans, and cities! There are things you have not even dreamt of!"

She recalled her early days on the Island, her longing to see all that could be seen.

"I could show you great nebulae and pulsating stars. I could take you to a planet where trees sprout from the ground in the morning, grow tall and bear fruit at noon, and die by nightfall. Or show you a world that has two atmospheres: one thick with vapor that covers all the lower regions of the planet's surface, while the air of the upper layer into which its highlands project is clear and rare. Some people live on these lofty lands, soaring in flying vessels over the Cloud Sea that separates them from one another as an ocean separates continents. The rest live beneath the gray canopy, never seeing the highland dwellers unless one of their ships crashes into the lower regions. And those that dwell in the upper realms cannot breathe the air of the lower; they stifle in it, as if drowning in water. No tales of the high lands come down to the people under the Cloud Sea," Mandrake said.

"And then there are Archons. They built great cities, whose ruins still lie on far-flung worlds. I could take you to a frozen world whose cities are made not of stone, but ice quarried from glacial fields. Lamps of many-colored venudor still stand in the icy chambers within, and their light shines through the cold walls as if through thick clouded glass, so that the cities glow in the night.

There are castles of ice, bridges of ice, towers and monuments and statues of ice in the shapes of strange beasts and beings. But no trace remains of their makers."

"Auron says they wore many forms on many different worlds. To his ancestors they appeared as dragons."

"That is true. What their own, true shape was no one knows: they never revealed it, and they did not bury their dead in tombs as humans do."

"Have you ever found anything that suggested what they were truly like?" she asked, curious.

"Not yet. On one small and lonely world I found remains I thought might be those of Archons: there were vast stone sarcophagi there with Elensi inscriptions, and inside lay huge skeletons, twice as tall as any human being. But I learned from the inscriptions that these were merely humans who had settled the planet in ancient times, developing huge bodies because of the low gravity."

"Giants—real giants." Ailia suddenly thrilled with the desire to see, to know. "So you haven't just been hiding all these years, but exploring, too."

He threw her a sharp look. "My dear Princess, I have had to hide all my life! My mother had to go into hiding to bear me, for fear the Loänan would kill her to prevent it."

"Oh, no! They *wouldn't*."

"Probably not, but she was afraid they would. And they would have taken me from her, I have no doubt: found a way to isolate me and confine my powers. Some of the Nemerei in Trynisia even wanted me dead. Ana wouldn't have it, but I was not allowed to go free either."

"And then came Andarion's court."

"My father . . ." Mandrake looked pensive. "He was terrified of me, and felt guilty for having loved my late unlamented mother. We never became close, though I tried hard enough to please him: all my greatest deeds were done for *him*, but to no avail. I had to call him 'sire' like everyone else—but since that could also mean 'father' I didn't mind so much." Mandrake paused, and his face grew closed, as though he had revealed more than he had intended.

It was a story Ailia had known for nearly all her life. At last she had a chance to know more of it, the facts the storytellers had not known. "Then why did you turn on him?"

"I never turned on my father! I truly didn't know what was happening to me—I had horrible dreams and sometimes thought I was going mad. But I had no idea that my moods were affecting the weather and the land. My Loänan powers didn't start to emerge until years later. Then the wind and clouds and rivers began to be disturbed by the energies I was unconsciously releasing. I had nightmares of being a dragon, of terrorizing the countryside. At least I thought then that they were nightmares: I didn't know that the images I recalled on waking each morning were actually memories, that in my sleep I was really leaving the castle, really *becoming* a dragon. I was two creatures in one, the dragon giving shape to my deepest fears, but I didn't know I *was* the rampaging monster from my dreams. When I was told that the attacks in those dreams really had occurred, I assumed I must somehow have developed a link to a rogue dragon's mind."

Ailia listened in fascination. There was conviction in his voice: she was sure he was telling the truth, or at least his view of it, rather than an outright lie.

"Eliana learned of what was happening, and she realized that my mother's talent had emerged in me. When Brannar Andarion heard, he thought I was doing it deliberately," Mandrake continued. "He had always feared me and was glad, I think, of an excuse to ride against me—destroy me at last. After the famous fight with Andarion and Ingard in the cave, I must have unconsciously assumed the dragon's form when I fell wounded into the water. A dragon can hold its breath for nearly an hour, long enough for my father to believe me drowned. When I came to myself again, all I knew was that I was lying on the shore of the subterranean lake, with a bleeding wound in my neck. It was deep but not mortal, and I staggered up through the cellars to the main floor of the castle, only to find it had all been laid waste, my loyal men killed. I found my way to the abandoned dispensary, where I bound up my injury, but I was afraid to leave the confines of the fortress and lived alone in its desolate ruin for weeks. It was my Zimbouran childhood all over again—but worse, for this time my attackers were those I hoped had some regard for me.

"As soon as I could, I made my way to an ethereal portal—there were a few left in Maurainia, and though all were closed I had learned the art of opening them—and I fled the world of Mera."

"But you came back," she said.

"Yes—many years later. I watched Liamar fall and the Dark Age begin. I returned to Mera only occasionally after that, to keep an eye on western scholarship—the legends of Trynisia particularly. As a dragon I built up hoards in other worlds, and I used riches from these whenever I needed wealth in Mera. Each time I visited I adopted a slightly different appearance, a new persona. I was always very careful to alter and age myself with glaumerie as time passed."

"I seem to recall," said Ailia thoughtfully, "a tale of a Marakite noble, a Lord Draco, who never aged. He vanished from his castle one day, only to be glimpsed again sixty years later by a woman who had once seen him when she was a little girl. The lord hadn't aged a day, the woman declared. A rumor arose that Draco was an alchemist who had discovered the elixir of eternal youth."

"Well, perhaps I have been careless on occasion," Mandrake admitted.

"And of course there was the Academy ghost—"

"Ah, but that was different! Ghosts are expected to hang about for centuries. Gullible people believed I was a specter and others dismissed my existence. Until Eliana discovered me lurking there in the ruins of my old home, no one in Mera knew that I still lived. When it became clear that she bore me no malice, and believed my account of what had occurred in Maurainia long ago, I rejoiced that I had one less enemy to fear."

"And then—I came."

"Yes. The priests who raised me used to terrify me with tales about the great witch-queen who would one day seek to destroy me. They believed my mother was a demon of some kind, and they told me that as the child of a demon I would be hateful to you, that you would want me dead. You figured prominently in my childhood nightmares."

"How dreadful! I am sorry."

"And you have been told similar lies about me, I am sure. My childish fears were abandoned in time, but I knew you were a creation of the Archons. How I came to hate you! Your birth was eagerly anticipated and celebrated—you were showered with gifts and love. I decided to steal you away from those who meant to mold your life—even as Ana had taken me from the Valdur coven and freed me from their schemes. And that was when I met Syndra, who was of like mind.

So Syndra had turned traitor all those years ago! "Go on," said Ailia.

"Your mother must have anticipated our plot—her Archon vision was always keen! She fled with the aid of a star-ship, not wanting to endanger her child any longer. I don't know what became of her, Princess: her body was never found. Neither was yours, so I assumed that you both had drowned. But I was never easy in my mind about it."

"So when you heard of Lorelyn—"

"Naturally, I thought she was you. The fact that Ana also seemed to believe she was the Tryna Lia helped to convince me. I led your little band to the temple and let you discover the empty sanctum. If the Zimbourans caught you, they would learn from you that the Stone was gone. All the cosmos seemed to be converging on the summit of Elendor that day: an Imperial dragon had also arrived, looking, as I suspected, for the Tryna Lia—he made the mistake of falling asleep while guarding the closed Gate, and I chained him as he slept. Then those two meddling friends of yours found me while I was resting on my hoard and seized the sword of my father and used it against me. But after all that they ran off with nothing but an empty box, so I did not pursue them.

"I carried Lorelyn away to Eldimia, knowing Ana must soon recover from her swoon and make use of Auron or the Guardians to follow us with the Stone. I had decided that I would let her think Lorelyn was the true princess, and then I would be safe forever. But I never suspected that *you* were the One—not until you were in your place of power at Halmirion, and then it was too late. So: that is my confession."

Ailia nodded in understanding. How much of it was true she could not know, but clearly he had struggled with his parenthood and destiny as she had with hers. And he had spared her life when he could have killed her.

In the great hall the music had started up again. Mandrake suddenly turned and took her hand. "But this is gloomy talk: I'm sure you have had enough of it. I meant to make you feel welcome here. Did you want to dance?"

She followed him back down the hall and into the ballroom. Dancing here was very strange, Ailia thought. There were no sets, no intricate figures: people danced in isolated couples strewn about the room, spinning slowly like double stars, paying no heed to the other dancers save to avoid colliding with them. They danced with their arms about each other in an embrace: to Ailia this looked almost indecent. But she could not refuse. Gingerly she placed her hands on Mandrake's shoulders, as the other ladies were doing. He put his about her waist: she could feel them trembling with suppressed mirth. "I was forgetting," he murmured, his face close to hers. "You don't dance this way in Arainia."

He was not so tall as she had thought—but then, of course, she had grown since last she met him. She let him guide her through the steps of the dance. It was not difficult, merely a question of matching her every motion to his, and it was slower than the set-dancing on Arainia. She could not meet his golden gaze for too long, however, and kept glancing away.

Suddenly a face in the crowd caught her eye: Syndra's. The woman was pale and her eyes filled with anger. Ailia gave a gasp.

"What it is?" Mandrake asked.

"Lady Syndra," Ailia said. "She is here?"

"You've nothing to fear from her."

"She hates me. You told me as much."

"She cannot harm you now."

But Ailia stepped back, out of Mandrake's arms. "Your Highness, I am—rather tired. I think I must rest."

"There are seats over there against the wall. Will you sit for a while? And have some refreshment—a glass of wine, perhaps? There are some bottles of excellent vintage, including a hundred-year-old red from the cellars of King Garon VII of Marakor. I was there when the grapes were pressed, and I can vouch that only the finest fruit went into it." He smiled.

She shook her head. "Thank you, but I don't drink wine. I would like to retire to my room, if I may."

"Certainly." It seemed to her that he was slightly displeased, but trying to conceal it under a veil of courtesy. "Until tomorrow night, then."

It was a warning that she had not yet won him to her side, and little time now remained to her.

DAMION STOOD ALONE IN THE DESERT, gazing at the stars.

The outcome of the raid was appalling, was worse than he had imagined. He had feared that his friends might be killed, but taken captive, taken alive—he knew enough of Zimboura now to realize what that meant. Then today Kiran Jariss had come again, with the news that Khalazar had posted notices throughout Felizia: if Damion, they said, did not surrender as well, his friends would be executed at daybreak.

There was, he had been advised, no hope of a rescue attempt. The stronghold of Yanuvan was impervious to attack. Only the greatest army could hope to break through—and even Khalazar's rebel army had been helped by traitorous zealots within the keep. Their own small group of Moharas and Zimbouran insurgents simply had not the strength to mount any assault.

"It is unfortunate," Makitu told him, "but we can do nothing." The Moharas had seen so much death already that they had become almost inured to it. They had received word of Unguru's loss and the capture of their Zayim with grief and anger, and then they had put their emotions aside and returned to the daily business of living. A hope had been lost, but not all hope, not yet. To Damion, though, the fate awaiting Jomar and Lorelyn was unthinkable.

He closed his eyes, seeing in his mind the dream he had had the night before.

In it Ailia had stood before him, clad in a flowing gown so white that it had seemed to shine with its own light: or perhaps it was she who shone. The dream figure both was, and was not, the Ailia he knew: she blazed before him like a star, transcendent, glorified. "You must help me, Damion," she had implored him, holding out her arms in their long trailing sleeves. "I will do what I must, but I cannot stand alone. Help me!"

He opened his eyes. The evening star shone above him, pale and solitary: he could still hear Ailia's forlorn cry as he gazed at it. *"I cannot stand alone!"* It seemed to ring from one end of the heavens to the other.

"Damion?"

He turned to see the shaman standing there. Wakunga's brow

was deeply furrowed. "Why do you stand out here, when all the rest are sleeping?"

Damion smiled wanly. "You're not sleeping, Master."

"I felt something from you. A strong emotion, filling the Ether. Have you been dreaming?"

"I'm not certain." He told the shaman what he had seen and heard in his mind. Dream or vision? It had seemed more like a memory—but of a time that had never been. He had never seen Ailia look as she had in that scene, robed in light. "Perhaps it's just my fear," he said as they walked over the dunes. "I'm so afraid for Ailia, and even more for Jomar and Lorelyn. You know that Khalazar has said they will be freed if I surrender myself."

"I know."

"Why am I so important, Master Wakunga? It's Jomar who has been the real leader. Why do they want *me* so much?"

"Perhaps the answer was in your dream."

He saw the beautiful, half-familiar face; heard the pleading words. "You mean it has something to do with Ailia? But what?"

The old man said nothing.

"Lori and Jo—I keep seeing their faces. They're in Khalazar's hands, and *I can save them.*" Damion groaned. "I want to go, Master! To hand myself over, to give them a chance to live."

Wakunga looked thoughtful. "You may go," he said. "There is no reason why you cannot."

Damion stared. "But you were against my going before. You said it would bring ruin on us all."

The shaman looked up at the sky. "That was when the dragon-sorcerer was here. He has gone now, back to his home in the stars. This path is not the one you would have trodden before."

"Then I can help Jo and Lori? And it *won't* bring harm to anyone else? How can I be sure?"

The old shaman faced him. "Why do you not go to the dream plane?"

"Meditate, you mean?"

"It is said among my people that when we think ourselves awake, we are in truth asleep," the shaman said. "And when we fall asleep, we wake to dreams. Rather than wait for a dream to come to you and give you answers, you can seek it out in the place where visions come from." And with that pronouncement he walked slowly away. Damion stared after the old man's stooped, shuffling figure. When it had blended into the night, he knelt and began to trace figures in the sand.

The carvings on the ruined walls in the oasis were a thing of the ancient past. The Moharas of this day and age made all their images in sand, not stone: for sand was by nature evanescent, shifting at every breath of wind, and any images that were drawn in it could not survive to become idols. Never again would their tribal chieftains go to war against one another's gods. Wakunga had taught Damion how to draw a shamanic circle around himself, each elaborate ring a layer of thoughts, brushing out and covering his footsteps as he went until he arrived at the still center. He drew one now. First came the outermost circle, with its fierce guardians: lions or jackals, or fantastic beasts of one's own devising. Next a ring of wavy lines created a moat or encircling river. Then the inner wall, with projecting tower shapes to suggest a citadel. Within this lay a ring of blank untouched sand, for tranquility. And finally the smaller circle at the center, in which he sat, legs crossed. As soon as his forefinger completed the circle shape, closing him in, he was aware of an easing of tension. The outside world might spin around him like a storm, but this was its quiet eye. He recalled the star-shaped city of Liamar on the summit of Mount Elendor. Like this circle, he realized, that city had been a mandala, the Temple of Heaven lying at its central point.

Damion closed his eyes and breathed deeply. There was no ambrosia here to make the passage easier: his mind must find a way into the Ether on its own. For a long time he sat motionless, as the stars slowly turned above him. A Mohara shaman would chant a mantra, over and over, until body and mind were composed. For some reason he found himself thinking of an old poem from his childhood, which he had memorized because it was about a knight:

My love dwelt in a golden hall
With many chambers, gemmed and pearled,
And muraled was each lofty wall
With wonders of the outer world,
And gardens grew with flowers fair
Whose perfume graced the gentle air.

O house divine! And there each day
We walked, and in the fragrant bowers
Did rest to hear the fountains play,
And while away the dreaming hours
With sweet embrace and tender gaze:
Such bliss we knew in kinder days.

Now he is gone on errantry,
With mail of steel, and shield and sword,
Upon a stallion tall rode he
To take—my love, my gentle lord!—
The steep path down to shadowed vale
And groves where paths and courage fail.

That way is dark and drear and hard
With peril great for wand'ring knight:
There serpents grim their caverns guard,
And couch their coils on jewels bright,
And cruel enchantress sets her snare
In guise of maiden passing fair.

Unto some dark and dismal keep
Beguiled and led by witchery,
Shall my dear lord in dungeon deep
Be bound by chain and iron key?
A prisoner wan and lost to woe,
No more his lady's love to know?

Or shall he, in some foul worm's den
The precious trove of gems behold,
And so may come to yearn again
For jeweled wall and tower of gold,
And to his house upon the hill
Return, where I await him still?

It was an old allegory, so the magisters had told him, of the division of soul and mind. The Elei believed that the latter became estranged from the former at the moment of birth, and its journey through the mortal realm in its new armor of living flesh was like the quest of a knight errant through unknown regions. The mind forgot its previous existence in the realm of spirit, leaving the soul there bereft, like an abandoned lover. Only the death of the body reunited them in Heaven.

But why did he think of this allegory now?

He sat motionless, centering himself within his own inner stillness until the outer world was banished from his thoughts—until thought itself was banished, and he drifted in a void where his consciousness was strangely altered, neither waking nor dreaming, yet somehow still aware. Aware of the dark inward abyss, of his own slow gentle breathing, and of something beyond these that was neither sound nor image but the constant flow and surge of some vast incomprehensible Power . . .

. . . *There was a glitter of many rainbow facets in the darkness. It was the Star Stone: Ailia's talisman. It glowed before him with its mysterious luminosity, calling out to him.*

"A thousand hues, one shining light. The many are One, and the One many . . ."

The figure of a bird arose from the Stone, as if hatching out of a radiant egg: a great bird of light that flew through the darkness, illuminating it. As it drew nearer he saw that it was made up of the flying forms of myriads of other smaller fowls, from doves to eagles, pheasants to cranes. They cried aloud in human voices as they flew in their bird-shaped flock, saying: "The Elmir! Who will show to us the Elmir, the Bird of Heaven?"

"You are the Elmir," he called back. "You are yourselves that which you seek."

"The many are One, and the One many!" they cried with a single voice.

The golden radiance brightened, and the thousands of winged shapes merged once more into the great bird of fire. But then the light seemed to be dimmed and tainted. As he watched in horror, the Elmir faltered in its flight. There was a serpent, a writhing coiling thing as black as night wound about its body. And the Elmir struck at the serpent with beak and claws, and the serpent buried its fangs in the Elmir's breast, until it seemed that the two would plummet through the darkness and perish together.

"No!" he urged the bird of light. "You must live! You cannot be overcome!"

The fiery eye of the bird turned to him, and he was dazzled by it as if by the orb of the sun. But he saw in it an appeal before the bird sank out of sight.

"Yes—I will help, if I can. Show me what I must do!" The cry came from his heart, from the very deeps of his being. And from the darkness came an answer-

ing cry, like the call of a wild bird in some desolate place far from hope or com-fort: "Akkar!"

The vision was gone. Damion came back to himself again, blinked, stared about him at the moon-silvered sand. "Akkar," he whispered.

The god-ever-returning. The old god of the Mohara myths, who died in the autumn to the sorrow of his consort Nayah: her tears were the winter rains, and in the spring she brought Akkar back to life again. So Kiran Jariss had told him, and the shaman also. "Each year the goddess goes down into the underworld, to bring forth her lost love," Wakunga had said. A fertility myth, Damion thought. There were many like it in pagan traditions around the world. As the sky goddess descends to the underworld to seek her lost con-sort, so the spring rain descends and seeps beneath the earth. As she frees him from death's dungeon and brings him back into the light of day again, so the seed is released from its husk and comes forth as a flowering plant: that was the basis of all these old tales.

But a myth was no mere fancy or fable: it was a living, potent thing, a part of the world of mind blending with that of matter, the dream realm acting upon the real. And now it had become his re-ality, and there was no escape. Every step he took, no matter in what direction, led him on to the same necessary destiny.

The bird of Heaven had shown him his path.

After Akkar dies, the sky goddess Nayah descends and weeps for him. The Morning Star's daughter also must descend to the earth and restore it to life and peace for the prophecy to be fulfilled . . . The myth-strands woven by the ancients had intertwined in this place, and held in their invisible mesh a possible future. As he pon-dered this he glimpsed, in a sudden burst of illumination, the shape that future must take. A place awaited Ailia here. She would com-mand the hearts of Zimboura, Mohara, Shurka, and make them one. She would become in their eyes the avatar of their most revered deity, forever thrusting aside the God-king and his cult. But Damion must first prepare the way for her. Khalazar would kill him if he turned himself in. He might kill Jomar and Lorelyn also, choosing not to honor the pact. But the myth was powerful, the myth was stronger than Khalazar—or death. Death would not de-stroy it, but reaffirm it. To these people he would become a living avatar—just as Ailia had been for the people of Arainia.

Ailia . . . He thought of her now as he had last seen her at Melnemeron, her large soft eyes full of concern for him. *Ailia, forgive me,* he said silently, gazing up at the Evenstar where it shone in the clear evening sky. *I love you, and it is for you that I do this . . .*

He felt, or seemed to feel, the presence of innumerable invisible beings about him—angelic presences, elusive, hovering, ministering. Almost he imagined that he could see them as bright, shining figures that surrounded him, soothing and encouraging him. He was awed, and yet also sensed a curious kinship with these invisible guardians, as though he and they were of one kind. It was as if the vision had unlocked a door at the back of his mind, which he had not known was there. Through that door came power, and more besides: the knowledge that he was a divine being. For was that not what a human being *was*—a spirit clothed and masked in flesh? The body was not all, it was but the outer garment. He knew his true, essential self as a core of imperishable fire.

Khalazar could not destroy that self, any more than he could extinguish the stars in the sky. He had not the power.

Damion rose in one swift decisive motion. The yearned-for answer had come to him, even as the shaman had known it would: he knew now what it was that he must do. He strode forward, and left the circle to the wind and sand.

19

Parry and Feint

WITH THE PASSING OF HER SECOND DAY in the Forbidden Palace, Ailia felt her anxiety begin to turn into fear. Mandrake, for his part, betrayed no sign of worry or impatience. He remained courteous and attentive, his treatment of Ailia that of a host indulging an

honored guest. He showed her around the castle, and told her all
its history, and took her for long walks in the pleasure gardens of
the inner ward. "You are not a prisoner here," he said, and it was
true. She could go where she willed, keep what hours she pleased,
have for her meals any delicacy she might desire. There were no
state functions or ceremonies, no government documents to study
and sign, no councils to attend. The burden of leadership, and the
need to earn all that she was given, had been lifted from her: she
had all the pleasures of a royal life with none of its onerous duties.
A bookshelf appeared in her apartment, laden with volumes of
alien scholarship, of history, of poetry. When she mentioned an interest in painting, she found a set of brushes and paints set out for
her the next time she went to her room. Entertainments of various
kinds were held for her, concerts and magical displays. During one
of the latter, the many-colored lights that she had observed before
were made to play about the towers of the keep and hang like
ghostly lamps in the boughs of the trees within the ward. They
were, as she had suspected, ethereal manifestations.

"They are harmless," said Mandrake. "These will o' the wisps are
akin to eidolons, but so weak they cannot assume material forms,
and so they remain mere masses of quintessence. The Nemerei, as
you know, summon them as lights to see by, though the Loänei used
them as prodigies to fill their subjects with fear and awe. There is an
undersea palace of adamant in the deep waters off the coast, where
once a Dragon King made his dwelling, and before him the Archons
who built it. There Loänei have lived in concealment for many centuries. That is why the dragon lanterns that your friend saw arose
from the ocean depths. My people wished to remind those on land
that the Loänei realm would one day be re-established. That has
now come to pass. But do not fear: as long as I reign I will not allow
them to enslave the humans as they once did."

Ailia spent much of her time in the palace library, where she had
leave to read any book that caught her eye. In addition to its many
volumes of long-lost literature and lore there was a large section on
black magic: shelves of dark-bound books that she carefully
avoided, recalling how Mandrake himself had first fallen from
grace. He laughed at her concerns. "There is no peril in knowledge, Princess," he rebuked her. "Only in ignorance." But many
other works she read with eagerness: histories written by explorers

and settlers of other worlds, tales of wars and great deeds in ancient times. Sometimes Mandrake joined her in the library, pointing out volumes that might interest her—he had of course read them all himself—and he spoke to her of the worlds he had visited, and people he had encountered there. He had known many historical figures of Mera and Arainia—figures that to her were mere names in history lessons—and had a disconcerting habit of referring to them as if they were people he had met in the street just the other day. "Oh, Ingard the Bold," he would say, "he was bold all right, and skilled with a sword. He was also loud, unkempt, and often boorish in his ways. He was raised by wolves, after all . . ." Or: "I told Valivar IX that Zimboura would never conquer Maurainia, but he insisted on conducting his forays," or, "I see you are reading Bendulus. He never could get his facts straight. He once told me, with a perfectly straight face, that an adder will lie with one ear to the ground, listening for the footsteps of its prey, while stopping up the other ear with its tail."

It was hard to realize that this genial host and companion would soon attempt to kill her if she did not turn to his side. It was, she thought, like playing with a half-tamed beast that might at any moment turn savage without warning. And as he showed no sign of being swayed by her arguments, she began to lose hope. She was running out of time, and she was also growing concerned about Syndra Magus. Though she never saw the woman—Mandrake must have instructed Syndra to keep out of her sight—Ailia half-fancied she could sense her presence always near at hand, like a taint in the air. Might Syndra poison Mandrake's mind against her?

"You are losing," remarked Mandrake as they played a game of Stratagem that evening in the treasure room.

Ailia looked up, wondering if he meant only the game. "I am losing because you are cheating," she replied in mild reproof, glancing down at the silver and gold pieces on the board. "Mounted knights don't take elephants. It's against the rules."

"So you *are* paying attention, after all. I never play by the rules," said Mandrake without looking up. "Those that attempt to bind themselves to a code of honor are always doomed to lose the fight. In any conflict, the strongest—or the most cunning—wins, not the most honorable." He leaned back. "Your move."

There could be no doubt now that he was not talking about a

board game. "It's still better to be honorable," she insisted after a moment's thought. "You must believe that, or you would not have honored this bargain you made with me."

"Do you really believe what you are saying, Princess, or are you merely repeating the lessons that have been drummed into you all your life? Remember, you are free here, and so are your thoughts. You may do and say and think anything that you wish, and no one here will condemn you for it. This little kingdom I am creating is to be a unique place. Nothing may enter it without my leave; neither Light nor Darkness, good nor evil, can hold any sway here. The storm that rages outside blows past my door—I will not let it in." He leaned his chin on his hand, gazing thoughtfully at her. "You desire freedom, too, or you would not be here. You escaped your keepers."

"Escaped? I sought you out to parley, and make a truce!"

"So you told yourself. But did you not, in some deep recess of your being, wish to be free? Did that part not rejoice when you struck out on your own, unfettered, unguarded?"

Again he compelled honesty from her. "Yes," she said in a low voice, remembering her wild joy when she captained her flying ship and sent it into the Ether.

"Well, now that you are here, why would you go back?"

"Because I cannot live only to please myself! The Arainian people need me."

"But do they? And what of you? What does Ailia need? Why sacrifice yourself for a people who have never done a thing for you? Do you truly love them, or are you bound to them only by joyless duty? Has the human race always been unfailingly kind to you?"

She recalled, unwillingly, the cruelty of the convent girls in Maurainia, the daily taunts and jibes that often had made her life there a misery. "You're trying to make me hate," she said calmly, sitting upright and looking him in the eye. He knew that she had suffered these things, and meant to use their memory to cause her pain and twist her thoughts. Yet in order to do so, must he not also understand what such suffering felt like? "They really hurt you, didn't they?" she added, in a sudden flash of insight.

"What?" said Mandrake, taken aback.

"Those children who stoned you and insulted you, when you

were a little boy in Zimboura—the scars have never healed, have they?"

For an instant, a mere breath's measure, he seemed to be taken aback. Then his golden eyes turned to shuttered windows. He rose abruptly from the table and went over to the tall bard-harp, picking out a rippling tune on its strings.

Unsure whether she had scored a victory or suffered a defeat, she sought to assume a natural tone. "I didn't know you played the harp, Mandrake," she said.

"One of the advantages of an extended lifespan is that one gets the opportunity to become an expert at almost everything. I have done, and been, many things in my time." He contined to strum on the strings.

"I know that song," she said, still trying to make conversation. "It is based on a ballad of the Bard's that I've always loved."

He made a face. "You have? It is overlong, and a trifle sentimental. I do not consider it one of my better efforts."

It took her a moment to realize what he meant. "You—!"

"I," he said gravely. "Yes, I was the so-called Bard of Blyssion. I went through a poetic phase once. Did it never occur to your estimable scholars that their anonymous bard was exceptionally long-lived? For any human to produce such a voluminous oeuvre in a mere four decades or so would have been quite impossible."

Ailia was stunned. He must be lying. This cold and cynical creature, the author of the poetic works she so loved? "But they are— so noble, so sensitive!" she protested, unthinking.

"And an ignoble, insensitive man such as I could not create such works. Well, you could be excused for taking that view, I suppose."

"Forgive me—I didn't mean—" It was too late: the words could not be recalled. His hand dropped from the harp-strings. "It is close in this chamber tonight. I think I will go up to the main tower for a breath of air. Would you care to join me?"

It was, she knew, a reminder of the unfinished duel that would soon take place if she did not either surrender to or convert him. Her heart seemed to plummet, but she again attempted a casual tone. "Yes, that would be—pleasant," she said, getting up and following him to the top of the tower.

The country lay spread out below, many-shadowed under Nemorah's three small moons. She went to stand by the parapet, struggling to compose herself. He moved to stand at her side, looking down at the lights of Loänanmar. Presently he spoke again. "So many lamps there are, now. I have watched this city and its inhabitants for centuries. It has been fascinating, in a way—"

"You make them sound like a lot of ants," she observed.

"Ants!" he snorted. "Ants would be more organized. From this height humanity is reduced to insect proportions—and it suffers by comparison. It is always the same story, played out again and again: the rebels set out to overthrow the tyrannical authority, but once they succeed they take the tyrant's place. That Overseer of theirs, now, is nothing but a tyrant."

"That's true," Ailia admitted. "Though I believe he meant well at first."

"Of course: his kind always means well—at first. He and his followers had a splendid time for a while, setting up their rules of order and justice—and killing everyone who disagreed with them."

She sighed. "I wonder what has happened to that baby I saw. The one whose mother looked drunk, or drugged."

"Very likely it is dead by now."

"I wish I had saved it."

"Why? The woman would only have another child, and it would starve in its turn. These people breed and die like the insects they are. You see, time makes a difference to one's perception, too. I can't seem to summon much compassion for these human mayflies. When I start to feel sorry for one, I feel the futility of caring for anything so evanescent."

Ailia tried desperately to think of an argument that would convince him. There would be peace then . . . peace won without war. She cherished no illusions about Mandrake. Even had she not known of his past crimes, she had glimpsed, despite his efforts to appear amicable, his callousness, amorality, and selfishness. But these faults were perhaps inevitable in one so exceptionally long-lived: watching generations of fellow beings die, it would become necessary to detach one's emotions to preserve one's sanity, and centuries of solitude would certainly make for a self-centered existence. And she found herself noticing, too, how unconsciously regal was his bearing, and how intelligent the gaze of his keen far-seeing eyes. She saw in him faint traces of the man he had once been, king's son and courageous knight, lingering even after five centuries. To destroy the creature he had become would be to deny that man a chance to live again.

He talked on softly, still gazing on the city. "When the Archons first visited the original world over a hundred million years ago, it was inhabited by reptiles and little else. You saw the great long-necked beasts in the jungle, the *tanathon*—descendants of those taken from that planet by the Archons. They only exist here now: their kind died out there long ago. When the Archons went again to that world it was to find birds and furred beasts ruling in their stead: among these, the forerunners of the human race. No one knows who lives on the original world now. It may be that humans never arose on the primal planet at all—or if they did, they may have died out in their turn. Perhaps humanity is like the giant reptiles that went before it—a failed venture of the life-force."

Ailia thought of the suffering populace here and in Mera, the wise and gentle Elei, her family and friends—all of these, merely a failure? Then she remembered Auron's kindly voice: *"We call you the Makers. You humans never cease to amaze."* She took a deep breath. "Mandrake, everything in me tells me that if one infant doesn't matter, then nothing does."

"Then perhaps nothing does. Leave humanity alone, Ailia. Let it go to Perdition if it wants to." He turned from the view, as if in disgust. "The people down there will tell you grand and glorious tales of their city, their history, their ideals. But from this height I have watched that city-state spread, and I have seen it for what it truly is: a great cancer, spreading uncontrollably and spoiling the land all around it. Humans like to think of the Morugei as unnatural, monstrous abominations. But they are monstrous only in their outward forms. War, murder, cannibalism—there is not a single thing they do that has not also been done by the human race at one time or another. Beneath their hideous appearance they are no different from you, and that is why you recoil from them. King Roglug, now—he is base, vile, treacherous, untrustworthy, devoid of conscience, scruple, or higher feeling. But he will never stab me in the back, because I know not to let him get behind me. The truly dangerous people are those who offer you their eternal friendship and loyalty. Rog might do me any sort of harm, but he cannot ever betray my trust."

Lies and distortions she had been prepared for, but not this relentless barrage of truth. She stood gazing silently at the city, and for an instant she saw it anew. It had all the contours of the human soul, she realized, its aspiring heights and hidden places, its blend of darkness and light. "I see good down there too," she insisted, thinking of Mag and her kindness.

"Yes, there is," he said, unexpectedly agreeing. "Good of a sort, though not the sort you are thinking of. Take the roses down there in the palace garden, for instance."

She turned to stare at him. "The roses? What of them? I think they are beautiful."

"Do you? I find them grotesque. Overbred, overlarge—many have no scent left in them. They have been tampered with, made to fit some human notion of beauty. And those fat, pampered little lapdogs that court ladies love: can you believe that their ancestors were wolves, hunting in the wild? Humans can't resist perverting nature to create monstrosities, and the same was true of the Archons. Look at the Elei, the result of eons of their tampering. The Old Ones sought to create a new version of humanity." He stood glaring down at the garden. "Pretty, docile, harmless. The lapdogs of the Archons."

"The Elei are happy."

"Too happy. They live in a fool's paradise, and that is why they are doomed: they will be no match for the invading Morugei and Zimbourans, for the strong, grasping, rapacious life-force those races represent. They will be swept aside."

"That's horrible!" she protested. But again she knew there was truth in what he said.

He shrugged. "It is the way things are. There is no god as such—merely a kind of idiot force, which generates life and living systems, but has neither the foresight to avoid mistakes nor the wit to remedy them. But it is still a kinder master than the Archons, who bent and twisted nature to their own ends. The life-force at least has no favorites: it treats all things alike, with the same sublime indifference. And through this randomness it has by sheer accident created something precious· freedom. That is all that matters: the freedom of beasts to run wild; the freedom of humans to manage their own affairs, even if they destroy themselves in the end; the freedom of Ailia to do as she wishes with her own life. You never chose this role they gave you. Let it go, free yourself from it. Remain here in Nemorah."

It was no use; their talks always came back to the same point. "Shall we be exiles together then?" she asked. "Both of us cut off forever from the human race?"

"Why should that trouble you? Now that you know you never truly belonged to it?"

By night his slit pupils dilated hugely, turning his eyes into pools of darkness: she wrenched her own eyes away, and a little silence fell between them. Ailia turned her gaze up to the emerging stars. One was large and red as a brand; another, paler one shone not far from it. She caught her breath. The configuration was slightly different from that she had always known, but there could be no mistaking them. There burned the fiery orb of Utara, the Eye of the Worm, and beside it was Lotara of the hidden companion—the Black Star no eye could see.

"They are so *near*!" she exclaimed involuntarily. "The Valei realms, I mean."

"Ah, yes." He too looked skyward. "I have visited them. I have been to Ombar, the world that circles Utara, and I can tell you—"

"Ombar!" Ailia gasped. "You have been—*there*!"

His pupils were dark holes that drank in light, as if they had themselves become little black stars. "Yes. It is a curious world. So slowly does Ombar spin that rotation and revolution are matched, and one side of it is turned forever to the sun while the other lies in perpetual darkness. On Ombar, night is not a time: it is a place. And it is a place that we all know, though few in Talmirennia have ever gone there. For the Morugei have told many tales of the Nightlands and the things that lurk there, and over the ages these tales have found their way into humanity's darkest dreams."

For some reason his words, and the knowledge that he had been to that evil world, filled her with a kind of dread. She drew away from him a little, and he hastened to say, "Enough. Let us talk of other matters. The second day has passed. Will you heed my offer?"

"What if I do not accept? I don't believe you would harm me, Mandrake," she declared, emboldened by a sudden memory of her dagger lying with its blade toward her. "You could have done so by now. Whatever others say of you, I have seen your true self, and you are not a murderer."

"I am flattered," he said dryly. "A murderer—no, I hope never to be that. I actually do possess a vestigial conscience. It gives me the occasional twinge, like gout. But the Stone and your so-called guardians are doing their utmost to transform you into an implacable, irresistible Power, and that is another matter entirely. You are a tool of the Archons, a last lingering vestige of their will to dominate the worlds. Have no illusions, Tryna Lia—I *will* fight you if I must, if you and your allies force me to. Don't imagine I will hold back out of some foolish sentiment, or because you are young, or a woman. I take *all* my opponents seriously, though I am not lawless as some would have you believe. On the contrary, I obey the only law the cosmos itself acknowledges: the law of the jungle, the law of survival. It is the Nemerei who flout the order of things, not I."

He did not say these things out of any intention to deceive, she sensed. His words were deeply felt and sincere, however mistaken the underlying beliefs, and she looked at him with sudden understanding. *Let me help you—let me save you!* she implored silently. *Leave the Valei and come back to us—poor old Ana would rejoice to have you back again . . .*

"The sight of the stars used to give me pleasure once," he said, gazing upward again. "They seemed to me mysterious and magical. But I can harbor no romantic illusions about them now. They are globes of flaming gases, nothing more. Though sometimes when I see them in the night sky, they make me think of dewdrops shining on a spider's web: they seem to betray some vast and sinister design. If this cosmos is not a mere chaos, then perhaps it is something worse still: a trap spun in malice, in whose meshes we are all snared. Perhaps we truly *are* fated to fight one another, Tryna Lia. Three times in the past I have sought to keep you from rising to power, to prevent this duel of ours from ever coming to pass. Three times I have failed. Perhaps it is simply meant to be, and no act of ours can avert it after all."

"No—there is free will, I'm sure of it! How could everything be preordained like that? There would be neither good nor evil then, because no real *decisions* could ever be made. Mandrake, you hate the thought yourself, and that must mean you don't really believe it, any more than I do."

"All I ever wanted was to be free. My life was my mother's first, because she bore me for her own reasons; then it was Valdur's because I was meant to be his tool; then the Tryna Lia's, because one day she would take it from me; then Ana's, because she saved it. I have belonged to many different people in my time, but never to myself. Until now." He leaned over the parapet, his long tawny-colored locks dancing like flames in the night-breeze. "This is an evening for flying," he said softly. "Do you ever wish to take the Loänan form, Ailia?"

"Yes, I have," she confessed. She had yearned for the power and the majesty, the freedom of flight, the superior strength that would come with a draconic body. To be a dragon was to fear nothing.

"I long for the day when I can set this human form aside forever, and with it every last tie to the miserable mass of humanity."

She looked him in the face. "It's not your humanity you hate, Mandrake, it's yourself. You can't be happy in any kind of body unless your soul is at peace."

"Ana again," he said curtly. "I had hoped it was the real Ailia I was talking with."

He turned abruptly and walked away from her, leaping up onto the parapet. For a moment he stood there, poised upon the edge. Then she caught her breath as he raised his arms and flung himself outward, as though he were diving into a pool. There came a sound of wings beating on air far below, and she saw the red dragon soar up into the moon-hung sky. Within minutes he had vanished from her sight.

Ailia remained at the parapet, her heart beating fast. He had shifted his shape in order to show her that his powers had returned: that the iron wound had healed. To show her that her one advantage was now gone. Another day had passed without success; only one more remained to her.

DAMION STOOD IN THE THRONE ROOM of Yanuvan. His hands were shackled, and armed guards stood behind him and to either side. He paid no heed to them, nor to the ornate splendor of his surroundings, but gazed steadily at the figure before him on its golden throne, with its jewel-encrusted garments and the sunburst symbol blazing on the wall above its head.

"He rode his horse directly to the gate of Felizia, explaining to the soldiers who he was. They bound his wrists at once and brought him to Yanuvan," the captain of the royal guard reported as servants and courtiers alike stared at the captive. Damion said nothing, and his gaze never left the king. Of all the emotions he had expected to feel, pity had not been one. But that was what he felt at the sight of this man, this thing of matter in its resplendent finery, believing that it could live forever and control the world in which it dwelt. Was Khalazar's mad desire not the dream of every human being? Who did not long to defeat death, to command the hostile forces of nature and render them harmless? And it was all in vain, splendid raiment and throne and temporal power notwithstanding. The figure before him suddenly became pathetic, its trappings of royalty and godhood sad and futile. A mist came before Damion's eyes, blotting it out.

"Ah, now you weep!" gloated Khalazar, leaning forward. "You believed yourself very noble coming here—did you not, Damion Athariel? Laying your life down for your fellow rebels. But now that you are here, you understand what is to come. You have not saved them, and you have doomed yourself. Go on—mourn!"

"It is your fate I mourn for," Damion told him quietly.

"Mine!" Khalazar bellowed, springing up from his seat. "You dare! Weep for me! Stop!" he screamed, lunging at Damion. "Stop, I command you!" He struck the young man's face, making him stumble back.

But, strangely, there was still no fear in the prisoner's eyes. Those eyes! So cool, so impassive, with their strange unsettling color, the hue of sea or sky. Khalazar seemed to glimpse infinite depths in them, and knew a moment of unreasoning terror. "I am the God-king!" he shrieked into Damion's face. But the cry sounded hollow as an echo. Before those calm unwavering blue eyes, all the magnificence of his throne room was reduced to nothing; all his triumphs and conquests were rendered meaningless. This man pitied him, and by so doing reduced him to something pitiable. For that the scoundrel must die—but not now, not yet. He must not only be killed, but also defeated and humbled. He must cringe in fear before the God-king, and own him master.

"Take this criminal, and beat him," Khalazar ordered the guards. "Then put him in a cell. Let him have neither bread nor water. We will starve the insolence out of him."

Damion offered no resistance as he was led away. Khalazar glared after him, his chest still heaving. He began to fear that he had lost face before his servants with his petulant assault on the prisoner.

The Zayim must be slain, but I will not kill this one. No! I will parade him captive before the people of Zimboura—those fools who tried to claim he was an angel. I will show them he is no more than a man. And I will use him to entrap the Tryna Lia, as Mandrake said!

JOMAR AND LORELYN HAD NOT been able either to eat or to sleep. Confined to separate cells far from the other prisoners, they had whispered to one another until a whip-wielding guard threatened to beat them if they did not desist. Having no doubt that he would follow through with the threat, they obeyed. On the first evening they had seen a gray-haired man in military dress dragged past their cell, head hanging. He looked rather like the general who had captured them. All through the night his tortured cries had torn at them, until at last he had fallen silent—forever, they were sure. If the Zimbourans could treat one of their own with such appalling cruelty, what fate awaited the rebel Zayim and his cohorts?

"Jo," Lorelyn called presently in a soft voice. "Someone's coming. Do you hear?"

Jomar lifted his head from the hard wooden bench on which he was lying. The footsteps coming down the passage were not the slow padding ones of the elderly keeper who brought their scanty meals of bread and water. It sounded to him like more than one set of booted feet. Soldiers. Now what? He sat up, staring as the men came in sight.

Between them, his face bruised with blows and his shirt torn at the shoulder, stumbled Damion.

Lorelyn gave a cry and ran to the door of her cell. "*Damion!* Not you too!"

He smiled at her. "I surrendered, to save you. The king said he would set you free if I came to him."

Jomar stared. "That was the bargain—us for you? Don't you

know you can't trust Khalazar's word? He'll just kill us anyway, and you too. You've thrown your life away for nothing!"

"Not for nothing," insisted Damion as the guards thrust him into a cell. "I can't explain, but this is something I must do. Trust me."

"I knew it!" exclaimed Jomar despairingly as he and Lorelyn were pulled from their own dungeons by the guards and led away. "Battle shock. He's gone completely mad! Now Khalazar's got all of us."

"You mean Mandrake," Lorelyn whispered back. "He's the real power here. But what does he mean to do with us?"

"Ailia," said Jomar. "He wants Ailia. That's what this is all about. If he—"

But at that point the guards dragged them apart.

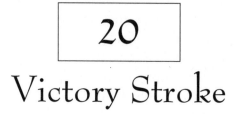

20

Victory Stroke

IN THE MIDDLE OF THE rough path that cut through the jungle's ferny growths walked two small and unobtrusive human figures: a short stout man with a long white beard, and a little sharp-featured woman with auburn hair. None of the other passersby paid any attention to them. Most walked at a brisk pace despite the heat, seldom glancing up from underneath the broad brims of their protective sun-hats. All of the traffic, the strangers noted, flowed in one direction.

"Tell me, friend, does the city not lie that way?" Auron asked a man leading an ox-cart piled with belongings.

"It does—but you may not wish to go there now," the man replied. "We are all leaving."

"Why is that?" Taleera asked. But he only urged his oxen onward.

The sky overhead was clear, but it had rained here not long ago: the red earth of the road was moist, and scattered with shallow temporary pools that steamed under the two suns, visibly returning to the air. It had been a curiously localized deluge, for only a hundred yards or so down the path there had been no mud or puddles to be seen. Auron and Taleera continued on their way. Presently they came out of the trees into an open area: the jungle did not so much thin as end abruptly, turning into a waste of toppled trunks and stumps. Beyond lay fields, and the wood and stone structures of a large city, with a towered fortress watching over it from a steep hill.

A group of shabby-looking men rested by the roadside, sitting on stumps and logs. "You don't want to be going there," one of them commented with a sour look as Auron and Taleera passed them. "There's been a change of leadership in Loänanmar. No more Overseer: he's packed his bags and fled."

Auron halted. "Who is the new ruler?"

"The old priesthood's come back, with all their rules: do this, don't do that. They've got all the power now, in the name of their Dragon King."

"Dragon King," Auron repeated. He and Taleera exchanged glances.

"That's right. So you'll not be wanting to go there, believe you me."

"I'm afraid we've no choice," Auron said. "We're looking for a friend of ours, who passed through there not long ago. You wouldn't have seen her, by any chance—a young lady rather slight in stature, with long golden hair and violet-colored eyes?"

The biggest and shabbiest of the men laughed and leered. "No, but if I had I'd know what to do with her. Your companion ain't half bad-looking, either, but for that nose."

He lunged to his feet suddenly and seized hold of Taleera's arm. At once she reached up with the other and struck him neatly across the face with her free hand. There was a distinct snapping sound and the man howled, putting his hand over his nostrils. Blood bubbled from them over his upper lip.

"You little witch!" he snarled behind his hand. His companions all got to their feet.

"I do wish you hadn't done that," muttered Auron in Taleera's ear. "Now an altercation is unavoidable."

"Oh, shut up, old Worm!" hissed Taleera. "Let's magic them and go!"

He answered her in a frantic whisper. "No sorcery! Not while we are so close to him! Her only chance is if we remain undiscovered. How else can we get close enough to rescue her?"

The men had moved in and encircled them. "What should we do with 'em, Rad?" one asked of the leader, who was still clutching his nose. "Let's have a bit of play. We've had no fun since the Overseer left. The snake pit, then—or into the river for the guivres?"

But even as he and his friends moved in, jeering and mocking, there was a sound of heavy footfalls from the green wall of jungle behind them, along with the rasping breaths of some enormous creature. Several cockatrices flew up screaming into the air.

"You stinking louts!" yelled Rad at his men, turning to flee. "I told you we should have took the river! Now you've been and brought a lindworm on us with all your noise—or something worse!" Without another word exchanged all the men turned and fled after him.

"Cowards!" Even in the face of an unknown peril Taleera could not resist a parting shot at their captors.

The crashing noises in the undergrowth grew louder. The trees quivered, and leaves and fragments of snapped vine showered in all directions as the jungle denizen burst out into the sunlight, bounding on four clawed feet and flexing giant wings. It halted in front of Auron and Taleera, gazing at them with great amber eyes.

They relaxed. "Oh, it's you, Falaar," the bird-woman said. "Well, thank goodness for that."

"I thought it best that I wait as near the city as possible," the cherub explained, "so that I might come more quickly at thy call."

"Well, you have saved us the need of using sorcery this time," said Auron. "And it is fortunate indeed those men left before they had a glimpse of you. They may not know what a cherub is, but they would have told the tale, and if Mandrake or his minions heard of it they would know a protector of the Stone is here. It would be best for you to go back and hide again, at least until we find the Tryna Lia." He turned to Taleera. "Let us go on into the city."

"I will never go anywhere in this world again in human form!" declared Taleera. "At least, not if I can help it."

"Neither will I." Auron shifted again, this time taking the form of a yellow-furred dog.

Taleera grumbled: "All very well for you. I can assume no other forms."

Wait here, then, both of you, and I will see what I can learn. The dog turned and loped off toward the city.

Within a few minutes Auron had reached the old stone gates. He stopped and stared at these, his hackles rising. The figures adorning them were not like the serene Loänan of the ethereal portals, but were carved to appear fierce and menacing, bristling with bared fangs and outstretched talons. *Loänei work,* he thought in distaste: these dragon statues were designed to fill human viewers with terror and awe. He padded on, through Loänanmar's streets. To all eyes he was no more than a mangy cur, one of many that roamed the city. Even other dogs were deceived, for his very odor was authentic. One or two snarled and tried to fight him as he approached, but he easily evaded them and ran on. He had always found the canine form useful when exploring human cities. In human shape he might be accosted and questioned, but as a stray dog he could wander freely—though, remembering the fondness of certain peoples for dog meat, he always took care to make himself thin and unappetizing in appearance. The dog's acute senses of smell and hearing were also very helpful, far superior to a human being's. As he trotted briskly through the grim streets his nostrils worked continually, deciphering scents. He ignored most of them—though if any humans eyed him he would sniff around the rubbish in the gutters, for the sake of appearances.

He hung about inns and taverns for the most part, ostensibly looking for scraps but really listening in on conversations. He also paused briefly by the large temple in the city center, peering in at its door and listening to the chanted liturgy until a shouting priest drove him away. Mandrake, he gathered, ruled here as a sort of god-king: the very thought made him growl and bristle. Ailia, it seemed, had made no move against her foe yet. Then where was she?

Weary hours of search yielded no answer. He was on the point of giving in when he turned down another alley and noticed a particular scent coming from the doorway of one inn. Ailia's scent.

He recognized it at once, and ran through the inn door into its main room, yelping as a large troll standing guard by the entrance made a grab at him. He dodged, darting under a table, and ran on into the kitchen.

A young girl was in there cutting strips of meat on a board. The scent he had caught came from her. Was this Ailia herself in glaumerie guise? But he sensed no sorcery from her. He sniffed, his sensitive nostrils flaring. Yes, it was definitely Ailia's scent. But how could that be?

The girl, who was little more than a child, saw him and recoiled, crying: "Mamma, there's a dog in here! A stray!"

A grizzle-haired woman with gold earrings came in from the inn's central court carrying a pot of steaming broth. Setting it down on the table, she stared at Auron. "Ah—poor thing! He doesn't look like a biter to me, Mai. More likely he's hoping for a handout. See how he's sniffing at that meat!"

It was not the meat, but the long filmy scarf binding back the girl's hair at which Auron's straining muzzle pointed. The Ailia-scent clung to the cloth. She too had worn this scarf, he was sure of it. The scent was fading, but she must have worn it a long time for the traces to linger so.

"Poor fellow," said the woman gently. "He looks half-starved— see how thin he is! You go into the dining room, dear, and I'll just give him a scrap or two." She turned toward the table again.

The instant the girl was gone and the woman's back was turned, Auron changed to his human form. He stood there quietly until the woman faced him again, the meat scraps in her hand. Her eyes widened, and the morsels of food dropped to the floor.

"Oh," she gasped. "Where did *you* come from? You gave me such a start!"

"Do not be afraid," he soothed, smiling and holding out his hands in a calming gesture. "I am only looking for a friend of mine, a woman named Ailia."

She looked puzzled and a little wary. "I know no one of that name. You've come to the wrong place, I think."

"I am certain she has been here. Your daughter's scarf—"

"That scarf?" she said. "What of it? I made it out of a young lady's petticoat."

"Lady?"

"Well, so I liked to call her, though she was poor and rather plain. But she was a lovely kind-hearted girl. Where she got that gorgeous fabric I don't know. Her name was Lia."

Lia. *Star*. Auron's human heart began to beat painfully fast against his ribs. He stared into the main room. Now that he had human eyes again he could clearly see that the girl's scarf was the same warm apricot hue as the chiton Ailia had been wearing when he last saw her. His dog's eyes with their limited color vision had not been able to perceive the delicate shade.

"You speak of her in the past tense. What became of her?" he implored her.

The woman looked away. "We don't know. The Dragon King's priests called for a sacrifice, and my Mai offered herself. Lia went with her, to comfort her. Mai was released by the dragon-folk later; but we never saw Lia again. And that is all I know. I can barely speak of it—I'm that worried about her."

"I, too," he said huskily.

She looked at him, then held out a hand. "I'm Mag, by the bye. This is my place, and any friend of Lia's is welcome here. There's one companion of hers staying with us already."

"Companion?"

"The little creature, there, was a pet of hers," said Mag, pointing through the open door to the courtyard. "You likely won't have seen one like it before. It's an amphisbaena, from the jungle."

Auron stared. The creature she was indicating was unlike any living thing he had ever seen: neither mammalian, reptilian, nor avian, with a head at each end of its bipedal body. It seemed impossible that such an oddity could exist in nature, but he had seen nothing like it in any listing of the Archons' creations. It huddled in a corner of the yard, eating a lettuce leaf with its larger head while the hind head swiveled to and fro. Keeping watch, he guessed. The rear head was, perhaps, also intended as a decoy to draw attention away from the true head—just like the dark eye-spots some fishes wore on their tails, to fool larger fish into attacking the wrong end of their prey.

"They are the shyest creatures alive, amphisbaenas," Mag told him. "It's rare even to see one, for they usually flee at the sight of a human, or so I'm told. This one attached itself to Lia—why I don't know, but it must have suspected she had a tender heart. I protect and feed it," said Mag, "for Lia's sake, to repay her for her own kindness to me and Mai."

Auron, remembering her gentle words to him when he was in dog form, was certain she would have done so anyway. He approached the creature, which dropped the leaf and backed away trembling.

"No! I mean no harm," said Auron, reaching out with his mind. He knelt, to make himself look smaller and less threatening. "I only want to ask you about the girl Lia."

"We don't know, we don't know!" it chittered, its thought-pulses coming in frightened bursts.

"There now, I do not accuse you of anything."

"Can you understand it?" Mag asked in surprise.

He nodded. "I am a friend of hers," he continued. "Please, where did you and Lia meet?"

"In jungle," said the thing's front head. "Deep, deep in jungle. We chased by manyhead."

"A hydra?" he guessed.

"Yes, yes! We thought we die then. But then she came, kind lady, walking out of trees."

"In the *jungle*? Alone?" exclaimed Mag when Auron had translated for her.

"She save us—make big monster appear, frighten off manyhead. Then make monster go away again. Magic, she is, Nemerei woman."

Auron urged, "Can you tell us anything else of her?"

"She look different, then. Slenderer, longer hair. Purple-color eyes, hair bright—like light from lamp. She change her looks with magic, later, when we go to city."

Auron's heart leaped. "It was she!"

Joy briefly blossomed and then withered in him, replaced once more by dread. Ailia was here in this city; but she had gone to confront the enemy, and she had not returned. What had become of her?

*　　*　　*

AILIA WALKED THROUGH an unfamiliar landscape, dun-colored with drought: her path wound among hills clad in parched grasses and a few thorny bushes, under a sky bleached to the hue of bone. A crowd of people in plain dusty garments had gathered about the mouth of a cave in the sun-browned side of the nearest hill. In their hands were sticks and stones, and sickles that they wielded like swords; and they were shouting together in anger and fear: "Kill it, kill it! The monster is there!"

Curious, Ailia left the path and ascended the hill, approaching the dark cave. Something moved within its mouth—

"I see it!" screamed a shawled woman behind her. "Beware!" She flung a fist-sized stone into the dark opening, and the others brandished their weapons and yelled. Ignoring them, Ailia went and peered into the dark opening, and then recoiled in shock at what she saw.

"Get back!" a man shouted at her. "It is the monster—the monster!"

"No!" Ailia cried. "Are you all mad? That's a child!"

The little boy crouching at the back of the cave was thin and pale, with long hair all matted and tangled. Ailia knelt and held out her arms to the ragged figure, but he made no move in response. "There—do not be afraid!" She spoke gently as she rose and moved closer, stooping beneath the cave's earthen roof. He trembled, but did not try to attack her or escape. His eyes were shut. Kneeling again, she put her arms about him, feeling the tension in his small body. "Let him alone," she told the villagers, who were crowding around the entrance and blocking the light.

She looked down at the child she held: despite his pallor and thinness and the dirt that blotched his face, he was delicately beautiful. Then as she watched he stirred, and his eyes opened. And she saw that they were inhuman reptile eyes, golden in color; and as he opened his mouth to cry out his teeth showed, sharp as fangs.

"Monster!" screamed the shawled woman in terror and disgust. Behind her a man raised a sickle, ready to strike. Ailia gave a cry, releasing the boy to hold her hands out protectively—and woke.

Golden afternoon light flowed in through her curtained windows. It had only been a dream. But she still felt Mandrake's presence, as close as though he were in the room with her. Suddenly she realized what had just happened. He had been having a nightmare, a recurring one no doubt, of his early childhood in Zimboura. It had temporarily reversed his mind to a childish state, and in it he must have sent forth a mental cry to which her own sleeping mind had responded, becoming incorporated into his dream. Now he too was awake, and aware of her, and she felt the brief comfort she had brought him turn to dismay as he realized how vulnerable he had proven to be. He was on the defensive now. What would his next move be?

She rose, and dressed with a heavy heart. Tonight: the duel would be tonight, if she could not stop it. And evening was already drawing near.

There was a knock on her door. "Who is it?" Ailia asked warily.

"It is only I, Highness." The old serving woman peered around the door. "I have brought you these, from the prince." She held out a crystal vase full of roses—the dark-red flowers from the palace garden. Ailia took them in reluctant hands, and the woman bowed and retreated, shutting the door.

Left alone with the roses, Ailia began to pace the floor. The heavy, opulent scent of them, which had been strong even in the open air of the garden, soon filled all the bedchamber.

"What if I were to go to him?" she murmured to herself. "What if I told him that I will stay, and join with him as he asked? Perhaps he is right after all, and good will come of it." Was she merely seeking desperately to avoid the fateful duel? But what if another's soul could be saved, and a war averted, if she surrendered and remained here? Such alliances had been made before: the offspring of rival royal houses had been joined in marriage to forge bonds of peace between their kingdoms. "He is not truly evil, and in many ways he and I are much alike. I never wished to harm him, and now that I understand him better I cannot bear the thought. But I must fight him, or else give in to him. *Could* it save him—and the Celestial Empire—if I gave in, and stayed here with him? Or would it only doom us both, make us renegades—despised and hunted by *both* sides?"

She reached for a rose. A thorn, sharp as any adder's tooth, sank into her finger and a red drop of blood welled up. Tears came to her eyes. She looked at her dagger lying on the nightstand. *Even a rose needs thorns*, Damion had told her.

She had dreamed about him also, a nightmare in which he struggled against a dark and hideous serpent. It was wound about him, and try as she might she was unable to free him: she had wakened from the dream with her hands still clenching in the effort to pull the black coils away from him. For some time afterward she had lain sleepless, convinced that he truly was in some terrible danger. Then she considered whether it might not be a manifestation of guilt. Was she not betraying him and all her friends by even thinking of accepting Mandrake's offer? The perfidy of Lady Syndra, a magus of the Nemerei, had been base enough. Was what *she* was doing not worse by far? And she was aware of another disturbing betrayal, from a still more unexpected quarter: her own body seemed to have grown an independent will in this place, and turned against her mind.

To the Nemerei the physical body was a beast, ruled from birth by the mortal realm of which it was a part, ruled by its appetites. The mind had to learn over time to control it, even as a rider had to rein in a horse lest it bring itself to harm. As a child Ailia had once seen a young boy whose pony would not obey his commands, but meandered over to eat the vegetables in a farmer's field. She could still recall the boy's flushed, humiliated face as he sought in vain to master his mount, and the jeering laughter of the passersby. When the body wars with the will, the Nemerei had taught her, the latter *must* guide the former, or a necessary balance has been lost. When she loved Damion, all parts of her being were in accord. But she had begun to feel only the deeper urge that was seated in the flesh: and against it her thoughts rebelled, until she felt torn in two opposing directions, for she sensed this longing not when she thought of Damion, but when she thought of the prince. Ashamed, she had forced the feelings into a far recess of her mind, refusing to acknowledge them even to herself. Only now, in the wake of the Mandrake dream and her own strong reaction to it, had she at last admitted the truth with great reluctance. It was no mere passing attraction, such as any girl might feel for a comely man, but something more. Her treachery against Damion was twofold.

Treachery—nonsense! said an inner voice. *Damion does not love you and he never will. You owe him no loyalty in that regard. You are free to seek for love elsewhere.*

She fled the room, unable to bear its heavy perfumed air any longer, and hastened down the stairs. There were still very few Loänei about, and when she paused by the ballroom door and peered in she saw it was still and empty but for one figure. Her heart gave a little jolt and began to race. Mandrake was there, pouring out a glass of some red liquor from a crystal decanter on the refreshment table. At the sound of her soft footsteps he looked up.

She opened her mouth to speak, but he held up his hand and she remained silent. "I was going to call on you. I want you to know," he said, "that I have come to a decision. I will go back with you—to Temendri Alfaran. You still have not convinced me. But I will not fight you, now that I have had a chance to know you—truly know you. I cannot find it in me to do you any sort of harm."

He had relented! She need not surrender herself, after all. Relief filled her, along with a small troubling tinge of disappointment that she was quick to quell. He would come with her, leave behind the Loänei and the servants of Valdur and submit to the true Loä-nan. Her friends would be safe, and there would be no more war . . . "I am glad—so glad," she said, entering the room, and she joined him by the table. "You won't regret this, Mandrake, I promise you."

"Will you join me in a drink?" He motioned to the decanter. "I know you don't care for wine, but this calls for a celebration, don't you think?"

Not wishing to refuse his hospitality in the face of his great concession, she took the crystal goblet he offered. In the light of the candelabra the dark red liquid had a fiery heart, like a ruby's, and its smell was rich and fragrant as the scent of the roses. She took a sip of it. The taste was sweet and strong, but it left a bitterness on the tongue. Still fearing to seem rude, she forced another mouthful down. Why was he not drinking, too? He had not once put his own cup to his lips, but only stood there watching her. A horrible suspicion seized her.

"No," she choked.

A wave of dizziness passed over her: the room seemed to spin slowly before her eyes. Had he poisoned her? She turned away from him, and the giddiness worsened. Mandrake took her arm. His face blurred and faded as she looked up at him. "I am sorry," his voice said, sounding strangely distant. "But it is for the best . . ."

"No—*no!*" She freed herself, took a lurching step away from him, and blundered into a chair, almost falling. She tried to run for the doorway. But it seemed to move, shifting about before her eyes and then changing into two doors. Which was the real one? She wavered. Then her vision clouded over completely, and she felt the floor come up to hit her.

DAMION STOOD LOOKING out through the bars of his cell. "What is it you want of me, Majesty?" he asked.

Khalazar paced to and fro before the cell, as though it were he and not Damion who was confined. His hands clutched great folds of his golden robe. He halted, and glared at Damion.

"I have had enough of your insolence!" he rasped. "I need nothing from you or anyone! I am the *God*-king, divine as well as royal. You must call me by my rightful title, or die. You must worship me!"

"But why, Majesty?" the young man asked. "You have a whole priesthood to venerate you, and many subjects. You say you need nothing from me. You certainly do not need my worship." His blue gaze was steady.

"I tell you, I am a god!" shouted the other.

Damion nodded slowly. "You *are* divine, Khalazar: that is no more than the truth. Your only error is in believing that the divine resides only in you, and not in all men and women, all things in earth and Heaven."

The king gripped two cell bars, peering in. His breathing was loud and labored, as though he were running. "They call *you* divine, do they not? A spirit, an angel. It is a lie. I will put you to the test, and expose that lie to all. For a divine being cannot be killed. I will send you to the arena, to be the fodder of bears and lions. The people will see you torn to pieces and devoured, and the beasts quarreling over your bones. Then they will know that you were never more than mortal." He released the bars and drew back, as another thought came to him. "Or . . . you could go to the temple. Yes, to the temple and the altar: for so it was done in ancient times to prisoners of war. A human sacrifice, the first in many an age—and not the last, now that I am king and god. You will be led to my altar for all to see—and they will fear me. I, who wield power even over spirits." The king swung away from the cell, and stormed down the corridor.

And I will show Mandrake who is the master! he raged to himself. *He dared order me to preserve this man's life—order me! Shall I obey my own servant? I will kill this Damion if I choose! And the Zayim also. Mandrake will come back to find his precious prisoners dead. As for his goblin-men, his spies, they will not prevent me because I will slay them also. I know now that a mere iron blade can defeat their sorceries.*

THE SOLDIERS CAME FOR DAMION a few hours later along with the jail keeper. He was taken from his cell and stripped, and clad in a plain white robe.

"To the temple of Valdur," said the keeper to the guards. "It is the king's order."

"The streets are not safe," one of the soldiers said. "The people have been restless ever since Gemala was slain. And the Mohara prophet is to die tomorrow too, in the arena. They remember that he saved the lives of Zimbourans, and they are angry."

The shabby old keeper shrugged. "That is none of my concern," said he, and returned to his bench and his wine flagon. "Do as you are bid."

Damion went with the guards, still not resisting. In the castle's outer courtyard a white horse with garlands of white chrysanthemums stood waiting with its handlers. Damion gazed at the horse in wonder. Was this not Artagon, Mandrake's white palfrey? He recognized a scar upon the horse's near hind leg, left there by the lash of a Zimbouran whip. The soldiers who had captured Damion and the others in Maurainia had also taken the white palfrey as a sacrificial mount for the Tryna Lia, and so Artagon had come to Trynisia along with their human prisoners. But how did the horse come to be here? Why had they brought him to Zimboura? Was it some sort of fate at work? The horse knew him: it whickered and nuzzled his face as he stood beside it. Yes: this was no coincidence, but yet another sign to him that his path was predestined. The Elei horse had been brought here not to bear Ailia to the altar of death, as they had no doubt originally planned, but to bear him there instead. He was going in her place.

"Artagon," he murmured, holding up his hand to rub the horse's nose.

They put garlands around his neck, too, and forced him up onto the horse's back. Then the two guards tied his hands, and mounted their own horses. Leading the white sacrificial mount on a long tether, they rode out through the mighty gates and into the city.

People in the streets murmured when Damion was led past, but he knew that their barely suppressed fury was not at him. The sight of a human sacrifice in ritual garb agitated them: no doubt they were once more afraid that this was only the beginning, that such sacrifices would soon not be limited to prisoners or captives of war. On through the streets he rode with his guards, and the crowds pressed closer to the flanks of the horses until the guards threatened them with their swords. At that their noise increased, until at the temple plaza it swelled to a roaring sound like a wind off a rising sea.

The guards pulled Damion roughly off the horse and led him up the vast central aisle of the temple, right to the very feet of the towering stone colossus. One man held the prisoner while the other knocked on the door of the sanctum with his sword-hilt.

"Let us in!" he shouted. "We come in the name of the God-king Khalazar!"

The door creaked open and a young acolyte in a dirty black robe looked out. His eyes were blank, uncomprehending: the eyes of a simpleton. The soldier shoved the gaping boy aside and strode in, followed by Damion and the other guard.

The chamber was dark, low-roofed, and reeked of blood both old and freshly spilt. There was a palpable atmosphere in it, too, of terror and despair, causing Damion to pause as he entered. His guards grinned, imagining that the sight had at last filled their strange unemotional charge with fear. They could not know that it was pity that moved him so deeply, grief not for himself but for all those human victims who had come here before him. This terrible room resonated with their anguish: traces of previous ordeals lingered on the very air. Then Damion calmed once more. These were not ghosts he was sensing. They were but echoes of the past—those ancient victims' spirits were long since fled, at peace, their sufferings over.

"We bring to you the heathen warrior Damion," the first soldier said to the elderly priest who stood before the plain stone altar, head bowed. "Servant of the Daughter of Night, a victory offering to Valdur."

"Pah! What is this?" spat the old man, lifting his gray head. His eyes did not turn to them, but seemed fixed on a far corner of the ceiling: their sockets were scarred and he was, Damion realized, completely blind. "Has Khalazar nothing better to offer than the blood of barbarians? First you send us goats and swine; then you send us unbelievers! Is there not a single loyal Zimbouran who will die for his god? In days of old nothing but the sacrifice of many fine youths and maidens would have sufficed for such a petition. Does Khalazar think that for this worthless barbarian's life Valdur will grant him victory over the Tryna Lia?"

"Blasphemy!" snapped the guard. "King Khalazar *is* Valdur's incarnation on earth. Do you think he does not know what pleases him? If he desires barbarian blood he shall have it."

The old man drew himself up. "It is you who blaspheme. When Valdur comes again it will be in might, as a great warrior, not as an aged dullard who never wielded sword."

"Ingrate!" the second soldier cried, letting go of Damion. "Khalazar-Valdur shall know of this! He brought your priesthood to power again, old fool: what he gave he can take away again." He drew his sword with a rasp of steel.

The blind priest did not flinch at the sound, but stood firm. "We owe him nothing. His role in this was foreordained: he was born for one reason only, to give us that power. When Valdur is done with him, Valdur will cast him aside. Already he has outlived his sole purpose, and his presumption grows and turns to sacrilege. As for this prisoner, I will accept him for the altar—but only so that I may bring a further curse on Khalazar. Unholy blood taints the holy place. At the close of the high festival tomorrow I will sacrifice him. He will die with the sun, as is the custom. But no sooner than that will I do it. And if the true god Valdur is angered by this act, then he knows that I am blameless, and his wrath will fall on Khalazar. Your God-king too may not live to see the day that follows."

The guards threw Damion to the ground before the altar, then strode out of the chamber, slamming the door. At once the sanctum was thrown into deep darkness. There was no lamp—the old priest, of course, having no need for any illumination. For many years he had dwelt within the temple, since he blinded himself to banish from sight the Creation that he held was a deception of lesser gods. He performed his duties by touch and memory, slaying his animal victims by feeling first for their beating hearts, groping his way about the sanctum until habit taught him how many steps lay between altar and doorway, and where in the floor the well-shaft opened, with no cover or raised rim to protect him from the deadly plunge. The acolyte never stirred from his post by the door, save at his master's command, following the sound of the priest's voice with unquestioning trust.

Damion lay in the black absolute darkness, feeling the chill stone beneath him, and the tremors that were beginning to shake his body. He had consented to this fate on leaving his circle in the sand, but the flesh had its own will, independent of the waking mind and even of the dream-spinning unconscious. An ancient purpose had been written into its every nerve and vessel, and that purpose was to live. The fleeting fear he had known on the threshold of the sanctum had roused it, and though he had conquered it again his hands of themselves began to strain against their bonds, while his feet made little running motions against the stone floor.

Then the image of Ailia once again floated before his eyes, and he knew in that moment how strong was his love and admiration for her, and how worthy she was of any effort he could make on her behalf—even this fearsome sacrifice. Closing his eyes, he retreated to his own inner darkness and the deep refuge where no pain could come. Ailia's face followed him there.

21

The Tide Turns

THE GREAT ARENA of Zimboura was a work of ancient times, built by slaves from massive blocks of red granite with a sanded oval floor large enough for whole battalions to fight one another. Here, trained gladiators in the prime of their strength dueled one another, and beasts were baited and slain, or themselves slew and devoured renegade slaves and other prisoners. Paladins had perished here in days of old, and even Nemerei been made to fight desperate duels of magic against still more powerful sorcerers. During Khalazar's reign the cruel spectacles were held more frequently than ever before, and were more extravagant and larger in scale. It was said that wild beasts had grown scarce throughout Zimboura, as many of them had been captured at the king's pleasure for his games.

In the upper levels the wealthy spectators feasted as they reclined on divans and watched the battles below, while statues of Valdur and the minor gods gazed down upon them with painted eyes. Far beneath these marble-faced pleasure halls, as if forming a hell to their heaven, lay a subterranean warren of torchlit tunnels and holding pens. Here condemned prisoners awaited their doom, while the captive beasts—bears, bulls, ostriches, rhinoceri, and great cats—paced restlessly behind iron bars, and gladiators honed their weapons and practiced battle strokes before their turn in the arena came. It was a strange combination of armory, dungeon, and menagerie. The dank walls seemed to absorb the anguish and despair of the lives they imprisoned, and to breathe it forth again as a sickly miasma. Some victims had scratched final messages on the reeking stone, in the tongues of the various lands from whence they came. Amid the pathetic graffiti and caricatures were marks a young Jomar had made years ago, as he awaited his turn to fight: insults leveled at the Zimbourans in mute defiance.

He had not known then that he would survive, nor dreamed that he would one day return here . . .

He sat now on a wooden bench, shackled, with several other prisoners: Mohara rebels, and Arainian captives taken in the desert battle. Lorelyn was not with them; he did not know where she had been taken. Some were Nemerei, including the great Ezmon Magus, but their iron bonds prevented them from using their sorcery. They had been here for two nights and two days, after being removed from the dungeons of Yanuvan. The others talked in low voices, but Jomar stared at the grimy stone floor, worn smooth by generations of doomed feet. How many had died here, he wondered—several wars' worth, perhaps, of helpless victims? And now he was here again—not even as a gladiator this time, but as an unarmed prisoner marked for execution. He gazed with dull eyes at the iron cages a few paces away, which housed a pair of lions with mangy manes and one saber-toothed cat. The latter somewhat resembled a maneless lion but for its bobbed tail, and its fangs: two long blades of bone like scimitars that hung below its lower jaw. The great cat reared up whenever anyone walked past its prison, roaring and thrusting its fearsome tusks through the iron bars.

He shuddered, filled with evil memories of fighting these beasts in the arena above. But this was not the foe he and his fellow captives were to face. There were new and more terrible arena beasts, it was whispered, creatures brought by the goblins out of their own world of Ombar.

A whip cracked on the air: he and the others looked up to see the slave master standing there, his broad scarred face mocking. "It's time, you sluggards! Up to the arena with you now—move!" The man leered at Jomar, whom he remembered well. He was plainly delighted to have "the Mulatto" in his power again. "You, too, my friend. Thought you'd got away, eh? They often think that, the ones that come in here. Somehow they'll escape, break free, find a way out. But they all die, man and beast: there's but one way out of here." He laughed aloud, as if at an exquisite jest. Jomar made no reply.

Shackled together, they trudged in single file past the iron cages and up the stair beyond, blinking as the short tunnel brought them into sudden sunlight. Before them spread the floor of sand, already patched in places with spilled blood, and all around them rose in tier upon tier the seats and marble galleries. But there was only a scattering of spectators in the upper tiers, and the royal box was empty.

The prisoners clumped together on the hot sand, waiting. Jomar stared at a nearby animal carcass, one of many strewn about the arena. Another sabertooth. The great cat had been literally torn apart, as if by giant claws. He swallowed. What were these beasts of Ombar like?

"I don't suppose," he said dully to the Nemerei, "any of you has animal-charming abilities?"

"Even if we had," said Ezmon Magus, raising his manacled hands, "we would not be able to use them."

"Take off their shackles and manacles," said the slave master to his thralls. "Except for those that wear the neckchain: they are Nemerei, and must remain bound with iron. But the others shall have the free use of their arms and legs. If all the prisoners are bound they will die too quickly, and Khalazar wishes to see some sport."

The Mohara prisoners and the soldiers of Arainia were released and forced at spearpoint to walk on, into the middle of the arena. Jomar now noticed some large indistinct shapes lurking behind the arched entrances of the three holding cells at the opposite end of the great stadium. He walked closer, his heart beginning to pound in a dismally familiar way. These were the chosen beasts, their adversaries—or rather their executioners, for he and his companions had no hope of surviving their attacks. As he drew nearer the shapes resolved themselves into huge creatures, the spawn of nightmares. There was a great bird taller than a camel, with a cruel hooked beak, long neck, and legs as thick around as young trees. When it saw him it rushed at the gate of its enclosure, clashed its beak against the bars, and screeched. In the second cell lay a heap of scales and horny plates that somewhat resembled a crocodile, only much larger. In the third—what in Valdur's name was it? It looked like an animal whose hide had been flayed off, or like something expelled from its mother's womb before it was fully formed: "mooncalf" was his first thought on seeing it. It was a shapeless, gelatinous thing, pulsing veins and pallid tendons plainly visible through flesh and muscle translucent as a jellyfish's mantle. From the center of the amorphous mass a single red eye stared.

A messenger ran out of the tunnel they had just exited. "The

king will not be coming after all. There has been rioting in the
streets and the guards cannot guarantee his safety. But he desires
that the prisoners be executed anyway. There are fears that their
rebel allies may try to free them."

"Well, what shall it be?" bellowed the slave master to the tiers of
seats above. "The boobrie bird, the afanc, or perhaps the nuckelavee?"

There was only a roar from the crowds in the lower seats, and
the voices of those in the upper levels could not be heard.

The slave master grinned broadly. "Did I hear them say *nuckelavee*? Yes—I'm sure I did." He and the other thralls strode back to
the tunnel. "Release the third beast!" he yelled as he passed back
through the entrance and closed and locked its iron gate.

The barrier to the third cell was raised with a grinding noise.
And the glistening bulk of the nuckelavee rose, and thrust out its
one-eyed head, and crawled out onto the sand of the arena. Now
that it was exposed to the light and no longer lying down, its true
shape became apparent to the onlookers. Twenty feet in height, it
stood on four splayed limbs, but from its sides there grew many
other strange appendages, flat and finlike, as though it were a creature of the water as well as of land. Its head was broad and split
nearly in half by a vast, grinning, whalelike mouth. Above it the
great crimson eye stared: it was set at the very front of the head, in
what would have been the tip of the muzzle in any other animal.
The color of the beast's body was pale purplish-red, and it was net-
ted with dark veins, and the shadowy shapes of the organs and of
its massive bones were visible as the suns' rays slanted through it.

Even a seasoned warrior could scarcely endure such a sight.
Cries of terror broke from the prisoners' lips, and those who had
been freed from their shackles huddled in a group, trembling.

"No! Don't all clump together like that! Separate!" Jomar yelled
at them. "The thing's only got one eye. Confuse it!"

The giant monocular head swung to and fro, seeming to debate
which victim to attack first. Then it lunged toward two prisoners
who were closer together than the rest. It moved with terrifying
speed for something so large: the prisoners screamed and fled,
both running in the same direction. Jomar swore and raced after
predator and prey. "No—no! Go in different directions! Confuse it,
I said!" he bawled at them. They were too panic-stricken to hear.

Jomar looked desperately about the arena as he ran. What was he to do without a weapon? Nothing but sand all around him—not even a stick or stone. There were a few bones from slain animals lying on the ground, but what use would they be against this monster?

Then his eye fell on the carcass of the sabertooth.

Stooping, he snatched up a large leg bone from those scattered on the sand without breaking his stride, and then he turned and sprinted for the dead cat's body. Throwing himself down on his knees beside it, he began to hammer at its muzzle with the bone, glancing over his shoulder as the nuckelavee harried its prey to and fro. With repeated blows he finally succeeded in knocking one of the huge curved teeth from the dead animal's upper jaw. As he stood clutching the tusk by its bloody root he felt courage flow back into him. Perhaps it was only the fact that he now had a weapon of sorts; or perhaps, as the shaman had said, the spirit strength of the dead beast was somehow entering into him. He yearned suddenly for Lorelyn, for her strength and speed and her own calm unwavering courage. She would have stood at his side, faced the monster with him.

There was a terrible cry from behind him. A huge bony claw lashed out, knocking one man to the ground and pinning him down. The beast's fanged jaws opened.

The creature's only got one eye. Blind it and it'll be helpless. But that eye was above a huge raging mouth, full of fangs. Could he climb onto its back and get at the eye from atop its head?

Avoiding the cyclopean stare, he ran for the beast's back and flung himself on it. The gelatinous flesh was sticky to the touch and the feel of it disgusted him, but he dug in the fang of the cat like a grappling hook. Tarlike black blood oozed forth from the wound. The beast, its jaws in the act of closing on its prey, bucked violently. Jomar fell off onto the sandy floor and lay for a moment dazed. Then he struggled to his hands and knees. The jaws of the beast were already filled with its victim, who was still screaming and flailing his limbs about. The nuckelavee shook its head from side to side, then lay down on the sand to worry its prey as a lion does.

At once Jomar ran in, attacking this time from the front.

He leaned over the thrashing man, leaned right into the monster's hideous translucent face. The single red eye glared out of the central socket in the skull. With his free hand he scooped up some sand, and cast it into that huge orb. A transparent lid shuttered the eye and the beast bellowed. As it did so its open jaws released their grip on their prey.

Jomar gave an answering yell. Then he hurled himself, not backward but *forward*, almost into the very mouth of the beast, a glistening red-purple cavern, from whose black throat came a foul stench and a deafening roar. He grabbed at the torso of the helpless man with his free hand, wrapping his arm about him, and pulled with all his strength. With the other he made chopping motions at the inside of the mouth and the flailing purple tongue, carving deep wounds into them. Injure an animal's mouth, he thought, and it may lose its eagerness to devour you.

One great yellow fang scored a bloody gash along his forearm as the jaws snapped shut. But neither man was trapped within the maw: the swooning victim had fallen to the sand, where he now lay insensible both of the danger and of his rescue, while Jomar sprang to one side and waved his arms again to draw the monster to him. The nuckelavee stood for a moment shuddering. Then it advanced, and its tremendous jaws opened wide again to engulf him.

Again he leaped forward, into the very mouth of the beast, using its lower jaw for a foothold. Seizing the upper jaw with his left hand and reaching up with his right, he plunged the cat's tooth into the giant eye.

There was a deafening bellow and the tooth was torn from his hand. He fell backward as the beast spun on its thick legs, flinging its head about and pawing at its eye. It succeeded in dislodging the bloodied tooth, which tumbled to the sand. But he had achieved his aim: it was blinded. Maddened with pain and terror it lashed out in all directions, and its frenzied gyrations brought it ever nearer to the prone body of its first victim, who was now stirring and trying to heave himself up. If it stepped on him he would be crushed. Jomar ran for the fallen cat fang and caught it up again. It was gored and slippery to the touch now: he rolled it in the sand, and then gripped it in both hands. The nuckelavee stood motionless again, heaving and quivering, its shapeless head cocked at an angle. Of course: deprived of vision, it was either listening or smelling for its prey. Suddenly it charged, straight at Jomar: striking out with its forelimbs, seeking to maul its unseen tormentor and avenge its injuries.

Dodging the blows, he ducked his head low and darted between the front legs, until he stood right underneath the sagging belly. Then standing straight again, he stabbed upward. The tooth, designed to pierce the thick shaggy hide of mastodons, sliced into the nuckelavee's soft underside with ease. It was a good thing the creature's vitals were clearly displayed, or he would never have known where to strike. With all his might he brought the tusk up, again and again. More black blood and foul-smelling fluids gushed out as he slashed at pulsing vessels and bloated organs, and at the baglike lungs. Then he flung himself to one side, rolling free as the legs bowed and collapsed like broken pillars, and the beast with a final howling cry collapsed upon the sand.

It was dead.

The din of the crowd was trebled. Jomar looked up, rubbing blood and sweat from his eyes, to see people pouring over the barricades and onto the arena floor. Screaming women and yelling men were everywhere. Had he survived the fight only to be torn limb from limb by a savage thwarted mob? One cat's tooth was no use against *this*, and his muscles shrilled with fatigue. He tried to rise, and fell back onto his knees.

The crowd streamed up and broke around him, like a wave. Hands seized hold of him. But their touch was not rough, nor were their voices angry. They were hoisting him into the air, onto their shoulders. And then he saw a familiar face in the midst of the throng.

"Well done, oh, well done, son of Jemosa!" Kiran Jariss was yelling. "Your fame will live forever after this day! I never saw such bravery!"

Seeing the smiles on the faces, hearing the laughter on the air, Jomar's wearied senses at last grasped the truth. The people had been on his side, all along! Their thunderous anger had been directed not at him, but at his captors. Now that he was free to listen, he heard through the clamor the words "Zayim" and "Jomar" being chanted in a booming chorus.

"We would have come to your aid before, but we were afraid of the beast." Kiran shoved his way through the crowd toward the exhausted Jomar as his bearers let him down again. "The people are angry about what was done to you—and to General Gemala, too. The army is divided: over half the soldiers have rebelled. Many are refusing to shoot at the crowds rioting outside Yanuvan; some even loosed arrows at their own comrades in arms who obeyed the order."

"I don't believe it," mumbled Jomar. Was it was really happening—had these people turned at last on their ruler? With a supreme effort he pulled himself together. "Help that man over there," he called. "The one the monster wounded. He's still alive, I think. Find someone to get the manacles off the bound ones too: they're Nemerei and we'll need their help!"

"You are hurt, too," observed Kiran, pointing.

Jomar looked at his bleeding arm. "A flesh wound. Give me something to bind it with, like a piece of your sash, and I'll be all right. We have to get to Yanuvan—I want to talk to these rebel soldiers, and I need a sword! Khalazar has more of my men in prison, and my two friends. Do you know what happened to Lorelyn, Kiran?"

Kiran's face turned grim. "She was sent into the harem wing to be a slave for the royal wives. And your friend Damion has been sent to the temple, for sacrifice."

"What!" Jomar paused in the act of tying a strip of cloth around his forearm.

"That is in part why the people are so angry—they fear the return of the old ways. Damion is to die at sunset. Jomar"—Kiran was now running to keep up with the long strides of the Zayim— "Lorelyn may be in greater danger. The crowds were already beating at the doors of Yanuvan when I left. If they break in, Khalazar will have to flee through one of his escape tunnels, and leave his harem behind!"

"So?" Jomar neither broke stride nor glanced at the man following at his heels.

"The guards will have to follow custom, to preserve the king's honor. All in the harem wing will be slain—including the slaves."

Jomar made no answer. His fatigue and wound were forgotten: shouldering aside the people in front of him, he began to run.

* * *

"WHAT IS ALL THAT NOISE?" asked Lorelyn, moving to the harem windows. She was clad in the thin brown robe of a slave, a thrall collar about her neck. Concubines and royal wives, bright as birds in their colorful gowns, looked up at her.

"It's like voices—hundreds and hundreds of voices," she said. "I can't see anything through these stupid curtains. How do you open them?"

One of the royal wives joined her at the window. "The curtains are always secured, so that only light may come through. We cannot be seen at the windows! We would be punished for immodesty."

Without another word Lorelyn reached up and wrenched away the thin white fabric, letting in the unmuted light and exposing a view of Yanuvan's battlements and the paved outer ward far below. The Zimbouran women blinked and protested, shielding their eyes as if the soft light of early evening dazzled them.

A pasty-faced boy of ten or so, who was lounging on a nearby divan, sat up and scowled at Lorelyn. "Get away from there, slave!" he called. "You will be beaten for that! And you, Arah"—to the woman standing next to Lorelyn—"you have shown yourself at the window, where one of the guardsmen might see you. A royal wife! You must be punished as well."

"Will you let him talk to you like that?" said Lorelyn in amazement as the woman recoiled with a cry.

"Silence!" the boy said. "She must do as I say. Get away from the window now!"

"Yes, my son." She moved to obey.

Lorelyn stared. "He is your son? You're not afraid of your own *child!*"

"He is the crown prince, Jari. With his brothers dead, he is second only to Khalazar."

Lorelyn snorted. "Nonsense! You ought to be ashamed, a grown woman like you, letting a mere child boss you about."

The dark-rimmed eyes dropped before her gaze. "It is the law. Men rule, no matter their age. If a man dies his son becomes head of the house, even if he is still a child."

"Well, it's a stupid law. It's high time it was changed." A commotion in the ward below caught Lorelyn's attention and she turned back to the window. "It looks like the army and the palace guard!" she exclaimed. "They're fighting *each other* down there! But why?"

Princess Marjana joined her at the window, and pointed. "Look there!" Hundreds of unarmed, ragged figures were running through the ward, following on the heels of the army.

Lorelyn gave a whoop of triumph. "The people! The people have risen up! Of course—the army's grown tired of shooting their countrymen. They've revolted—they've breached the fortress, and they're coming after Khalazar!"

The women began to wail and keen. Lorelyn turned to them. "Don't be afraid! You'll not be blamed for Khalazar's wrongdoing. You will be set free, I am sure, to go back to your homes. This is the best thing that could happen to you!"

"No," one royal wife said tearfully. "You do not understand. We cannot survive this. You will see."

"Whatever do you mean?" Lorelyn asked. But the woman only wept, and many of the others began to weep as well.

The face of the chief eunuch was gray as ash. "The palace guard have their orders, for such times as this," Yehosi quavered, but he too would say no more.

As they watched the battles below, the door at the end of the chamber suddenly burst open. Two fully armed palace guards entered. One's sword was drawn; the other carried a huge flagon, which he set down on a table.

"It is over. You must perform your final duties," the first guard said.

"The king is dead?" cried a wife.

"No, he lives yet; but he must flee the palace and Jari must go with him. But we cannot take all of you as well. You must die, rather than dishonor him by becoming spoil for other men. The slaves too must die," he added, looking at Marjana and Lorelyn, and Yehosi standing behind them. "All within the harem walls must take poison. Be brave, and die honorably for your king, serving him to the last."

"Why is your sword drawn?" Lorelyn asked him boldly, eyeing the weapon.

"If any one of you refuses, she shall be slain. It is the law."

The women wailed again and clung to each other sobbing. Some of the eunuchs wept too. If only they had the courage to charge the guards, Lorelyn thought in frustration—they vastly outnumbered them. But these were not free men and women, they were timid creatures bred for docility. As well try to set a herd of sheep on a pair of wolves!

Lorelyn set her jaw. "I'll be the first, then." She pushed her way past all the others and went straight to the table. The second man was filling a goblet with a dull-brown liquid from the jug.

"Wives, then concubines," he snapped. "Slaves go last."

"What does it matter?" she challenged.

"Let her do it," the guard with the sword advised. "This one *must* die, by sword or poison, lest her companions free her. It is Khalazar's command."

"Very well," said Lorelyn. "I'll drink the poison. Let me take my own life at least, and not die on a coward's sword." She took the cup from the table, raising it to her lips.

Then with a sudden flick of her wrist, she dashed the contents in the second guard's face.

He screamed, clawing at his face as though terrified that the poison might somehow seep through his skin. Blinded by his own frantic efforts, he stumbled backward, and Lorelyn seized his sword-hilt, yanking the weapon from his belt. The other guard, recovering from his own stupefaction, raised his sword—too late. Lorelyn's blade had already plunged in under his arm. He crumpled to the floor.

"Take his sword," she yelled at Marjana while the Zimbouran women screamed and milled about, looking more like frightened sheep than ever. The surviving guard was curled up in a corner, moaning with fear and clutching his face. Marjana looked at Lorelyn in disbelief.

"What are you doing?"

"We've got to get out of here," Lorelyn urged. "I must help the rebels. Here, help me into his clothes and armor"—indicating the slain guard—"and take his sword for yourself!"

"I can't," said Marjana, shrinking. "I have never wielded any kind of blade. It's no use, Lady Lorelyn—I'm not as strong as you, nor as brave!"

"You *must* be," insisted Lorelyn, struggling into the armor. "You're the Queen of Shurkana. You must be brave for your country's sake, Your Majesty."

Marjana stared at her. Throughout her captivity it had never once occurred to her that the deaths of her father and brothers made her the heir to the throne. Shurkana was fallen: how, then, could the Lotus Throne have an heir? But now Khalazar had been toppled from his own throne. At last she understood. She was free—and all Shurkana with her.

Queen. With shaking hands Marjana took up the fallen scimitar. It was a well-balanced weapon, not so heavy as it looked, and to her surprise she hefted it with ease.

"Good," approved Lorelyn, putting on the helmet. "Oh, do stop the noise"—this to the gibbering guard—"If the poison were going to kill you, you'd be dead by now. And after all your talk of *dying honorably*, too!" Lorelyn snatched up the flagon and, smashing the windowpane with her sword-hilt, flung it together with its contents into the court below.

"Now, Your Majesty!" she cried, running to the door.

Lorelyn and Marjana rushed out into the hall, heading for the great central staircase. Noises came from the ward outside: men cursing and the clash of steel on steel.

KHALAZAR STORMED ONTO THE battlements. A roaring, ravening crowd had converged upon the central keep, and the palace guard had stationed several battalions in a protective circle around it. Khalazar clenched his fists, staring with bloodshot eyes at the rebels below. From this height they looked to him like insects, minute scurrying forms he could crush with his foot. Would that it were so!

Again and again he had ordered the army to fire the cannons and shoot arrows into that hateful mob. They had obeyed, wreaking death and injury—and still the mob grew, like some noisome monster sprouting many heads for each one cut off. And with every attack on the people, dissent grew within the army. Attacking Moharas and Shurkas was one thing; firing on their own fellow citizens was another. Some of the conscripts had been born in these very streets, had wives, friends, family living here. Many were now in open revolt. Someone had cut General Gemala's body down from the gibbet on which it had hung: they had removed it for burial, no doubt. It was a flagrant violation of his royal command.

He gnashed his teeth. Mandrake had not answered his summons for aid, either. "I will punish him for this disobedience!" he snarled. "When next he comes, I will be waiting for him with cold iron to bind him as I bound his goblin servants!"

Gemala had warned him before dying: "That Mandrake is no spirit," he had insisted. "A magician of terrible powers, but mortal all the same. He bled, Majesty: you saw it! When did a spirit ever bleed? He has deceived you from the first."

"Gemala spoke true," fumed Khalazar. "Mandrake gulled me. Well, I will make him bleed again, wizard though he be! I will hang him from the gibbet in Gemala's place!"

He ran down from the battlements. Seizing a sword out of the hands of a terrified guard, he ran on down the wide main staircase of the keep.

Suddenly two figures raced across the hall below: a woman in brown slave's garb, and a palace guardsman. "Here are the main doors," called the slave whom he recognized as Princess Marjana, "we need only unbar them, and the people can come in."

He glared at the guard in fury. Here was yet another traitor—within his very household! And the guard had given the slave woman a sword! At that his anger wholly possessed him: he charged down the stairs like a mad bull, brandishing his own blade.

"Treacherous filth!" he howled. "Aid my enemies, would you?" He ignored Marjana, flinging himself on the armored guard in a frenzy of hate. The guard's sword came up and Khalazar's blade glanced harmlessly off it. Raining blow after blow on the guard's weapon, the king sought to strike it from his grip and slay him. But then there was a stabbing pain in his shoulder and he cried out, turning. Marjana stood there, her own sword held out in shaking hands. Its tip was bloodied.

"No!" the guard shouted. "Leave him to me—"

The young man's voice was familiar—but the king was too furious to ponder further. Khalazar struck Marjana's weapon from her unskilled hands and raised his blade again to behead her. But the guard's sword sliced into his arm before he could strike. He turned, striking back, clumsy with pain, but throwing his whole massive weight behind each blow. The guard gave way. And then, even as he raised his blade high for another mighty downstroke, there was an agonizing jab in his left side. He looked down, staring blank-eyed at the sword-tip protruding from his upper chest.

He turned himself slowly about, and saw her—Marjana: she had taken up the sword again, and run him through. But no. It was not possible. A woman could not do such a thing . . .

He sagged to his knees, his sword clattering to the floor. He, who had commanded countless legions, could not now exact obedience from his own limbs. They betrayed him, failed to respond. He collapsed onto his side. And there, flowing away across the floor: his own blood—deserting his body in long red runnels. His strength was fading, his sight dimming. He was no god, but only a man—a man with not much life left in him. A man dying by a woman's hand—not even the hand of the Tryna Lia, but the hand of a lowly slave.

It could not be. Khalazar-Valdur could not die—not this way. A groan arose deep in his throat, the sound of a stricken animal. Or of a man, a mortal man who was not and never had been a god . . . He felt himself falling into lightless deeps, beyond healing or hope. Not Khalazar-Valdur, only Khalazar who must die as other men. At least let him die by a man's hand, and not a woman's! Why did the traitorous guard not strike, curse him, now that his master lay helpless before him? Khalazar's life was ebbing fast, but there was still a chance to be slain honorably—by a male hand. He stared up at the guard in impotent entreaty. *Kill me! Kill me now! If I die of the woman's wound I die in dishonor. Let me die by yours . . .* The man, he saw, was removing his helmet—

At the sight of the face beneath, Khalazar gaped in horror and despair. Then a long shriek of utter defeat burst from his lips.

THE MAIN DOORS BUCKLED and burst wide open, and a torrent of rioters poured in. The beleaguered palace guard had broken and fled at the overwhelming onslaught. People trampled those who did not flee fast enough, and seized tapestries, gold fixtures, vases, whooping and yelling as they pillaged.

One of the men looked up as Lorelyn hastened through the hall. It was Jomar! She ran to him with a cry, and he grinned at her. "What a day! Isn't this amazing? The mob freed me! But where is Khalazar?"

"Over there," Lorelyn waved her hand at the bloodied corpse on the stone floor of the hall. "He's dead, Jo."

"You're sure?" Jomar prodded the corpse hopefully with his sword, but it did not stir. "A pity," he grunted. "I would have liked that pleasure myself. Oh, well, at least one of us got him."

"It wasn't I," said Lorelyn. "Marjana struck the death blow."

The Shurka woman still clutched the bloodstained sword. "It is over," she said in a quiet voice, throwing it down. "My father and brothers are avenged."

Jomar turned back to Lorelyn. "Are you all right? Did he hurt you?" he asked, laying a hand on her arm.

She shook her head. "Jo, are the other warriors with you? We must set a guard on the harem. The women are terrified, and I think the children are in danger from the mobs. Some of them are little monsters, Jari especially, but they can't help being Khalazar's children, and they don't deserve to be killed for it."

Still holding her arm, Jomar began to run, pulling her along with him. "The Arainians are here with me. I'll send them to guard the women and children. And Marjana too. Go back to the harem, Majesty, and wait there!" he shouted over his shoulder. The young queen, who had been following them, stopped short. "Please. You'll be safe there, I promise. Lorelyn, come with me!"

"Where are we going?" she panted as they ran.

"The temple of Valdur. Damion was sent there—to die at sunset."

Lorelyn gasped. "Then we must hurry, Jo," she cried. "The sun is setting *now*!"

DAMION WAS ONLY DIMLY aware of the hard stone of the altar on which the priest and acolyte had laid him. The latter, at his master's command, had gone back to the door and opened it a crack to watch the sun's progress down the sky. The priest now held in one withered hand the ancient ceremonial dagger, with its bronze blade and hilt of human bone. But Damion spared no thought for these things. He lay still and closed his eyes, entranced by the procession of images playing out in his mind. Against the darkness of his eyelids they grew clear once more. His procession through the crowded streets—the oasis refuge—the battle in the desert, all rushed by, like a tide reversing its flow. And then he was back in

Arainia again, at Halmirion, and Ailia was looking up at him from under her crown of flowers.

Ailia, he thought, then: *Ailia, I love you!*

Now their first adventure swept before his eyes; the Stone, the island of Trynisia. The images flicked past with breathtaking speed. Ana—Lorelyn—the scroll—the seminary years—the orphanage . . .

Somewhere, very far away, the voice of the old priest said, "Is it time yet, boy? Tell me when it is time."

The acolyte's slow halting voice answered. "The sun dies, Master. The sky is red. But, Master—"

"What is it, boy? What is all that noise outside?"

"People coming—shouting. So many angry, angry people—" The acolyte's voice trembled.

"Close the doors and bar them!" There was no fear in the priest's tone, only a curious gloating. "The reign of Khalazar is over. One thing only remains: the last act of blasphemy, to condemn him for all eternity."

There followed the sound of the doors slamming, and the darkness behind Damion's eyes deepened as the light was again shut out. But against that blackness the images of his inner vision grew clearer. With a thrill of wonder, Damion felt his mind go back further still: to a far shore beyond the seas of thought, where lay the flotsam and jetsam fragments of a still earlier past. Lost memories of—a garden—flowers—two faces: a woman, a man—*Father and Mother.* No, this last was no memory, but a real presence. A white-clad woman with green eyes and golden curling hair stood before him, in the darkness, calling out to him . . .

I remember you now, he said to her in his mind. *I remember it all! Is that what death is then—the recalling of what we have lost? Is death truly a sleep— or do we dream our life, and then wake from it?*

Her hands and eyes beckoned him onward, into her embrace.

22

The Dragon's Bride

AURON CIRCLED HIGH above the towers of the Forbidden Palace. He flew in the guise of a cockatrice, but even so he risked much in coming so near the enemy's keep. Desperation and his anxiety for Ailia had pushed him to this hazardous gamble. He could only hope that, with so many Loänei dwelling in the keep, the pulse of ethereal power coming from his transformed body would be dismissed as one of their own sorceries, should any of them happen to sense it. It was said that the dragon-folk slept through the daylight hours, so there was a chance that he would be safe, and escape the notice of their sentries. Even so, this pass above Mandrake's fortress must be swift.

He flapped his leathery wings and dared to skim down lower, under the shadow of the central tower. He had seen something below: a lone figure, female, walking in one of the courtyard gardens. *Could* it be—

He spiraled down on the heavy warm air and alighted on the lawn a few paces away from her. She was dressed in a robe of red silk patterned with gold dragons, and her hair was bound up in an unfamiliar style. But it was she. He could not believe his good fortune. She started and stared at him with wide, wondering eyes as he transformed to his customary human shape and whispered, "Ailia."

She gasped. "Auron."

"Highness, don't worry, we have come for you—Taleera and Falaar and I. Come, let us flee while Mandrake's eye is off you! I will carry you away on my back." He drew on his power again, preparing to change to his dragon's shape. By now his use of power would have alerted those within. The prince would be upon them in an instant, calling on his own Loänan. But they would escape, if

Auron flew at his greatest speed and called upon his weather-power—

Ailia gave an odd little cry, and retreated a couple of steps. "No—go away! Leave me alone!" she exclaimed.

In his surprise he lost hold of the power he was summoning. He ran to her, holding out his hands. "Ailia—it's I—I'm here to rescue you! I would have warned you I was coming, but I dared not speak mind to mind through the Ether, for fear of Mandrake overhearing. Quickly, now—I can fly you away from here!"

Again Ailia backed away from him. Her face was pale, and contorted with something like loathing. "Don't you come near me!" she screamed. "I *hate* you! You and your friends carried me off and held me captive on your world! Mandrake warned me you would come and try to abduct me again! Mandrake," she turned and shouted in the direction of the doorway, "Mandrake, help me!"

"Ailia—"

There was a noise of running feet. Dismayed, Auron turned at once back into his cockatrice's form, and flew away over the wall even as the Loänei guards poured into the garden.

"SHE HAS TURNED ON US!" cried Taleera in horror. She was sitting, transformed to human shape, with Auron and Mag in the latter's kitchen. "Do you think that Mandrake has corrupted her—made her believe his lies?"

Auron shook his head. "No! She is under a spell of some kind— she must be!" But he was miserable as he recalled the revulsion in Ailia's eyes. *Could she really have learned to hate us? Has Mandrake won her over and twisted her thoughts?*

"I have heard of potions that enslave the will," said Mag suddenly. "The dragon-folk used such things in olden times. And there is one that creates absolute devotion to another person."

"What is that?" demanded Taleera, turning her auburn head sharply to stare at the innkeeper.

"The love-philter, it is called. It makes a person fall deeply in love with the first person she or he sees."

"Of course! Ailia wouldn't ever turn against us!" exclaimed Taleera, as though that had been her position all along. "Is there an antidote to this poison, Mag?"

"Yes—it's in an old book of my grandmother's. I never had any call to use it before. I'll go look at the ingredients this minute."

When Mag left the room Taleera said, "We must go to the castle, Auron, in disguise."

"The prince will be on his guard now, and increase the number of his sentries. And if Mag is right, Ailia herself will fight us," said Auron. "She will use all the powers at her disposal. Ah, clever Mandrake—he has turned the strength of our own champion against us!"

"Well, we must do something. We can't just leave her there."

There was a long pause as the two of them sat pondering. A small head poked out from underneath the table, followed by a larger one that emerged on the opposite side. Twidjik plucked a fruit out of the bowl sitting unregarded between them, and then withdrew both his heads from sight again. "I have an idea," said Auron at length. "We will need Falaar's help to execute it, but I believe it can succeed. We must also have someone whom Ailia still trusts, to take her a message. She will believe neither one of us now."

"Can you not disguise yourself again?" asked Mag, coming back in with the book.

"Mandrake would sense my sorcery at work—as would the Loänei. I barely got away the first time, with most of them still asleep."

"I'll do it then," Mag offered. "Ailia trusts me, and I owe her a debt for Mai's sake."

"Would the guards admit you, though?" said Taleera. "Someone might recognize you: it's well known that you and your daughter gave shelter to Lia. Nor is it any secret that you are a Nemerei. They may suspect that you know she is the Tryna Lia, and want to help her. I think they will not let you in."

"Maybe *we* get in?" said a voice from somewhere at their feet.

All three stared in astonishment. It was Twidjik the amphisbaena who had spoken. His front head reappeared and looked at them with its round dark eyes. "We go," it said. "Dragon-people not afraid of us. Nobody afraid of amphisbaena. We go, for sorceress-lady."

"Well I'll be—blessed!" said Mag once Auron had translated for her. "A two-head do such a thing? I never heard the like! But will he be able to do it, or will he lose his nerve and run away?"

"We do it," Twidjik said, coming out from under the table and training the eyes of both heads on them. "For her. For sorceress-lady."

The nights were very beautiful here—she had not noticed that before. The sky turned from green to the deepest possible turquoise, and the moons lay scattered in it like pearls. And the Loänei palace, though made like a fortress without, was luxurious as Halmirion within.

Halmirion . . . It seemed to her more than ever in memory like an exquisite prison, a cage in which she had been trapped and confined. How could Auron have been so foolish as to believe she would ever return there? Ailia reveled in her stay in the Forbidden Palace. All worries had been banished from her mind: she had lounged at ease all last night with the other courtiers, being waited upon by slaves who brought them sweetmeats and cooling cordials. She had soaked herself in a perfumed bath and been anointed with fragrant oils.

And there was Mandrake, her beloved. All her hours were filled with the thought of him. He was teaching her to take a dragon's form herself, through deep meditation exercises: giving her the feel of its vast armored body, its clawed limbs and mighty wings. Soon he would teach her to take that form in reality, and she would fly the skies with him as a Loänan, knowing a freedom beyond any she had ever yet experienced. The only thing that cast a slight shadow on her happiness was the thought that *he* did not always seem as happy as he should. He would look away from her at times and sigh, and she would quickly put a hand upon his shoulder or stroke his long soft hair.

She reclined on her divan in the ballroom while the indoor fountain splashed soothingly. The carp in their basin rose greedily for the delicacies she cast to them, while people played stringed instruments and chatted and laughed. Light patterns reflected on the ceiling from the fountain rippled like music and laughter made visible. She took in a deep breath, scented richly with the jungle flower perfume she now wore. The Loänei had been right all along, she thought. They understood how to live. And they loved all beauty, including hers. The blue shadowing they had rubbed on her eyelids and the paint on her lashes made her eyes seem even larger, the rouge on lips and cheekbones accentuated the fetching pallor that layers of rice powder created. Her hair was dressed with jewels and rose in a mass of twisting interwoven braids, echoing the sinuous coils of the dragons worked into her scarlet lounging robe. Her fingers were tipped with long red artificial nails, in imitation of a dragon's claws.

Pleasure: it was the goal and the very essence of life. For this alone did one come into the world, to take all one could of what one wanted. To be like the beasts, who did not ponder or puzzle their minds with questions, but only ate and bred and then died. To live as long as possible, to preserve one's youth and health and beauty for as long as possible. She looked up at the frieze of capering marble nudes on the walls above. No fat or coarse-featured or elderly figures there! They were all young and beautiful—*too* beautiful for her liking, suddenly. She frowned. The sculptor's chisel had given them an impossible perfection of smooth skin, rounded muscle, and classical feature. No living person could look like these idealized stone idols, nor could the passage of time work any change in them. She fretted—for a moment was actually jealous of the stone figures. What if Mandrake were to compare her beauty with theirs, and find her wanting?

I must learn to alter myself with shape-shifting. There must be no flaw in me, no imperfection. I will change my height—my face—my limbs. I will make myself perfect, so his gaze can never stray to any other woman. For it stood to reason that if people were animals, then the best animal would always win. The more beautiful and virile among beasts distracted potential mates away from their rivals, flaunting their glorious plumes and manes and horns. She sat up and looked suspiciously about the room. Rivals! *Had* she any? Would anyone dare? That young Loänei woman now, by the window—she was tall and slender and lovely, too lovely by half. Mandrake must surely have noticed her, and admired her: how could he not? A hot anger rose in Ailia's breast, burning through the drowsy haze of indolence. In Nemorah people moved from lover to lover as from one meal to the next, with no more emotional attachment than one gave to eating. It was the animal's way. But it was not Ailia's: she loved Mandrake to the exclusion of all others. If she could only be sure of *his* love!

No one must take Mandrake from me. If any woman so much as tries, I will kill her!

A shrill, inhuman cry rang out in the corridor and she looked toward the doorway, annoyed. What games were the courtiers up to now? There was another scream and a sound of laughter and running feet, and several of the younger Loänei charged into the room bowling what looked like a thick gray hoop before them with a stick.

"What is it?" someone asked as the hoop rolled over on its side and became the huddled shape of a small animal with a head at either end.

"We don't know—some jungle creature," laughed a youth as he prodded it with a stick. "It got into the castle somehow—through the tunnel, I'll wager—and we've been having a bit of fun with it."

"It's an amphisbaena," said Ailia, rising to take a closer look. "I had one for a companion, when I came here through the jungle. They can talk, if you have the power to hear. I am surprised it would dare to come to this place: most fear the Forbidden Palace, and amphisbaenas are very cowardly."

The creature raised its front head, still panting with fright. "We come to help you, beautiful sorceress-lady," it chattered.

Ailia was astonished. "Twidjik, is that you? What are you doing here in the castle, you silly creature? I told Mag to take care of you."

"We came here to be your servant, carry messages and things for you. We have not forgotten your kindness, your protection. Don't send us away!"

"Honestly, what a little limpet you are! Never mind, you may stay for now." She returned to her divan and he scuttled underneath it.

She paid him no more heed, for Mandrake had entered. Delight filled her when he was present, and pleasurable anticipation when he was absent. His attentions were what she lived for: a soft-spoken word, a caress, a cut flower placed in her hand.

"I want you to be as happy as I am," she murmured as he sat down beside her on the divan. "Don't you love me as I love you?" She waited anxiously for his reply.

He turned and kissed her hand. "Of course." She breathed a sigh of relief and reached up to stroke his hair: he seemed to want to pull away, and also to enjoy the caress, at the same time. What could be wrong with him? She posed the question to his mind, and he answered aloud, as though he did not want to share the intimacy of thought. "It is nothing."

"I will always love you," she said softly.

"I know." He looked at her oddly. "That is the difficulty."

And then he rose again, and left her alone and desolate. When he had departed from the room, she turned over and buried her powdered face in the cushions.

"So! When is the wedding to be?"

Ailia glanced up at the mocking voice. Syndra was standing over her divan, smiling down at her.

"What do you mean?" asked Ailia. "Whose wedding?"

"Why, yours, of course. To Prince Morlyn." Syndra sat down uninvited on the divan cushions.

Ailia looked at her with contempt. "Do you know so little of this world, and you here longer than I?" she retorted. "You know there is no marriage among the Loänei. They do not own one another that way."

"A pity, that. It helps keep the men from going astray."

"Mandrake is not like other men. He loves only me."

"Are you so sure of that?" Syndra leaned close. "Why has he not claimed you and taken you for his own yet? Can it be that he is only amusing himself with you?"

A hot flush swept over Ailia's face, and she leaped up. "Take that back," she hissed, "or so help me, I will slay you where you stand—for Mandrake's sake and mine. You dishonor us both."

Syndra's face retained its mocking expression. "I am merely trying to help you, my dear Princess. You might show some gratitude. As for killing me, well, you might find that harder than you think." Naked hate flashed in her narrowed eyes.

"You treacherous snake!" screamed Ailia. "You cringing little gutter-witch! Don't you know that my powers are many times greater than yours? Mandrake has been teaching me how to use them. I could blast you to a cinder if I chose!" She flung out her hand and from her sapphire ring there shot out a small bolt of pure quintessence. It struck Syndra, knocking her to the floor. But the other woman was on her feet again in an instant, eyes blazing, attacking in her turn. Disdainfully, Ailia deflected the other sorceress's bolts and sent another fiery blast at her, hurling her against the far wall. She crumpled to the floor again.

"Enough!" a voice snapped from the direction of the doorway.

Ailia stood stricken, one hand still raised. Mandrake was standing there, and he looked angry. Her beloved prince was angry with her. No, more than that—there was real distaste in his eyes as he looked at her. He averted his gaze, then turned without another word and strode away.

Syndra crawled across the floor to a nearby divan and hauled herself up onto it. "You saw that? You saw the look on his face?" she spat. "He hates you—actually hates you! You might as well die, for you'll never have him now!"

Ailia's heart faltered at those words, and the whole world seemed to darken. Ignoring Syndra, she rushed from the room.

MANDRAKE FOUND ERRON KOMORA taking his ease in his private apartments. "What have you done to her, blast you?" he shouted, striding into the room and seizing the Loänei by both shoulders.

"To Ailia? I have done nothing, Highness," Erron replied, cowering. "Nothing! It is the philter that has done its work, as I told you it would."

"You did not tell me it would alter her character completely!"

"Nor has it. You see merely another side of Ailia's character, a side that she has hitherto kept carefully suppressed. Her dark, secret side of hidden emotions and desires. The potion has taken away certain . . . restraints she previously imposed on herself. That is why the Loänei no longer use this potion on our vassals. It was thought that it would compel obedience from them by filling them with adoration for us. But it only set them to fighting one another for our favor."

Mandrake said no more, but turned away from him and left the room. Shame was an emotion he had not felt in literal ages: he had forgotten its peculiar sting. Ailia's downfall had come about because of her trust in him—she had taken the draught believing he would put nothing in it that would harm her. And now . . . Mandrake recalled the writhing medusan hair, the powdered face and scarlet lounging robe that showed off her long graceful neck and slender waist. His hands clenched tightly at his sides. That look in her eyes of utter devotion, where only sympathy had shown before—he was utterly repelled by it. In a sense it was not Ailia who had stood there before him but an automaton, a being without real feeling and subject to commands. He, who loved freedom best of all things, had stolen it from her.

But it is better this way, his other side insisted. *This way she does not control me, but I her. I am the one in power.* It was true that under the influence of the philter she would never harm him—could not even think to harm him. Her power was rendered null: she would use it only at his command. They would not have to fight the duel he had dreaded, and he would not have to kill her. Together they could defy both Nemerei and Valei, their blended strength a match for any foe.

But to keep her in that loathsome enchantment—!

There was a counter-potion, that likely would not be difficult to obtain. But he could not afford to release Ailia from the philter. Mandrake saw, too late, how perfectly he was trapped. Were he to free her, she would realize his treachery as soon as her normal state of mind was restored, and turn on him in anger. Perhaps the sly Erron had even planned it so? No, he was seeing conspiracies in every corner now. But to release Ailia was impossible. Then was killing her the only solution?

The last report from the goblins in Mera had told of Damion Athariel's capture. But though he had instructed them to watch over the priest, he had also realized that the holding of such hostages was a futile gesture. Ailia was not one to put her personal feelings before her duty. He could no longer hope to control her that way.

He had tried to turn her to his side, playing on her love of knowledge and her desire to escape confinement. He had sought to interest her in learning to become a dragon, to throw off her humanity; instead she had hesitated, and it was he who had been obliged to spend more and more time in human form. And in consequence he had grown more *human* with every day that he spent in this body, while his thoughts and his nature became correspondingly petty. He was reminded suddenly of the temple virgin who had lured him from his lair centuries ago. He had been besotted with the girl, never looking ahead, never wondering what he would do when her shorter lifespan began to tell, her beauty to wither, and her vitality to diminish while his own remained unchanged. He had had some vague idea of "aging" himself with glaumerie for her sake, but his mind had shied away from the future. One did not think of a flower fading after it was cut and placed in the vase. What a fool he had been! This was the folly he committed when in human form. If he did not find a way to cast it aside forever, he would be lost.

He could feel the dragon within him as a palpable presence: writhing, struggling, beating its wings in the desperate effort to break through, to be free. The iron-wound in his chest had remanifested, as had the older scars in his side and neck: they throbbed with a dull, nagging pain. He glanced in a mirror in the hall: yes, there were the angry red welts again.

He took the long stair up to the top of the central tower, seeking the clarity of mind that came with the dragon's form. He felt a lift of the heart as he put off his humanity and all the frailties connected with it and raised his wings to the wind. He was a master of the elements now, equally at home in earth, air, or water. Out over the city he flew, watching its inhabitants look up and point and scatter. Then on over the river and the fields. Several goats and their herdsman fled before him, the man as panicked as his beasts. Mandrake could now feel pity for all the little human creatures below. Human weakness he could easily set aside, it was for him only a temporary inconvenience; no such escape was possible for them.

Once in draconic shape his troubles, as always, ceased to seem so overwhelming. His feelings for Ailia faded—he could view her, now, as a small and frail creature who was of no importance to him, save for the potential threat she still presented.

Why, after all, *should* it be so hard to kill her?

THE AIR WAS HOT AND HEAVY, and Ailia's skin was filmed with perspiration. She went restlessly to the main window of her chamber and looked out. Day was breaking: the clouds were stained a lurid sulphur-yellow on their undersides, and the air was yellow, too. It was as if light and air had congealed together into some thick resin, encasing every leaf and twig in the garden below and holding it motionless. Ailia leaned against the pane. She felt as stiff and exhausted as though she had been running. All was still: no creature stirred or made a sound. It was a prestorm stillness, breathless, charged, fraught with tension. This was no ordinary storm: the local climate reflected Mandrake's mood. If this stress in the atmosphere were any indication of how he was feeling, everyone must tread carefully, even herself.

Something suddenly showed through the steam clouds suspended above—something that swept through them, circling the four-horned tower that stood in its wreathing mists dark and solitary as an island in a stormy sea. It was a red dragon with a russet mane, looking no larger than a bat beside the great thrusting pinnacles. It was Mandrake—she was sure of it. Ailia drew back from the window, suddenly afraid of this Loänan, this other Mandrake, even as she loved him. Why had he taken his dragon shape? As she watched he swept upward, vanishing into the low-hanging sulphurous clouds.

She remembered the repugnance in his eyes as he looked at her: it was too much to bear. She sobbed, pulling off the various pieces of jewelry he had given her. She was unworthy of it, unworthy of his love. And this accursed sapphire ring, cause of all the trouble—she cast it to the floor. It would have been better had she stayed in that empty life on Arainia, imprisoned in her palace, despising herself for letting the people believe she was divine. But there was no going back, either. She could not live without her prince.

As she paced about, weeping quietly, her eyes fell on the silver dagger resting on her night table.

Her Thorn. Someone had given it to her, long ago—not Mandrake, but another. She had forgotten who it was. No matter. Its sharp blade, she saw now, offered the only possible escape. Syndra was right. To live without Mandrake's love was impossible. Far better not to live at all. She took the weapon from the table and weighed it in her hand.

A humble scratching noise at the door, rather like that made by a dog, caught her attention. "Who is it?" she snapped.

"It's we—Twidjik."

Irritated, she opened the door. The amphisbaena sidled through, his front head drooping on its long neck, his hind head nervously scanning the hall behind him. But he had seen the dagger in her hand, its point still aimed at her own breast. That, and the tears streaking her face, told him all. He stretched out his foreneck and interposed his front head between her bosom and the blade. "No—no, lady! Mustn't hurt yourself!"

"Don't interfere!" She pushed his head away.

"Please, mistress. The Loänei said we might serve you. And the prince gave us message, to tell you to come to him."

"Message—for me?" Her heart lifted, but she could still not quite believe it. Mandrake hated her, would always hate her. She could still see the disgust in his eyes. "Why did not he summon me in my mind?" she asked.

"He not want Lady Syndra and other sorcerers overhearing. He want you to come see him alone, in secret cave at heart of hill."

"In his lair? When?" she asked breathlessly.

"Now—this minute. Bring lamp, and come!"

Odd: she had just seen the red dragon flying through the skies moments ago. But perhaps that was but a ruse, to throw Syndra and the others off. He would come back disguised in another form, and enter the cave, and they would be together once more. She hugged Twidjik, squeezing a startled breath from both his heads. "Oh! I'm so glad, Twidjik, so glad! He doesn't hate me after all then—he *doesn't*! He would have me come to him—a secret tryst. And no one else shall know!"

"Come." The little creature ran for the door. "Quick, quick!"

She followed him down the stairs. The castle was silent, its inhabitants asleep or retreating from the heat in the comfort of their private chambers. The lower halls were empty. Twidjik led her to the door and the rough-hewn tunnel—down, down to the cave with its steaming pool. At its edge she paused, peering through the dense vapors for a sight of the crimson dragon. Nothing stirred in the dark water.

"Up other tunnel," urged Twidjik. "Up, to entrance."

She followed him, and still she saw no sign of Mandrake in any of his accustomed forms. Then as she approached the tunnel's mouth there was a rush of wings, and a dragon alighted on the threshold, thrusting its great head inside the cavern. In the suns' light its scales gleamed not red, but the color of gold. It looked like—

"No," she said, stopping short.

Hello, Ailia, said Auron in her mind. With a flutter the firebird alighted beside him. In her beak she held a glass flask, filled with some pale green liquid.

Ailia rounded on Twidjik. "You!" she cried. "You deceived me! You're on their side!"

"You must come with us now," said Taleera. "Don't be afraid, Ailia. We won't harm you."

"You think I would go anywhere with you?" Ailia cried. She strode up to them. "I hate you! Go! My prince will be here soon: if he finds you here it will be the end of you."

"Mandrake can do nothing, nor can you," Auron rumbled. "No sorcery will harm us. Look up! There, in the sky."

He pulled back, to let her see. There was flash of golden wings high above the mounting steams—a cherub, stooping on them like a hawk. How could she ever have thought such a horrible, mutant monster beautiful? And then she saw in horror that the creature clutched in its beak a black lump of rock, a rock from which came a terrible roar. Cold iron! Of course, the cherubim were immune to its magic. In mere seconds she would be powerless, unless she acted swiftly.

Spinning around, she bent and caught hold of Twidjik's leg and foreneck, and with one swing of her arms she hurled him out of the cave mouth, out over the sheer side of the volcano. His double scream faded as he dropped.

"Well?" she cried in triumph. "Will you save your spy, or not?"

Auron had no choice. He whirled and flung himself over the edge, going to the amphisbaena's rescue. The cherub spread his wings to halt his dive and hovered high above, knowing that the iron would take the dragon's power of flight from him. And as Taleera flapped to one side, still gripping the vial in her beak, Ailia sprang past her and launched herself into the abyss.

She had never before shape-shifted, never taken dragon form: but Mandrake had been thorough and patient in his tutelage. She felt her body expand, quintessence pouring into it out of the Ether to increase its size: saw the great red wings unfurl to either side of her. The wings seemed to know what to do: they lifted her up, up into the sky away from the cherub. The Loänan had caught the amphisbaena, as she had known he would, and had wasted even more time setting him down safely on the ground. He was now rising again, but he was too far behind her. She screamed a dragon scream of pride and defiance at him, and flew on.

And now at last the storm broke, its pent-up energies unleashed by her wrath, with a great flash and a roll of thunder. Out of the midst of the dark clouds she saw her beloved come flying to her, his flame-red wings spread wide. Coming to her aid. She winged her way toward him as fast as she could. But the winds surrounding her were wild and she did not know how to fly in such a turbulent atmosphere. She was buffeted and tossed from side to side like a falling leaf.

She beat her dragon wings wildly, flying on. But already she was weakening, and her wings and dragon body were dissolving, fading like mist in the sun . . . The cherub! He was pursuing her, gaining on her: she could hear in her mind the fearsome noise of the sky-iron. Ailia screamed, hearing this time her own woman's voice. Her wings were gone, her magic banished. She was falling—falling . . .

"Catch her!" Auron cried, behind her.

And she was seized: Falaar's claws closed upon her. The talons did not so much as scratch her, but cupped her gently like enfolding hands. The green face of Nemorah was no longer hurtling up to smash her life from her.

Ailia turned her head, saw the red dragon engaged in aerial combat with Auron. Taleera with the glass vial clenched in her beak was flying with all her might toward Falaar. Ailia wailed aloud in impotent fury and anguish. Her prince was in pain—she could not sense his suffering through the iron's clamor, but she heard it in his cries that rose now above the thunder. She twisted in the cherub's furred claws, but could not free herself. *Oh my love, my love—how dare they hurt you! I will punish them for this—I will blast them from the sky!* But she could do nothing.

More dragons arrowed out of the clouds: Mandrake's Loänan and the firedrakes from Ombar, come to help him and her.

Taleera shifted the phial from her bill to a claw. "Auron! Leave him!" she screamed. "We are at the portal's threshold!"

The golden dragon broke away from the fight and sped toward them.

"Now!" cried the firebird. "The portal is near! Open up the dragon-way, and let us be gone!"

"No! Let me go!" Ailia shrieked, and she wept as she struggled in Falaar's claws.

Then the roiling gray tumult of Nemorah's sky vanished as they plunged together into the twisting tunnel of the Ether.

23

The Leavetaking

THE FLOWERS OF SUMMER bloomed all around Ailia as she sat in the gardens of Halmirion: hibiscus with blossoms the size of dinner plates, billows of pink and wine-purple bougainvillea, huge heavy-headed roses. Butterflies dipped and flickered among the flowers like airborne petals, their painted wings greater in span than those of their kin in Mera, while beyond hedges and rose bowers the plumes of fountains soared higher than any fountain of that distant world. It was the "golden hour": the sun was setting slowly, its mellowed beams glancing through fountain spray and flower petals.

Mag's antidote had done its work: Ailia's mind was fully restored. But gray depression shrouded her thoughts as she sat alone in the pleasance. She had nearly brought disaster on them all, she reflected, with her mad flight to Nemorah. All the warnings of Mandrake's deceit she had willfully ignored. She would have ended as his mindless thrall: worse, he would have used her powers to strike at those she loved best. And all this would have been her own doing. This much she was able to confess to her father and her guardians. She was filled with revulsion at the memory of what she had done while under the philter's influence: her savage assault on Syndra, her betrayal of poor faithful Iwidjik. The vile draught had not altered her character, but brought up from hidden depths its darker, bestial side: and she saw that darkness and was forced to acknowledge it, shamed and terrified. *Is that what I am really like—deep down?* she wondered in horror. And now that these evil concealed passions had been unleashed, could she ever hope to force them into hiding again—or would they always be near the surface now?

Her most dreadful secret she kept to herself.

She had been falling in love with Mandrake. That was the cruel irony: the prince, had he but known it, had not needed the philter to win her. Had he not enslaved her with it, she would soon have been willingly his.

Her mission had not been an utter failure, her father assured her gently. Most of the other races of the Celestial Empire had now taken Ailia's side, so deeply impressed were they by her desperate effort, at extreme risk to her own person, to avert a war. That her attempt at diplomacy had been met with hostility and treachery had turned them against Mandrake and his allies. So something had after all been accomplished: but this was little comfort when a war now seemed inevitable.

And it was not enough to assuage her guilt. *I saw something in him—perhaps an echo of his father's nobility, or perhaps it was something that was his own—a buried good. He wrote the poems of Blyssion—how could he write such words and not have some good in him? It was only a glimpse, but it made me want to help him.* To her own ears these sounded like excuses. Perhaps it had been easier to make herself believe this than to do the harder thing and attack him—to destroy him. *Did I just take the easy way, out of weakness?* She had ignored the advice of Ana and warnings of her guardians, and gone rashly to try and bargain with her cunning foe. And this had all come of a false humility that was (she thought now, feeling wretched) in truth a masked arrogance. "I am not so important as they all believe" she had thought—yet in thinking this she had set her judgment above theirs. She had convinced herself she was unworthy of her position and her appointed task, and persuaded herself that she knew better than they. Had she only placed her whole trust in Auron and Taleera and Ana, she would never have gone to Nemorah.

She looked up, dull-eyed, as her father walked toward her through the garden. Tiron's face was strangely pale and drawn. He came up to her and took her hand. "Ailia my dear, the Loänan have brought Jomar and Lorelyn back safe from Mera. They wish to speak with you," he added in a low voice.

Only Jo and Lori? A spasm seized Ailia's heart, but she could not move or speak. She watched as Jomar and Lorelyn came to her, walking slowly, their faces as haggard as her father's. They stood looking at her in silence, and she looked back, saying nothing. There was no need for words. Nevertheless, Jomar cleared his throat and spoke. For the first time she heard his deep voice tremble.

"Ailia . . . Damion . . . he—"

Sorrow hung about her, a thick engulfing mist. He tried again. "Damion—Damion . . ."

"I know," she said.

"I'LL KILL THEM ALL!" Lorelyn cried.

She and Jomar stood alone in the lengthening shadows of the garden. "The whole rotten, miserable crew—Morugei, Valei—I'll *kill* them for this!"

Jomar saw the savage gleam in Lorelyn's once clear and innocent eyes, and was disturbed. She looked, for an instant, like a terrifying stranger and not the woman he loved. "No, Lori!" He stepped toward her, caught her wrists. She shook him off. "You're a Paladin. If you kill for revenge you'll have to do penance. Remember?" he pleaded.

"I don't care!" she said wildly.

He caught hold of her again and she struggled in his grip, then suddenly sagged against his chest and cried—not like a girl but like a man, in great wrenching sobs that shook her whole body.

"Listen," he said when at last her grief had subsided. "Khalazar's already paid his debt. You saw to that, you and Marjana."

Lorelyn looked up at him with red-rimmed eyes. "Mandrake's alive still. So help me, he'll pay for his part in this. You can fight him now, Jo—you've got the Star Sword. And I've brought Damion's back with me—the adamant sword that belonged to King Andarion. It's wounded Mandrake twice before—he'll feel it again, Jo, and may the third blow do what the first two didn't!"

His arms tightened their hold on her. "An oath, Lori! When everything in Mera is settled, you and I will go after him together. We'll hang his head over the door of his own temple. Let his subjects worship him then!"

Lorelyn's bright blue eyes stared into his, fierce as flame. "Agreed!" she said.

From a high branch in one of the tall perindeus trees, where they were both perching in bird form, Taleera and Auron watched as the two young humans walked away toward the palace. Presently the firebird spoke within Auron's mind. *The danger is not yet over, and the harm that is done I fear cannot be reversed. Mandrake has taught Ailia to use her Loänan powers—powers that she is not yet ready for, that she feared to use when she was in her right mind.*

Auron's own feathered form, an ercine with keen night-piercing eyes, shifted uneasily from one foot to the other. *But she is in her right mind again,* he replied. *He has no influence over her anymore.*

That makes no difference, Auron. She has tasted those powers now, and she remembers what it was like to wield them. Who can say she will not be tempted to take draconic form again, and to rule the elements, now that she has the knowledge? That is how Mandrake himself fell, remember. Ana was right. Ailia's powers were always a danger to her, and she cannot unlearn what she has learnt. What will become of her, and all of us?

Auron made no reply. They sat together in silence as the dusk around them deepened.

MANDRAKE PACED ALONG THE PARAPET of the Loänei castle, his cloak flowing around him like a shadowing cloud. Once again destiny had intervened at a crucial moment. Or was it his own fault? Had he been as blind as Khalazar?

The former God-king's body, he heard, had been hung by the crowd on the same gibbet on which Gemala had been displayed, giving rise to a popular jest in the Zimbouran marketplace: "Khalazar has risen above all other men!"

"Do you know what they are saying?" one of the surviving goblins had told him after fleeing Mera. "They say that Damion truly was an angel, as the Moharas believed. Now that there will be no more sacrifices and Valdur's temple is abandoned, they say this was a plan of the Zayim all along! That he sent one of his angel servants to the altar, to be a divine substitute for all the human victims who now will never have to die upon it. The Zayim himself denies this, but most people cling to the fanciful tale and love Jomar all the more for it. They will never retrieve Damion's body: the sacrificial well shaft is too deep. So they are saying that he simply vanished, moving onto a higher plane. Even Farola, the blind priest who slew him, says this."

"The killer of Damion would say anything to save himself from the mob's wrath."

"Not so, for he would not change his tale, not even under torment. Farola declared that after striking the fatal blow he heard a sound like the rushing of a great wind, and then the body was gone from the altar. And he says that in that moment something smote him lightly upon the face, so that he flung up his arms. Then he felt it one more time, on his hands—a thing like a feather-fan; but even as he grasped at the thing it was no longer there. He does not know what it was. The people say, of course, that it was an angel's wing, and that Damion was in that moment transformed to his true shape, and departed for the heavens. As for the priest's halfwit acolyte, he would say only that he saw a great light that hurt his eyes, and made him close them and cower."

"The testimony of a blind man and a simpleton," said Mandrake. "But they will believe." And it was true, in a sense. Damion Athariel had indeed been transformed into something more powerful, something that no weapon could destroy. *That Zimbouran archpriest did not slay a man, he birthed a god. If Damion was hard to deal with as a man, how much worse is he now as a divinity! He lives, forever and ever, in the mob's imagination.*

And he will be enshrined in Ailia's heart and mind, until she herself dies. An ideal beloved, who will grow in memory ever more perfect, ensuring that she will never love any living man again . . .

His own anguish was suddenly unendurable. He reached out to Ana through the Ether, along the delicate cord that was her bond with him, the bond he had always chafed against. But now there was no one there: the cord had been severed—at her end, not his, this time. She had abandoned him to his fate at last. He was beyond forgiveness now, as Ana had warned. Ailia had given him a chance at peace, and he had in the end proven unworthy of it. There could be no reconciliation. Forgive him—for his part in her beloved Damion's death? She would surely destroy him—and she could do so now. He himself had shown her the fullness of her power, even taught her to take draconic form And his pity for her—that fatal flaw!—had allowed Ailia to survive her sojourn here, and escape him in the end. His one chance to eliminate her—the chance that she herself had given him—was now gone. When he and the Tryna Lia met again, it would be as two powers equally matched, in a duel that would end only in death for one or the other.

Mandrake fled blindly down the staircase, out into the inner ward, then stumbled and fell his length on the ground. He looked up at the sky, saw the constellation of the Worm with its red eye glaring down. There was no escape. Ailia was back with her guardians. The Star Stone was in her hands again. If only there really were a Power of some sort, a dark primal power one could call on, adding its strength to one's own . . . "Help me," he whispered to the shape outlined in stars. He regretted the words at once: they seemed to hang dark as smoke upon the still air, to stain it and accuse him. They were an admission of weakness, and worse, of belief. Belief in Valdur—not a long-dead Archon, but the god of the Valei! Had he really come to this?

He took his dragon-form, casting weakness aside, and winged away from the castle into the night.

THE BLASTING HEAT OF THE SUNS woke him. He stretched, became aware that he was lying on something hard: a surface of stone. He had returned to man-form.

A voice was speaking nearby.

"A worthy vessel," it said. He opened his eyes, blinked up at the figure of an aged man, whose crude features suggested he was at least half-goblin. Mandrake sat up, and realized that he was naked. His robe lay discarded on the ground a few paces away: he must have clawed it from his body when he reverted to man-form. Why could he not remember?

He looked about him. He could not recall coming to this place. Broken ruins lay everywhere, the remains of some ancient city from before the time of the Loänei. They were half-buried, and a few leagues away a vast volcano raised its smoking cone—the author of the city's destruction.

The old man continued to look down at him, smiling and nodding. "Yes—a fitting vehicle for my Master's will. You know that you are his now."

Mandrake stood. He had little patience with human notions of shame and modesty, but something in the old man's gloating look made him reach for his robe and cast it about him. The wizened creature chuckled. "Ah, it's too late now! You can't take back what you've given. You've made your bargain and must keep it."

"I don't know what you're mumbling about, old man," the prince snapped. But a chill ran through his flesh, though the air was warm.

The aged man waved a clawlike hand at the large rectangular stone on which Mandrake had been lying. "You know what that is, don't you? It's the high altar of the old temple, Valdur's fane. He was worshiped here, along with Elnemorah, before your dragon-kind came. Victims were offered up to him on that stone slab, long ago. And now you've offered yourself to him: a living sacrifice."

"Don't be foolish," said Mandrake shortly. "I had no knowledge of what that stone was." *But how did I come to be lying on it?* he wondered, unsettled.

"You're afraid," the old man accused. "You needn't be. With your self-offering will come great honor, and power too."

Mandrake stood still. "Power?" he repeated sharply.

"But of course." The man pointed skyward. "Even now, whole armies of Morugei and firedrakes await your command. You can lead us to victory!"

"He speaks the truth," another voice said. Mandrake turned. There in the ruins stood the two ethereal forms that Naugra had summoned into Khalazar's throne room. Elazar and Elombar. He lifted his hands in a futile warding gesture.

"Stay back!" he cried. "Is that you, Naugra? Do you mean to threaten me?"

"Fool. We came to help you. You are our prince, our chosen champion. Your father and mother were two of the most powerful Nemerei who ever lived. You bear in you the blood of Archons and of Loänan. You are the culmination of the Master's greatest plan, your parents the unwitting instruments of his will. You will defeat the Tryna Lia!"

"No," he rasped. "I will not do it. I will not be part of your schemes any longer!"

"Then you will be slain by Ailia and her followers. Do you think they will let you live, renegade Nemerei and dragon-spawn that you are? The warriors Jomar and Lorelyn have sworn publicly to slay you with the iron sword and blade of adamant, and hang up your head in your own temple. The Loänan and cherubim are ready to make war against you, and they have the support of nearly all the worlds. You can die like a beast backed into a corner, or you can fight, and live. It is your choice. We will aid you—but you must proclaim yourself the Avatar."

Mandrake's head came up. "Very well. I *will* fight—but only for myself, do you understand? Never for Valdur!"

An enigmatic smile touched Elombar's lips. "It is the same thing," he replied. Nearby, the old man cackled with glee.

Mandrake turned away. "I agree to your terms."

"Done," said the apparition. And in Mandrake's ears the word had the ring of a knell.

FOR WEEKS NOW IT HAD RAINED in Mirimar, though this was not the season for it: an effect of Ailia's grief upon the climate, it was said. The faithful believed that her goddess-mother mourned with her. There had been no word from Ana, who seemed to have gone into hiding with her Nemerei, but the old shaman of the Mohara had been in communication with Arainia's sorcerers, apprising them of all that took place in Zimboura. "Many claim to have seen visions of Damion in the ruined temple," Wakunga told them. "They await the coming of the sky goddess to grieve for the earth god and make the desert bloom with flowers, as the prophecy foretold."

"She must go to Zimboura," Marima told the court. "He is right. I feel here the hand of destiny."

Lorelyn shook her head. "She won't! Do you think she would ever go to that place? She was so close to Damion!"

Ailia had not left her room in days, and it was feared that she was ill. Swans and Elei, so a popular saying went, mate for life. If one should die, the other will not be long in following. Ailia had long ago made her heart's choice in Damion, and in her mind at least she was paired with him forever. Alone in her chamber, Ailia raged at Khalazar and Mandrake; she railed even at Damion, for going to Mera when she had begged him not to—for giving up his life when she needed him desperately. Then with her anger spent grief would overwhelm her again, sweep her down into depths where there was neither light nor hope. Sometimes in her dreams Damion would come into her room and sit by her bed. She could clearly hear his voice as he spoke to her, telling her it had not really happened, that it had all been a misunderstanding. And then she woke up, as she always did.

Soon the longing arose to cease waking, to dream on without any interruptions of reality.

One dismal night she could not find sleep, but tossed and turned ceaselessly, yearning for a sleeping draught to give her the escape for which she longed. At last she rose from her bed. The room was blue with moonlight: quietly, so as not to disturb the sleeping Taleera, who was perched on a chair nearby, she pulled on her robe and left the bedchamber. Benia was slumbering in the outer chamber, slumped on the divan: Ailia tiptoed past her and opened the door to the passage. It was empty.

She walked in her bare feet along the carpeted hall, passing by her father's door. No light showed beneath it, but under the door of her mother's old chamber a crack of warm radiance glowed.

He must be in there. She would talk to him, seek comfort in his arms and gentle voice. Ailia knocked softly, then pushed the door open. "Father?" she whispered.

The room was a rose-colored cavern of warmth and light, the curtains drawn before the windows, the lamps lit. Her father was nowhere to be seen.

But the room was occupied.

A figure sat in a chair by the window: a woman clad in a simple rose-pink gown that fell to the floor. She had long golden hair, gleaming in the lamplight, and it too reached her feet. Her head was bowed, her face lost in the drooping cowl of hair.

Ailia stood transfixed. *"Mother?"* she choked.

The woman raised her head, and there was the face from the portrait on the wall—the blue eyes, the smooth white skin and fine features. But no: her mother could not look like this, not now. Even an Elei woman must show some signs of change in twenty years. "I'm dreaming!" said Ailia bitterly, forgetting how she had longed to do just that.

The woman held out her hands. "Elmiria—daughter. Come to me."

And then Ailia no longer cared if it were a dream or not. She ran to the woman's arms and buried her face in the silken lap, the soft falling hair. "Mother—Mother, you've come back!" she sobbed.

"Daughter, I have never left you. Oh, my dear child, I would gladly have suffered all this in your stead. But take heart! For all hope is not lost."

Smooth hands cradled Ailia's face, brushed her tears away. On the right hand something shimmered blue: a star sapphire set in a ring. "I am in the Ether now, and so too is your Damion. He has not left you forever. Look." She reached out, pulled the silk curtain away from the window. One lit tower window shone through the night beyond. "He awaits you in the Ether, like me. You shall see us both again before all is over." Elarainia took the star sapphire ring from her finger, and gently slid it onto Ailia's. "It is your own ring, the same I bequeathed to you long ago. Receive it again, and remember," she said, and leaned forward to kiss her daughter's brow.

The room faded. Ailia was rising through layers of soft radiance, up toward a brighter luminosity. Was this the Ether—or High Heaven? Was she dead, too? Her eyes opened to light, a blurry blaze. And now a shape was taking form out of that luminosity—a bird-shape, with plumage of fiery hues, its plume-crowned head sunk upon its breast. The Elmir? Then she was in Heaven—she would see Damion again, be with him once more! They would never be separated again . . . But as she sat up eagerly, she saw that it was only Taleera, roosting on her chair; and the light was that of the morning sun blazing in at the window. She was still in bed. Despair seized her mind, a crushing weight. But her body was young; it welcomed the renewal of life in its limbs. With treacherous eagerness it recovered itself, stretching and moving almost of its own volition.

She felt a sudden sharp pang of compunction at the sight of the sleeping Taleera. The firebird looked exhausted, but she had not put her head beneath her wing, fearing perhaps to miss any sign of returning life in her princess. Taleera, and Auron and her father and friends—what worry and misery had they been suffering as she slept? Then through the window she saw the black banners flying from each tower, and recalled that she herself had ordered this display of public mourning. "It was a dream, just a dream. Mother is gone, dead, and so is he . . ." Not only dead, she knew, but vanished beyond recall, leaving not even his body to bury.

No light would shine at his window across the way, ever again. Ailia rolled over, tears welling in her eyes. Then she started, sat bolt upright staring at her right hand. Her eyes went wide, though she made no sound.

On her ring finger the star sapphire glinted.

Impossible. She had lost it, left it behind in Mandrake's palace in Nemorah. How then could it be here, on her hand . . . ?

She leaped to her feet and tore through her rooms, waking a startled Taleera. "Ailia—merciful Heavens, what is it?" the firebird squawked. Ailia paid her no heed, did not even hear her. She flung on a chamber robe and burst out into the corridor. Jomar and Lorelyn were standing there, keeping vigil along with the door guards and her father. They all gaped at her.

"Damion isn't dead!" she cried.

They stared at her in consternation. Barefoot, wild-eyed, and disheveled, she looked half-mad. "Ailia," began Tiron tremulously, "Ailia my child—Damion is gone—"

"Yes," she gasped, "gone—that's it, gone but not dead! I have seen him, and Mother too. I was right, she's not gone and neither is he!" She turned to the guards. "Tell the people I have recovered, and am going to make a journey."

"But where, Highness?"

"To Mera. To find Damion." She turned back to the others. "I saw him in my dreams—only they weren't dreams, but visions. He went into the Ether, he escaped death—just as Mother did, years ago. Those Zimbouran people have really *seen* him, lingering between the two planes. The old priest and the acolyte told the truth!"

"Ailia, I cannot allow you to travel anywhere," said Tiron. "You are not well—"

"No! I know I'm right!"

Tiron and the others exchanged looks. A wild hope sprang into Lorelyn's eyes. "She's not dreaming, Jo—look at her! She's *seen* him."

"Jo." Ailia put her hands in his. "Will you help me? I must leave Arainia in my father's care, and go to Mera. Will you follow me there, and help me restore it? We will find Damion there, Jo. All they say of him in Zimboura is true—he has only changed, become something new and powerful." She turned as a large group of palace guards ran up, alerted by her shouts. "Take down those black banners. They aren't needed. And call the councillors," she told them.

They stared at her. "But, Your Highness—"

"Do as she says," rumbled Jomar.

Ailia turned back to her apartments. "And I *don't* want priestesses with candles walking in front of me all the time. I will no longer have the light ritual performed."

"But—"

Ailia swept past them impatiently.

Hope and joy had returned to her, sweeping away doubt, grief, and self-recrimination like a flood. Damion—she thought of the hovering butterflies down in the flowered pleasance, glorious winged creatures sprung from the cocoons of the lowly, wormlike larvae. *He has changed, become something greater and stronger.* She knew now to whom her heart belonged, and where her true destiny lay.

A FEW HOURS LATER AILIA, still pale but with a new look of determination on her face, walked out onto the roofs of Halmirion, accompanied by her friends and advisors. She wore her white mage-robe, and her only adornment was the sapphire ring.

In the sky something gleamed like a golden star—a dragon, hurtling through the air toward them. A great cry went up from the crowds assembled below, who had kept an anxious vigil during Ailia's illness and now gathered in hope at the news of her recovery. Ailia lifted a hand in response to the sound, an oddly assured and gracious gesture so far removed from her former timidity that even her friends were awestruck.

"Look at her!" Lorelyn whispered. "I wouldn't want to be one of the enemy, would you?"

As Jomar gazed at the princess he felt hope stir in him. "By all the gods, maybe she *can* lead us to victory after all!"

Ailia kissed her father, and looked solemnly at her friends. "Look for me in Zimboura, when you come there in your turn."

Auron alighted in a storm of golden wings and lowered his neck for her. She climbed up and settled herself behind his mane. Then the dragon sprang skyward. As they watched, his shining form grew ever smaller, a tiny glimmer against the Arch of Heaven, a flicker passing across the face of the moon, seeking a distant door in the air and the world that lay beyond.

"She's left us!" sighed Lorelyn.

"We'll join her soon," said Jomar. "In Mera we'll put everything to rights."

And then they were silent, watching the golden gleam until it vanished in the sky.

Here ends the second part of
The Dragon Throne
The third volume,
The Archons of the Stars,
will tell of the war between the worlds and the
final battle for the throne of the Celestial Empire.

APPENDIX

PRONUNCIATION OF ELENSI WORDS

Elensi words are pronounced as follows:

Vowels

A—always has the short sound, as in *flat*.

AA—has a long, drawn-out "ah" sound; before R, pronounced as in *Car* (in some instances I have rendered it as A for easier reading, as in Aana—Ana, Loanaan—Loänan)

AI—as in *rain*

AU—another "ah" sound; before R, pronounced as in *oar*

E—always has the short sound, as in *bed*

EI—like the German *ei*, an "eye" sound

I—like the French I, an "ee" sound

O—always the long sound, as in *bow*, except when it is the penultimate letter in a word (i.e., *Damion, Halmirion*), in which case it has the short sound, as in *iron, lion*

OA—not a diphthong as in *road* but two distinct sounds, as in *co-agulate*

U—always the long sound, as in *tune*

Y—always a vowel, never a consonant: has the short I sound as in *win*, except before E, when it takes the long sound, as in *wine*

Consonants

G—always pronounced like the G in *goose,* never as in *gin.*
S—pronounced as in *so,* not the Z sound in *phase.*
TH—always pronounced as in *thin,* never as in *then.*

Note: these rules do not necessarily apply to words in languages other than Elensi, i.e., Zimbouran, in which the letter Y *is* a consonant.

GLOSSARY OF
EXTRATERRESTRIAL WORDS

Ailia: (AY-lee-a) Elensi *ai* + *lia*, "lode star." Island girl who joined the quest in Mera to find the Star Stone; later revealed to be the Tryna Lia.

Akkar: (AH-kar) Moharan. God of the earth, consort of Nayah the sky goddess.

Ana: (Ah-na) Elensi. Wise woman and guide to the Tryna Lia. See *Eliana*.

Andarion: (an-DAR-ee-on) Elensi *aan* + *darion*, "Lord Knight." Title given to King Brannar of Maurainia in the Golden Age.

Arainia: (a-RAY-nee-a) Elensi *ar* + *ain-ia*, "bright homeland/sphere." Second planet in the Auria system.

Arkurion: (ar-KYOOR-ee-on) Elensi *ar-kuri* + *on*, "bright torch bearer." First planet in the Auria system.

Auria: (OR-ee-a) Elensi *aur* + *ia*, "place/sphere (of) life." Elei name for the sun.

Auron: (OR-on) Elensi *aur* + *on*, "vessel of life." An Imperial Loä-nan, friend and protector of the Tryna Lia.

Azar: (AZ-ar) Elensi *azar,* "calamity." Name for the planet of the dwarf star Azarah. See *Azarah.*

Azarah: (AZ-a-ra) Elensi *Azar'ah,* from *azar + rah,* "bringer of calamity." Name of a small dim star that became trapped in the Auria system's gravitational field. See Terrestrial Terms: *Disaster, the.*

Byn-jara: (bin JAH-ra) Kaanish. A martial art practiced by the Kaans, emphasizing posture and breathing as well as meditation.

Damion: (DAY-mee-on) Elensi *dai + mion,* "welcome messenger." (I have simplified the spelling of this name from the phonetic *Daimion* as there is an English name, Damien, pronounced similarly.) Priest of the Faith and companion of the Tryna Lia.

Dogoda: (duh-GO-duh) Dogoda. A race of the southern peninsula in the Antipodes, possibly a survival of the Neanderthal species long extinct in our own world.

Elaia: (el-LAY-a) Elensi *El'aia,* from *el + laia,* "lower gods."

Elarainia: (el-a-RAY-nee-a) Elensi *el + Arainia.* Name of the goddess of the planet Arainia; also, the mother of the Tryna Lia.

Eldimia: (el-DEEM-ee-a) Elensi *Eldim'ia,* from *el + dimi + ia,* "(the) gods' beauteous country." Land in the world of Arainia to which the Elei fled after the Great Disaster.

Elei: (EL-eye) Elensi *el + ei,* "children of the gods." Ancient race now vanished from Mera. They had special powers of the mind, believed by them to be the result of a divine ancestry.

Elendor: (el-EN-dor) Elensi *el + endor,* "holy mountain." Sacred mountain in Trynisia, on whose summit the holy city of Liamar was built.

Elensi: (el-EN-see) The language of the Elei. From Elensi *el + ensi,* "holy tongue" or "gods' tongue."

Eliana: (el-ee-AH-na) Elensi *el-i* + *aana,* "lady (of the) spirit host," or "queen of the faeries." Former queen of Trynisia; see *Ana.*

Elmir: (EL-meer) Elensi *el* + *mir,* "spirit power." The concept of Spirit, represented in Elei art as a bird.

Elmiria: (el-MEER-ee-a) Elensi *el* + *Miria.* Birth-name of the Tryna Lia.

Elyra: (el-LIE-ra) Elensi *El'yra,* from *el* + *lyra,* "higher gods."

Falaar: (fuh-LAR) A cherub guardian of the Tryna Lia. This is an approximate phonetic rendition of his name, which means "Sun-hunter."

Gemala: (gum-AWL-a) Zimbouran. General of King Khalazar's army.

Halmirion: (hal-MEER-ee-on) Elensi *Halmiri'on,* from *hal* + *Miria* + *on,* "Castle Moonbearer." The palace of the Tryna Lia in Eldimia.

Hyelanthia: (hye-el-AN-thee-a) Elensi *Hyelanth'ia,* from *hy-el* + *antha* + *ia,* "cloud-country belonging to the gods." Land in Arainia where the Elaia were said to have dwelt.

Iantha: (ee-AN-tha) Elensi *i-antha* + *a,* "of many clouds." The sixth planet of the Auria system, a gas giant.

Ingard: (EEN-gard) Elensi. Famed knight and friend of King Andarion.

Jomar: (JOE-mar) Moharan. One of the Tryna Lia's companions, a warrior of mixed Moharan and Zimbouran heritage.

Kaans: (KAHNS) Kaanish. The inhabitants of the Archipelagoes of Kaan in Mera.

Khalazar: (KHAL-a-zar) Zimbouran *khal* + Elensi *Azar,* "born under Azar." Name of the king of Zimboura in Ailia's day. The "kh" sound is pronounced like the "ch" in the Scottish *loch*. (The western peoples, who had no such sound in their language, pronounced the name "Kalazar.")

Kiran Jariss: (KEER-an JAH-riss) Zimbouran. A Zimbouran ally of the Zayim.

Liamar: (LEE-a-mar) Elensi *lia + mar*, "star city." Holy city atop Mount Elendor in Trynisia.

Loänan: (LOW-a-nahn) Elensi *Loanaan*, from *lo + an + aan*, "lord (of) wind (and) water." See Terrestrial terms: *Dragon*.

Loänanmar: (low-A-NAHN-mar) Elensi *loanan + mar*, "city of dragons." Largest city in the world of Nemorah.

Loänei: (LOW-un-eye) Elensi *lo + an + ei*, "children of wind and water." Race of beings descended from unions between humans and Loänan transformed into human shape.

Lorelyn: (LORE-el-in) Elensi *Lor'el'yn*, from *lora + el-lyn*, "daughter of sacred sky (heaven)." A gifted Nemerei and friend of the Tryna Lia.

Lotara: (low-TAR-a) Elensi *Lot'ara*, from *lot + tar-a*, "tail of the worm." A star in Entar, the constellation of Modrian-Valdur. It is companion star to Vartara, the Black Star.

Marakor: (MA-ra-kor) Marakite. Country to the south of Maurainia in Mera.

Maurainia: (mor-AIN-ee-a) Elensi *Maur + ain + ia*, "homeland (of the) Maur (tribe)." Principal kingdom of Mera's western continent.

Meldramiria: (mel-druh-MEER-ee-a) Elensi *meldra + miria*, "throne (of the) moon." The Tryna Lia's throne in Eldimia.

Meldrian: (MEL-dree-un) Elensi *meldri + aan*, "lord of thrones." An ancient world, the capital of the Celestial Empire from the days of the Archons.

Melnemeron: (mel-NEM-er-on) Elensi *Melnemer'on,* from *mel + ne-Mera + on,* "repository of the lore of the Not-world (Ether)." Place in Arainia where the Nemerei gather to learn and share their knowledge.

Mera: (MARE-a) Elensi word for "earth" or "soil," also used by the inhabitants of the third planet of the Auria system as the name for their world.

Meraalia: (mare-AWL-ee-a) Elensi *Meraal'ia,* from *mera-al + lia,* "star stone." The star stone of the Archons.

Merei: (MARE-eye) Elensi *Mer'ei,* from *mera + ei,* "earth children." True humans (as opposed to Elei, Loänei, and other altered races).

Miria: (MEER-ee-a) Elensi *miri + a,* literally "of radiance." Elei name for Arainia's moon.

Mirimar: (MEER-eem-ar) Elensi *miri + mar,* "radiant city." Capital city of Eldimia.

Modrian: (MO-dree-un) Elensi name for a deity, chief of the sky gods (but subordinate to the supreme deity of High Heaven). Said to have rebelled and been defeated by the other gods of earth and sky, who confined him to the Pit of Perdition. See *Valdur.*

Mohar: (MO-har) Moharan. Country south of Zimboura, now an occupied territory.

Mohara: (mo-HA-ra) A people of the southern Antipodes.

Moriana: (mo-ree-AN-a) Elensi *mori + aana,* "lady/mistress of the nights." A title given to Mera's moon deity; also the name of Brannar Andarion's queen.

Morlyn: (MORE-lin) Elensi *mor* + *lyn*, "night sky." Son of King Brannar Andarion and Queen Moriana.

Morugei: (MOR-oo-guy) Elensi *Morug'ei*, from *moruga* + *ei*, "children (of) the night-haunts." Also Demonspawn. The mutant humanoid races that worship Valdur. These creatures are reputed to be the misshapen offspring of true humans and evil incubi. They include numerous races, whom I call here Anthropophagi, trolls, ogres, and goblins. The first three subspecies breed "true," passing on their characteristics to subsequent generations, but among goblins no two individuals are alike, and even their offspring do not resemble their parents. However, the goblins have a higher intelligence than the other races and are more skilled in the arts of sorcery.

Nayah: (NYE-uh) Moharan. Goddess of the sky in Moharan myth.

Nemerei: (NEM-er-eye) Elensi *ne-Mera* + *ei*, "child/children (of the) not-world." ("*Ne-Mera*," "Not-world," is a literal translation of the immaterial dimension here called the Ether.) Beings able to communicate with their minds alone, in addition to other psychic powers.

Nemorah: (nuh-MOR-uh) Loänei-Elensi. A world once inhabited by the Loänei, now home to human beings.

Numia: (NYOO-mee-a) Elensi. Elei name for Mera's moon.

Orbion: (OR-bee-on) Elensi. Name of the Celestial Emperor.

Rialain: (REE-a-lain) Elensi *Riala* + *ain*, "home (of the) Riala (tribe)." Country north of Maurainia in Mera.

Shurkana: (shur-KAN-a) Shurkanese. Country to the north of Zimhoura in the Antipodes.

Syndra: (SIN-druh) Elensi. A Nemerei woman of mixed Elei and Merei parentage who betrayed the Tryna Lia.

Talandria: (tal-AN-dree-a) Elensi *Talandri'a*, from *tal* + *an-dri* + *ia*, literally "all salt water place/sphere." The fourth planet of the Auria system.

Taleera: (t'yuh-LEER-a) T'kiri. A friend and guardian of the Tryna Lia. (The name is pronounced with a little roll to the R that makes it sound almost like an L.)

Talmirennia: (tal-meer-EN-ee-a) Elensi *tal* + *mir* + *en* + *ia*, literally "all-power-great-place." Elensi name for the Celestial Empire.

Tanathon: (TAN-uh-thon) Elensi *tana* + *thon*, "tree eater." Species of large saurian inhabiting the world of Nemorah. There is reason to believe these giant reptiles are not indigenous to that planet, but are descended from sauropods of our own Jurassic period, brought to Nemorah from our world by the Archons.

Tarnawyn: (TAR-nuh-win) Elensi *tar-na* + *wyn*, "white serpent-foe." Unicorn.

Temendri Alfaran: (tem-END-ree AL-fa-ran) A world colonized by the Loänan, where many races dwell and meet.

Tiron: (TEER-on) Elensi *tir* + *on*, "blessing-bearer" or "blessed one." Name of the father of the Tryna Lia.

T'kiri: (t'KEER-ee) T'kiri. An avian race, called "firebirds" by humans because of their brightly-colored, bioluminescent plumage.

Tryna Lia: (TRY-na LEE-a) Elensi *Tryna Li'a*, from *tryna* + *lia-a*, "Princess of the Stars." Prophesied ruler awaited by the Elei, said to be the daughter of the planetary deity Elarainia.

Trynel: (TRY-nel) Elensi *tryne* + *el*, "royal and divine." A title of the Tryna Lia.

Trynisia: (try-NEE-see-a; try-NEEZH-ee-a) Elensi *Tryn'isia*, from *tryne* + *is* + *ia*, "royal beloved country." Land of the Elei in Mera, abandoned after the Great Disaster.

Trynoloänan: (try-no-LOW-a-nahn) Elensi *tryno* + *loanaan*, "dragon prince/ruler." A male leader of the Loänan.

Twidjik: an amphisbaena of Nemorah.

Unguru: (oon-GOO-roo) Moharan name, derived from the Elensi name of the Maurainian hero Ingard. A warrior of the free Moharas who fought and gave his life for the Zayim.

Utara: (yoo-TAR-a) Elensi *Ut'ara*, from *ut* + *tar-a*, "eye of the worm." Red star in Entar, the constellation of Modrian-Valdur.

Valdur: (VAL-dur) Elensi *val* + *dur*, "dark one." Name given to the god Modrian after his fall from grace. Later appropriated by Zimbouran clergy as the name for their chief deity.

Valdys: (VAL-diss) Elensi *val* + *dys*, "dark dwelling." The fifth planet of Auria's system.

Valei: (VAL-eye) Elensi *val* + *ei*, "children (of the) dark." The followers of Modrian-Valdur.

Vartara: (var-TAR-a) Elensi *var* + *tar-a*, "mouth of the worm." Black star in Entar, the constellation of Modrian-Valdur. Also called the Mouth of Hell.

Wakunga: (wuh-KUNG-guh) Moharan. Shaman of the last free tribe of Moharas.

Yehosi: (yuh-HO-see) Zimbouran. Chief eunuch in Khalazar's palace.

Zayim: (z'eye-EEM) Moharan. According to Mohara legend, a divinely appointed savior who would one day free them from enslavement.

Zimboura: (zim-BOOR-a) Zimbouran. A country in Mera's Antipodes.

GLOSSARY OF TERRESTRIAL TERMS

The words below are taken from our own terrestrial myths, languages, and cultures. I have utilized them for parallel concepts found in the worlds and cultures described in this book.

ambrosia: the Elei possessed an elixir, given them by the gods, according to tradition, which was taken from a fruit called the "food of the gods." It was said to augment the latent powers of Nemerei.

amphisbaena: name of a two-headed snake in medieval myth, here used for a creature of Nemorah.

Anthropophagi: deformed humans, one of the races of the Morugei. This name (meaning literally "eaters of men") belonged to a similar race featured in medieval European mythology.

Archons: a term used for an ancient race of beings that once dominated the galaxy and were worshiped as gods. Believed by some to be the origin of the Elaia, "lower gods," in Elei mythology.

aspidochelone: a whalelike creature from our own mythology, which was sometimes mistaken for an island by sailors. If they lit a campfire on its back, the creature would submerge and drown them. It would seem that the inspiration for this myth is an actual beast in the world of Nemorah, though how our own storytellers learned of it remains a mystery.

avatar: a term taken from Hindu tradition, here meaning either the physical manifestation of a god or else its representation by a mortal being in such a way that the divine being can be said to be literally present.

barometz: in medieval lore, the barometz or Vegetable Lamb of Tartary was a species of mythical sheep that grew on a tree. The word is here used for the planet-creatures of Temendri Alfaran.

Celestial Empire: the realm of the Archons. The constellations in Mera's night sky were seen as hegemonies of these divine beings, the star-states in which they dwelt. Later mythologies during the Dark Age came to describe this stellar empire as a mystical country in the sky.

cherubim: gryphons; winged creatures who serve the heavenly powers as steeds and guardians. The word *cherub* comes from ancient Hebrew mythology, and was used for a divine gryphonlike creature (not to be confused with the Renaissance version, a cupidlike winged figure).

demon: an Elaia; spirit closely linked to the plane of matter. The word is here used at times in its classical sense, the "daimon" of Greek myth being a supernatural, but not necessarily malevolent, being; very different from our modern understanding of demons.

Disaster, the: I have translated the great cataclysm of 2497 N.E. as the "Disaster," since it literally involved an "evil star." Approximately ten millennia ago, a small "rogue star," probably a brown dwarf, entered Mera's solar system and became caught in the sun's gravitational field. In passing through the cometary cloud, it sent dozens of comets plunging towards the inner planets. This bombardment continued sporadically over thousands of years. From descriptions of the Disaster in Mera—"stars falling from the sky," earthquakes, volcanic eruptions, dust-clouds obscuring the sun (hence the appellation "Dark Age")—it would appear that one or more fragmented cometary nucleii impacted with the planet. The damage to the moon and other planets is also consistent with a cometary bombardment.

This accords well with the mythical account, in which the god Modrian-Valdur sent his lieutenant Azarah to destroy the world; all such higher spirits being associated with stars. Azarah also brought with it a single planet, the ill-omened Azar of Elei lore.

dracontias: according to folklore, a "magic stone" or jewel that lies inside the head of a dragon. There is in fact a crystalline substance located in, and extruding from, the Loänan braincase, which is said to amplify the creature's extrasensory powers.

dragon: the oldest intelligent race in the known universe, the dragons or Loänan are giant saurians that do not in the least resemble the monsters of Western myth but are closer to the *lung* dragons of China: supremely wise, almost godlike beings, benevolent in nature (with a few exceptions). They are able to shape-shift, can exercise power over the elements, and may live for a thousand years or more. They come from the area of the galaxy known to Merans as the constellation of the Dragon, and travel between the stars by entering a hyperspatial dimension known as the Ethereal Plane.

dragonet: the juvenile form of a dragon. The youngest have not yet developed legs or wings.

eidolon: on the Ethereal Plane, the illusory "body" of a spiritual being that enables it to interact with other such bodies; also anything on the Ethereal Plane that resembles something on the material plane.

Ether: a dimension of pure energy beyond or "above" the material plane.

glaumerie: an illusion cast by faerie beings on mortals. Some human sorcerers are also able to create illusions.

Mandrake: (*man* + *drake*) English equivalent for the Maurish name Jargath, "dragon-man."

ornithopter: literally "bird wing," a term for any craft that flies through the air by mimicking the wingbeats of a bird. In our world such craft are not practical on a large scale, but the flying ships of the Elei stay aloft in part through sorcery.

quintessence: The "fifth element" in old Meran cosmology, a substance superior to the four material elements of earth, fire, water, and air. Celestial objects and divine beings were believed to be composed of quintessence. The term most likely derives from the old Elei concept of *elothan*, what we might call "pure energy."

Sibyls: prophetesses; holy women of the Elei faith who are believed to commune with the gods and receive from them visions of the future.

Translation: the process whereby a mortal bodily enters the Ethereal Plane, becoming a being of pure quintessence (energy).

Tree of Life: the ambrosia tree; also, the symbolic representation of the universe as a tree.

venudor: a gemstone that shines with its own inner radiance.

ypotryll: in heraldry, a beast with the body of a camel, boarlike head, and serpentine tail. Possibly inspired by an Arainian creature, for whom the word is here used.

About the Author

Alison Baird is the author of *The Hidden World, The Wolves of Woden, The Dragon's Egg,* and *White at the Waves.* She was honored by the Canadian Children's Book Centre Choice Award, is a Silver Birch. Award regional winner, and she was a finalist for the IODE Violet Downey Book Award. She lives in Ontario. Her Web site is: http://webhome.idirect,com/~dbaird.